Brianna stood, stiff, her hands clenched in fists at her sides, fighting the magic of Creighton's fingertips as they drifted over the bared curve of her shoulder.

"I wanted there to be starlight when I took you thus." His voice wooed her. "I wanted strains of music, drifting up from a gallery soft with candle-shine; and goblets, iced, with finest of wines. I wanted, just once, to make you mine, Tigress, as I would have had there never been a war."

Against her will, Brianna felt herself drawn by the throbbing longing in Creigh's voice, her gaze lifting to his dark-lashed eyes. She was stunned to see the stormy gray oddly misted.

"Dance with me, Tigress. Let me feed you sweet cakes dipped in honey. Let me weave flowers into your hair, take your body in tenderness and passion. For just this day, let us both dream that you are not just my lady, but my wife. . . ."

Kimberly Cates

POCKET BOOKS

New York   London   Toronto   Sydney   Tokyo

*To my husband Dave,
for giving me the greatest gift of all—
our daughter, Katie.*

Another *Original* publication of POCKET BOOKS

POCKET BOOKS, a division of Simon & Schuster, Inc.
1230 Avenue of the Americas, New York, N.Y. 10020

ISBN: 0-671-63394-5

First Pocket Books printing July 1988

10 9 8 7 6 5 4 3 2 1

POCKET and colophon are trademarks of Simon & Schuster Inc.

Printed in the U.S.A.

Chapter One

Ireland, 1649

Weep not the brave dead!
—from the Ballad of Cean-Salla
by James Clarence Mangan

The banshee worked a-weaving, snarling silken webs of death about the ancient walls of Drogheda. Seventeen-year-old Brianna Devlin clenched trembling hands in the folds of her heavy green cloak, but the fur lining crushed beneath her fingertips did naught to banish the chill that prickled her skin. *'Tis only the mist,* she chided herself. *Aye, and the cry of the wind.*

But as she peered down from the steeple of St. Mary's to the Irish countryside beyond the massive city wall, it was not the army of Oliver Cromwell she saw, straining to entrench its daunting train of artillery upon the hillside. Instead, it was the banshee's face grinning back at her, the old hag's fingers dancing like a puppet master's over the sea of Sassenach invaders blighting the land.

Brianna shivered, the sound of screams long silenced clawing at her ears. Aye, she had heard the white fairy's keening before . . . stumbled into the stark black vortex that was death.

"Shane . . ." she whispered the name, her arms clutching tight under her breasts. Yet, still the pain came, slashing beneath that fragile skin as the dawning sun blurred into tawny, windblown hair, a distant sweep of hill transforming into wide, roguish lips twisted in agony. Agony born of an Englishman's sword. Born of her own selfish pride.

"So ye deigned t' drag yerself from yer blankets at last."

1

Brianna jumped, a voice behind her cracking the silence like iron slamming stone. Frieze skirts swirling about her ankles, she spun, hand instinctively flying to the wire-bound hilt of the rapier that never left her side.

"What the—" Thick fingers gripped her wrist, the rasp of her blade half-yanked from its scabbard ringing to silence. "Hold, ye little she-cat! Th' enemy be out *there!*"

The wild bounding of Brianna's heart eased at the affronted, familiar tones, her eyes locking with the disgruntled glare of Fergus MacDermot. Cheeks burning, she slammed the rapier down into its casing, nerves, jerked whip-taut, snapping into anger.

"Plague take you, Fergus!" Brianna blazed. "What do you expect, creeping up on me like a—"

"Creeping?! *Creeping?!*" The wily old war veteran bellowed, his own cheeks staining a dull red. "It's mindin' me own concerns, I was, comin' t' get the bit an' sup ye should have had here an hour ago, and *ye* nigh sent me soarin' down t' Cromwell like a cursed tiercel!"

The image his words conjured ghosted a smile across Brianna's lips. She could almost believe he would take flight, he looked so like an old falcon, bushy brows crashing low above his great hooked nose, eyes black with righteous indignation.

She had seen that glare cow a dozen seasoned soldiers who towered above the barrel-chested MacDermot. But instead of filling her with fear, the scars slashed across his craggy features merely deepened the shroud of foreboding that clung like breeze-born cobwebs in her mind. The short sword bound to his side was ludicrous against the gleaming mass of Sassenach steel beyond the city's wall. A hundred nicks and dents upon the ancient blade stood testament to feats of daring, of death-defying raids and yet . . .

"Musketballs care naught of courage." She whispered the words, scarce aware she had spoken them aloud as she watched a distant cuirassier cantering his mount through the maze of English tents.

"What?"

"I . . ." She flushed, chagrined at being caught in her childhood trick of spilling her thoughts into words. "I said bullets care naught of courage."

2

"Bree."

Her gaze leapt back from the hills, expecting the censure or amusement her verbal stumblings had always sparked from her brothers, but Fergus's gruff baritone was soft, probing.

"Brianna, no chains bind ye t' the battlefield. Ye'll not be branded coward if ye do na choose t' fight."

"I'm not afraid . . . afraid of their muskets, their cannon. 'Tis just that . . ." She groped for the words. "Doyle and Daniel . . . Shane, too, they used to torment me whenever I'd try to explain. But betimes I get these feelings . . . as though there are things just beyond the mists."

"Things?"

"Aye. Hauntings from beyond . . . spirits. I don't know what they are. I-I can *feel* them, almost *see* them. But I can never *stop* them." Her voice trailed to a whisper, hand clenching again in the softness of her cloak. "They taunt me, dancing always at the tips of my fingers."

"And when they dance, Bree, what do you see?"

"War . . . death. Crazed, is it not?" Brianna gave a shaky laugh, surprised at the total seriousness in Fergus's keen eyes. "Doyle would say 'tis little wonder such scenes are playing before my eyes. That it takes no spirit whisperings to see that the Sassenach will soon be pounding at the gate. Shane used to bid me to doff his hat to the fairies when next I met with them, and ask them for fair weather for a ride or a hunt. Still . . ." She raked slender fingers through the curls at the end of her braid, the soft gold strands twining about her hand. She dared a look at Fergus. "Most like you think it a fool's tale as well."

"I've seen my share of things to turn yer hair t' white, these four and fifty years. Far too many things to scoff at ye, Bree," Fergus said. "Who knows, mayhap what ye see is the Sassenach's destruction. Mayhap 'tis our own." His voice fell to the softest burr. "But no matter the which of it, I must believe I can change what's destined to be. That somehow, someway me doin's can turn the tides."

The tides . . . Brianna's gaze shifted to the hills framed in the steeple window. Could any man or woman roll back the waves that would soon crash down on Drogheda? The great iron siege guns crouched atop the hill, savage beasts poised

3

to hurl claws of fire into the city, while the soldiers swarmed across the countryside like an apocalyptic plague, back and breastplates gleaming. Soldiers of God, the Puritan commander, Oliver Cromwell, claimed. Or were they the vassals of Satan himself? Devil-soldiers spawned of hate that had gnawed like rats in the bellies of two nations for five centuries. A hate that had festered since the day the sly prince the masses called John Lackland had swaggered ashore to plunder the country his father, Henry II, had tossed beneath his trampling feet.

Brianna shivered. For ten lifetimes the English had swept across Ireland, a savage torrent of war, oppression, death that crashed over the land, ebbing only to return with more brutal fury. And now, after waging a civil war that had culminated in the beheading of a king, the tempest had once again returned to Eire.

"Fergus."

The old soldier looked at her, his own face silent. Still.

"There . . . there are so many of them."

"Aye." Fergus reached up one gnarled finger to scratch at his bewhiskered chin. "I was judgin' yesterday, tryin' t' gauge their number. There be ten thousand of the bastards if there be a one. And ol' Crom, he's makin' certain we've had plenty of time to let that stick in our gullets afore he calls for surrender. A week he's been out there, arrangin' his cannons just so, grindin' his troops in our faces like a blasted headsman sharpenin' his axe. Christ, 'twill nigh be a relief when he makes a start of it."

Brianna's stomach churned. "Ten thousand!" she breathed. "But—but how many have we?"

Fergus snorted. "Sir Aston'd be lucky to number two thousand fighters within these walls, let alone have enough powder an' shot to—" He stopped abruptly, sweeping one gnarled paw across his sweat-beaded brow. "Damn, me throat's parched as an old whore's stuffin'. Did ye bring me any brew?"

Brianna fumbled with the strips of leather that laced a flask to the band of soft doeskin cinching her waist, pressing the vessel's leatheren neck into his hand. "If you're right— about Cromwell's army, and . . . and ours—they outnumber us five to one."

Fergus downed a swig of the *usquebah*. When he turned

4

back to Brianna, the smile half-hidden in his grizzled red beard was strained.

"Whist, Bree," he said, tugging at the gold plait draped over her shoulder. "Ye of all people should know 'tis not size that matters, but the heart in the fighter. Two thousand the like of yer brothers an' that flame-topped Rogan Niall should have little trouble drivin' such a pack of Bible-bearin' sops back into the sea, think ye not?" He pointed one gnarled finger to the nearby summit of the city's wall. "That is, unless I toss the lot of 'em off the stones meself, first."

Aware that Fergus was attempting to distract her, yet grateful for his attempt, Brianna followed the path his finger directed to where the six-foot-thick barrier snaked beneath them, ringing the town in medieval arrogance. Even the sun, as it danced across the stone, seemed to join in the frolics of her brothers, Daniel and Doyle, who stood atop the wall's narrow crest four cart-lengths away.

Morning scattered rich gold sparkles across the cheeks of Doyle, her oldest brother; the breeze, sweet and cool on its sweep down the River Boyne, tousling mischievous Daniel's honey-colored curls. Despite the grim scene on the hills beyond, Brianna had to smile when, with a mock innocence that belied his skill, Daniel, fourteen years old, whooshed a pikestaff about. In a deceptively awkward path, the seasoned ash end whisked bare inches from Doyle's nose, the pike's iron point neatly plucking a slab of buttered fadge from the brooding Rogan's hand.

Purpose served, Daniel snatched his booty with a whoop of glee, pausing but a second to drop the pike before scampering off down the wall top. Robbed of his breakfast, and whatever scraps of good humor he had left, Rogan gave chase, hurling threats that would have made a seasoned soldier blanch. But Daniel, his brown cloak streaming behind him, merely pulled a face, cramming the hearty bread into his mouth as he skittered to the streets below to lose himself in the crowds. Thoroughly enjoying the frolic, the ever-patient Doyle threw back his head, letting one of his rare, yet beautiful, laughs trip along the dawn.

Brianna lifted her hand in silent greeting as his gaze swept to the steeple, but memories of a distant twilight haunted her mind. Doyle screaming at her for the first time in his life, raging—irresponsible, he had called her then, but in

5

truth she had been *responsible* . . . responsible for the disaster that had struck that fateful night . . . and for the nightmare that followed.

Her fingers dropped to the window ledge, the smile that had touched her lips fading. Yet even from so far away, Doyle's soft brown eyes seemed to soothe her. Brianna blinked the veiling of tears from her lashes. No blame clouded his face. Only love. Always love.

Her heart twisted as Doyle grinned up at her. Pressing his fingertips to his lips, he threw his hand outward, sailing the kiss toward her as he had when she was small. Brianna reached out, pretending to catch it. But instead of the gentle sense of security that had always stolen through her from the imaginary kisses, self-loathing seared through her, leaving her empty, hollow as the blown glass orb Shane had brought her once from Rosecrea.

She looked away, fastening overbright eyes on a distant Roundhead banner, but it was not the folds of billowing silk she saw, but rather fragments of crystal, scattered like broken dreams across a wrapping of tawny linen. It had been but two months since Dame Death robbed her of one brother. When the fighting did begin, would the old hag be so greedy as to steal Daniel and Doyle as well?

"Ye've naught t' fear, Bree."

Brianna started, Fergus's voice more gentle than she had ever heard it. "They be a fine brace o' boys. Erin's finest." The tender light in his dark eyes was that of a weary father as he turned his gaze away from the young men, letting it drift again to Brianna.

The keen, questing expression beneath the scarred lids made her squirm. "It's quiet ye are of a sudden," Fergus said. "Are yer fairies whisperin'?"

"No. It's—"

"Rogan? Ye and the lad a-warrin' again, Bree?" He glared down at the sullen young man. "I vow, if words were sabers, that stubborn oaf'd have cut 'is way through every man in this garrison by now, what with 'im constantly twistin' every word ye say to him into a slur on 'is sainted father's honor. Betimes I could thrash 'im meself, plaguin' ye as 'e does."

"He tries not to," Brianna said softly. "'Tis just that he . . ."

6

"Loves ye?" Fergus snorted in disgust. "Well, 'tis no excuse fer drivin' a body mad. Ye've made yer feelin's on the matter clear enough. The boy had best to honor 'em an' find some other poor wench to foist 'imself upon." For all his bluster, Fergus's mouth widened in a disgruntled grin. "Ah, well, mayhap I be too hard upon the boy," he admitted grudgingly. "Can not be easy, bein' the son of the man who turned traitor at Gobbin's cliffs—"

"Tomas Niall was no trait—"

Her indignant defense was cut short by Fergus's battle-hardened hand against her lips. "I mean the boy no harm, Bree. 'Tis just hard for people to forget . . . women, babes bein' driven off the cliffs as though they were—" Fergus stopped, his eyes roving out to the English encampment below.

When at last he dragged his gaze back to Brianna, he raised her chin up with a finger so stiff from past injuries its joints were nigh useless. One corner of his mouth tipped up in a gentle smile. "'Tis little wonder the poor lad's so smitten wi' ye, cailin. It's passin' fair ye be, bristlin' up t' shield 'im so. I vow I could vanquish thrice the number o' Cromwell's army, had I but a dozen wi' courage such as ye."

Even as her cheeks flamed with pleased embarrassment at Fergus's blunt words of praise, Brianna detected a wariness beneath the old soldier's scarred eyelids. He stared over the heads of his three young charges, out across the myriad of tents blighting the grassy swells beyond. "Ye'll take care, child? In what is to come?"

"Aye. And you?"

"My eyes have seen a lifetime o' wars." Fergus's broad shoulders squared, stubborn, proud, facing unafraid what Brianna was certain, he, too, knew was disaster. "Ye'd best go down, Bree. There be fires, now, near th' cannons." She turned, a first, distant rumble sending tentacles of fear unfurling inside her.

"Fergus, I—"

"Whist, now. There be naught either of us can do but fight bravely. Bree?"

She turned. One corner of Fergus's mouth twisted up, the smile tragic, tired.

7

"Aye?"

"Ye might speak t' yer fairies fer me, if ye chance t' see 'em."

Icy fingers of foreboding trickled down Brianna's spine.

"'Tis passin' miserable . . . fightin' in the rain," Fergus said softly. "An' I think I hear the thunder."

Chapter Two

The dank hovel reeked of unwashed bodies, excrement, and the far subtler stench of human bondage as violet chains of night shackled the hills. Lord Creighton Wakefield thrust the blood-colored folds of his casaque over wide-set shoulders. Eyes, gray as a gale-tossed sea, narrowed as he stalked toward the eerily shaded building that cowered in a crook of the hidden glen.

Curse them! Curse them all! Cromwell, his blasted army, Charles Stuart, and himself. Aye, most of all God curse Creighton Wakefield as a dundering fool. Four-and-twenty years he had plunged from one grand adventure to the next, savoring danger as though it were but another roll of the die in a bout of gaming. Yet this time he had not only cast his own life to the tables of chance, but the life of his best friend as well. And it seemed that for the first time Dame Fortune had turned against him.

Creigh peered over his shoulder, eyes straining to penetrate the darkness of the tree-shrouded path he had ridden moments ago. Moonlight rimed the far-off walls of Drogheda, the distant glow of Roundhead campfires dancing flame shadows up the crumbling stone. *A dance of death for the defenders within the walls,* Creigh thought grimly. Yet he could mourn with them as they awaited Armageddon. For this night had also seen the end of his own reckless plan. The desperate plot in which he had risked his honor, his loved ones, his life. His life . . . he cared naught if they cast it to the winds. But Michel's . . .

Frustration, helplessness brassy in his mouth, Creigh

raked strong fingers through untamable waves of hair the rich dark shades of rosewood. It had all seemed so simple while he and Michel had lain sprawled in the Comtesse de Alimagne's chambers after a night of wenching. They would dupe the stodgy Cromwell and his plodding Parliamentarian government with the same finesse with which they had fooled a score of jealous husbands, then return to the exiled court of Charles II in glory.

Creigh's eyes skimmed to where the peak of Oliver Cromwell's tent rose midst the distant glow like the shield of some vengeful saint. Simple . . . Nay, for Creigh this mission had never been simple . . . for its goal was to free the man he hated most in the world from the dread Tower of London. Free the man he hated, yet loved. Galliard Wakefield, Duke of Blackthorne. Galliard Wakefield . . . his father.

Creigh forced the thought away, fighting to banish with it the jagged-edged emotions tearing through him. There was no time for anger, pain, regret. No time for anything except snatching Michel from the greedy hands of death.

They had been betrayed. Creigh had seen it in the lord lieutenant's dour, siege-worn face, felt it in the stiff shoulders and hooded stares of his fellow officers clustered around Saul Ogden an hour past in the canvas shelter. Ogden . . . Aye, Creigh had seen it especially in the disquietingly familiar sneer of the mercenary colonel: a triumph glimmering beneath the slit of his drooping eyelid, pock-ravaged jowls ruddy with loathing. Nothing, Creigh was certain, would please the sadistic Ogden more than to see Creigh's head adorning a traitor's pike on London Bridge. Yet, for reasons a mystery to Creigh, the wily Cromwell had done nothing, merely biding his time . . . waiting . . .

Creigh's mouth twisted bitterly. Mayhap the high and holy commander had petitioned God to split the earth and hurl Creigh to Hades. Well, so be it. Cromwell and his avaricious savior could cast Creigh wherever the impulse struck them. But he'd not drag Michel with him, by the saints. Creigh reached beneath his casaque, fingering the smooth shape of a silver flask, the jeweled hilt of a dagger. No, he'd not drag Michel with him.

Striding to the heavy oak door, Creigh cracked his knotted fist against it as though it were the face of some unseen enemy.

There was clattering within, followed by a muffled curse, then the heavy oak door swung open, feeble light from a single candle within silhouetting the skinny form of guard Perkin Ulger. "Who goes there?" the man barked, tardily fumbling for the hilt of his sword.

"Colonel Lord Wakefield."

Eyes dull as rain-sodden mud flickered with recognition and barely checked insolence. "Ah, yer lordship." Thin lips snaked over rotting teeth, the lopsided grin foul with cunning. "I was e'spectin'—uh, hopin' someone 'd be about."

The veiled insult of the guard dropping his military title set Creigh's nerves on edge. He stiffened, leveling Ulger a steady glare. "You said we're expecting someone, *Private* Ulger," Creigh prodded coldly. "Why? Is there something you or your prisoner have need of?"

The man cleared his scrawny throat and spat on the ancient rushes strewn across the floor. "I be 'fraid milord marquis be nigh out 'o eatables," the guard said, his ingratiating grin turning Creigh's stomach. "Made the 'ristocrat dog so surly I had t' give 'im the flat o' me sword but an hour past."

A muscle in Creigh's jaw tensed, as he ducked beneath the doorjamb, pacing past the guard's fetid bulk into the filth-ridden room. Creigh turned, a silky edge to his voice. "The marquis was ever . . . surly."

"'Tis a common fault wi' Royalist scum. Too much time slaverin' over fancy laces, an' silk-dressed strumpets. But we'll soon ha' the traitors beggin' fer mercy, eh, yer lordship?"

One corner of Creigh's mouth lifted in a brittle smile, instincts honed in a lifetime of court intrigues snapping whipcord tight at the odd glint in the guard's eyes. "No one will rejoice more at the traitor's fall than I." The words were steely challenge cased in velvet. "After all, 'tis why I rode here from camp tonight. To tip a flask to their impending defeat." Creigh reached beneath the scarlet folds of his casaque, withdrawing the small silver flacon. "To the fall of Drogheda, and the death of Le Marquis de Charteaux."

"Aren't you a trifle premature, *cousin?*"

Creigh wheeled toward the sound, the light from the candle casting eerie shadows on a form in the corner of the cottage. "It may yet be *your* traitor's head bedecking the tower." Sharp, patrician features seemed ludicrous beneath their coating of dirt, a fall of dark-blond curls, once the pride of Paris's most dashing cavalier, falling in a nest of dirty tangles across the remains of a velvet doublet.

"Michel." Creigh tried to sneer the name, but the moon, streaking through the still open door, skated silver across a bruise purpling one finely carved cheek.

Creigh yanked the flask's stopper free with a force that nigh twisted the neck from the silver vessel. "Come now, milord marquis, is this any way to bid farewell to your most trusted friend?"

"I can think of a hundred ways I'd like to bid adieu to you, Wakefield. All at the point of my sword."

"T'would seem you've fared badly enough in swordplay this day." Creigh gave a short laugh, brushing his cheek with his knuckles. "You would do well to check your temper, my lord, lest your betters check it for you."

"You? My better?" Michel Le Ferre's face twisted with contempt. "Do you know what your traitor comrades call you? Wakefield the betrayer, the jackal who waits to scavenge the lands of his father and brother over their corpses—"

"Damn you!" Instinctively Creigh's fist flashed out, the blow connecting with Michel's jaw despite Creigh's attempt to stop it. Slowly Le Ferre raised a shackled hand, one elegant finger wiping a trickle of blood from the corner of his mouth. Brows swept low over eyes suddenly confused as a huntsman whose hawk has flown, talons spread, into his face. Bile rose in Creigh's throat, horror rushing through his still-throbbing knuckles as he realized what he had done.

"Well taken, yer lordship! That'll school 'im t' keep 'is Royalist yap shut!" Perkin Ulger's high-pitched giggle made Creigh want to drive his fist into the man's stomach. "'Risticrat bastard, th' colonel 'ere will show ye how we deal wi'—"

"Get out." The command was all the more dangerous because it was scarce above a whisper.

"Yer lordship—"

"I said *get out.*" Creigh spun to face the private. "The prisoner and I have some unfinished business to attend to."

"B-but sir, if Colonel Ogden was t'—"

"Colonel Ogden will be sequestered in the lord lieutenant's tent all night, making plans for tomorrow's assault on Drogheda," Creigh said, fingers clenched about the neck of the flacon still in his hand. "He'll never know that you stepped outside for a trice, to . . . shall we say, *brace* yourself for the ordeal of battle?"

"Battle?" Perkin squeaked, scuttling toward Michel, as though to use Le Ferre as a human shield. "I be goin' t' no battle!"

"A fine *disciplined* soldier such as you, who cannot be coaxed to relax his duty a trifle, even at the bidding of an officer? I can well imagine your disappointment at being cheated out of the morrow's excitement. Of course, one of the cavalrymen under my command fell from his mount this morn. Mayhap before the assault I could request—"

"Nay, Colonel Lord Wakefield. I—" The bony private gulped. "I don't be above skirtin' me duty a bit now and again . . . an' I be sore 'fraid o' horses . . ."

"But not, I trust, afraid of brandy?" Creigh extended his flacon toward the skittish Ulger and nodded to the open cottage door. The etched silver flask trapped the glow from the smoldering fire, strewing silver-orange glimmers of light across the rushes.

"N-nay, sir. Th-thankee, sir." The guard snatched the flask with trembling fingers, skittering toward the doorway. "I-I'll be outside, lest ye ha' need o'—"

Striding to the door, Creigh slammed it shut behind the guard, so quickly Perkin had scarce time to yank his scrawny buttocks through the aperture. Creigh wheeled, lips stiff with remorse as his eyes locked on the scarlet smear still visible on Le Ferre's mouth. "Michel, by God I meant not—"

The Frenchman grimaced. "I see your skill with your fist has suffered much since our last bout of brawling at the Griffin's Claw. You were supposed to make *pretense* of striking me, not fatten my lip like a cursed pastry."

"I know. 'Tis just . . ." Creigh ground his fingertips into his eyes. "You struck a tender spot with me."

"*A tender spot?*" Michel yelped, glaring in total disdain.

13

"There is not a spot on my entire person that has not been feasted upon by vermin, rubbed raw by these God-curst shackles, or bruised by that miscreant Ulger. And now, thanks to you, cousin, 'twill be weeks before I can . . . *amuse* myself with the ladies." Michel fell back into the tattered blankets, affecting such a look of wounded dignity, Creigh felt the ghost of a smile tug at his mouth.

"Fear not, Michel. I warrant there are few beauties on this barbaric isle worthy of your discriminating tastes. Besides, in your present state of dress, I doubt even Juliet would deign to speak to you."

"You think not?" The words were quiet, bemused, a rare tinge of brooding clouding the pale blue of Michel's eyes. "Your sister was ever given to tossing livres to starvelings."

Creigh looked at his best friend sharply, but there was none of the usual lazy mockery in Michel's face. All pretense of arrogance had vanished from his features, a sudden softness touching the haughty curve of his lips. As if suddenly aware that silence shrouded the room, Michel's gaze snagged Creigh's, then leapt away, a tinge of rose dusting the crests of the Frenchman's cheekbones.

Chains rippled, chinking together as, with a restless laugh, Le Ferre pushed himself up from the cot. He swept fingertips accustomed only to the finest of silks over the soiled blue velvet nigh fused to his chest with sweat and dirt. "What think you, Creigh? Would I not make Mauricheau Bouret a fine scullion lad? I am told your sister's husband is hard put to keep servants in his employ."

"Despite the shackles and grime, you've not yet acquired the look of a whipped cur." Creigh paced to the tiny window and stared moodily into the blurred square of night visible through the greased paper pane. "'Tis the single requirement to gain entry to Chateau aux Marées Vengeresses. Be it as hireling or . . . wife." He fairly spat the last word, the taste of it bitter on his tongue. "Dear God, how could Father do it? Christ, even *he* has to love Juliet."

Creigh wheeled, pain raking claws through his belly, but he found no answers in Le Ferre's face. Traces of unnameable emotion lined Michel's brow, mixed with resignation.

"Love has naught to do with marriage, Creigh. Never has. 'Tis but a game we play, tossing our hearts like quoits. And

14

'tis our own foolish fault if the iron rings sweep back to crush dreams we should never have dared hold in the first place." The touch of melancholy disappeared from Michel's face, yet Creigh sensed the arrogance being carefully schooled into features reluctant to fall into their accustomed bored lines.

"So." Michel's voice was suddenly brisk. "Since I see no fresh doublet or scented soap, I assume you've not risked coming here to rescue me from the horror my person has become?"

"No. I've come to leave you these." Creigh slipped free a disreputable looking bundle secreted beneath his casaque. "'Tis a peddler's shirt, breeches—"

"I am . . . speechless with gratitude," Michel interrupted, nudging the bundle with one finger, as though expecting a rat to leap from the dingy gray folds. "Just because *you* choose to lower yourself to be seen in the raiment of the peasantry, Lord Creighton, does not mean that *I* can be cozened into wearing it. The very thought is enough to make my skin burst into a pox." Michel shuddered. "Jesu', next you'll be slipping me a scissors, expecting me to shear my hair like you have."

"There was no room in the bundle for scissors. You'll have to use this instead." Creigh unsheathed the dagger at his side, pressing its jeweled hilt into Michel's hand. The Frenchman's other fingers leapt to the dirty locks falling past his shoulders, blue eyes widening in a genuine horror that would have been comical in other circumstances.

"Creigh, what—"

"Damn it, Michel, for once your needs must sacrifice your vanity—that is unless you want your curls *plus* your head adorning London Bridge." Exasperated, Creigh raked his fingers through his own dark, collar-length mane.

"I had not planned to relinquish either. Perhaps if you would explain?"

"It's Ogden. Somehow the bastard discovered what is afoot. Or at the very least, tenders strong suspicions. And Cromwell, it seems, is heeding them. There was a meeting tonight—advisors, officers, to plan for the storming of the city tomorrow. Every commander in camp was ordered to be there, Michel. But when I arrived, I was told that since I was the newest addition to the ranks of Parliamentarian officers, I was being charged to inspect the sentries and check the cavalry mounts during the meeting."

Michel's brow wrinkled in thought. "'Tis not such an odd request. Someone has to—"

"Michel, it was not just the orders, but the way they were given. Cromwell was staring at me cold as Christ facing the devil, and Ogden, God curse him, was grinning at me like a wolf who has just torn out a stag's throat. There's naught to do now but get you away from here, then slip from the ranks myself."

"But Lindley . . . your father . . . 'Tis but six weeks 'til they fall before the headsman's axe."

"Damn it, you think I don't know that? I've agonized over it for hours. But if we are both taken prisoner, what hope do they have? All our plotting to secure their escape will have been in vain."

"Yet our plan depends upon one of us being in the Tower, or have you forgotten why I am allowing myself to be subjected to this?" Michel crinkled his nose at the stench rising from his soiled clothing. "Without someone to inform them of the plot, guide them, do the last bits of bribery necessary from within the prison walls—"

"Unless one of us remains *outside* of the prison there will be no plan to explain." Creigh stalked across the room. "We have to escape Ireland as best we can, then travel to London and hope, please God, that we can contrive a way to get word to Lindley and Father before . . ." Flattening his palm upon the wall, he leaned his forehead against the crook of his elbow. "Damn it, Michel, I feel so cursed helpless!"

"Helpless?" Creigh heard the stirrings of the rushes, the clink of chains. Hard and warm, Michel's hand gripped his shoulder. "Even without your hair, you are more than a match for those Bible-bloated bastards in England. We'll just divest Private Ulger of his senses, then dash off for the ship Charles comissioned us in Carikbrah. With the battle in the offing we can easily elude—"

"Nay."

"What?"

"I'll not be leaving with you tonight. I purloined the key to your shackles from Ogden's quarters before I came, and I vow he fingers it more often than Sister Clementia fingers her rosary beads. Unless I return it, t'will alert him to your escape. I'll allay their suspicions by going back to my tent, gather some things, then slip away before the battle."

"Providing our beloved Colonel Ogden is not waiting in your quarters with a set of irons to match these lovely ones he gifted me with."

Creigh's jaw hardened at the memory of the slack-lipped eagerness that had fouled the colonel's face the day he had first shoved Michel's wrists into the iron bands. It had taken every ounce of control Creigh had not to draw sword on the brute as he had leered at Le Ferre with an almost ghoulish greed, as though Ogden were some pagan priest about to feast on human flesh. Creigh pulled his gaze away from Michel's and busied himself searching out the heavy iron key that lay in a leathern bag at his waist.

"There's naught to fear, Michel," Creigh said, working the rusty locks at Le Ferre's wrists. "Cromwell is clutching tight to Ogden's chain for the present, and if 'twas the lord lieutenant's intention to imprison me this night, he would have done it the moment I entered his tent. You and I will meet in Carikbrah two weeks hence, board the ship Charles stationed there at our disposal, and have the captain put us ashore somewhere near the mouth of the Thames."

"Agreed. By the time we strike out on English soil, we'll have come up with some other—ah, what did Juliet call it? *Some other brainless scheme to get us both killed.*" Michel slipped the iron circlets from wrists chafed raw. He flexed his fists. "Well, it seems there is naught left to do but allow myself the pleasure of repaying Private Ulger for his tender care."

"I am afraid you could thrash him until your knuckles turned black, and he would never know it," Creigh said. "I slipped a sleeping philter into the brandy. When the coward wakes tomorrow, Cromwell will be well into the battle, and I doubt Ulger will risk coming within musket range bearing the news that the Marquis de Charteaux has vanished. And by the time Cromwell makes an end of the poor bastards inside Drogheda's walls, you and I should be well on our respective ways down the coast."

Unbidden, the memory of stone sprang into Creigh's mind, courageous fighters entrenched behind their failing shelter. His allies they were, though they knew it not.

Charles II's allies. An odd flash of guilt jabbed Creigh. There was naught a single man could do to turn back the tide of destruction that would soon sweep over the city. And yet . . .

"Creigh, you are not telling me all." Turning back to Michel, Creigh saw his friend regarding him through questioning eyes.

Creigh dropped the key back into the pouch, forcing a bantering tone. "Aye, you're right," he said, slanting Michel a grin. "The real reason I dare not flee with you is that t'would ruin my reputation. No self-respecting cavalier would suffer being seen with a mangy lowling the likes of you."

"M-mangy!" Michel sputtered indignantly. "At least I still have my hair."

"Aye, God help the virgins of Carikbrah," The laugh that tumbled from Creigh's lips was like a river bursting its banks, the waves sweeping snarled emotions that had plagued him for days, cooling them, soothing them, like the waters of a spring freshet. It had ever been easy to laugh with Michel, no matter what befell them. War, betrayal . . . death. Creigh clamped his hands on his friend's broad shoulders. "I vow Ireland's mothers had best look sharp to guard their daughters' maidenheads."

"If there be a maidenhead on this whole infernal island worth the plucking."

Creigh turned to the door, but the familiar cool brushing of an object against his chest made him pause. He reached beneath the wide fallen ruff about his throat, drawing out a slender gold chain. The ivory disk it bore shone softly in the candlelight.

"Here, friend," Creigh said, pressing it into Michel's hand.

Le Ferre opened his palm, his face suddenly still. Fireshine stroked soft color into the face captured on the ivory miniature. Hair that glowed all the warm lovely shades brown can be, swept back from delicate cheeks, dark eyes alive with unbridled merriment peering out above a soft mouth, all the more vulnerable because it seemed fashioned solely to smile. Michel's fingers closed over the painted face with a gentle reverence. He raised eyes devoid of careless jest, his handsome features flushed as a village lad caught in his first throes of impossible passion.

"'Tis a talisman to protect you from the hordes of barbarian maidens who will no doubt give you little peace on your journey," Creigh said. "St. Juliet, the ever loving."

"And who, my friend, will be your patron, then, against these warrior maids?" Michel's voice wavered, the attempt at his usual light-hearted humor failing.

Creigh's mouth tipped in a grin. "I needs must fend for myself." Pacing to the door, Creigh opened it a crack. The sleeping draught had worked its magic well. Ulger lay sprawled amongst the roots of a nearby oak tree, his sagging mouth emitting snores that rivaled the rumblings of the now silent cannons entrenched upon the hills.

Creigh turned again to Michel. "I tied a horse for you about a mile west of here, in the ruins of an old monastery. And there is enough coin in the bundle to take you to Carikbrah in a style befitting a poor peddler."

Michel nodded, his hand still clutching the miniature.

"Godspeed, friend," Creigh said softly.

Michel closed the distance between them in three quick strides, embracing Creigh in arms from which hunger had robbed a measure of once steely strength. "We'll find a way, Creigh, to spare both Lindley and your father. I swear it."

"Aye."

"And Creigh—" Michel grabbed up his bundle starting toward the open door. "Quit the Roundhead camp as soon as you can. If I reach Carikbrah before you, I vow there'll be not a drop of ale left in the whole port."

"After all you've risked for the Wakefields," Creigh said, following Michel into the cottage yard. "If I reach Carikbrah first, I'll *buy* you every barrel of ale in the city."

"I'll hold you to that." Le Ferre's voice was solemn, rife with cautions neither man could utter aloud.

Creigh flashed him a taut grin. "I'll have my coin ready."

Striding to where his own mount was tethered to a tree, Creigh swung into the saddle with the lithe grace of a man bred to ride. He paused, lifting his hand in return to Michel's silent salute, watching as his friend's pale shadow dissolved into the shrouding of darkness.

The wind's chill fingers crept beneath the folds of Creigh's casaque. By hour's end the key would be safely on the peg driven into Ogden's field desk. And by dawn, Creigh would be miles on his way toward Carikbrah. 'Twas a child's game, Creigh thought. Simple as fighting a battle against merchants and yeomen had seemed before the defeat at Nasby. Simple as holding a crown.

Creigh fought to suppress the thought, the unaccustomed weight of failure settling upon his shoulders like a mantle of chain mail. Why, then, did he feel like a green country lad, hurling his weapons to the grass, to flee from the horror of battle? And why did the walls of Drogheda clutch at him, like claws of the damned plunging into hell?

The darkened interior of the forest-green tent seemed to burn Creigh's flesh like flaming pitch as he stalked across its familiar confines. The sandalwood scent that had whispered of home to him on a dozen separate battlefields mourned now for hope buried. It was over. Nigh an hour had passed since he had hung the key to Michel's shackles in Ogden's field tent. The roan stallion stood ready in the shelter of a copse of trees half a mile from the outskirts of the encampment. And Colonel Lord Wakefield? Creigh swore, cramming a wad of white linen into the recesses of his saddlebags. Before the moon softened into dawn, that leader of a dozen daring cavalry charges, that rakehell friend to Charles II, would be skulking through the shadows like a whipped cur.

Creigh's fist knotted in the cloth, the fabric snagging on his sword-roughened hand. Sweet Christ, he should be rejoicing that all had gone well. Michel was free, and, he, Creigh, would soon be extricated from this sham of allegiance he had been forced to show his enemies. Yet even as he had crept through Ogden's musty tent, he had nigh longed to see the man's pockmarked countenance, nigh wished that the cruel colonel would return so that he could pit his blade against a tangible enemy.

Creigh loosed his hold on the linen, but the soft folds clung like a gentle, staying hand. He fingered the gold threads of embroidery, worked by Juliet's own needle last Michelmas. "What would you think of your brother now, Jolie?" he asked bitterly. "Now that I've failed Lindley . . ."

Lindley. Eyes guileless as a child's despite their six-and-

20

twenty years rose in Creigh's mind, their gentle blue light staring out at the world with the patient suffering of St. Sebastian 'neath the knife. Was that innocent face ravaged now by the horrors that lurked within London's fearsome Tower? Those eyes turned expectantly toward the horizon, watching, waiting for Creigh to come as he always had before? To rescue him as he had the night Penrose Trowbridge and his band of stripling ruffians had locked a ten-year-old Lindley inside the abandoned cottier's hut the peasant folk claimed was ruled by the dark one.

Creigh shut his eyes against the agony that twisted in his belly, the image of his brother's face that long ago night rising to haunt him. For hours every kern within the castle had scoured the lands in search of the missing boy, a frantic Galliard Wakefield tearing about at their head.

But when at last Creigh had thrown open the door to the dark, cobweb-dusted room, Lindley had merely smiled a serene, yet sad smile and said: "I knew that you would come."

Creigh's fingers clenched on the half-filled leather pouch upon his cot, the hammered iron fastenings of the container cutting deep into his palm. 'Twas as if he could feel Lindley's slender, pale hand reaching out to him from across the wild-tossed sea, sense the bewilderment that would savage Lindley's gentle soul if he were prodded through a jeering crowd of London rabble to meet his death.

"Marquess de Lackwit," the cruel boy-nobles had labeled him, when the Duke of Blackthorne had gifted his heir with the title of Arransea. The cowardly varlets tormented Lindley, Creigh knew, whenever he was not there to serve as his champion. Yet what fate had slighted Lindley in powers of reason it had gifted richly in sensitivity, and to face the blood-drunk joy of the masses at his execution would snuff out not only the spark of Lindley's life, but the essence of his soul as well.

Iron bands seemed to crush Creigh's chest as he turned, sweeping up the rest of the objects scattered across his cot. Nay. If he had to plunge a dagger into Lindley's heart himself, he would spare his brother that ghoulish rite.

Creigh jammed the tangle of clothing, leatherbound volumes, and a scattering of jewels into the pouch, caring naught what became of the jumbled mass.

Swirling a sable-lined mantle of velvet shot with gold about his shoulders, Creigh enveloped himself in its midnight folds, shielding from curious eyes the silvery gleam of back and breastplates encasing his chest, the glistening visor and jaunty burgundy plumes of the cuirassier's helmet affixed to the leather strap of his shoulder belt. If he were stopped by anyone, t'would be nigh impossible to explain why he was leaving camp laden with the accoutrements of war.

Pacing to the table at the far end of the tent, he took up the jeweled butt of his pistol, shoving its barrel into the band of his breeches. 'Twould no doubt prove useful in convincing the sentries to let him pass, in the event of any difficulty. Creigh let his eyes rove one final time about the canvas walls that had served as his sanctuary these weeks within the dragon's jaws.

The glow from the one candle stub he'd dared light cast a rich patina of shadow over those articles of armor he was being forced to abandon, and glossed the flame's reflection over chests inlaid with ivory. Let Ogden and his vultures have it all, Creigh thought, slinging the pouch over his other shoulder. It mattered not.

Easing aside the tent flap, he peered out into the sea of canvas shelters. They seemed to stretch forever, blanketing the earth with ten thousand different hopes and fears on this, the eve of battle. Three tents away, Creigh could hear crabbed Grover Sproule grousing about his bunions to his long-suffering comrade Dolittle Makepeace, while somewhere, toward the back of the encampment, incorrigible jester Harston Walcott spun a bawdy tale for Creigh's solemn aide-de-camp, Jules Dunley.

Creigh's mouth twisted into a cynical curve as he pictured Dunley's boyish features taut with shock at Walcott's lewd story. No doubt Michel would laughingly discount it, but Creigh had but to close his eyes to imagine himself back with a Royalist camp. Exchange the plainer raiment of the men for a few velvets, replace the page-worn psalters in the tents for equally dog-eared Catholic tomes, and there would be little difference in the armies that would murder each other on the morrow. Each bore its fanatics. Each bore its heroes. And each would bury its dead.

Creigh grimaced, as he slipped silently through the moonlit night. Was he becoming an old woman, with no stomach for war? Or was that double-edged feeling of betrayal buried in his chest because for the first time the soldiers whom he had opposed on a dozen different battlefields had faces? Names? Even though the majority of men had never fully accepted him, he had shared their firesides, their exhaustion, the rare missives from mothers, sisters, wives who loved them.

And he had shared their fears. Creigh tightened his grip on his pouch as the maze of tents before him thinned, giving way to dark, empty countryside but a hundred steps beyond. The low murmur of sentries posted nearby rose and fell amidst the quiet that edged the encampment.

Creigh narrowed his eyes, trying to gauge the position of the guards. If he could only—

Suddenly he froze, the hair at the nape of his neck prickling as a shriek spawned of hell split the night. Chilled to the core of his being, he wheeled toward the sound, the screams of terror now mingling with a sickeningly familiar laugh.

Silhouetted in the moonlight, the bearlike bulk of Saul Ogden grappled with a wild-eyed urchin so filthy half his weight could be measured in the mud encrusting his ragged trews. Beefy fingers forced the child's arm toward a tree stump, the Roundhead's huge hand crushing the boy's wrist until it seemed that the delicate bones must surely snap.

"Strike me again, you thieving Irish bastard, and I vow I'll cleave it at the elbow!" Ogden's lips curled back from his teeth in a blood-hungry sneer. "You'll be cutting no more purse strings with that hand!" The child shrieked, sobbed, clawing and kicking at Ogden like a fox kit in the jaws of a bear. Sick horror tore through Creigh, as Ogden hissed out a laugh cold enough to freeze the river Styx, the man's thick fingers grasping the hilt of his sword.

All thought of Michel, Lindley, and the sanctuary of darkness but a whisper away vanished from Creigh's mind. There was the sound of running footsteps, other men's shouts, but Creigh scarce heard them. Hurling the encumbering pouch and helmet to the dirt, Creigh lunged out of the shadows, racing across the distance separating him from the child as Ogden's blade whisked free of its scabbard. The sword arced upward. Hurtling himself toward Ogden,

Creigh grabbed the man's thick wrist with fingers strong as tensile steel, tearing the colonel's heavily muscled arm to one side. Ogden gave a bellow of rage, his face contorting as he tried to hold the weapon to its path. There was a gut-wrenching sound of the blade biting deep.

Horror jolting through him, Creigh's eyes flashed to the tree stump's surface. He had but an instant to see that only the wood lay mangled, the silvery edge of Ogden's sword buried deep within the chunk of oak a blade's breadth from the child's small fingers. Then Ogden spun on him, eyes bulging with the crazed fury of a boar robbed of its kill.

"Od's feet, are you mad?!" Creigh yanked the child free of the colonel's cruel grasp, shoving the scrawny lad behind the shield of his own broad shoulders. "For God's sake, Ogden—"

"God's sake!" Blood rushed to the Roundhead colonel's face flushing the pouchy sags of flesh so red they seemed ready to burst. "What would *you* know of God, aristocrat cur, aside from the crosses piercing your harlot's ears? The brat is a thief! I saw him—"

"I don't give a damn *what* you saw! Christ's blood, you can't cleave a child's hand!"

"A *thief's* hand! I was but serving God's justice. 'Tis written in the Bible: *If a hand offends ye, cast it from—*"

"The hand of a six-year-old child?" Creigh grabbed the little boy's small fingers, thrusting them toward Ogden. "Look at them, for the devil's sake! Your great and vengeful *God* hasn't seen fit to give *this* lad's hand enough strength to 'offend' anyone!"

The sound of approaching footsteps stilled, night-blurred shadows of men closing about the three, quiet, watching.

"Sir, sir!" A little voice snuffled through sobs, as the boy tugged at Creigh's cloak. "I be . . . nae cutpurse! Me ma'd flay . . . me hide if I stole a . . . a egg from a linnet's nest! She bakes little cakies an' I—I was jest peddlin' 'em t' the soldiers, when—"

"What is your name, boy?" Creigh interrupted gently, crooking one finger beneath the quivering little chin to tip the child's face toward him.

"J-Jemmie, yer honor. J-Jemmie MacGregor."

"'Tis a trice late to be out peddling this night, is it not, Jemmie MacGregor?"

"Do you take me for a half-wit?" Ogden bellowed. "The whelp was thieving! I saw him creep into Private Sproule's tent, but the little ferret wriggled out the other side before I could catch him!"

"I weren't thievin'! I—"

"What is the meaning of this!" Sharp, clear, a voice well-accustomed to command cracked through the child's protest, every spine in the circle of soldiers stiffening to attention as the stocky figure of Oliver Cromwell stalked into their midst. Night-shadowed eyes glowered ominously from beneath a shelf of brows, the lord lieutenant's mouth set in a frown. "Colonel Ogden? Colonel Lord Wakefield?"

"T'was naught but a misunderstanding, sir," Creigh began. "This lad—"

"The boy is a thief!" Ogden blazed. "Colonel Wakefield interfered with just discipline."

"Begging your pardon, sir. Lord lieutenant, sir." One of the shadowy figures stepped into the moonlight. Private Harston Walcott fingered the brim of his hat sheepishly.

"Private? I was addressing my officers," Cromwell snapped.

"Aye, sir. But Colonel Wakefield's tellin' you true. Young Jemmie's no cutpurse. T'was me, sir, what sent him to Sproule's tent."

"You?"

"Aye, sir." Walcott shuffled his feet nervously. "T'was meant as a jest. There be a man in our regiment, Grover Sproule, an' he's always croakin' 'bout his . . . uh . . . bunions. Well, three days past I sent a message home with Jemmie, askin' his ma t' work me somethin' on her needles for Sproule. She finished it tonight, an' I gave Jemmie, here, a shilling t' sneak it into 'is tent."

"T'was a bunion cap," Jemmie piped up, eyeing Oliver Cromwell with a total lack of awe. "A fine 'un, wi' a crim-sum tassle on the top an' blue ribbands. But *he* made me tear it." The boy poked a dirty finger accusingly at Ogden's paunch. "Then 'e tried to chop me hand right off! But *he* stopped 'im," Jemmie said, turning to jab a thumb toward Creigh.

"Hush, Jem." Walcott swallowed convulsively. "We've done enough damage for one night. My 'pologies to you all, sirs, lord lieutenant, sir, Colonel Wakefield, an' Colonel

Ogden, fer settin' up this ruckus. And thank you, Colonel Wakefield, fer stepping in when you did. Praise God, no harm was done."

"Aye. Praise God no harm was done." Ogden's voice rasped unpleasantly. Creigh's gaze snapped up, locking with Ogden's slitted eyes. The muddy green depths were murky with hate, resentment, cunning, the subtle twisting of Ogden's lips warning that the colonel liked not appearing a buffoon in front of their commander. He gave Creigh a serpentine smile. "'Twas most fortuitous that the notoriously *loyal* Colonel Lord Wakefield happened to be such a . . . *distance* from his own tent on the even of battle, to save me from wreaking such an *inhuman* act upon this innocent child." Creigh felt every nerve in his body jerk taut. "Of course, one might wonder exactly what business drew him here . . ."

"Mayhap, Colonel Lord Wakefield, you would see fit to enlighten us in regards to whatever errand you were about here, at the very outskirts of camp?" Cromwell said.

There was a sudden scuffling sound to the back of the group as a gangly young man elbowed his way toward the knot of officers. Jules Dunley rushed forward, the gleaming object he held in his hands bumping sharply into the lord lieutenant's shoulder. Creigh's stomach lurched as a drifting of moonlight touched the russeted iron, burgundy plumes of his cuirassier's helm.

Cromwell's eyes flashed to the glimmering metal, his mouth hardening. Saul Ogden's blunt features radiated victory.

"Your explanation, Colonel Wakefield?" Cromwell demanded.

A heavy, suffocating silence fell over the soldiers surrounding them. Despite the roiling in his belly, Creigh squared his shoulders with the careless arrogance of a cavalier facing the headsman. A cynical smile touched his lips. "I was—"

"He was searching for me, sir."

Creigh's stunned gaze leapt up to the flushed Dunley. The aide-de-camp seemed to shrink into himself, clutching the helmet to his breast as though it were some holy relic. His soft brown eyes were wide as a startled child's. Confusion, gratitude, and fear coursed through Creigh, and he felt a sudden impulse to pull the younger man into the circle of his protection as he had Jemmie MacGregor.

"Searching for you?" Cromwell prodded, the echoed words a command to continue.

"Aye, sir. See, I was . . . polishing Colonel Lord Wakefield's cuirass in readiness for the assault tomorrow, and—"

"Polishing his armor half the camp away from his tent?" Ogden challenged derisively.

"No, sir. I was polishing it *in* the tent. But when I began on the helm, I found the visor was loosening. On my way to the armorer to have it repaired, uh . . ." Dunley twisted a wisp of the burgundy feather. "Uh . . . Private Walcott informed me of his gift to Private Sproule. We commenced talking, and . . . the time escaped me, sir."

Creigh stepped forward, easing himself in front of Jules's lanky frame. "'Tis of no consequence, private," he said, eyes hazed with solemn gratitude as he caught Dunley's gaze with his. "I had but a trifling question to ask you. I am glad I could be of aid to little Jemmie, here."

"'Twas most fortunate for the boy at least," the lord lieutenant assented cryptically. "But know you this. I will brook no more warring between my officers. 'Tis task enough to keep the troops at bay, with the scent of battle in the air. And Colonel Lord Wakefield—"

"Aye, sir?"

"I will expect you to remain with the men of your command until the assault commences." Creigh could feel the canny battery of Oliver Cromwell's eyes boring into him. "One never knows when a soldier might bolt for the hills. And deserters will be dealt with in a manner befitting their crime."

Ogden's smile slithered over Creigh like the underbelly of a snake. "I can post extra guard, lord lieutenant, sir. Strategically placed to—shall we say—*avert* any such temptation."

Cromwell nodded. "See to it at once." The lord lieutenant's eyes affixed on the violet sky, as if seeking some vision he alone could see. "'Tis God's sword we carry into Drogheda on the morrow, and any who stands in its way will face His righteous judgment."

Creigh drew his casaque more tightly about him, watching

27

in silence as the lord lieutenant strode off through the camp, the other soldiers and young Jemmie melting into the darkness as well.

Wispy memories from childhood swirled through Creigh's mind. Lindley standing in the shadow of the statue of Christ adorning the chapel at the Wakefield country estate of Wrensong, the image's marble hands reaching toward his brother in the gentlest of comfort. There had been no thirst for vengeance in the face that had taken the tortures of men's irrational hatreds onto His own flesh. Only a weary sorrow that had touched the beautifully wrought stone face like the kiss of a penitent child.

And when dawn broke, Oliver Cromwell would drown his hands in blood in the name of that gentle, tormented Being.

"Sir?"

Creigh started. Jules Dunley peered up at him, his face childlike as Jemmie MacGregor's, his brow furrowed in a puzzlement seeming strangely to reflect Creigh's own confused musings.

"God . . ." Jules hesitated. "God does want us to drive out the heathen Papists, does he not?"

"Who can say?" Creigh looked up into the silver countenance of the moon, but it held no answers, merely peering back at him with a face distant and cool as that of an empress, oblivious to the woes of those beneath her.

Dunley shifted uneasily. "I . . . I hear the Irish are fearsome fighters."

A smile tipped Creigh's mouth. "They should be. They've done little else these centuries past."

"Are you . . . afraid, sir?"

"Only a fool fears not on the eve of battle."

Creigh's skin crawled as fetid breath brushed upon his neck.

"And the great Colonel Lord Creighton Wakefield is of a certainty no *fool,* eh, Dunley?"

Creigh slanted his gaze to where Ogden stood, flanked by two hulking soldiers. Ogden's jowls stretched in a malevolent sneer. "I am assigning Seabert and Thorley, two of my most trusted retainers, to remain in your company until the battle begins, Colonel Lord Wakefield. In case any other part of your armor needs repair."

Ogden's fingers closed on the hilt of his sword, still buried in the stump. He yanked it free. "Make certain your aide, here, hones your weapons well, Wakefield," Ogden purred, caressing the blade as though it were a woman. A line of blood welled on the man's thick finger. Ogden smiled. "Aye. Hone them well. For you needs must fear far subtler steel than an Irish sword this night."

Chapter Three

Brianna clutched her rapier in fingers so swollen they could not uncurl from its wire-bound hilt. Only the viselike grip of Rogan's hand crushing her other wrist kept her from crashing to the cobbles, as he dragged her through the street. Behind them the sea of Roundhead invaders welled, a bright gash of crimson set against a maze of crumbled stone.

Scarlet with the blood of a thousand deaths, the blades of Cromwell's army slashed, hungry, greedy at ought that moved before them as the soldiers poured across the drawbridge linking the town across the river Boyne. Women clutching babes, grasping at scattered broods of children, struggled desperately to keep ahead of the sparse shield of Royalist survivors, the straggling ranks of wounded, battle-dazed soldiers their only defense against the seething mass of the New Model Army.

Brianna turned burning eyes back toward the roiling scene of destruction, fighting yet again to free herself from Rogan's crushing grasp, to run and aid their embattled comrades. But 'twas as if her numbed limbs belonged to someone else, exhaustion robbing her muscles of all strength, all will.

"Damn it, Bree, stop fighting me!" Rogan snarled, yanking her into a darkened lane with a force that nearly jerked her arm from its socket. "You'll do naught but die back there. Think of Doyle."

Doyle . . . Brianna stumbled, her shoulder slamming into the wall of a shadowy building, the rough stone tearing the worn stuff of her bodice, the delicate skin beneath, but she felt naught but the hot, rending pain clawing her heart. Had it been only yesterday that Rogan had picked his way through the rubble to where she knelt among the wounded, binding up yet another suffering lad's ghastly wound?

"Bree, I bring you two wretches who vow they saved Duleek Gate with but their two swords . . ."

She had turned, a joyous cry on her lips as she leapt to her feet, flinging herself at the two grimy figures at Rogan's side.

A weary, yet ever jaunty Daniel had flushed crimson with boyish embarrassment as she kissed him full on the lips, but Doyle, solemn, patient Doyle had clutched her tight in his arms, until she could feel the horror within him like some hideous, living thing.

"Bree, we routed them! Doyle . . . I vow he took out nigh a hundred of the Sassenach bastards himself." The shrill cracking of Daniel's rejoicing blended into the unintelligible tide of groans, cries, welling from the men around them as Brianna looked into Doyle's pain-filled face. She had seen the twisting agony in him as he looked down at the wounded boy at their feet. The toe of Doyle's shoe snagged a bit of cloth. He stared at it, long minutes, then his eyes raised slowly to Brianna's. Her lips parted in silent pleading. Then Doyle had quietly nudged the bright red casaque of Cromwell's army deeper into the fallen roof-timber's shadows . . .

Brianna forced back the images of what seemed an eternity past, blinking hot tears from the corners of her eyes and struggling to urge her numbed feet onward beneath the tangle of her skirts as Rogan pulled her on. "'Tis Doyle, Bree . . . a bad blow 'neath his ribs . . ." Rogan's words of but minutes before tumbled through Brianna's mind. She swallowed, a sob choking her throat. He had ripped her from the battle just as the Parliamentarians broke through the drawbridge's last defenses. She had tried to pull away, fight, a soldier still, despite sorrow, fear. But Rogan's face went rigid with some emotion Brianna could not name. "Damn it, he's dying, you little fool," Rogan had ground out. "Asking for you. And by God, you'll be at his side if I have to drag you by your cursed hair!"

Dying . . . Brianna bit her lip, her battered sword slipping from numb fingers, but she had not the will to reclaim it as it clanked onto the cobbles. Jesu, she had known, *known* last eve, with a certainty that had steeled her courage in this battle, that all she loved would die this day. Yet suddenly the thought of seeing Doyle, his pale hair tangled across his deathly gray brow, his body torn, bleeding like the countless others she had bandaged, poulticed, trodden upon in the heat of fighting, held all the more horror because somehow she had known . . . *he* had known . . .

The roar of the conquering army faded, their distant clamor eerie as echoes from a crypt as Rogan tugged her down yet another twisted lane. Shrouded in the shelter of an ancient well, Brianna could make out a clump of broad shoulders melting into the shadows, the dull glow of weapons bared, battle-ready in the hands of three figures.

Brianna swiped her arm against her burning eyes, struggling to focus on the hazy shapes before her. Fergus MacDermot's burly hulk nigh burst the confines of his dented armor, Daniel's thin shoulders ludicrous as he pressed near the veteran, the boy's prized pike in one thin hand, while behind them, silhouetted against the well's pitted stone . . .

"Doyle?!" The name ripped from Brianna's throat, jagged edged with joy, disbelief, fury. She pulled free of Rogan's grasp, sensation surging through her weary limbs in a dizzying rush as Doyle stepped from behind his two companions. She froze between Rogan and the small cluster of men, unable to pull her gaze away from the forest green tunic covering Doyle's chest. No gaping crimson slash carved deep into the flesh, the breadth of his chest wondrously, infuriatingly whole. "You're safe . . ." Brianna's eyes leapt up to bore into Doyle's pale face. "Hale." The gut-deep fear, grief that had been tormenting her at the thought of Doyle injured, burst into full-blown fury.

"Aye," he admitted softly. "We could think of no other way to lure you from the battle, so we—"

"You *lied?* Sent Rogan to tell me you were *dying?*" Rage, betrayal seared through Brianna, her blazing eyes sweeping an accusing path about the circle of sheepish, yet steely faces surrounding her. "I left mayhap forty men behind me, warring for their lives. All that remains of two thousand—"

"Bree."

She spun back to Doyle, eyes spitting fury. "They stood

fighting for their lives while the four of you hid plotting in the shadows."

"Curse it, Bree, that's enough." Rogan's face was white, his lips a gray line.

"Don't you dare tell me when 'tis enough, Rogan Niall! You saw them, Flannery, O'Toole, Paddy Tiernan . . . You saw them fighting! But still you dragged me away! Made me as much of a coward as—"

"Brianna, hold!" Fergus's voice was gravelly, angry as the burly veteran's hand closed on her arm.

"Nay, old man," Rogan said, stepping between them, his eyes hot, hurt as they pierced hers. "I would have dragged you away, Bree, were the whole of Ireland to be lost! And I vow I—"

"Christ's blood," Fergus exploded. "There be scarce space enough t' get her safe as it is, let alone waste precious time slingin' fury an' blatherin' love words! The girl be right about one thing, we have a need t' get back t' the others. We'd best get her parceled off, then be away to the fighting ourselves."

"Parceled off?" Brianna sputtered.

"Aye. Ye're t' go down the well, here. Wait until nightfall," Fergus said. "The river be but a little down the lane. Daniel an' me, we hid an empty cask, bound wi' ropes for ye to hold to. 'Twill float, an'—"

"Nay! I'll not run!" Brianna whirled on the grizzled Fergus, her chin thrust out. The tiniest of quavers beset her voice as she glared into his impassive face. "I thought *you* at least understood. I'm a soldier, not . . . not a child to be trundled off to bed when the game grows too rough."

"I wish to God I *could* bar you in your room as I did when you were small." Doyle gripped her arms, exasperation shredding the edges of his voice. "But you're not a child anymore, Bree. And the Sassenach, they'll not use you as one. What . . . what happened to you after Shane died will seem like a day at the fair, compared to what will happen if the Roundheads fall upon you this day!"

"I-I care not—" Brianna cried, fighting to quell the sharp stab of terror that pierced through her at the memory of sly, drooping eyelids, thick slavering lips.

"You damn well better care! A woman, any woman, will be just prey. But you . . . You think they've marked you not,

33

fighting in their midst? A woman bearing a sword is odd enough, but one who wields it with the skill of a man . . ."

Brianna tore away from Doyle's grasp. "Aye. I wield it with as much skill as any of you. And I blasted well intend to turn my blade against the Roundheads until they or I or neither of us can stand. You can all huddle here in the corners the night through if you chose. I'm going back to aid whoever's left to fight." Anger poured a surge of strength through her exhausted body. She turned, her soft leather shoe biting into the cobbles as she made to run back up the lane.

A raw oath sounded behind her, the clatter of a sword being flung to the stones. Suddenly something round, hard slammed into the back of her head. Through a splash of gaudy color she saw Doyle's features, shocked, yet oddly relieved, Rogan's set face, a stunned smile tugging at Daniel's lips. Then the colors spun away, leaving the sinking emptiness of midnight, the only image remaining that of Fergus MacDermot, rubbing his burly fist with stiff, gnarled fingers.

Sobbing. Someone was sobbing. Brianna struggled through the webs of blackness, mists the shade of poppies beckoning her in the distance like silk ribands trailing from an old woman's basket. Brianna tried to catch them between her fingers, stop the crone, to ask who was weeping. But the riband ends danced just out of reach, sweeping down into the dawn-lit cottage window, across the scarred oak table to the straw-stuffed pallet upon which Brianna had spent a thousand childhood nights.

She drifted down into the pallet's softness, but instead of the comforting warmth she had always felt there, the tattered coverlet tangled about her ankles, cold . . . strangely cold. Why did Doyle not stir up the fire? Summer was nigh past and the morns were waxing chill. Daniel would be catching a fever, dashing about the cold floors . . .

Danny . . . Aye, 'twas Daniel a-sobbing. Shane was riding off to the hunt again, leaving the boy behind . . .

Through the thick wall of clay she could see as if by some sorcerer's spell the five-year-old running after Shane's great white gelding, chubby legs churning, bare beneath his patched white longclothes. She had to get up, catch him before he tumbled into the nettles, but the cursed gullsdown comforter clutched at her, its worn folds clinging, binding, cold, oddly wet . . .

Nay, hot . . . Brianna crinkled her face, straining away from the drops of wetness splatting onto her brow, burning her . . . hot.

"B-Bree." She stirred at the broken sound of her name, the strange deepness of the voice she knew was Daniel's. "Bree—"

She struggled to open her eyes, but the lashes seemed to have fused to each other, blinding her to all but the horrible sense that something was wrong, terribly, terribly wrong.

Aye . . . there had been sounds, she thought, fighting to peel away the gaudy haze still gripping her consciousness, ripping it back bit by agonizing bit. Sounds that were not the scuffle of boyish scrapes, the stompings of a toddler's tantrums. Other sounds, that struck her through with fear, the clash of steel, shouts, screams drifting down to her as though she were at the bottom of some great void.

The damp, close air pressed down on her chest, suffocating. Something thick, slimy lapped against her bare forearm. She tried to sit up, sudden horror racing through her as her back and knees scraped scum-rimed stone. The bone-chilling sensation of awakening in the midst of a nightmare swept over her, and she felt herself scream.

A thin, wet hand clamped over her mouth. Ribs, yet too prominent, pressed into her side, someone whose whole body shook with silent sobs. Driving pain spiked down from the back of her head, unfurling sharp tendrils of pain along her scalp, spine as she writhed, kicked at the stone, at her captor.

"Q-Quiet, Bree, please." Daniel's voice echoed in the darkness. "Th-they'll hear you. The Roundheads . . ."

"Daniel." She gasped his name against his palm, her whole body quaking with unleashed terror as she realized her eyes were open, the blackness crushing down upon her growing but deeper, more suffocating.

"Aye. 'Tis me. W-we're in the well," Daniel whispered, easing the pressure of his hand upon her lips.

"The—the well?" Brianna repeated, trying to grasp the

threads of reality that yet eluded her. She shoved with the soles of her feet, forcing herself upright against Daniel's narrow shoulder.

"The well at the end of the lane," Daniel said. "F-Fergus and Rogan, they lowered us in. Doyle made me come down, hold you—your head above water. Didn't know how deep it was, how long you'd be unconscious. But they—they had no time to get away. The Roundheads . . ." He choked, and Brianna felt a raw sob tear through him, the sound of it ripping through her own consciousness, clawing at her shaken self-control with savage hooks of terror.

"They broke into the lane just as I touched the well bottom," Daniel wept. "I heard 'em, Bree. Doyle, Rogan, Fergus . . . heard 'em fighting, but I c-couldn't help them. You . . . your head would've slipped 'neath the surface. I couldn't help them." Daniel buried his face in her hair, crying, crying the awful, painful sobs of a boy battling desperately to cling to the fringes of manhood.

A giant fist seemed to clutch Brianna's throat, strangling the cries of denial that rose within her. She wrapped her arms about Daniel, seeking, needing something to hold onto midst the brutal tides of agony hurtling through her.

They had no time to get away. Daniel's words pounded in her head. *No time . . .*

Nay! Brianna wanted to scream. Rogan and Doyle were fearsome fighters, and Fergus . . . he'd outstripped his enemies for nigh two score years. They would have bested the Sassenach soldiers, struck down a goodly number, then slipped out the other end of the tiny courtyard to join whatever remained of Drogheda's defenders.

Aye, a tiny voice whispered inside her, unless they stood guarding those the English could not see—herself, Daniel . . .

She tried to tear the thought from her mind, but the walls of the well seemed to fling it back at her, tormenting her with her own image, arguing, stubborn, furious with the three men. *No time . . .* If she had but listened to them or left without stopping to vent her fury . . .

"Daniel." Her fingers tightened on the boy's thin arms, unable to bear not knowing for another instant. "We have to get out of here. Find out what . . . Find Doyle, the others. They have to be alive—have to be—"

"Damn it, Bree, they're dead!" Daniel's voice rose, edged with hysteria. "I heard . . . heard them scream. Heard the Sassenachs' swords tear through them."

Brianna's hand flashed out, the sound of her wet palm crashing against Daniel's cheek resounding through the well. Then, horrified, she tugged the boy tighter into her arms. The awful tension she had felt within him had snapped, and he clung to her, sobbing brokenly.

"Danny, forgive me." She choked, stroking his tangled hair. "'Tis just that we have to—to stay strong, think what to do . . ."

"Doyle—Doyle said I was to wait 'til nightfall, get you away from the city even if I had to—to jam you into a piggin and carry you."

Brianna's jaw clenched against the tears that welled inside her. In the darkness she could see Doyle, his long fingers raking the lock of hair that always straggled across his forehead, his face clouded with the loving exasperation and weary pride he had always reserved for her.

"It must be past nightfall already." Brianna forced herself to say.

"What light I could see through the top of the well faded a long while back. Ever since, there's been but little noise nearby. Only sounds far distant . . . fires . . . musket shots."

"Then we'd best get started. We've little time." Brianna gripped a bit of protruding stone, hauling herself to her feet. A wave of dizziness swept over her, the throbbing in her temples nigh driving her to collapse back to the well's floor. She clung to the wall, the knee-deep water wrapping her skirts tight around her. Her fingernails dug into the slime coating the stone, the sickening, foul-smelling layer clinging to her fingers. She leaned her brow against her arms, struggling to still the swirling in her head.

"Daniel, how did—did they say we were to get back up to the street?"

"Fergus fastened a rope to a ring just inside the well's rim. We're to climb it and . . ."

Brianna shut her eyes, skimming her hands around the curved wall until her palms brushed a coarse length of hemp. "Here it is," she managed weakly, her stomach churning. "I'll start up first, then you follow."

37

"Nay," Daniel objected. "Doyle said—"

"If there's anyone about, they'll think me just a lass, hiding, afraid. But you, they might suspect you were with Aston's forces." Brianna reached out a hand, touching Daniel's chest, the fabric of his tunic rough against her palm. "You'd best shed your colors," she said. "The Sassenachs will know the Devlin green if they get but a glimpse of it."

She heard Daniel tearing at the fabric, the tunic he had donned with such pride but a month ago dropping with a dull whisper into the stagnant water.

Brianna could almost see the gold-embroidered griffin, proud claws outstretched, sinking into the darkness, vanishing like Drogheda's hopes, like the hopes of all Ireland. For if Cromwell could drive impregnable Drogheda to its knees, what of the rest of Eire? Her verdant hills lay open, vulnerable, the lands but sparsely dotted with strongholds powerful enough to check the Sassenachs' bloody marches for even a day's time. And Cromwell . . .

Brianna shut her eyes, trying to blot out the memory of swords slashing down wounded, blades biting into the innocent flesh of women, babes. Aye, Cromwell had made well certain that word of this horror would spread through Ireland like the cacklings of demons, seeping through the very stones that guarded any who would say him nay.

Gripping the rope in wet hands, Brianna strained to pull herself up, the weight of her soaked dress dragging at her ankles. The muscles in her arms shook with weariness as she tugged herself upward, the toes of her shoes fighting to retain their hold on the treacherous stone.

Frayed hemp sliced palms raw from the hilt of her rapier, yet she felt no pain, only a terrible dread as her hand at last closed upon the well's outer rim.

They're dead, Bree. Daniel's agonized words echoed in her mind. *I heard the Sassenach blades tear through them.*

Brianna's fingers tightened on the unyielding stone endless moments, but she did not haul herself up, out of the black void. She merely gripped the well, a chill piercing to the core of her being as the night air struck her wet skin.

"Bree?"

At the sound of Daniel's worried whisper she bit her lip,

38

heaving herself in one quick pull over the well's edge. The worn stone cut into her stomach and scraped her arms as she slung her legs over the wall, her feet landing upon the ground below.

'Twas as if she had been hurtled from the stillness of a tomb into the bowels of Hades. Fires roared, devouring hovel and cathedral alike, a building set ablaze at the other end of the lane shooting an eerie glow across the cobbles. Snaking tongues of light flicked across the shadowed streets, orange-gold reflections sweeping eagerly across Armageddon.

Brianna stared at the devastation in the distance, unable to will her eyes down, terrified of what might lay there, upon the dark, cold ground. She heard the sounds of Daniel starting up the rope, the scraping of bootsoles, rasping of hemp against stone. Daniel, who had tramped along in Doyle's bootprints since the day of the boy's first steps. Daniel, who had endured the horrible eternity of hearing the men he loved battle, while he lay helpless below. Nay, she could not let him be first to face whatever agonizing secrets the tiny courtyard might hold. Slowly, painfully, she forced her gaze down, following the flame's writhing path. The light leapt, greedy, defiling treasures abandoned as their owners had fled. A gilt-framed portrait lay coated with muck beside a crudely wrought cradle, its pieced blanket spilling out across the ground.

Brianna felt a sudden, irrational fury that the child's coverlet should be strewn into the street, its embroidered corner stained dark, rumpled over something yet secreted in the shadows.

She walked toward the quilt with wooden steps, grasping its soft edge, pulling it upward with trembling fingers, just as the distant flames flared into the building's thatch, setting the sky ablaze.

Her mouth opened in a horrible, silent scream. Pale gold hair tumbled across a ghastly white face, its beloved features, even in death, etched with desperate worry.

"No." The denial scarce stirred the air as Brianna sank to her knees, mindless of the blood soaking through her skirts, heedless of the far-off figures of the conquerors wreaking their vengeance on the defeated city.

"No." She whispered the word, her icy fingers reaching out to the still hand that stretched toward the well as if in his last agony, Doyle had yet fought to protect those he loved.

She lifted the lifeless fingers . . . warm, still warm. She could feel them smoothing the battered comb through her hair, gently working free bits of twigs tangled in the golden strands as she wriggled with childish impatience . . . could see the rough fingers as they had been but days before, sailing a kiss to her across a September sky.

With aching slowness she raised Doyle's hand, pressing it against her cheek. Cry . . . she should cry. The way she had wept over the myriad of injured creatures she had tended as a girl, the way she had wept for Shane. But no tears would come. The banshee had borne them away in her rapacious hands along with hope, love, joy.

At the scrape of wooden boot heels striking the well's rim, Brianna glanced back over her shoulder, catching but a glimpse of Daniel's soiled linen shirt as he pulled himself up. Her fingers clutched fiercely at Doyle's for an instant, then she forced herself to lay his waxen hand upon the griffin emblazoned across his chest and draw the soft folds of the babe's coverlet gently over his face.

Awkward, numb with the chill of the well, she pushed herself to her feet, her sodden skirts snagging upon the splintered frame of the abandoned portrait. The visage of another age peered back at her from beneath a pearl-encrusted bongrace. The woman's face, framed by the azure headdress, gazed out over the shattered buildings, her oil-painted eyes haughty, serene. Hating the long-dead woman for her complacency, Brianna yanked her skirts free, sending the portrait skittering across the cobbles.

Only then did she notice that the canvas bearing the beauty's rose-tinted cheek had been slashed. She stared as if trapped by some macabre spell at the silvery blade of the sword that had lain beneath the portrait. Doyle's sword. She could see him in the shade of the cottage yard, his mouth nigh cracking with the strain of quelling his laughter as he parried a thousand clumsy thrusts, schooling her awkward adolescent arms and legs in the graceful postures of the riposte, the wily feint.

"Bree?" Never had Daniel sounded so wrenchingly lost.

She swept the weapon up, sliding it into her own empty

scabbard, wanting to spare Daniel the sight of Doyle's treasured blade forsaken on the ground. But as she turned to face the boy, his eyes were already locked upon the griffin's head crowning the brass hilt, Daniel's thin face robbed of all color.

"Nay!" His scream ripped through the night, agony bursting over his features, and Brianna could sense the horror he had suffered those endless minutes in the well, could hear the sounds of Doyle warring . . . dying . . .

She reached out to stay him, keep him from where Doyle lay, but the boy slammed her hands away. Stumbling across the bloody cobbles, he ripped the coverlet from Doyle's face, hurling it from him with a tormented sob.

"Daniel, don't. There's naught we can do for him now."

"I could have—could have wielded my sword at his side. But I—I lay down in that cursed well, and let them murder . . . Damn them!" he cried. "Damn . . ."

"Quiet, now. Hush!" Brianna ran to him, trying to take him in her arms, soothe him, as she had when he was small. "You'll bring the whole Roundhead army down upon us."

Daniel's face contorted, terrifying, wild. "'Twill save me the labor of seeking them. I vow they'll pay for this night's work. I'll drag a dozen Sassenach bastards with me into hell. I'll—"

Brianna's hands clenched on his arms, shaking him fiercely. "Do you think Doyle would want you to hurl yourself on some Sassenach blade . . . get yourself killed? Doyle died to give us a chance to escape the city. You owe it to him to *live.*"

"Nay! I care not! I won't leave him here for the cursed Sassenachs to—"

"There's no other choice left to us." Brianna's jaw clenched in an agony of grief, only the feel of Daniel's arm through his shirt—warm, *alive*—keeping her from hurling herself back to Doyle's side. "He would have wanted—"

"Doyle's dead! They're all dead! I hope the Sassenachs kill me. I want to die!"

Brianna struck Daniel full in the mouth, pain exploding in her raw palm. His hand swept up, his fingers death-white against the crimson mark left by her hand. The hysterical lines of his face shifted to a stark betrayal that tore at Brianna. Daniel's face crumpled, horrible, broken sobs

41

ripping low in his throat. She wanted to hold him, comfort him, cry, but the first stirrings of dawn circled the horizon like vultures hungry for fresh kill. She steeled herself, forcing her eyes to blaze fury.

"We're getting out of this city, Daniel," she said, shoving him toward the lane that snaked in the direction of the river. "Now. If I have to drive you the whole way at the point of my sword."

Burned buildings lined the streets, their windows, doors gaping at her like vacant eyes as she propelled the shaking boy down first one winding street, then another. Blood-drunk shouting, laughter echoed from the victorious Roundhead troops still swaggering through their conquered domain, while cloak-wrapped specters with faces carved in fear scurried in the shadows, their arms weighted with what few treasured belongings they could carry as they sought escape. And the dead . . . They littered the earth, twisted, maimed, like puppets cast from their master's hand.

Brianna's fingers clenched tighter on Daniel's arm as she forced herself to search each grisly death mask, hoping, praying that Fergus, Rogan lay not among them. Yet even in the horrors of the siege, she had seen naught to compare with the hideous sights that now met her eyes.

They'll murder all who bear arms, Fergus had warned. Bile rose in Brianna's throat as her eyes locked on the cottage they were passing. A dark-haired boy of no more than seven years lay sprawled across the threshold of the tumbledown hovel, his small hand clinging to a pike four times his size, while curled on the dirt floor behind him, a tiny golden-curled waif clutched at his leg even in death.

Brianna tore her gaze away. Dear God, had they murdered *children* pathetically trying to defend their homes? What price, then, would Cromwell's soldiers exact from any who could truly issue them challenge? Instinctively her fingertips touched her tangled hair. *You think they marked you not?* Daniel had said. *A woman who wields a sword with more skill than a man?* And if they did run afoul of some Roundhead troops that recognized her, 'twould not be only she who suffered.

She dared a glance up at Daniel's face, wanting to hasten to the nearby river, but the sight that met her eyes filled her with fear. The sharp bones of his face pressed pasty white against his skin, his eyes wild, glassy, fixed upon the inky shadows at the side of the cottage.

Brianna froze, a sudden, stealthy sound of metal scraping wood knifing fear through her. She spun, the image emerging from the night burning into her mind in but an instant, like some nightmarish embodiment of her worst fears.

Parts of a cuirassier's armor flashed upon a broad chest, bisected by a sapphire silk sash whose soft knot caught above sinewy, long-muscled legs. A plumed helm seemed but a black, soulless void, so hidden was the face within the shadows beneath its upraised visor. While a sword, hellish orange by the light of the raging fires, poised in the air graceful, dangerous as the head of a serpent.

Brianna groped for her own weapon, oddly awkward, slow, but in the space of a heartbeat the menacing figure had vanished, obscured by Daniel's shoulders as the boy hurtled past her with a chilling cry.

Chapter Four

Brianna lunged to stop Daniel, but the full sleeve of his shirt wisped just out of reach. Horror crushed her chest as the Roundhead's blade hissed through the air, yet as if deflected by her very will, the sword swept out of Daniel's path.

With the lithe grace of a panther, the Roundhead leapt aside, evading the boy's clumsy lunge. Brianna grasped Doyle's sword as the man's gauntleted hand shot out, clenching Daniel's shirt, sending the boy sprawling to the street. "Damn it, boy, hold. I bear no quarrel with you." The man's voice grated, its aristocratic tones incongruous with the stark Parliamentarian armor.

The words died on the man's lips as Daniel leapt to his feet, flinging himself at the Englishman with a sob of rage. Brianna wheeled, the wicked blade clutched in her aching fingers, but just as she faced the towering man, the Roundhead slammed the jeweled hilt of his sword down on the back of Daniel's head. Brianna felt the blow as though it had exploded upon her own flesh, the sight of Daniel crumpling to the street nigh snapping the wire-taut rein she had held on her roiling emotions.

Fear, rage raced through her veins, but she yanked the fury in check, forcing herself to stay icy calm as she circled the fallen lad. She had to draw the cuirassier's attention away from Daniel at any cost. But the hours of battle yet numbed her limbs, the chill of the well dulling her usually lightning-quick reflexes. And the Englishman facing her held all the menacing grace of a silver wolf stalking.

44

Doyle's sword weighted her arms, heavier far than her own light blade. She clasped it in both hands, swiping it in an awkward pass at the soldier's belly. The cuirassier stepped from its path with an ease that infuriated her, driving her swing wide. Fear prickled the back of her neck. This was no bumbling crofter, wielding a sword like a hayfork. The razor-sharp weapon danced with the elegant finesse of a man bred to battle, only the set of the shoulders beneath their armor betraying his weariness.

"Milady, put down that blade," the man's deep voice held the resigned exasperation of a man much tired of his mistress's nagging. "'Tis passing sharp, and you're like to do yourself harm."

Brianna slashed down at one thigh, oddly bared of a cuirassier's protective tassets, the blue velvet of his breeches serving a vulnerable target. The rich cloth yanked taut over the coiled muscles as the Englishman lunged from beneath the bite of her blade. Brianna tightened her grasp on Doyle's sword, shifting her fingers on the hilt, battling to accustom herself to its weight, the play of its finely honed steel.

"'Tis your own black heart you'd best be tending," Brianna hissed. "'Twill not be my blood bedecking these cobbles."

"Damme, girl," the Englishman cursed, flinging his sword up, to deflect another wild thrust. "Been fighting since dawn," he grated, the words punctuated by the clash of steel against steel. "No time—to battle—a wisp of a wench—who can scarce lift—a sword—let alone put it to any—good use."

The rough hilt of the sword dug deep into her raw palms as with one mighty swing his steel slammed into hers, driving the point of her sword to the ground. Terror shot through her, fragments of a second stretching into eternity. She struggled vainly to rip her sword free, expecting his boot to slam onto the bowed steel, cracking her sword in half, piercing her body with his own blade. But instead the heavy leathern sole raised up, connecting soundly with her ribs, the elegant polished boot shoving her backwards.

With strength borne of desperation, Brianna clung to the hilt of her sword, the tender flesh of her derriere cracking hard into the cobbles. Her teeth crashed together, her eyes smarting with needlelike tears of pain, fury.

As if to mock her, the roof of a nearby shop crashed down, the flames gutting the structure flashing orange light across infuriatingly handsome features reeking with masculine arrogance. Then, with no more thought than if she'd been a nettlesome gadfly, the despicable cuirassier turned on his heel, striding toward the river with a nigh jaunty gait.

Devlin rage, legend in five counties, rushed through Brianna with more force than even the notorious Shane could have boasted. She sprang to her feet, the bitter bile of defeat, humiliation driving strength through her aching limbs. "Turn, you bloody murderer!" she cried. "Stand and fight!" Swift, sure, she leapt toward the retreating cuirassier, sword high.

The Englishman spun, diving to the right with a savage curse as her blade slashed down in biting challenge, but even his lightning movements could not fully save him the edge of her sword. The full, gold-cloth sleeve shielding his left arm caught on the deadly point, fabric rending in a jagged tear. Blood seeped in a slow trickle, dulling the material's rich shine. The Englishman stared at it for a heartbeat, the mouth that had smirked but a moment ago setting into a grim line.

She shifted her feet, centering her balance, ready for attack. But the man moved not, only watched her as if truly seeing her for the first time, his face inscrutable. 'Twas as if he were some Druid god, the deserted lane nigh swallowed by death, destruction, yet eerily untouched at his command. Firelight flickered over sharp-hewn patrician features. The open visor cast in soft shadow high cheekbones, night-black brows, strongly carved lips that seemed to mock the world with their arrogant curl. A strange tension built within Brianna that had naught to do with the matching of their skills.

"'Twas most unwise." The words fell from that aristocratic mouth like killing frost. "The first rule of battle is ne'er begin something you have not the stomach to finish."

A bitter, sickened laugh escaped Brianna's lips. "Roast in hell."

Eyes turbulent gray as ice shards in the sea locked with hers, haughty features whipcord tight as the man sketched her an unsettling bow. "I've ne'er been known to disappoint

46

a lady." 'Twas as if he graced a ballroom, sweeping out across the floor to a much-anticipated pavane. But this dance, Brianna knew, waxed far deadlier.

She could nigh feel the touch of his blade trailing up her ribs as the man raised his sword to the ready, its honed edge glowing like newly fired steel.

One dark brow arched in sardonic challenge, gleaming leather boots planting in a wide, graceful stance as he started to circle her with the lazy confidence of a wolf closing in on weaker prey. "At your pleasure, milady," he said softly.

She clutched Doyle's sword, and eased slowly in a ring around the soldier. Her palm stung with the salt of sweat, every nerve in her body burning with the need to humble the arrogant Sassenach before her. She slashed out, the Englishman's blade barely turning aside her sword point as it sliced but inches from the colonel's ribs. Surprise flashed across his face, followed by a disturbing half-smile of respect.

As if galvanized into action by the first evidence of her skill, the Englishman rushed at her, his weapon striking through the air in blinding arcs of silver. But 'twas like Doyle's sword itself bore tempestuous Devlin blood. The griffin-carved hilt settled deeper into Brianna's hand with each blow she parried, the weapon seeming to meld with her palm as though it had rested there forever.

Despite the Englishman's daunting strength, she held her ground, a sudden surge of confidence washing through her. The man was a sham, Brianna thought incredulously, lithely dodging the path of his blade. He swept about like a swordmaster, each shift of his muscles gauged for maximum effectiveness, yet still not a single thrust came near to cutting her flesh. The blade danced ineffectually about her sword arm, its honed point catching at the quillions that curved about her hand.

The compelling gray eyes no longer spilled arrogance, boredom. Black-fringed lids narrowed now in a steely mask of concentration as her own blows cut ever more true, the brow visible beneath the cuirassier's helm gouged with deep lines.

Brianna felt a feral smile twist her lips, the pleasure this warring stirred in her shaking her more deeply than the horrors of battle. Dear God, had she become one of the soulless soldiers that infested all armies? Taking a twisted joy in the killing? She bit her lip, faltering for but an instant.

Swift as the strike of a snake, the Englishman's blade flashed toward her. She lunged to the side, but his weapon slipped between the curved guard that shielded her hand, the point of his sword gouging her fingers. The man yanked his blade up, its point entangled in the handguard of Brianna's, but she clung to the hilt, gritting her teeth against the horrible grating sound of metal against metal.

Blood streamed down her injured fingers, but she felt no pain, only clutched at the hilt with a strength born of sheer will. A savage curse exploded from the Roundhead's lips as his sword tore free, casting him off balance for a fragment of a second.

Brianna dove forward, her blade flashing under his. With a skill gained in eternities of practice, she slammed her sword into the Englishman's, the angle of the blow driving the jeweled hilt from his hand. Gauntleted fingers closed on air, silvery eyes widening in shock as the blade clattered ignominiously across the cobbles, its jeweled hilt thudding into a pile of refuse beside the cottage wall.

The Englishman started to lunge for the weapon, then froze, Brianna's sword point bare inches from his aristocratic nose.

"Cailín, hold!" A gruff, sharp voice cut the night, the sound of it piercing Brianna more deeply than the Englishman's blade ever could. "Th' Sassenach colonel may be our only key t' unlock this livin' grave."

She didn't so much as flick her gaze to the shadows from which the sound had come, but tears blurred her eyes, a sob of joy catching in her throat. "Oh, sweet Christ . . ."

"Nay, it be but me, Bree." Fergus MacDermot's gravelly tones were edged with the merest touch of wry humor. "Though I vow only the savior himself and Widow O'Flannigan could have brought me through this hell wi'out my dyin'."

"F-Fergus . . ." She said the name over and over, shaking as the vanquished Englishman's oddly hued eyes followed the tracks of tears down her cheeks. But she cared naught, as the familiar thump of Fergus's bootheels drew near. There

48

was a sound of stirring from where Daniel lay. She rejoiced in it, clutching to her this brief, tiny spark of triumph as she faced the English officer.

"The boy, Bree, is he . . ." she heard Fergus pause beside Daniel.

"He but took a clout to the head, but Doyle . . . he lies dead. And we've seen naught of Rogan."

Something soft brushed her skirts, a second sword point, aged, battered, joining hers at the Englishman's throat. "Last I saw Niall, he was fightin' like the very furies, but outmanned five to one. I was going to aid him when some bloody bastard tried to sink a musketball in my brain."

"Are you—"

"Nay, girl. My head be far too hard to let a Sassenach's bullet pierce it. Besides, the man was a damned poor shot. Just stunned me. Woke in the widow's flour chest, wi' the whole o' Satan's army a-poundin' in me brain."

"Flour chest?"

"Aye. Dragged me there herself, she did, hidin' me from the soldiers. We had a'—uh—understandin', the widow woman an' me, an' she said she'd hate to see th' waste o' . . ." Fergus cleared his throat. "Ah, well, leave it to say she helped me get out of me predicament best she could."

Brianna dared a glance up at Fergus's beloved features, but the vision that met her gaze nigh made her dissolve into hysterical laughter. The grizzled red beard had vanished, the craggy, scarred features hidden in the folds of a woman's hood. A linen headpiece wrapped his broad brow, while his bearlike body strained against the bodice of a brown-stuff gown.

She could sense the flush rising on the old warrior's cheeks. "I only let the wench trap me in this foofarah so I could rescue ye and the lad, ye ungrateful chit," he growled. "An' if I hear but a peep out o' either o' ye, I'll toss ye on your hinderparts."

"I'm quite bruised enough there," Brianna returned ruefully, surprise coursing through her as she saw the Englishman's ice-gray eyes thaw, just a bit. The tiniest of smiles tipped the corner of his mouth.

"Bruised?" Fergus echoed.

"The lady became intimately acquainted with the cobbles," the Englishman offered, his silvery eyes flashing boldly from Fergus back to Brianna's heating face, "and I performed the introduction."

Fergus's eyes narrowed. Brianna sputtered with rage, but the Englishman calmly went on. "Had she but listened, and not waxed so stubborn, I'd have explained—"

"He was trying to kill Daniel!" Brianna snapped.

"Kill him? I all but shattered my sword hilt on his thick skull to avoid it. If I'd meant to kill the boy, he would lie dead," the Englishman said, arching one infuriating brow. "And so, milady, would you."

"Damn you!" Brianna's blade jabbed closer, only Fergus's hand on her wrist staying her from swiping that arrogant grin from the Roundhead's lips.

"I was trying to quit the city myself when the lady here insisted upon delaying me," the man continued, patently unconcerned about the razor-sharp blade that had nigh sliced his skin.

"Quitting the city?" Brianna spat. "Why? Are there no babes left for you to murder?"

"I kill not children," the Englishman said, his voice hard as velvet-sheathed steel.

"I trow, then, 'twas my imagination that conjured all the babes I stepped over in the streets. And the lad in this cottage, he must be but slumbering upon the doorstep. No doubt he will waken if we but pull your dagger from his side."

"I kill not children." Quiet, deadly, the words fell from his mouth. Despite the fact that the man was unarmed, Brianna flinched beneath the fierce light in his gray eyes. "I bear urgent news to my liege, King Charles."

"King Charles?" Brianna forced a disdainful laugh from her lips, glancing at Fergus for support, but the bemused expression on the veteran's face stilled her biting retort.

"What be your name, Sassenach?" Fergus demanded, his gaze searching the Englishman's face.

"Colonel Lord Creighton Wakefield."

"Wakefield!" Fergus's voice held the stark accents of betrayal. "I should slit your lying throat! I fought beside Galliard Wakefield at Nasby when I roved with the Irish Brigade, and in a hundred years there's ne're been a Wakefield turned traitor."

"I stand loyal to the crown."

"Then it seems, sir, that someone switched your uniform," Brianna said with acid sweetness. "Or did you find yourself confused on your way off to battle?"

"I—" the man's retort was bitten off by Fergus's sharp command.

"Take off that helm." Scarred eyelids yanked taut with challenge.

"What?"

"Take it off, an ye be a Wakefield."

Fingers, long and slender beneath the soft leather gauntlet, reached up, unlatching the helmet and drawing it off the Englishman's head. A fall of thick hair the rich hues of rosewood tumbled about his face, the silken, wayward mass a perfect foil for his aristocratic features.

"Damme, ye be the image of the duke," Fergus cried, dropping the point of his sword. The cuirassier's features paled, the unfathomable gray eyes turbulent, oddly vulnerable under MacDermot's scrutiny. "What are ye about, lad? The son of Galliard Wakefield consortin' with Cromwell's dogs?"

"I have my reasons." The words seemed ragged, raw, unbreachable.

But Fergus heeded them not, only pierced the man's eyes with his own keen gaze long moments, a slow assessing look spreading across his grizzled face. He nodded, clapping the Roundhead on the shoulder. "Well, lad, the word of Galliard Wakefield's son be good enough for me. Blackthorne be a fine man, he be. A sire to be proud of. And your own prowess, Lord Creighton, 'twas nigh legend when I—"

"Fergus, have you gone mad?" Brianna blustered, waving the point of her sword at the Englishman's face. "The Sassenach bastard nigh killed Daniel! What's to stop him from betraying us to—"

"God's feet, Bree, put that thing down!" Fergus grasped her hand, forcing her sword to her side. He reached beneath Wakefield's sash, shoving it aside to reveal a loaded pistol. "If Creighton Wakefield had wished either of ye to heaven ye'd be halfway there by now."

The Englishman flashed her a smile so smug, she fought the urge to drive her knee into his groin. Her cheeks fired with humiliation, rage spiraling through her as Fergus regarded her with strained patience.

"The uniform says he's a Roundhead!" Brianna cried. "Fighting at Cromwell's side. Blast it, Fergus—"

"For the love of God, Bree, ha' mercy," Fergus said, pressing gnarled fingers to his temple. "My skull feels like to split as it is, without you shriekin' in my ear like a cursed harpy."

"Bree?" Patrician accents interrupted, the hesitation at the end of her name deeming it a question.

Fergus turned to the Englishman with a grin. "Aye," he said. "'Tis neglectin' me amenities, I am. My name be MacDermot. Fergus MacDermot. An' this hellcat"—he jerked a thumb in her direction—"be Brianna Devlin."

"Charmed, gentle lady." Amused gray eyes flicked to hers, the voice weighted with so much male superiority, Brianna half expected the wretched man's head to burst. He turned back to Fergus, effectively dismissing her. "Captain MacDermot, we must away from here at once. There are many making it their purpose to see that no one who raised a sword escapes death this night."

"Patrols?" Fergus asked.

"Aye. One is posted just at the end of this lane." He gestured to the exact place Brianna had been heading and flashed her a grin. "And Ogden's command is sweeping the streets for any combatants that slipped through their fingers. Thanks to the chit's foolishness, we've scarce time to gain the river."

"Foolishness!" Brianna blustered. "Go to—"

"Hold, Bree," Fergus commanded. "We've flung away too much time already. Be a good lass and fetch Lord Creighton's sword."

Blue curses, gleaned in weeks of living in a military encampment, spewed from Brianna's mouth in a rush. Creigh's eyes widened in amazement, their corners crinkling in an amusement that made Brianna want to scream.

"Damn it, girl, I'm yet your commanding officer, and ye'll follow my orders!" Fergus said sharply. "'Tis no place for tempers." He turned back to Wakefield. A feeling of betrayal sluiced over Brianna as Fergus spoke to the Englishman in rushed tones, the two men going to kneel where Daniel had pushed himself to a sitting position, his face sickly green. Her brother, at least, showed good sense, glaring at Wakefield with mistrustful eyes. But Fergus fawned over the man as though he could walk upon water. Well, mayhap 'twould make their escape far easier, Brianna thought bitterly, that is, if his high and mighty lordship would allow such lowly creatures to use the same river as he.

She stalked to the refuse heap, kicking a clump of rags savagely. But the deceitful folds concealed something so hard it nearly cracked her toes. Pain shot through Brianna's foot, hateful tears pricking at the back of her eyes. She swept up the jeweled blade, and stomped back to where the two men were helping a groggy Daniel gain his feet.

Without sparing her so much as a glance, Creigh held out his other palm for the weapon. Brianna slammed the jeweled hilt into his hand with all the force she could muster, wishing she could have 'mistakenly' used the cutting edge. Ice-gray eyes flashed toward her, and she could have sworn dry humor lurked in their depths.

"'Tis a brilliant plan, my Lord Creighton," Fergus lauded him. Brianna gritted her teeth against the camaraderie in the veteran's tone. "With the keg Danny-boy and I rigged, we'll be out from under the Sassenachs' noses before they can say 'fool's bluff.'"

"Aye, with a touch of fortune," Wakefield said. "I'll bear the lad, and you keep the girl from scratching my eyes out."

Fergus's laugh rumbled deep in his chest.

"Damn you both, I'll—"

"Cleave me in two? Grind me to dust?" Wakefield offered helpfully, linking his arm about Daniel's unsteady form. "I fear 'twill have to wait, Tigress. But I vow to give you fair chance to unleash your claws upon me after our dip in the Boyne."

"Damme, I hope you drown," Brianna grated between clenched teeth.

Laughter burst from those arrogant lips, the sound so rich and unaffected it skated an unwelcome tingle of pleasure down Brianna's spine. She quelled it ruthlessly, glaring as his bold eyes raked her.

"Aye, I wager you'd love to see me kissing the bottom of the Boyne," he said, one gauntleted finger reaching up to trace her cheek. "But I'd not dream of sleeping in the river's bed when I might share the company of such a *refined* maiden."

Brianna snarled a curse, dashing the hand away, excruciatingly aware of the layer of grime and powder dust sticking to her skin. Her hands knotted into fists, her teeth grinding as Fergus guffawed as though the veteran thought Wakefield the most amusing of jesters.

She tried to summon hate, fury as they turned their backs on her, guiding Daniel into the slivers of shadow between the savaged buildings. But as she followed them into the maze of houses, 'twas hurt that stung her eyelids. She fingered the scraggly ends of what had once been smooth, neat braids, her broken fingernails and calloused palms snagging on the soft strands. They had laughed at her, Fergus and the Englishman, the Sassenach lord's drawling voice leaving no doubt that he thought her a woman scarce worthy of his scorn.

Well, she had had precious little time to play at being a lady of late, with the war in the air. And God knows, with four mouths to feed at the Devlin cottage, and the English raping the land, there had been no coin for the silver laces and plumes that would no doubt satisfy Lord Creighton Wakefield's discriminating tastes.

As if he could hear her very thoughts, the Sassenach glanced over one broad shoulder, his sensual mouth curving into a knowing grin. Her chin jutted in stubborn defiance, her eyes schooled into a mask of patent indifference as his gaze turned back to the winding maze of gutted cottages, looted shops. Yet even the sinking feeling his mockery had conjured within her, even her own stiff pride, could not wholly banish the sensation of the Sassenach's slight touch. It lingered upon her cheek, warm, strong, unconscionably thrilling, as though within the threads of gold embroidering the gauntlet had lurked some philter, slipped from a sorcerer's hand.

She shivered, but 'twas not the wind skimming in from the Boyne, nor the peril lurking around every corner that chilled her. 'Twas a far subtler sense of danger that drifted over her with each sinuous shift of Creighton Wakefield's well-honed muscles, each ripple of the dark waves that tumbled in glorious disarray about his proud head.

54

The magnificent locks begged to be tamed by a woman's fingers, the rosewood tresses smoothed in sensuous contrast against the muscled column of his neck. Brianna's hand knotted in a fist, as she forced a disdainful sniff. No doubt Lord Creighton would have to examine most thoroughly any hand honored enough to touch his exulted brow. Why, then, did the thought of running her fingertips over those arrogant lips set a hundred butterflies to fluttering their wings against her stomach?

'Twas absurd, Brianna thought grimly, stomping behind the men as they passed the darkened stable of a once-lavish inn. Just because Fergus had been duped into believing the man's crazed story, meant not that it held any truth. Mayhap instead of leading them toward safety, he was herding them along like sheep to the slaughter, only awaiting the perfect time to betray them.

A sudden din of hooves made Brianna's heart drop to her toes, a contingent of Roundhead cavalry thundering in a wild, whooping sweep but a horse's length from the clump of discarded kegs beside which the tiny party had been walking. She lunged behind the barrels, reflexively grabbing for Doyle's sword. The others dove in behind her. Holding her breath endless seconds, she waited, half expecting to hear Wakefield cry out and betray them, the meager shelter of the barrels seeming ludicrous to protect them all from the searching gaze of the blood drunk soldiers. But the Roundheads rode on, bent on some other errand of destruction.

"Disappointed?"

She spun at the sound of the voice scant inches from her ear, more shaken by the warmth of Creigh's breath upon her skin than the contingent of Roundheads fast disappearing. His face was so close she could see each long, curling lash that fringed his gray eyes, the tiny scar that bit into one dark brow, making his face seem but more dangerous, exciting.

"I could call them back, you know," he said, low in his throat. "With a single cry. And even if those soldiers couldn't hear me, there would be a hundred others within reach of my voice."

She jerked her face away, wanting to scream at him to go ahead, summon his cohorts, that she dared him to. But she only bit her tongue and started again down the street.

He helped Daniel up, falling into step beside her. "What? No gracious thanks for shielding you from harm? No token of gratitude? Maidenly kiss?"

"I'd sooner kiss a rat!" Brianna hissed. "God knows, you cling to the walls like one."

"Surely you might think of a more flattering likeness," he teased. "A fox, mayhap? A wolf?"

"It matters naught. You skulk about like a cutpurse."

The grin had faded, his eyes, oddly somber. "One learns to watch his back at court, lest a knife—verbal or steel—be slipped twixt one's ribs," he said. "And you, milady, might be grateful that 'tis one skill I've mastered, as 'tis all that stands between your beautiful neck and the edge of a Roundhead sword."

"Bastard." She flung out the word, wanting to hate him, but at that moment Daniel stumbled. Gentle as a father teaching a babe to walk, Creigh shored up the boy's wobbly legs with his own strong body. The Englishman said something Brianna could not hear, and Daniel's peaked face angled up to his, creasing in a wary smile.

Then suddenly the little party stopped, Creigh hunkering down beneath the shelter of a low-hanging roof. Brianna crouched behind him, staring across a patch of open ground to where the Boyne river spread like liquid onyx from the edge of its rocky shores.

Pools of flame splashed crimson upon the dark water, reflections from torches that turned the veiling of night to the rose of false dawn. In the hellish glow three-score yards from where the little party stood, lobster helmets gleamed, buff coats set against the night dull as corpse's eyes, while casaques the color of blood rippled in the wind.

Brianna felt fear constrict her throat as she stared at the hated uniforms of the Parliamentarian foot soldiers. Their voices were gloating with victory, drunk with the spilling of their enemy's blood. To reach the river unseen would be nigh impossible, even for one lone person, and to battle the Boyne's swift current . . .

Brianna kneaded the aching muscles of her arm, her eyes shifting to the still-unsteady Daniel. Creigh's hand circled the boy's arm, the sight of those strong fingers supporting her brother oddly comforting.

Brianna raised her eyes, to find Creigh's gaze fastened

upon her. "What say you, Tigress?" he asked softly. "You bested me in swordplay. Are you as fleet on foot?"

"St. 'Bastion, there be no way, lad," Fergus growled. "Look at 'em, swarmin' like maggots on carrion. If she's seen, they'll be upon her in a trice."

" 'Tis the only way," Creigh said. "You can't manage the lad and get the keg adrift at the same time. And the girl, of a certainty, can't be the one to set the hovel afire."

"I can walk, now, Colonel. I vow I can," Daniel insisted, his reedy voice belying his words, but Brianna cut off his protest.

"Fire? Kegs? What in the name of God are the three of you babbling about?"

Creigh smiled at her, reaching up to draw her close beside him. "See that man?" he said, pointing to a swaggering captain in the distance. "Greediest officer in Cromwell's whole army. I vow Captain Grimbol was pulling rings off dead men before he was a sword's length past the breach. Stored his little cache in that building there. If, perchance, it caught fire . . ."

"Fire?"

"Aye. Say from a stray spark." Creigh's mouth tilted in a grin, and he flicked his fingers as if they bore flint. "I trow he will send his entire command scurrying through the flames to rescue his treasures."

"And when he does?"

Creigh's face angled down to hers, and, beneath the taunting light in his eyes, she saw an unmistakable trace of respect. "While they are thus occupied, someone, swift, stout of heart, could dash across to that pile of turf, dig out the keg Fergus rigged and get it into the river."

"Damme, lad," Fergus blustered. "I don't think she can do it. That keg be passin' heavy. An' she'd have t' hold it against the current 'til the rest o' us break water."

Creigh lifted one finger, laying it along his granite-hewn jaw. He sighed. "Mayhap you're right. I forget she is but a frail maid—"

"One who held you beneath the point of her sword." Brianna bristled. "You just concentrate on sending Captain Grimbol's stealings to the devil, Colonel Lord Wakefield." She spat the title like a curse. "And when you split the sea I'll be waiting for you."

57

"Split the . . ." Fergus's brow crinkled in confusion, but Creighton Wakefield's eyes twinkled with suppressed merriment.

He stretched one graceful hand toward the tumbled pile of turf, teasing, "I'll meet you at the chariot, milady. Count to five hundred, lass. Slow. If I've not reached the shore by then, you start off without me."

"Nay!" The word was out before she could stop it, shocking Brianna even more than the three men who stared at her, roundeyed. "Well 'tis—'tis like that he might be delayed. Or—or get cut off and have to take a longer route back. Or . . ." she stammered, blushing hotly at the slow smile that spread like honey across Creighton Wakefield's handsome face.

"Tigress, I had no notion you were so concerned for my safety," his voice was sweet as summer berries, but his eyes fairly danced with mischief. "Fear not. I'm not about to let you travel the Boyne without me."

Brianna wanted to slap him, furious at herself for spilling out one word of caution. But before she could spit out a retort, his head swooped down. Lips, incredibly soft, firm, taunted hers with a whisper of their moist warmth, sending a despised shaft of heat through the pit of her stomach. She expected revulsion, disgust, her body's response to the slavering mouth that had crushed hers but a month before. Yet soft as angel's wings Creighton Wakefield's kiss whispered across her flesh, then vanished, filling her with the hateful, nearly uncontrollable need to catch that face between her hands and pull his lips again to hers.

But he had already turned, running lightly, lithely through the shadows toward the whitewashed building. Furious with him, more enraged still at herself, Brianna muttered a string of Gaelic curses. Yet even before he disappeared into its shadows, the anger faded, leaving her strangely bereft, forlorn.

She'd not bandied jibes about with such zest since before Shane died. Nor taken such pleasure in matching wits. And yet, 'twas disloyal, despicable, to feel any spark of anything but hatred for an Englishman when both Shane and Doyle lay dead.

She closed her eyes, the image of Doyle's broken body chastening her. She should lay keening, crying, mourning.

Daniel still bore the aura of a battered pup, his grief stark on his face. But she . . . Wakefield had kept her raging like a termagant from the first moment she had set eyes upon him.

"Bree."

Her eyes snapped open as Fergus touched her arm. She looked out over the river bank, to where flames were already lapping at the building's roof. There was a cry of alarm from one of the soldiers, and Brianna saw the swaggering captain rush toward the hovel, his men on his heels.

"The keg be buried on the opposite side," Fergus hissed. "'Bout three slabs deep."

Bree nodded. Scooping up her heavy skirts, she dashed for the turf pile. Out of the corner of one eye, she saw a Roundhead start running toward her, saw another soldier grab his arm, yanking him back toward the blaze. Men poured into the building, out of it, crashing into each other, their arms laden with chests, heaps of cloth.

With more speed than she'd known she possessed, Brianna gained the shelter of the turf. It seemed an eternity as she dug through the slabs of peat, uncovering the keg, dragging it free by one of the sturdy hemp ropes Fergus had bound it with. As she lugged the keg across the rocky bank, she saw Daniel, leaning on the veteran's arm, stumbling toward her. Cold water sucked at her feet, skirts, as she splashed waist-deep into the river, the Boyne's current wrapping the single petticoat she wore into a tangled mass about her ankles. She stumbled, the rocky bottom slick, treacherous, nearly causing her to lose her grasp on the length of hemp that bit into her palms.

Bracing herself against the weight of the keg, she clung to the ropes, but her eyes followed not the trek of her brother and Fergus across the clearing; rather, her gaze sought Creighton Wakefield's tall figure near the flames. The man she had fought and nearly killed . . . the man who had kissed her.

A fist seemed to tighten in her chest, spilling a flood of heat, confusion through her body. He was a Sassenach, a turncoat, aye, and a liar, no matter which side held his true loyalties. No doubt he had murdered in the name of Oliver Cromwell, even as he vowed fealty to Charles Stuart; had led Roundhead troops into battle, then betrayed them by aiding enemy soldiers. Brianna shivered. What manner of man would kill to maintain some twisted facade of loyalty? Sell his honor? His soul?

And why was it that she sensed in the very core of her being just how much that betrayal had cost him?

Yet had not Creighton Wakefield caused her to commit her own, more subtle betrayal? That she had begun to believe . . .

A sudden splashing sound made her nearly drop the rope, the sound of Fergus's voice shattering her tangled thoughts. Her eyes flicked to where he and Daniel were slogging through the water to her side, gasping for breath.

Fergus's gnarled hands closed on the keg's hemp bindings, easing their pull on Brianna's tired fingers. "Well, we've made it thus far, thanks to my Lord Creighton," he breathed. "If we can but gain the current, 't should sweep us past the guards right quick."

"How long," Daniel panted, "can we wait for the colonel?"

"But a minute's time," Fergus said in the barest of whispers. He ripped off the last of his disguise, tossing the linen headdress into the river. "We dare not tarry more, or we'll ha' the whole lot o' the red-bellied devils down upon us."

"They may have us twixt their musket sights even now," Brianna grumbled, *"thanks to Lord Creighton."*

"Damnation, lass, do ye think if his lordship intended to throw us to Cromwell, he would'a gone to the trouble o' lightin' that fire?"

"How would I know?" Brianna snapped, her temper sharp with her own tearing doubts. "If his family is so notoriously loyal he must've put himself to considerable bother to weasel himself into the lord lieutenant's good graces. God knows what lengths he would go to in order to—"

"Well, it matters naught. The Sassenachs are spillin' out o' the house. We daren't wait any longer."

Brianna felt something twist inside her. "Nay, we can't—can't just leave—"

"Girl, for the love of St. Savior, make up yer blasted mind! But a breath ago, ye had Wakefield a black-hearted traitor ready to fire half the city to get us in 'is trap, an' now ye want us to fling away our chance of escape waitin' fer 'im?"

"But . . ."

"Bree, our only chance lies in slippin' past the guard while they be busy wi' the fire. An' in but a little no man'll be able to brave it. Wakefield knew—"

"But—but if what he claims is true . . . if he is a vassal of King Charles . . . He might—might lie wounded, or . . ." She stopped, suddenly aware of Fergus watching her with his keen hawk eyes. Hateful tears stung her lids. Sweet Christ, she sounded like a babbling idiot, crying yea, nay. From the time she had been three, Doyle claimed she made decisions with the irreversible swiftness of a ruling queen, never wavering, never giving in to the bouts of fluttery indecision other girls indulged in. She had trusted her instincts, but now . . . 'Twas as if Creighton Wakefield had stirred a tempest inside her, battering her emotions about like twigs in the midst of a torrent. She spun back toward the flaming building, willing Creigh's broad shoulders, dark hair to emerge from the haze of smoke. But nowhere in the confusion surrounding the blaze was there any tall enough, lithe enough to be the glittering Englishman.

"We shove off as agreed, *cailín,*" Fergus said quietly. "'Tis what his lordship would want."

"There's no well for you to dump me in this time, Fergus," Brianna thrust her chin out defiantly. "And I'll not leave—"

"Leave whom, milady?"

Low, musical, the voice at her shoulder made Brianna wheel, her heart lurching at the sight of Creighton Wakefield's soot-smudged face. The damp ends of his hair clung to the muscled column of his throat, the rich blue of the embroidered doublet that had taken the place of his armor clinging wetly to every rippling sinew of his chest.

How had he broken water without making a sound? How long had he stood there, listening? Brianna wanted to cry with relief, scream, rake his perfect countenance with her fingernails. His lips still curved in that arrogant grin, but in his eyes lurked a softness, the barest shading of his own confusion . . .

His eyes flashed down to her lips, then back to her face. She dragged her gaze away.

"It seems the lass was loath to abandon ye, yer lordship," Fergus snorted in disgust. "That is when she wasn't caterwaulin' that ye were draggin' yer Roundhead troops to capture us."

"The troops!" Creigh exclaimed in mock chagrin, snapping his fingers. "By the saints, I was certain I'd forgot something!"

Fergus guffawed, and Daniel stifled a weak laugh. Brianna shot Wakefield a murderous glare.

"If you'd like I can summon them to you," she snapped, more surly than ever. "I vow, 'twould nigh be worth it to see you lose your head."

A flash of some unreadable emotion hardened Lord Creighton's features, the corner of his mouth tautening dangerously. "A lust for blood, milady?" He gestured to the shore. "You may yet have your appetites satisfied."

Brianna followed the line of his hand to the river bank. The men who had been dashing in and out of the burning house but moments ago, now clumped together on the shore, their captain stamping about in a screaming frenzy. While at their center . . . Brianna flinched inwardly at the hulking man who sat sawing at the reins of a magnificent stallion, the gleaming front of his helm turned out toward the waters . . . the makeshift float. A shiver skated down her spine, her throat constricting as she felt the man's eyes, secreted from her by iron, by distance, bore into her, as though he could see . . .

"That bastard took my horse!" Wakefield cursed, and Brianna could see his jaw clench at the distant Roundhead's cruelty to the beast. Creigh started forward, stopped, swearing. "Grab on and kick. We have to get as far from shore as possible before the current carries us past them. Ogden'd make a pact with the devil himself to serve me a traitor's death. Damn it, *kick*, Tigress, an you want to live to flay some other poor man with your tongue!"

A sudden sharp tug on the ropes scraped the rough hemp in a stinging path down Brianna's arm. She felt the small barrel list to one side, then bob into the waves as their feet left the river bottom. Her fingers closed convulsively on the rope, the icy waters tearing at her skirts, yanking her downward as Lord Creighton's mighty strokes dragged them out into the swift current. But even the roar of the river as the current caught them in its jaws could not muffle the sounds of shouts raising the alarm from the riverbank.

The keg whirled amongst flood-tossed tree limbs, debris, like a child's wooden top, twisting the ropes about Brianna's hands with crushing force, then spinning them nigh from her grasp as the keg lurched over a whitecapped swell.

"Cling close to the keg," she heard Creigh bark. "Stay low, and—Damme!" A shaft of raw terror jabbed through her, as she glimpsed the Roundhead colonel's hulking body, the stallion's thrashing legs, as the keg swept toward the soldiers. The waning moon glinted on iron, tiny glowing sparks at the musketeer's sides glowing like scattered embers as they poised the long, smoldering matches above their weapons' powder pans.

"Faster, damn it," Lord Creighton hissed.

Musket fire cracked through the night, the blaze from the Parliamentarian's muzzles spitting death into the river's dark waves. Brianna stifled a scream as the barrel stay inches above her head splintered. There was a guttural moan from the opposite side of the keg.

"Daniel! Fergus!" Brianna choked out.

"Is anyone hit?" Wakefield's voice, brusque with command, demanded.

"Nay. Barrel but struck—sore shoulder," Fergus called. "Get—the devil outta here."

Brianna's eyes locked upon the soldiers now lining the riverbank, reloading their muskets, cradling them at the ready in their stands. Merciful Mary, she could nigh see their blurred faces, buff coats . . .

"Damn it, Tigress, don't gawk. *Kick!*" Wakefield grated savagely.

Anger seared Brianna, warming her numb limbs. She started to kick with all the strength she could muster, her mouth opening to deliver Lord Creighton a scathing reply, but suddenly a wave crashed over her face, its force driving water into her lungs. She fought, choked, battling desperately to kick, but her skirts dragged at her legs, making them nigh useless.

She tore at the fastenings of the simple gown, but the hooks and knots seemed fired together, fused. She had scarce fumbled with the first fastening when something hard cracked into her thigh. Sharp, fingerlike projections of a

63

huge tree branch ensnared her arms and skirts, the limb tossing crazily in the current, fighting to tear the rope from her hands. Wakefield muttered an oath, straining toward her to tear the clutching wood free of the heavy water-swirled folds of her skirt.

"Sweet Christ, what the—"

The oath died on his lips as he released his hold of the keg's rope with one hand. A cry of terror breached Brianna's lips as the current started to yank the limb away, sucking it into some swirling vortex of blackness. The water closed over her head, her lungs screaming for air as the rope slipped in her fingers.

But just as the hemp was about to snap free, something warm and hard manacled her wrist. She thrashed furiously, trying to break the water's surface, but the tree limb, tangled in the cloth of her skirt, dragged her inexorably deeper. Suddenly something dug into the firm swell of her stomach, jerking savagely. The horrible crushing pressure dragging at her body disappeared, the thing banding her wrist jerking her upward as her skirts swept clear of her body. She burst into the cold night air, choking, desperately fighting to drag air into her lungs.

"Grasp on, Tigress! Grasp on!" The voice, hollow, distant, sounded as though it came from the depths of a cave, but its fierce tones wouldn't be denied. Her icy fingers clutched at the length of hemp, and she forced her eyes open, to see Creighton Wakefield's worried countenance scant inches from her own.

Another volley of musket fire split the night, the sound tearing away the last webs of near-unconsciousness that clung in her mind. She saw Creigh lunge closer, his body blotting out the bright blaze of flame from the Roundhead muskets.

For an instant, through her still-blurred vision, she saw his mouth snap taut, felt his body, so close to her own, lurch as if yanked by the river's capricious whim.

Then the current whirled the keg yet again, sweeping it far past the borders of the city, batting the fragile wood barrel between its claws like some brutal beast a-toying with its kill.

Chapter Five

Creigh grasped the exposed root of a dying oak, digging his fingers into the rotted wood as he dragged his battered body onto the Boyne's dawn-glossed shore. A white-hot brand seemed thrust through his leg, the torn muscle afire with the chunk of lead buried in his flesh.

He rolled onto his side, clamping one palm on the throbbing wound, the cold of the river water blending in sickening contrast to the warm, sticky flow of his blood. Sweet Jesu, the cursed musketeer on Drogheda's quay had borne the devil's own aim. But then, as Michel had always claimed, 'twas always passing easy to strike down a fool.

Creigh's pain-whitened lips thinned as he glanced over his shoulder at the three others who had slogged their way onto shore a dozen feet up river from where he lay.

'Twould serve him right if he bled to death right here in this blasted wasteland, fool that he was. The gates of the city had been open to him, an officer in a conquering army. He could easily have slipped from Drogheda under cover of darkness, aye, and have been far into his ride to the coast. But no. He needs must play knight errant. And now . . .

Now he was saddled with an old man, a half-dazed boy, and a lady more troublesome by half than the musketball embedded in his leg.

A *lady?* The ghost of a laugh escaped his stiff lips as he imagined Le Ferre's horror at his labeling her thus. Michel had nigh fallen into apoplexies the time Creigh had championed a poor ratcatcher's daughter bedeviled by a brace of drunken cavaliers. If Le Marquis could but have heard this wild-eyed Irish witch spitting curses the entire trip down the river, no doubt he would be off summoning a surgeon, demanding some physick to make Creigh regain his sanity.

A taut smile tugged at Creigh's lips. He *had* goaded her, the sparks in her eyes, her quick, searing sarcasm the one thing that had distracted him from the agonies in his leg.

She had snarled like a wild thing. And in truth, even now, the little barbarian had more the look of some creature Bouret should hold locked up in his menagerie than anything remotely feminine. She crouched with her back to Creigh, a mass of tangled, sodden hair all but obscuring the dirt-streaked remains of a petticoat long overdue for the ragman's trade. One bare arm, its finely muscled length infinitely different from the dimpled limbs of the pampered court belles he had danced attendance on, was looped around the lad's narrow shoulders. The girl's face, its sharply carved planes half-hidden, was turned toward the lad as she murmured something into his ear. Yet even though distance veiled her eyes, Creigh could still see in his memory their intriguing golden lights flashing hatred, fury, and a stark courage that had pierced him to the very core of his being.

He struggled painfully to force his body upright, bracing himself against the trunk of the oak. Her eyes had not been all that pierced nigh through him. Had MacDermot been but a heartbeat later in arriving at the deserted lane, Creigh bore no doubt that the tawny-curled hoyden would've driven her blade straight to the center of his "black Sassenach heart."

He gritted his teeth, the play of his muscles grating the musketball against bone. Yet even the waves of fire pulsing in his leg could not fully banish his sensation of rueful amusement as he heard the termagant's voice raise in argument with the hapless MacDermot. Aye, "Sir Gallahad Wakefield," as Michel had been wont to call Creigh, had nigh had the Grail smashed over his head this time, what with being so careful not to hurt the helpless, fragile damsel. Helpless? Creigh grimaced. Mistress Brianna Devlin was nigh helpless as the tigress he had named her, and as ready to tear off a man's arm . . . or leg.

Creigh sobered, looking down at his injured thigh. He

could feel the blood welling beneath his fingers, running in thick rivulets to drip on the carpet of moss below. Damme. Mayhap he should've let the wench run him through. At least 'twould have spared him the unraveling of this latest disaster—thrown ashore God knew where, with no horse, wet gunpowder, and a leg that felt like a petard about to explode.

He shut his eyes, arching his head back into the oak's rough bark in an effort to stem the nausea that swept over him in dizzying waves. He had no time to wax faint. There was a fair chance contingents of English soldiers might be sweeping the countryside for Irish deserters. And if Saul Ogden had as yet discovered that Colonel Lord Wakefield was missing, somehow Creigh sensed the bastard would be out prowling, preying, sifting his greedy fingers through the Leinster Hills seeking his most hated rival.

"So, your high and mighty lordship, do you intend to lounge here all day? Or are you waiting for your coach-and-four?"

Creigh winced, the acid-sweet lilt of Brianna Devlin's voice grating on his nerves. He raised one eyelid with feigned boredom. "I'd not deign be seen in any conveyance with less than eight horses," he said, his hand tightening over his wound. "So if you'd be a clever child and fetch one . . ."

"Go to hell."

"'Tis a thought. Old Hades might have a chariot to spare. But, ah, I'd forgotten." Creigh let his eyes light, as if having made some brilliant discovery. "You're hardly in any condition to go a-hieing off, even to the devil." His eyes swept a disparaging path down her body, his intent to torment her about her bedraggled appearance. But whatever words had been playing upon his tongue trailed silent, his throat suddenly dry as his gaze skimmed the fine linen that had once been her chemise. The honey-hued tone of her skin glowed through the transparent dampness of the cloth, its wet folds clinging like a lover's kiss to the smooth curves of a body anything but childlike.

High, peach-tipped breasts thrust in impudent mounds against a meager ruffling of lace, slender hips tapering down into legs so long and delicately muscled that he had to clench his fist to keep himself from curving his palm around one perfectly turned calf. His gaze traveled back up to the soft, dark shadow at the joining of her thighs.

A shaft of desire drove deep in his loins, shocking in its raw intensity as his mind scrambled desperately to reconcile the filthy urchin of Drogheda with this nymph's body. From the day he had turned fifteen, and gained his manhood at the hands of a fading court dame, Creigh had sampled at will the sweetest blossoms France and England had to offer. Scented with costly oils, their arms powdered, hair bedecked with jewels, the Court's most desirable women had dropped like ripe fruit into his hands. Why, then, did this wench stir him so with her wild eyes, her biting temper, her fall of untamable hair? 'Twas absurd! The weary months of war without a woman was no doubt affecting his brain. By sheer force of will he dragged his eyes back to her face.

Chin jutting defiantly, the girl regarded him in belligerent challenge, her countenance chiseled with the strong perfection of Artemis on the hunt.

"You needn't gape!" she snapped, her cheeks washing crimson. "'Twas you who divested me of my gown!"

"Aye." The single word caught low in his throat, the teasing tone he had tried to effect snagging in his belly. What had seemed a mass of snarls now caught the sun in tumbled tawny waves, the slightest of trembling at the corner of her lips betraying a hint of vulnerability that made Creigh want to mold his mouth to hers . . . taste . . .

"'Tis no great achievement, Lord Creighton, I vow," her blade sharp voice snapped him back to attention.

"Your pardon?"

"I said, 'tis no great achievement. Your stealing my gown. No doubt a blackguard such as you has had much practice filching ladies'—"

"Bree!" Fergus bit out a warning, and the girl wheeled to where the veteran sat, supporting an ashen Daniel with one thick arm. "If ye be in such a dither to roast something alive, go off an' snare us a coney for breakfast, an' leave off tryin' to ram Lord Creighton on yer spit. I trow ye're as surly as the day Rogan an' Doyle slipped rats into yer stew."

"Rogan? Doyle?" Creigh repeated, heaving a gusty moan. "Dear God, don't tell me there are other men so unfortunate as to be subjected to your tantrums, Tigress. 'Od's blood, I—"

"Keep your filthy Sassenach mouth from sullying their names." Brianna glared at Creigh, but even through the hard glint in the amber eyes, he could see an edge of pain.

"Tigress, I . . ."

"My name is Brianna!" the girl grated. "And I intend to have myself and my brother far beyond the Roundheads' reach before nightfall. So, unless you plan to run up your standard and hail the murdering bastards, my lord colonel, I fear you're going to have to soil your fine leather boots with the rest of us." One small foot flashed out, dealing the offending article a sharp kick.

Spikes of pain exploded in Creigh's thigh, a savage oath tearing from his lips. "Little witch!" he grated. "I'd trek—to Connaught to escape your viper's tongue—that is, if I—could stand."

"Stand?"

"Aye, *stand.*" Creigh glared at the girl's confused countenance, and ripped his hand defiantly from where it clamped over his wound. " 'Tis passing difficult with a musketball buried in one's leg."

The girl sucked in a sharp, hissing breath, her hand flying to her mouth for but an instant as she stared at the bloodied silk of his breeches. A fierce sense of triumph, as though he had dealt her a masterful swordstroke, swept through Creigh at the quicksilver flashes of guilt, consternation, and concern that whisked across anger-flushed features. Then, more rapidly, still, shame claimed him as he saw her soft lips quiver. Yet he scarce had time to take in their slight trembling, before they set into a firm line, and a whirlwind seemed to descend upon him.

The girl dropped to her knees beside him, slender fingers deftly unsheathing the dagger at her waist. "Dear God," she said between gritted teeth. "The cloth of your breeches is driven halfway through your leg. If I don't cut it away . . ."

"What the devil?" MacDermot's harsh voice cut in, his bulky shadow falling across the girl's face as he strode up beside them.

"The blasted witling is wounded!"

Creigh felt a grin tug his lips at the girl's affronted cry. Her eyes blazed as though the musketball was a personal insult. "Come, now, Tigress. 'Tis hardly mortal," he teased, her tempers stirring an odd sense of delight in him in spite of his throbbing leg. "I've run afoul of enemy fire before. The only difficulty is that somehow this cursed musketball had not the good manners to carve its own exit."

He saw the girl wince, but she never hesitated, merely swiped the flat of the already bright dagger blade upon a clean spot on her chemise. A tiny, cold lump of unease knotted in Creigh's stomach as her eyes narrowed on the torn flesh a hand's length below his hip.

"Why didn't you say something?" she demanded.

"As I remember, milady, *you* were saying a great deal," he said, eyeing the blade warily. "'Twould hardly have been chivalrous of me to interrupt. I—Nay!" Creigh stiffened against the tree trunk, dragging his leg from beneath the dagger's edge as a sudden, sharp nausea assailed him. He felt his cheekbones heat red, his voice quavery even to his own ears. "I—I would much prefer you did not come at me with that thing," he managed. "Considering our past exchanges, you might—er—might slip and cleave a vital part of my anatomy."

"The only thing I might be tempted to sever is your tongue if you keep making jest of this. 'Tis a wicked wound. Let me clean away the cloth before your leg festers."

"Better my leg than my—Damme!" Creigh grasped her wrist, struggling to evade her hand as she reached for the corded silk covering his thigh. Horror that this little harridan could even think of touching his wound made the bile rise in his throat. "Just give me that dagger, girl, and let me—"

"I can take that lead from your leg now, or wait 'til you faint of bloodloss, Colonel Lord Wakefield. 'Tis entirely your choice."

"If you think, for a trice, I'm allowing some half-breeched girl near me with a knife, you're sadly mistaken! Mac-Dermot!" Creigh looked desperately to the older man, expecting rescue.

But the veteran merely peered down his hooked nose, an infuriating smile twitching beneath his red beard. "Whist, m'lord Creighton," he said, his voice so soothing Creigh wanted to strangle him. "Bree, here, be a right capable healer if ye can bear her caterwaulin'. Ye can't go traipsin' clear back to merry King Charlie wi' a hunk o' lead in yer gam, an' ye can count on me to guard yer privies if she goes too free with the knife."

"I can make it to the nearest village. Find a surgeon, if I can just—gain my—feet," Creigh argued, digging the heel of his other foot into the turf, trying to shove himself upward. A thousand acid-tipped spikes rammed into his thigh, tiny black dots whirling in front of his eyes. With a blistering curse, he sagged back to the ground, his pride nigh as damaged as his leg. He looked up to see Brianna regarding him with a smile sweet as new cream.

"At that rate, my lord colonel, you should reach Slane-town sometime next summer."

Anger, frustration warred with the sudden need to laugh, and Creigh felt an urge to crush the girl's complacent smile with his lips. " 'Twould be preferable to having you carve away at me," he said. "However, I'm afraid my . . . business . . . can't wait that long." Creigh ground his fingertips against his eyelids, desolation stealing over him as the image of Lindley and Galliard Wakefield assailed him. "Slice away, Tigress. I've no doubt you'll take joy in it."

Creigh waited for a sharp rejoinder, indignation, anger. But the voice that ordered Fergus to start a fire, Daniel to tear strips from his tunic, was even, calm. While the hands that peeled the bloody silk from his wound were gentle as an angel's wing, the sharp edge of her dagger was unerringly deft as it cut away the torn cloth, baring the wound beneath. The river water had at least kept the cloth from fusing to the torn flesh, and when she eased the tattered bits from the wound, Creigh was stunned at how little it pained him.

He looked up sharply, but she didn't see, busied as she was with the doeskin pouch he had seen bound to her belt. A square of wet linen lay spread on the moss, a few crude instruments arranged upon the piece of cloth in precise rows. A small blaze crackled to life beneath Fergus's flint, the glowing tongues streaking the tiny metal teeth, long pincers gold, red. The girl's fingers closed around the dagger hilt, and she buried it in the flames. Creigh's jaw clenched.

"You needn't fear, my Lord Creighton."

He jerked his gaze up to Brianna's, seeing in her face a compassion that touched her strong features with the subtle beauty of heather clinging to barren cliffs.

Slender fingers drew out bundles of sodden herbs, bound with bright gold strands that could only be her hair. "I grew up amongst three brothers." Her rose-tinted lips curved in a smile, distant, beguilingly vulnerable. "I've stitched up more gashes, lanced more boils, and plucked out more splinters than I can count. And as for bullet wounds, Shane took his first when he was scarce thirteen, his last at four-and-twenty, and in the years between the two, gathered up enough musketballs to lead the roof of Castle Kilcannon."

The eyes that had spit hate now glowed the hue of burnished gold, their dark-fringed depths seeming to strip away all defenses, to pierce his very soul. 'Twas as if she could sense his fears, his failings, and gifted him with her own.

Creigh summoned a smile, chagrin reddening his cheek-bones. "In truth I feel better already," he said in the intimate tone that had charmed more than one reluctant maiden out of her virtue. "That is, Tigress, if you can assure me your Shane lived to the great old age of five-and-twenty?"

He watched the girl's lips, waiting for them to part in the anticipated smile, but instead a look of such torment streaked across her face that the depth of her pain seemed to lodge in his own breast.

Three brothers she had claimed, Creigh thought, his gaze straying to the gangly lad who still huddled like a lost child on the riverbank.

A sudden surge of understanding went through Creigh, as he remembered the look in the girl's golden eyes in the dim light of Drogheda. The same expression he had seen as a child, the day he and his father had come upon a she-wolf whose den had been ravaged by a boar.

Though twenty years had passed, the horror Creigh had felt struck him like a fist in his belly, the savaged wolf cubs littering the earth, their silvery coats stained with blood, their bodies torn by huge tusks, while the wounded mother wolf battled the boar in agonized frenzy.

Blackthorne had commanded his retainers to kill the

boar, and ordered them to do away with the she-wolf as well. Creigh had never forgotten the desperation in the creature's eyes. Even while a sword bit into her belly, she lunged in front of the smallest cub, trying to shield it as she died. That same desperate courage had blazed in Brianna Devlin's face when she had charged across the cobbles to defend her fallen brother, if only Creigh had not been too blind to see it.

The soft chink of metal jarred him from his musings, gentle, probing fingers circling the gouge in his flesh. His breath hissed, sharp between his teeth. Brianna's fingers stilled.

Uncinching the belt from around her waist, she doubled it, pressing the cream-colored leather smooth upon her thigh. Creigh saw her lift one hand. Tentatively, soothingly, her fingertips skimmed his jaw. The warmth of her palm seeped into the rigid flesh, and Creigh fought the need to turn his cheek more fully into the comforting lee of her fingers.

"The musketball . . ." she said softly. "It looks to be passing deep."

"If it was but a simple wound, I'd have ripped the blasted nuisance out myself." He tried to brush aside her concern with a smile, but his face felt too stiff, what little strength he had left seeming to fade away like the sheen of dampness drying on his skin. He surrendered, his jaw tightening in pain.

"Bite on this." She held her folded belt to his lips.

"I need no—"

"You will, my lord."

Creigh regarded her long seconds, icy rivulets of dread trailing down his spine. Christ, she sounded so certain. Her full lips pressed together in a somber curve, all the sweeter because they were shaded with such unmistakable regret.

"Please."

If she had slashed him across the face with the strip of leather, Creigh could not have been more stunned. His eyes locked with hers. Slowly he opened his mouth.

She eased the folded belt between his lips, holding it there until he clamped his teeth upon it. He watched her take up the pincers, settling her fingers about their curved handles. Creigh stiffened against the tree, steeling himself for the agony of those thin spikes of iron delving into flesh that

73

already burned like fire. Poising the instrument inches from his wound, the girl glanced up.

"I would that I had whiskey," she said. "Something to deaden—"

"I'd much prefer you refrained from using the word *dead* at the moment," Creigh groaned, the belt making his words all but unintelligible. But Brianna must have understood, for her eyes warmed, gold as honey, before they again shifted to his wound.

Metal bit into savaged flesh, Creigh's fists knotted on the unyielding roots of the oak. His teeth sank fiercely into the belt, his head arched back into the rough bark until the sharp bits of wood cut into his scalp. Raw agony raged within his thigh as the pincers drove deeper. Each fraction of an inch within the torn muscle seemed to pierce the flesh anew, ripping away his will, suffocating him in a leaden coverlet that crushed his chest, hazed his eyes.

"Don't . . . don't fight it, my lord," he heard a faraway voice plead, its gentle accents blurred with torment nigh great as his own. "Fergus . . . I can't—can't hurt him any—"

"Hurt him? Damn, if ye don't be quick, he'll be halfway t' hell by the time ye do the burnin'," a gravelly voice warned.

The instrument's handles dug into the rim of his wound, the points deep in his thigh seeming to split the muscle within. Creigh groaned, his teeth nigh cutting through the leather as the pincers sliced, twisting along the path of the musketball. Blood gushed from the wound, but he felt its heat as though 'twere another man's life spilling to the earth. He was being sucked into inky velvet, the heavy folds shrouding him, bearing him down.

"Losing too much blood," he heard the deep voice grumble. "The lad can't last."

"Damn it, he *will*. Faint, you stubborn bastard! Faint!"

The words seemed so far away, yet the voice pulled at him, relentless. Suddenly something buried in his thigh wrenched, yanked. Agony exploded in his leg. His pain-glazed eyes flickered open but an instant, focusing on the blade of the dagger, glowing like a sword from hell. A scream lodged in his throat as the white-hot blade plunged deep. Muscle, skin seared, a horrible stench rising from the blackened flesh. Creigh's head thrashed against the tree trunk, his hands clenching on the roots, but agony drove its talons deep, dragging him down into welcome blackness.

With a shaking hand Brianna tore the blood-cooled blade from Creigh's flesh, a sigh of relief quavering in her lungs as she stared at the burned flesh. Horrible as the blackened skin was, 'twas far better than the flow of lifeblood now pooled on the turf beneath Creighton Wakefield's leg. Far better than the possibility of putrification setting in, a curse which had left more than one soldier with a gruesome stump where their arm or leg had been.

" 'Tis for the best," Fergus said at her shoulder. "The lad's losin' himself for now. 'Twill give ye time t' bind the wound wi'out dealin' him more pain."

She nodded, letting the dagger fall into the dirt beside the discarded pincers, the instrument's tiny teeth still clamped about the bloodied chunk of lead. She looked from the deadly missile to the face of the man who had borne its removal so stoically.

Slumped against the tree, his face had the look of a beleaguered David, having at last bested a pack of Goliaths. Beads of cold sweat clung to his broad brow, testament to the torture he had suffered. The belt had slipped from his mouth. The arrogant curve of his lips, though lined with pain, was oddly soft in the morning light, easing the mocking bent that had infuriated her from the first time she had seen it. She smoothed a curl of rosewood hair back from his temple, and the wrenching wave of emotion that went through her struck to her very soul.

Sweet Christ, how had he done it? He had battled the current, driven them all through the treacherous waters by sheer force of will, his own leanly muscled body guiding the pitching keg, keeping it steady when the rest of them had no longer had the strength. He had alternately teased, goaded, commanded, threatened, all the while bleeding from a wound that would have driven most men to screaming frenzy. And he, a vile, hated Sassenach bastard, had suffered being shot, while aiding three Irish in escaping a fellow Englishman's "justice."

Guilt was bitter in Brianna's mouth, as if each scathing word she had uttered to him was layered across her tongue. Who was this man—Colonel Lord Creighton Wakefield? And why did she feel so desperately the need to plumb the

75

depths of those silvery eyes, to run her fingertips over those marble-hewn features?

"Ye'd best be bindin' 'im up 'fore he wakes," Fergus prodded, hunkering down beside her. "Spare 'im that much pain, at least." Gnarled hands, gentle as a woman's, lowered Wakefield's limp form back onto the mossy earth. "Galliard Wakefield would've waxed full proud of the lad this day."

Brianna nodded, a lump lodging in her throat. She turned to her medicines, mingling the herbs into a healing poultice, but the image of a child Creigh, basking beneath a father's fierce pride, stirred something illusive, unnameable, deep within her. She could nigh see Creigh, bolting about on plump, stubby legs, hurling himself into the outstretched arms of his father, while the glittering, laughing nobleman tossed his son high. She swallowed, an odd longing stirring in her belly.

With fingers strangely lacking their usual efficiency, she smoothed the pungent mixture of the poultice across the sleek, hard sinews of Wakefield's thigh, wrapping the muscled length in the snowy strips of cloth.

"We'll have to be partin', Bree. The lot o' us, I mean." She glanced up to see Fergus run one hand over his furrowed brow.

"Parting?" she echoed. "But . . ."

"Aye, an' the quicker the better. 'Twill be far too easy fer Cromwell's hordes to spy us, clumped together like a flock o' geese. Especially bearing a man wi' a slug in 'is leg. An' someone needs must reach the Marquis of Ormonde soon as possible, to tell him . . ." the old soldier's eyes turned in the direction of what had once been Sir Arthur Aston's impregnable city. "Tell him the garrison o' Drogheda is no more."

"Ormonde will have to wait," Brianna insisted. "My Lord Wakefield will not be able to travel for days, and, even when he can, t'will be so slowly we'll not reach the Marquis's forces for weeks."

"Weeks might be too late. With Cromwell rollin' his bloody army across the land, Ormonde will need every man. Danny-boy an' I'll ride to his aid, while you hie Lord Creighton off t' heal at Heatherspray."

"Heatherspray?" Brianna rounded on the old soldier, bristling. "Oh, nay, Fergus MacDermot, you'll not trundle me back to that empty cottage like a recalcitrant babe! I battle for Devlin land, just as you fight for your plot of ground, and—"

"And while we're battlin', who's to tend to the man who kept us all from bein' drowned?" Fergus barked, gesturing to where Wakefield lay. "Do ye plan to abandon him here? Or shall we but drag him along behind us 'til he has the good manners to die?"

"But Daniel . . . I'll not leave—"

"The lad stays with me. Look at 'im, *cailín.*" Fergus's hand closed on her chin, forcing her to turn to where her brother sat curled upon the turf. The once-sparkling eyes were blank, thin shoulders shivering beneath the remains of his tunic. "Tell me, what would ye do with the both of them? Lord Creighton an' the lad? Dame Fortune'll be smilin' on ye if ye're able to get a one of 'em out of this hellhole."

"Then *you* tend Wakefield," Brianna said almost desperately. "Daniel is all I have left."

"If Lord Creighton hadn't aided us, there'd be no Daniel for you to blather about. You're the healer, Bree. An' even if we be the only ones left of Drogheda's forces, I'm still your commanding officer. I'll take care of your Danny, lass. But you . . . I order you to stay with Lord Creighton, help him reach wherever 'tis he's bound for."

Chapter Six

Hours later Brianna could still picture the stubborn jut of Fergus's grizzled jaw, the implacable set of his shoulders as he had settled her and the yet unconscious Creigh in a secluded, flower-spangled glen. She had pleaded, cajoled, ranted at the old soldier, even trailing him and Daniel to the rim of the glen in one final attempt to make the veteran see reason, but Fergus had held firm. And when she had embraced Daniel those last horrible seconds before he and Fergus started down through the open fields, it was as though the last vestiges of the child she had been were being ripped from her breast.

Daniel had cried, wracking sobs torn from his thin chest. But she had only watched him as he disappeared into the glow of afternoon, his broken farewell leaving her empty, aching, afraid.

And now . . . Brianna curled her knees further beneath her, blinking eyes parched from their lack of tears. 'Twas as if some cruel hand had dashed her into nothingness, abandoning her to a stark barrenness such as she'd never known. She was alone—alone with a man she scarce knew, a man who intrigued her, infuriated her. Aye, and terrified her. Her eyes skimmed over his death-pale features, the straight patrician nose, strong, lightly stubbled chin, the bruised shadows beneath lashes curled luxuriously as wisps of sable.

The first ribbons of twilight kissed the exquisite planes of his face with fingertips dipped in rose, accenting the blatant sensuality in his mouth, the latent danger etched into the tiny scar biting into his black brow.

Danger? Brianna shivered. He lay so still, so pale, only the slight stirring of the blue velvet covering his chest showing he was alive at all. Yet somehow, watching him thus, she felt more vulnerable than ever in her life.

More vulnerable, even, than she had felt crushed beneath the heaving body of that other Roundhead, so many weeks ago. She tried desperately to banish the agonizing memories, but they seared through her relentlessly, tormenting her with such stark clarity her flesh crawled. She could feel slack, pockmarked jowls crushed against her, a slavering mouth raping her lips, brutal hands savaging her body.

The nameless Sassenach had stolen a thousand girlhood dreams from her, as he'd forced himself between her thighs. Dreams of gowns woven of gossamer lace, strong arms tumbling her back into featherbeds sprinkled with wild rose, of a phantom lover teaching her with passion, fierce, yet gentle, what it was between a man and a woman.

But as if the sadistic monster had not deemed the subtle hauntings of the rape enough, he had carved his mark into her skin, assuring that she'd never be free of the horror. Her hand drifted to the fabric of her chemise, her fingertips tracing the thin, upraised scar beneath her breast. Even if she did gain the courage one day to let another man make love to her, the Roundhead's brand would always be upon her, never allowing her to forget the terrible brutality of the first time a man had used her thus.

An osprey's cry rippled over the glen, lonely, aching, and a knot lodged in Brianna's throat at the sadness of it. Nay, for her there would be no tumbling of innocence into wonder, no unbridled ecstasy in the arms of a dashing rake the like of the man lying so still beside her.

She looked down into Creighton Wakefield's aristocratic features, so tantalizingly perfect, so temptingly near. The barest shading of color had returned to the sharply drawn cheekbones, the rosewood waves of hair clinging in silken wisps along his granite-hewn jaw. And his lips . . . they beckoned with a hundred whispered mysteries of pleasure, aye, and pain.

Brianna reached out trembling fingers, their tips hovering endless seconds above that strongly chiseled mouth. What would it be like, to be wooed by that sweet curve, to hear love words rasp low in that throat as Creighton Wakefield's slender, bronzed hands awakened her to bliss? To be touched by a man, body, soul, and to touch him without horror . . . fear . . .

Of its own volition, her hand drifted down, his breath, warm, moist, misting her skin with a hundred nameless longings. She wanted to press her mouth to his, to taste again of its magic, but instead she traced the lines pain had dug into his taut face, the bristly stubbling on his lean jaw, the black satin of one arrogant brow. The fever she had known would come after bearing such an angry wound was setting in, but she tried to imagine Creighton Wakefield gripped in the throes of a far different heat, one that would consume them both.

One fingertip wisped down, and she closed her eyes as it touched the sensual curve of his lips. The silky heat of his mouth burned into her hand, piercing her to the pit of her stomach. Shivering with a raw delight that terrified her, she let her hand savor their fullness, the sweetness of his breath sifting between her fingers.

She started, guiltily snatching her fingers away as the lips that had been so still moved, his moan barely reaching her ears.

Brianna bent closer, unbound hair spilling in a golden fall across his chest. "Colonel Lord Wakefield?" she said, touching his shoulder gently. "Sir?"

Wakefield's eyelids fluttered half open, his hands plucking restlessly at the velvet of his doublet as though trying to grasp something just beyond his reach. Brianna touched his forehead, his skin ablaze with fever.

"Lord Creigh—"

His face twisted in a torment that clutched at Brianna's heart. "Lin—Lindley . . ." the word, squeezed from a throat parched, fever dry, rasped so softly Brianna scarce heard it. "Don't . . . don't let them get the axe . . . hurt . . ."

"I'll not, my lord." Brianna tried to soothe him, smoothing her fingers in a comforting path down his now-rigid jaw as his torment raged through her. Torment, doubtless spawned of the fear that someone would amputate his wounded limb. "They'll be no taking off your leg. I've bound it up and—"

"Nay! Kill him . . . they'll . . . Bastards!" His face was

tight with fear, fever-bright eyes glazed with desperate fury. "Father . . . Curse—curse you . . . murdered . . ." A choked sound, akin to a sob snagged in his chest, and he struggled to force himself upright. "Jolie . . . can't—can't find him—can't . . ."

"Whist, my lord. Whist," Brianna hushed him, her own throat tight with misery at seeing this man in such inner pain. Gently she pressed his shoulders back to the turf. "Rest, now, and—"

"Have to—have to find . . ."

"Aye, my lord. We'll search for . . . *him*. As soon as you're better. Just—"

"God . . . Sweet God, don't hurt—Lindley!" Creigh's mouth contorted in agony, his arms, legs thrashing as he fought against her restraining hands. Fear bolted through her. Dear Lord, if he kept battering himself about so, he'd split open his wound. "Don't kill him! You bastards! Don't—" He screamed a savage battle cry, hurling himself upward, but Brianna held him, her arms straining against the still-mighty strength in his broad chest.

One rock-hard fist crashed up, bruising her cheek. Brianna gritted her teeth as her jaw seemed to explode, but she clutched Wakefield all the tighter, desperate to keep him from ripping open his torn flesh. "Stop! Lord Wakefield . . ."

The fist arced up again, and she braced herself for its punishing blow. Yet instead, the bronzed fingers swept lower, groping at her throat. She tried to yank away, evade them, but his sinewy hand locked about her, tightening.

A startled cry caught in Brianna's chest, died there as his fingers strangled all sound. She grabbed at his hands, her nails digging into his flesh as she struggled to work his fingers loose. Yet even through the alarm that clutched at her she fought to pin him to the ground to keep him from doing himself harm. Wedging her knee against his chest, she shifted all her weight upon him, straining the rest of her body backward to break his hold. But despite the grip of fever, the finely honed muscles held the strength of tensile steel, whatever hauntings torturing him in his nightmare prison driving him to battle like the demons of hell.

She clawed at his fingers, arching her head to the side in an effort to sink her teeth above his wrist. She bit down. With a

81

fierce oath he tore his hand away, delirium-clouded eyes narrowed in a hate that chilled her blood. She sucked in harsh breaths, fighting, kicking to break free, but his muscles snapped taut, bunched, as in one lightning movement he rolled, tumbling her over. A jagged stone raked her back, the heavy plane of his chest crushing what little breath she had managed to squeeze into her lungs.

A thin blade of fear cut deep.

"Kill you. Kill . . . bloody Roundhead murderers—"

The mouth she had caressed but moments before twisted in a feral snarl, his unfocused eyes heavy with some fear-hazed scene that he alone could see. But the strength of his hands was very real, powerful enough to crush life out of any he saw as enemy.

Brianna balled up her fist, slamming it into one patrician cheekbone with strength born of a hundred childhood brawls. "Lord Creighton Wakefield!" she bellowed, infusing her voice with all the steely command she could muster. "'Tis me, Brianna." She clouted him on the side of the head. "Listen, you great oaf!"

A muffled sound tore from his lips, as his body collapsed atop hers. "Listen. Can't—can't stop . . ." he moaned, shudders wracking his tall frame. "Crying for me . . . Lindley crying for me . . . Juliet, can't . . . I can't find him. Oh, sweet *Christ.*" Agony, more devastating than any physical pain, ripped through his voice, the sound of it rending Brianna's heart as he buried his face in her breasts. Instinctively she flinched from the heat of his skin against her soft flesh, a ripple of panic starting in her stomach. But then the odd, strangled sound tore again from Creigh's throat, and she felt a hot wetness dampening the chemise crushed beneath his face. Tears . . .

The sudden certainty rocked her to the core of her being, the sight of this arrogant man's grief moving her with an intensity that left her shaken. Fierce protectiveness welled inside her, her trembling fingers feathering over his hair, smoothing the tousled waves as horrible, silent sobs wracked him.

"Hush, now, 'tis not your fault," she crooned, her voice catching in her throat. "We'll find . . . Lindley." She brushed the wispy curls from Creigh's sweat-sheened temple, pressing her lips to the skin she bared. Hot, faintly salty, she tasted of the sorrow that clung to his lashes.

His arms tightened convulsively around her. "Late . . . too late . . . they'll—"

"Nay!" Brianna burst out with a savage tenderness that shocked her. "'Tis not too late. I swear it. All will be well. Just . . ." She kissed him, stroking his beard-stubbled jaw. "Just close your eyes, rest . . ."

"Need—need to . . ." A sigh shuddered through him, the arms that had been crushing her easing their desperate grip. She felt his face lift from her breasts, and her pulse thundered as her gaze caught the stormy gray of his eyes. "Soft . . ." he murmured, with a dazed wonder, shaking bronzed fingers trailing up to trace her cheek. "So soft, warm. So long since I've felt . . . peace." Her heart gave an odd lurch, the fear she had experienced at his fever-spawned rage moments before paling to insignificance in the light of a far deeper terror. Fear born of the sudden heat firing his gaze.

Brianna fought to breathe, couldn't, as he lowered his head, burying his lips in hers. Her mouth opened to protest, but he merely groaned deep in his chest, crushing his lips more tightly over hers. Hungry, demanding, his mouth delved into hers with a fierce need that set her whole body quaking. His tongue thrust deep into her mouth, filling her with liquid fire.

Brianna whimpered, the waves of pleasure he evoked in her body so great, so consuming, 'twas as if her very being would burst. Some trapped, fluttery part of her beat fearful wings within her, goading her to flee, but as though they possessed a will of their own, her fingers twined in the thick waves of his hair, drawing him closer.

With a groan of satisfaction, Wakefield shifted, cupping his body more fully over hers. The lean hardness of his hips crushed the soft swell of her stomach, his uninjured leg curving over her thighs. Shivery heat built in Brianna's breasts as the soft hairs bared by his partly open doublet tickled her skin, sensation swelling inside the rose-tipped mounds until they throbbed. Fear, desire lashed needlelike tentacles around her.

She dug her head back into the turf, her eyes squeezing

shut as Creigh's mouth left hers, his teeth taking half-savage bites along her jaw, throat.

"No." Her denial was scarcely a croak, as his hand took in her breast, fingertips molding it through the worn linen, demanding every mystery from the delicate flesh. His breath scorched the lace edging her chemise, his mouth searing kisses down the soft mound to fasten upon the nipple thrusting against its shielding of cloth.

"Hot, soft . . . feel like fire . . ." Feverish hands fumbled with the frayed ribbon lacings of her chemise, shoving the linen from her breasts as if he would rip every veil from between them. A hungering moan broke from his lips, half pleasure, half pain, knotting in her heart with a need so strong her throat ached.

His mouth opened over her nipple, drawing her deep. Brianna's teeth clenched against the exquisite torment, and she wanted to clasp those incredibly soft lips to her, give herself over to the drugging passion of the hard, lean body, wanted to be naught but a woman being wooed into the wonder of her first loving by this magnificent man.

Her fingers tangled deeper in the silken waves of his hair as if trying to cling to the illusion . . . the illusion of being untouched . . . loved.

Almost as though the sudden cooling of her response to him penetrated his fevered haze with a vague dissatisfaction, his bronzed, rein-hardened hands cupped around her breast, molding it more tightly into the heat of his mouth. His tongue, lips, fingers skimmed over her flesh, wooing sensation from every nerve in her body. He tracked kisses to the hollow of her throat, then down to her other breast, trailing the tip of his tongue over creamy smooth skin. Trailing closer, closer to—

Terror bolted through Brianna with a force that tore the breath from her lungs as his tongue wisped over the raised length of scar marring her breast. And suddenly the flower-spangled glen spun into a muddy roadside, tangled branches of the trees snarling in hideous patterns over her head as thrusting porcine hips drove her into rain-sodden ground. A scream clawed at her throat, and she kicked, fought like a wild thing, her only reality the horror that robbed her of all reason.

Reflexively the hands that had been stroking her grabbed

at her wrists, trying to bind them. She lashed out savagely, driving her knee up to slam into her captor's groin. But instead of crashing into the apex of his thighs, the hard bone of her knee cracked into thick cloth wrappings . . . bandages . . .

A cry of agony pierced the fear that enveloped her, the manacling fingers loosening, the body crushing her down falling still, unmoving. She struggled from beneath the ensnaring weight of arms, legs, and scrambled away from the inert form of Creighton Wakefield.

Clutching her chemise about her, her whole body drenched icy with sweat, she stared into his pain-savaged face. Wayward dark locks tumbled over his clay-colored brow, agony gouging lines in his countenance, as though a master sculptor had been careless with his chisel.

Even though unconscious, Creigh had clamped his hands over the newly-stained bandages, the burnished strength of his fingers smeared with the freshet of blood. Brianna choked down the bile that rose in her throat, aftershocks of horror at what she had done rushing through her in sickening waves.

He was injured, crazed with fever, and she, who had seen the extent of his wound more clearly than any, had driven her knee into the angry flesh, breaking it open yet again.

Coward, she derided herself. *'Twas not his fault! He knew not what he was about. Had no way of knowing about the other.*

But I was so afraid.

She clutched her arms tight about her breasts, her skin crawling as the hideous images of rape, death surged over her. She bit her lip, her fingernails digging into her flesh. *Aye,* a voice mocked within her. *And now, he may well bleed to death because of your cowardice.*

Brianna stiffened, forcing the haunting memories away. Nay, she already had paid too high a tithe to the horror that had befallen her so long ago. This man would suffer no further because of it.

She dropped to her knees at Creighton Wakefield's side, her fingers peeling his hands from the bandages. The strips of linen sagged in grisly loops about the hair-roughened flesh as she worked the dressing's knots. But as she opened the wrappings to peer beneath, a sigh of relief shuddered through her. Silently, Brianna blessed the thick poultice of herbs that had, apparently, saved Creigh's wound from the full impact of her knee. Much of the cauterized flesh had held firm, only the edge nearest his groin bleeding freely.

Wadding up the hem of her petticoat, Brianna pressed the cloth onto the wound, holding it there with fingers still lacking their usual deft assurance. She had broken open a wound on this man, still too fragile to be healed, and yet Creigh had slashed wide her own inner scars, releasing a torrent of poison within her. *Remembrance, aye, and hopelessness,* Brianna thought numbly. For though he, no doubt, would recall little of the moments of the fire that had flared between them, Brianna knew that she would never forget them. They would dance within her memory, silvery stars always just beyond her reach, mocking her with the certainty that never would she be able to capture the glory his loving had promised. For even if some man loved her, she would never be able to offer herself to him, sullied as she was by the shame of that distant, muddy roadside.

She reached up one hand, wiping away the sweat beading Creigh's brow, the boyish cast to his face tugging at her heart. He lay so still, so vulnerable beneath her hands, despite the daunting breadth of shoulders, power of sinewy muscles cording his body. Brianna swallowed, letting the pads of her fingers trail down to his lips. For these hours, days, that he lay, unknowing, he would be hers. She would watch every movement of his arrogant, beautifully carved mouth, every kiss of sunshine gilding sable lashes, rosewood hair, and mourn for what she had lost.

Brianna huddled deeper into the meager shelter she had worked of scrub branches and rubbed her palms against her arms in an effort to warm herself. The breeze skating in from the nearby river darted beneath her petticoats to nip at the bare skin beneath and sifted chill fingers through Creigh's tumbled hair. Three days fortune had smiled upon Bree and her charge, blanketing them in robes of heather-scented air warm as goosedown. But as the sun dipped low behind the hilltops this night, 'twas as if that capricious Dame had turned against them, spinning from her fingertips mounds of slate-colored clouds that whispered of rain.

Brianna pulled a bit of tough meat from the coney she had

spit-roasted that morning and chewed it slowly. There had been little enough she could do for Creigh these days past—wiping away the sweats of agony that drenched him, changing his dressings, feeding him morsels of meat she had pounded soft between two stones. But once the inevitable Irish mists began to fall, there would be naught she could do to keep him warm, dry. And if his fever worsened . . .

Nay, he was strong, this man. A fighter. She glanced down at his face pillowed on sweet moss. A tearing ache gnawed at her heart as his brow creased with pain.

How had he done it? Burrowed past all her defenses to the very core of her, without so much as opening his eyes. The planes of his face were branded upon her soul, every nuance of his pain, torment, melding with her own. A hundred times she had touched him, soothed him, stilling his tortured mumblings with the tips of her fingers. But never had she expected the velvet-sheathed blades of peace and desolation he had buried within her.

Tearing a tiny bit of coney from the fire-blackened bones, she parted Creigh's lips, slipping the morsel onto his tongue. But as she reached to stroke his throat, aid him in swallowing, his pale lips contorted in a sour grimace, his head twisting away from her grasp as he spat the offending piece of meat onto the grass at his side.

"T-trying to . . . bloody poison . . . me."

Brianna's gaze darted up at the sound of Creigh's raspy voice, expecting the haze of nightmare to lay again over his features. But instead of the tortured lines that had etched his face as his demons had claimed him, gray eyes glared up at her, their disgruntled light infusing her with the sudden, unleashable urge to laugh out loud.

"Not jesting," he ground out. "Tastes . . . like inside of . . . chamberpot."

"'Tis one confection I fear I've missed," Brianna chuckled. "I searched for hummingbird tongues broiled in honey, but it seems there is a shortage hereabouts, so you needs must make do with charred rabbit. However, in a fortnight or so, when you're able to travel—"

"Nay! Not fortnight," he said, struggling to push himself up on his elbows. "Have to . . . hasten."

"The only thing you *have* to do, Colonel Lord Wakefield, is lay still and not ruin my handiwork." She gently pushed him back to the ground. "Your leg is mending nicely, and—"

"Plague take . . . leg! Lindley . . . I promised Juliet I'd—" He tried to put pressure on the bandage-wrapped limb, lever himself up. His lips whitened. Brianna's fingers tightened on his arms, an odd imp of jealousy pricking in her stomach that for this woman—Juliet—he would endure such agonies.

Brianna's own mouth thinned, and she was furious at herself for the very real feeling of betrayal that swept through her. "Well, whoever the chit is, she will have to wax patient," Brianna snapped. "I went to a deal of trouble to save your Sassenach hide, leg and all, and I'll not have you splitting it wide for some pampered little—" She stopped, acutely uncomfortable beneath his gaze, but the eyes that had been so clear but a moment before, were fraught, now, with desperation.

Her voice gentled. "'Twill do your Juliet little good if you collapse. Trust me. I know the way to the sea passing well. We'll regain whatever time we lose now a hundredfold if you'll but let yourself grow strong. But if you persist in this folly of rising too soon . . . well, Colonel Lord Wakefield, Fergus's orders or no, you'll be fumbling about the countryside alone."

A blue curse broke from Creigh's lips. "MacDermot!" he bellowed. "Where the hell is MacDermot?"

"I'm afraid if you shout 'til next Michaelmas 'twould serve you no good, as he and Daniel are most like halfway to Ormonde's headquarters by now. But seeing as they did leave you in my charge, you have little choice but to heed me."

"Abandoned me with a headstrong . . . witch . . . in middle of . . . nowhere?"

Brianna smiled at Creigh's affronted tone.

He shot her a thunderous glare, but she could feel the surrender in him. "Take flat of . . . sword . . . to your backside. If could reach it." He cast a longing glance at the scabbard and baldrick laying near his feet.

Despite herself, Brianna felt a laugh bubble in her throat. "I've dealt with you and your blade before, sir, and as I recall, you came out of the encounter much the worse." Her gaze snagged his, all jest vanishing at the sudden, questing heat firing his eyes, infusing her words with other, more sensual meanings.

"Remember . . . remember something. You . . . I . . . Did we—"

Brianna's cheeks burned. "You were delirious," she snapped. "No doubt 'twas but the wanderings of your mind."

"My *wanderings* . . . turning your cheeks to roses?"

Anger welled inside her at the sight of his pale lips widening into a weak smile. "Real. It must have been real." His eyelids drooped shut.

Brianna swallowed, mortified at the expression on his handsome face. 'Twas as if he were recounting every caress, mating of their mouths, rasping of tongue against flesh. But he had been so ill, incoherent. Surely he couldn't recall—

She started to spin away, but his hand caught at her petticoats. "Nay, Tigress, don't," he whispered. "You felt so warm . . . sweet."

Brianna's mouth went dry. "C-colonel Lord Wakefield, I—"

"Creigh. My name is Creigh." He reached out to her, silvery eyes supplicant. "Tigress, lay with me."

Fire raced through Brianna's veins at the throaty tones of his voice, her whole body alive with desire, terror. But before she could pull away from his grasp, bolt, a shudder went through him, the force of it jarring his teeth together.

"Cold . . ." he grated, his jaw clenching. "Sweet Jesu. So . . . cold."

She lifted a shaky hand to dash away the rivulets of sweat running down his face. The lean cheek was chill, clammy, tendrils of hair sticking to the beard-stubbled skin. Even though he was strong, the cold might settle in his lungs, hurling his life into jeopardy yet again.

His hand caught her wrist, and her pulse bounded beneath his fingers. "Tigress," he said. "Warm me."

Slowly, Brianna lowered herself beside him, every muscle in her body steeled as though for some hideous pain. But as he drew her into his arms, she felt only the hardness of his broad chest, the silkiness of his hair brushing her temple, and the sweetness of his sigh wisping across her neck as he closed his eyes.

She lay awake, watching him, as the mist began to fall.

And when the day had again melted into night, she slept as well, cradled close in the circle of his arms.

Dawn was lacing the sky, when she heard it, the sound of hoofbeats nearing the rim of the glen. She eased from beneath the weight of Creigh's arm, and crouched low at the edge of the shelter hoping, praying that some simple crofter's sons were but out for a ride. But even before the horsemen crested the rise, her stomach clenched with the knowledge that 'twas no gaggle of rakehell lads shaking the ground with their mounts' thundering hooves. She reached for the hilt of her sword, catching a glint of armor, flash of red casaque as five Roundhead cavalrymen spilled into the glen. But before her blade could clear its scabbard, a hand caught hers in an iron grip.

"Nay!" A voice hissed in her ear. She spun around to see Creigh's face inches from her own. Silvery eyes narrowed, he peered from beneath the tangled branches of the shelter, watching the soldiers as they pounded toward them.

"Are you mad?" Brianna whispered. "If they see us, they'll—"

"Draw that sword and you'll bring them down on us like the Furies."

Brianna tried to jerk her wrist from his grasp, but his fingers clenched with startling strength. "The blade, you little fool!" he snapped. "'Twill catch the sun. If we stay still, mayhap they'll think this *thing* you built is but a pile of refuse, cast away from some peasant's axe."

"Damn you, I—"

His other hand clamped over her mouth, stifling her protest as he yanked her tight into his body.

Brianna started to struggle. Froze. Flashing hooves, heavy, muscled flanks thundered but a little to the west of the ramshackle shelter. She felt Creigh's breath catch in his chest, held her own as she marked the pounding of each horse as it passed. She clenched her fists, willing the riders to bolt onward, to fade into the distance.

But at the sound of a sudden cry, hope twisted. Died.

"Hold!" The distant voice was obscured by the clamoring of five racing horses being reined to a halt just within view of the shelter. She felt Creigh stiffen against her, his hand releasing her mouth and inching toward the hilt of her sword as whoever had barked the command neared the other Roundheads.

"Colonel, sir, we've been combin' the river-bank for three days," a paunchy private whined. "He be a hundred miles from here by now."

A great roan stallion plunged into sight, its helmeted rider wheeling the magnificent beast in a path that cracked its great haunches into the private's mount. A gauntleted fist shot out, slamming into the little man's jaw. "Wakefield's here, God curse you!" the Roundhead colonel raged. "I know it."

The faintest of hopes stirred. Brianna felt Creigh still.

"But sir—" The tentative, doubtful voice of another man began. "Crowley is right. Even if the traitor went this direction, he's long since gone."

"Not unless the bastard is crawling on his belly!"

Brianna flinched at the cruelty in the voice, a prickle of some nameless fear icing down her spine.

"Sir?"

"I shot him myself, you cursed witling! I know I did. And I'll not rest until I hold that traitor cur's severed head within my hands."

The colonel yanked savagely on the stallion's reins, and Brianna could see the beast's mouth fleck with blood. One huge hand slammed up, the commander shoving the visor from his fury-reddened face.

"Now, *ride*, you cowardly knaves!" he shrilled. "And I vow that 'less you flush out Wakefield, 'twill be your heads adorning a pike!"

Relief drained all life from Brianna's limbs as she heard the other riders race off in another direction, waiting for their leader to join them. But she scarce drew breath before terror clenched razor-sharp talons about her throat.

The Roundhead colonel spun his mount around, his eyes searching the horizon once more. Brianna fought desperately to tear her gaze away from the pockscarred, evil face beneath the battered helm, but she could not. She froze, prisoner of the greatest horror she'd ever know, as she stared into the countenance of the man who had raped her.

Chapter Seven

Creigh sagged against the rooted sapling supporting the shelter's roof, disbelief and jubilation warring with the throbbing in his leg as he watched Saul Ogden spur the stallion out of the glen. The bastard had missed them, by the saints! Ridden but a stream's breadth from his quarry, and spared not a glance at the clump of sticks hidden in the crook of the valley. 'Twas amazing. Aye, a miracle worthy of a hundred lighted candles upon Cathedral de Chartres's grand altar. And, Creigh vowed, if he ever escaped this infernal island, he himself would light every one of them.

He turned to the girl, grasping her shoulder to spin her about, rejoice, but the feel of her flesh beneath his hand made him hold. Like marble it was—icy cold, stiff, lifeless.

"Tigress?" Digging his stockinged toes into the ground, he shoved himself around, maneuvering until he crouched in front of her. His fingers clenched on her arms, forcing her to face him, but 'twas as if she were staring into a druid's crystal, seeing all, seeing nothing.

"Brianna?" he said her name softly, soothingly, peering into the pale oval of her face. The wild, honey tangle of her hair tumbled about her stiff cheeks, liquid gold eyes that had flashed with courage, wide now, with the mindless terror of a child.

Terror of what? Creigh wondered. The danger was past, the soldiers gone. And God knew this she-cat had faced death at the point of Parliamentarian swords far too many times to crumble at the sight of them.

Creigh stroked back the wisps of her hair, fragments of

three days past drifting through his memory. He had been delirious, aye, but he could still feel the heat of her mouth under his, feel her passion . . . then fear smothering the eagerness of her body beneath him. Blind fear, that had changed this most valiant of women into a bewildered, frightened waif.

His hands cupped her face, threaded back into her hair, protectiveness surging through him. "Tigress!"

Her horrible fixed stare shattered beneath the steely velvet of his voice, her golden eyes darting about like a sleepwalker awakened.

Two spots of scarlet sprang to her cheeks as her eyes locked with his. "C-Creigh." His name was but a choked little breath, and he could feel her whole body wrack with tremors. He wanted to hold her, to kiss the blush of color back into her lips, but he only traced the curve of her chin with his fingertips.

"They are gone, Bree."

The too-bright smile that curved her mouth wrenched Creigh's heart. She tossed her head, whirling away from him in a pathetic show of what he knew she hoped passed for elation. But he sensed she wanted naught but to escape the touch of his hand.

"So we—we duped them," she said. "I—I always told Fergus you Sassenach wax half-blind."

"Not all Sassenach."

She flashed him a glance, her smile faltering but an instant before she pasted it yet again on her lips. "Well, at least we'll be safe enough here, now, until you gain your strength back. They'll hardly search this dell again, and even if they did, they'd not spy us. Of course, I could search the area. Mayhap there's a cave, or a—"

"Hold!" Creigh snapped, more harshly than he intended, unable to bear her nervous babbling a second more. She turned toward him, the smile on her lips dying. More gently Creigh continued. "We're not safe here. And there's not a cave deep enough to keep me from Ogden's grasp. Our only chance will be to get horses, ride like the devil to the coast."

"Horses? Ride? But—but your wound . . ."

"It matters naught. If we hasten we can reach Carikbrah before a fortnight is out. From there I sail—"

"On the point of my sword!" Amber eyes blazed, anger

93

quelling the hauntings in their depths. Creigh started, then smiled slowly, welcoming her fire.

"If you believe for one minute, Creighton Wakefield, that I'll allow you to traipse across half of Ireland with a leg still reeking of gunpowder, you are most certainly mistaken!"

"I know how saddened you are, milady, that our little— interlude will soon be at an end," he said, a goading quirk at the corner of his mouth. "But we've got no choice. Ogden will not rest until he's brought the wrath of God down upon me. And if he captured you—"

Her lips whitened, and Creigh saw her fists dig into the folds of her petticoats, but he forced himself to go on.

"You wax passing fair, since you scrubbed the grime of battle from your face," he said, reaching up a fingertip to brush a smudge of dirt from the tip of her nose. "And even in *God's* army, there are those who are hungry for a woman."

He hated himself for the fear that flickered in her eyes, and he could feel her forcibly dragging pride, courage about her slender shoulders.

"We've eluded the soldiers thus far," she said. "Most like our luck will hold if you give yourself time to heal."

"Time?" Creigh raked his fingers through his hair as images of Lindley tormented him. "Even if Ogden was roasting in hell, I'd have no time. I may already be too late."

"For what? To serve *Jolie's* whims?"

Creigh wheeled, more stunned by the distinct edging of dislike Brianna infused in the name, than by the fact that she had flung it out at all. "Jolie?! What the hell do you know about Juliet?"

Crimson stained Brianna's cheeks, and he saw her chin jut out in defiance, defiance and some other, barely veiled, emotion. Despite the vague feelings of unease Juliet's name had spawned in him, complacent amusement tipped his lips in a half-grin. Sweet savior, could the little hellcat be *jealous?* God knew he had seen that emotion in the faces of court belles oft enough to recognize the signs. And those golden eyes that had seared him with courage, ensnared him in their terror, now snapped and sparked like La Marchioness de Bongre's had the eve he had dared a pavane with her beauteous stepdaughter.

Unable to restrain himself, lest he laugh aloud, Creigh

looked past Brianna and let a languorous light steal into his eyes, as though he were fingering some cherished, sensual memory. But he had little time to savor the stinging irritation in her gaze before her delicate brows slashed down in a scowl.

"I'd not wax so haughty, my lord, if I were crying out in a fever," she said.

"Crying out? What—"

"You were taken with a nightmare, and—"

Creigh swore, the visions that had tortured him for so long spinning in his head. Christ, how much of his torment had spilled into words before this girl? Sudden unreasonable anger crashed over him, and he felt as though she had stolen not only his secrets, but his pride as well.

"I'll wager you reveled in listening, did you not?" he blazed. "Pawing through things that were none of your concern?"

Brianna thrust her hands behind her back, and Creigh detected what looked to be a flush of guilt dusting her cheeks.

"It would have been passing difficult *not* to hear you, the way you were sprawled atop me!"

Creigh's face flamed. "Well, in truth I must have been more ill than I knew," he said silkily, letting his eyes trail in a disparaging path down her body. "I'd best hie to a surgeon with all haste."

Hurt flickered in her eyes, and he felt, rather than saw, her stiffen her spine. Disgust at his deliberate cruelty left a foul taste upon his tongue, but he forced his eyes to dismiss her, struggling not to acknowledge the way her simple chemise accented the perfection of her breasts.

Desire flashed through him, quick, sharp. He snatched up his boots, wedging his feet into the stiff leather, welcoming the throbbing pain that pulsed up his leg to drain away the unwanted sensations that had stirred in his loins. He grabbed his baldrick, the scabbard attached to the gold-embroidered band swinging to crack into his thigh. Red-hot spikes of pain drove into the half-healed wound. Creigh clamped his fingers over the thickness of bandaging, an oath tearing from between his lips.

"No doubt you'll reach the sea before nightfall, your lordship, fit as you are for a-journeying," the girl's honey-sweet voice crooned. "We'd best send a messenger ahead, tell your ship to rig full sail."

"I've borne worse wounds and gone a-hunting next day." A muscle in Creigh's jaw clenched, unclenched, as he battled the need to knot his hands in her hair and dunk that damnably superior smirk of hers 'neath an icy stream. "Just mind that you keep stride with me, milady. I've no time to coddle fractious children this day." He flung the baldrick over one shoulder, yanking at the buckle to fasten it as he stalked from beneath the shelter's leafy edge.

A perverse satisfaction warmed him at the rage etched upon the girl's face. Her delicate brows crashed together above her nose, her eyes flashing as though she'd barter her soul for a dagger to stick in his back.

"Keep *stride!*" He heard her echo as if repeating his words to herself. "Keep *stride!*" Her voice rose, or was it that Creigh could hear her very temper threatening to burst? Before he had taken three steps, she was behind him, her petticoats whirling past his leg as she stamped up the hill. She flung a glare over one shoulder.

"Do cry out, your lordship, *when* you collapse," she said in tones of acid sweetness. "I've heard such tales of the grace and courage of King Charles's Cavaliers, I'd not want to miss the pleasure of seeing one sprawled in the dirt."

"'Tis one spectacle, milady, I swear *you'll* never see," Creigh vowed.

She smiled—damn her—her mouth so smug in its rosy-tinted fullness. His own lips set hard. He matched his gait to her militant strides, feeling, in truth, he was girding himself for battle. But even before they crested the hilltop, slipping into the wild, deserted countryside beyond, the pain began, gnawing at the savaged muscles of his leg. And he began to wonder if, for the first time in his life, he had met the opponent who could best him.

Creigh glowered at the derriere swaying along so jauntily before him and gleaned the greatest of pleasures in imagining his hand plying a willow switch to that perfect curve. Plague take her, the witch! She had fairly skipped through the meadowgrass mile after mile, pausing with infuriating frequency to ask how he fared. Even now her sugary tones clung in his ears. *Is your worshipfulness wearied? You seem a*

bit gray about the lips. That heather looks soft as goosedown.
Mayhap you'd care to rest a bit.

"A bit," Creigh mused sourly, his jaw aching from hours of grinding his teeth. If he ever *did* sit down, 'twould be All Hallow's Day before he could rise. And he'd be damned before he gave the little harridan the satisfaction of hearing him cry *enough.*

Oh, aye, a goading voice whispered inside him, *'Twill do your blasted pride worlds more good to walk until you pitch, nose-first into the grass.* Despite the pain, Creigh felt a smile tug the corner of his mouth. *At least if I do that, I'll not have to see that cursed smirk of hers.*

The heel of his boot caught on a stone, the jarring of his ankle twisting coils of pain up into his thigh. An oath hissed between his teeth.

In truth he was looking forward to sinking into a faint. Every muscle in his body screamed in exhaustion. His empty stomach had given up growling an hour past, and now 'twas as if some taloned beast was trying to slash its way out of his belly. But Brianna— His eyes narrowed in a mixture of exasperation and grudging respect as his gaze followed the girl's graceful form. She drifted across the endless countryside like a tumbled angel, her petticoats swirling about her trim ankles, her face cool, serene as a marble madonna's.

Creigh's mouth twisted in a wry smile. His tigress a madonna? If a supplicant knelt at Brianna Devlin's feet, she'd most like box his ears. She was more of a kind with the Amazon maids he had read about in ancient tomes of mythology, wild, fiery warrior women who drove men from all but their bedchambers at the point of their spears.

Yet surely even termagants the like of Brianna needs must eat. And if Creigh could avoid sacrificing either his consciousness, or his pride, so much the better. He scanned the countryside, spying a humble cottage nestled in the lee of a nearby hill.

"Milady?"

"Yes, my lord colonel?" She turned, her delicate brows arching up in question, the fluttering of gold-tipped lashes failing to wholly hide the expectancy in her face. For a moment Creigh searched for any innocuous subject to comment upon, the weather, the clouds, anything that would keep a glint of triumph from her gaze. But then his belly wrenched with hunger. Creigh rolled his eyes heavenward in surrender. The leg he could tolerate. He was a soldier, well trained in the art of keeping physical pain at bay. But it had been five days since Drogheda fell, and the few pieces of beefsteak he had managed to choke down in his tent with Jules Dunley that distant morning had long since passed into oblivion.

"My lord colonel, you addressed me?" Brianna repeated.

"Damn it, woman, I bid you to call me *Creigh!*" he snapped. Creigh stopped, stunned at the violence in his tone, the roiling emotions it exposed, but 'twas as if, in clinging so assiduously to his formal title, the little barbarian had turned it into a subtle form of insult. He was allowing her liberties rarely bestowed upon those of her class, and—plague take her—she was flinging his kindness in his face like a cursed gauntlet.

Indignation burned in his belly as he glared into her chill amber eyes.

"'Tis a kindness, gifting you with the use of my Christian name." He bristled. "A boon not given lightly. But as you proved yourself courageous for a wench, removing the musketball, binding the wound, I thought to honor—"

"Honor me?"

He saw her chin thrust upward, her eyes narrowing in belligerence, and suddenly his words lashed back at him, their insufferable arrogance making him wince.

"Well, mayhap *your lordship* is well used to your English vassals' falling upon their knees and thanking you for such an *exalted honor,"* she said, sweeping into a mocking curtsy. "But *I* have the good fortune to not be bound to you in any way—to your commands, your purse strings, or your tempers, my Lord Creighton. So you may take your cursed name and bear it to the devil."

Creigh stared at her, the small fists planted on her hips, dark-lashed eyes spitting fury above a mouth absurdly kissable even in rage. He had a fleeting image of Maryse Houblon's simpering face as her rouged lips had first formed his given name. She, daughter of the wealthiest viscount in all France, had fairly purred with pleasure, brushing her lush breasts against his doublet in a way that invited intimacies far greater. But this wild Irish wood-witch had flown at him, spitting and snarling, laying bare his ridiculous conceit.

Creigh struggled to suppress the mirth that welled inside him, but despite the gnawing pain in his leg, his merriment was too great to contain. His laughter rang out, deep, unbridled, until his ribs ached with it.

"You bastard!" she sputtered. "Don't you dare make jest of me! I'll—I'll . . ."

He felt her glaring at him, groping for some threat dire enough to satisfy, rage boiling in her eyes, but even the dangerous scarlet that stained her cheeks couldn't stay him. He reached out, his hands tangling in the tumbled curls at her temples. She started to jerk away, but his fingers held her captive as his eyes skimmed her face, a face that had been taut with jealousy, gilded with longing. Endless moments he stared into her mutinous eyes, then, with a curious catching in his chest, lowered his mouth to take hers in a kiss.

Her lips opened beneath his in a startled gasp, the taste of her mouth innocent, sweet as wild berries. But his eyelids had barely drifted shut to revel in them when sudden sharp pain drove into his lower lip.

He yelped, shoving the girl away, swiping his hand across his stinging mouth. The fingers came away smeared with crimson.

"You bit me!" He glowered at his hand, then at Brianna, disbelief turning to righteous ire. "Damme, I but tried to kiss you."

"And I *tried* to get you to release me," the little termagant observed calmly. Her eyes raked his swelling lip with a smugness that set his teeth on edge. "Mayhap next time, my Lord Creighton, you'll let me go."

"*Next* time!" He swore. "'Twill be winter in Hades before I risk any part of my anatomy with you again, milady. Now, even if, by God's own fortune, we do find food, I'll not be able to eat it."

"Eat? Food?" Brianna repeated, her face wreathed in confusion.

"Aye, *food*," Creigh barked. "Something you blasted Irish have obviously learned to live without. The reason I was so foolish as to pause in the first place was to ask if, by Peter's holy grace, we dared stop somewhere to eat. There is a cottage just below the crest of the hill, and my belly has nigh

99

caved in upon itself, what with that tripe you were attempting to poison me with while I lay ill."

He thought he saw a flicker of concern cross her features. Her gaze darted down to his thigh. Anticipation curled his mouth as he saw the fresh staining of blood, and he crossed his arms over his chest, expecting Brianna to wax contrite.

Instead she seemed to mull his words over, her mouth at last curving in barely veiled victory. "'Tis most fortunate that you deigned to admit you are . . . starving, Creigh," she tossed over her shoulder as she started toward the cottage. "That is, *before* you pitched into a faint."

He scowled after her, fuming that a wisp of an urchin the like of her had managed yet again to best him. But as he limped down the twisting path behind her, stingingly aware she had slowed her steps to salvage what remained of his pride, the realization struck him. That taunting, silkily triumphant voice had called him Creigh.

His fingers raised of their own volition to touch the lip she had bitten. The tender flesh pulled into a predatory smile as he recalled the sparkings of jealousy in her eyes, the feel of her writhing beneath him so hungrily her passion had penetrated even the shroudings of fever. Mayhap there was more than one way to wipe that cursed superior smirk from Brianna Devlin's face. A way he would take much pleasure in . . .

The image his mind conjured was so mesmerizing, as he trailed the girl down the hillside, the pain in his leg faded to but a dull throb. Remembered sensations, gleaned from those fever-hazed minutes when he had made love with her, flashed across his memory so vividly he nearly crashed into her backside, when she stilled, midstride, beneath a dying hawthorne. One slender hand raised to bid him to silence, and Creigh froze, as the sound of a distant, high-pitched cry carried on the wind.

Chapter Eight

Creigh's fingers grasped the hilt of his sword, every muscle in his body snapping taut, battle-ready as he jerked the weapon free. A flash of steel slashed bare inches from his belly, the razor-sharp edge nicking his wrist as Brianna swept her rapier free. He leapt aside, a thin line of blood welling from the cut, but before he had time to curse, Brianna grabbed his other arm, yanking him around.

Creigh started to jerk away, more irritated by the knowledge that she had drawn her sword a split second faster than he had, than by the tiny wound that stung his skin. But her fingers clenched tighter, her eyes narrowed, alert. "Quiet, damn you!" she hissed.

"Damn *me!*" Creigh grated. "You nigh cut off my—"

"Listen!"

Creigh clenched his teeth, intending to bellow at the insufferable little witch, yet just as he was wheeling upon her he heard it—something, someone crashing through the tangle of bracken to the west.

Cursing Brianna for being right again, and himself for being caught off guard, he squinted against the late afternoon sun, fully expecting to see Ogden's men bursting through the undergrowth. But as he strained against the glare to define the shape of whatever approached, 'twas no plunging stallion that neared. It had more the sound of an overgrown colt, galumphing awkwardly toward them.

Creigh dashed his hand over sun-stung eyes, as a mop of straggly hair thrust through the undergrowth. Almost lashless eyes gaped up at him in a peaked face, the pale blue orbs ringed white with fear as they darted to the remnants of Creigh's English garb.

Creigh heard Brianna call out in Gaelic, her voice reassuring, but the urchin only flung her a terrified glance. His gaze snagged Creigh's for an instant, the mud-smeared features imprinting themselves upon Creigh's consciousness as the boy paused, stumbled. Then the child wheeled again, crying out some unintelligible warning before hitching up his ragged trews and bolting, headlong, up the hillside.

Creigh stared after the fast-disappearing waif, groping for what it was that made the little wild man seem so disturbingly familiar. "What in the name of Hades—" Creigh turned to Brianna, but she had already spun away, peering back into the bracken with a face chill, pale as iced marble.

"Roundheads," she said. "Roundheads on horseback, riding this way."

"Ogden. Damn it, it has to be Ogden." Creigh's fist tightened convulsively on the hilt of his sword.

He heard Brianna's breath hiss between her teeth, felt her stiffen. Yet, as his gaze swept the tangle of brush, he had little comfort to offer her. The hawthorne by which they stood was rotted, sagging beneath the meager weight of its own gnarled limbs. And to charge into the maze of bracken beyond would, in truth, be bolting into the dragon's jaws. Yet except for that isolated thicket, the countryside spilled about them, devoid of aught that could even remotely afford them protection. Aught, save the ramshackle cottage . . .

As though she'd read his thoughts, Brianna wheeled to face him, and he could see the fear in her, and the fire.

"Tigress—"

"Nay!" Her gaze flashed to the aged thatched roof. "If we're discovered in that cottage, 'twill most like be put to flame, mayhap all within it slain for shielding us."

"There is nowhere else to go!" Creigh swore savagely, grabbing Brianna by the wrist. "If they choose not to give us shelter, we'll not press—"

"M'lord, lady!"

Creigh felt Brianna jump at the nasal cry, as they both whirled toward the source of the voice. The cottage yard that had been so quiet but a moment before seemed to suddenly burst into a frenzy of scrawny chickens, and flapping geese, the squawking fowl scattering from beneath the feet of the tiny woman dashing through the cottage's wood gate.

Cranelike legs churning 'neath a whirl of dingy homespun, her black linen headdress askew, she ran down the hill, the ragged urchin trailing in her wake. "Hasten!" she called, waving stick-thin arms frantically. "Hasten, m'lord! There be a place ye can hide!"

Creigh glanced at Brianna's face, seeing shadings of terror that yet lurked beneath the stiff set of her lips. She had claimed Ogden would fire the hovel if he discovered this peasant woman had aided fugitives. Aye, and Creigh well knew the bastard would revel in it.

But, damn it, he had seen the fear in Brianna's face, felt it, cold, beneath her skin, when Ogden and his cronies had ridden past the shelter in the far-off glen. And though, with his own life, he'd bow to fate's whims and meet whatever Ogden might deal him, rather than cast this peasant woman and child into peril, the terror in Brianna Devlin's golden eyes spawned within Creigh a savage protectiveness stunning in its power—a need, soul-deep, to take her into himself, shield her, no matter the cost to himself or others. He cursed.

Gritting his teeth he grabbed her wrist, dragging her toward the cottage. The ragged peasant woman caught Brianna's other arm, the voice, heavy with Scottish accent, prodding them forward. "Me name be Mary," the woman gasped as they ran. "Mary MacGregor. There be a space in the wall me husband's grandda built when the clans were a-warrin'. Used to secret 'is bairns away in it—aye, an' a bit o' treasure. Ye can hide there 'til the peril be past."

"But if the Sassenachs find us—" Brianna protested.

"I ken, child." The woman threw open the cottage's rickety gate, hustling Brianna and Creigh toward the door set in the hovel's crumbling walls. "But 'tis but the least we can do, me lad an' me."

The woman's hand, reddened, calloused, closed upon the door latch, flung the portal wide. Her sunken, world-weary eyes fastened upon Creigh as the ragged urchin tumbled past them into the dimly lit room beyond. "MacGregors pay their debts," Mary said softly, urging them into the cottage's cool interior. Brianna saw puzzlement crease Creigh's brow as they stepped into the tiny room, then a flash of what seemed to be recognition. Quicksilver emotions played across his features as his gaze flicked to where the lad was dragging a pallet from the corner of the room.

A dull flush crept up the arrogant planes of Creigh's cheekbones, and suddenly the rakish curve of his mouth faded into a strange mixture of irritation and sheepishness.

Brianna saw his fingers twist about the large ruby crowning the hilt of his sword. "Mistress MacGregor," he began, shifting his feet with a discomfort Brianna sensed was not wholly due to his wound. "You bear no debt."

"Nay? Then ye've ne'er known love, sir, for ye know not its worth," Mary said, bolting the door. Confusion jolted through Brianna at the woman's words, and she stared at Creigh.

"You—you know these—"

"'Od's Blood!" Creigh's hands knotted into fists, and she saw his eyes flash as if he wanted to strike the hovel's crumbling walls. "Will you both quit blathering like you're at a cursed garden party and hasten! I vow I'd as lief be waiting to greet Ogden's bastards outside the gate."

Brianna's lips thinned as she saw Mary MacGregor's shoulders square, the poor woman hurrying toward the flooring bared by the displaced pallet with a quiet dignity.

Bony knees thumped against the worn wood, and Mary wedged dirty fingers into a wide crack where the boards were joined, the only betrayal of her true emotions the quivering at the corners of her wide mouth.

Brianna hurled Creigh a murderous glare. "You conceited, pompous, ill-mannered *bastard!*" she snarled between gritted teeth. "That woman is risking her life for your worthless Sassenach hide."

Insolent silver eyes, glinting with barely leashed anger, raked Brianna. "As I remember, milady, you didn't find my *hide* quite so worthless that afternoon in the glen."

Hot shame washed over Brianna, then was quickly swirled away in waves of searing anger. But the diatribe she had been girding herself to flay Creigh with was stilled by the sound of wood scraping wood. Brianna looked down to see the square of planks come away from the rest of the flooring, revealing a dank, dark space beneath, a space that seemed scarce big enough to hold Mary MacGregor's son, let alone secrete away Creighton Wakefield's long form.

"Mary, he can't . . . we can't both fit in—" Brianna swallowed. But Creigh had already stalked to the opening in the floor, slamming his lean body into the nook with a force that raked the uneven edge of a plank across his injured thigh. Brianna heard him bite out something in French, and a tight smile tugged her lips.

But as she peered down to where Creigh lay curled against the rich blackness of the dirt that formed the nook's walls, the smile faded. An unwanted trickle of fear crept down her spine as she remembered the tales Shane had delighted in spinning by the fireside, when she was small, stories of witches, demons, spirits haunting the night. She had loved to listen to them, loved the prickling of hairs at the back of her neck, the shivery feeling she had gotten when she thought of the tales 'neath the safety of her coverlet. Only one story had terrified her . . . the story of the old woman the kelpies had buried alive.

Brianna swallowed, that childhood fear clogging her throat, but at that instant her eyes caught the glowering countenance of Creigh Wakefield.

"Well?" he barked, attempting to scrunch his tall frame tighter against the loamy walls. "Do you want me to send you a royal invitation?"

"Hasten, milady," Mary urged in a voice rife with apprehension. "Methinks I hear hoofbeats."

Quickly Brianna swung her legs into the space by Creigh's belly, and wedged herself down into the tiny area. He grunted in pain as her elbow dug into his ribs, and Brianna had a sudden urge to drive her other elbow backward as well.

"Blast it, lay on your side," he ordered, shoving her arm out of the way. She saw him clench his teeth as she squeezed in next to him, curving her body to fit tight against his. Her legs crooked about the hard length of his thighs, the muscles of his chest imprinting themselves against her back, while her thinly clad rump was cradled in the lee of his hips— lean, hard hips that left no doubt he was a man.

One arm looped around her waist because there was no

105

room to fit it anywhere else. She flinched as its warmth burned through the thin lawn veiling her skin, his touch infuriating, frightening, disturbingly intimate despite the fact that he was not holding her by choice.

She stiffened as Mary lowered the section of boards into place, the darkness and the dirt clinging to Brianna's skin making her feel as if she were in a tomb. She shuddered, grateful, in spite of herself, for the virile warmth of Creigh's body, the stirring of his breath at her temple. There was a soft, rasping sound as Mary dragged the pallet back into place, then the shush of bare feet upon wood overhead, the low murmurs of the MacGregors' voices.

Brianna held her breath, feeling, in the earthen hiding place, the rhythmic pounding of approaching horses. Creigh's arms tightened around her, and she thought she felt him press his lips in a grudging kiss behind her ear. "All will be well, Tigress," he whispered. "Cromwell told me a dozen times that he's leading God's army, and the Lord would never inflict your temper upon His own ranks."

Brianna jammed her elbow back into his ribs, delighting in his grunt of surprise. But as the seconds ticked by endlessly, she clung to the spark of anger his words struck, warding off the horrible sensation of helplessness, of not knowing what was happening above them.

A shout rang out in the cottage yard, and Brianna fought to quell the image of Mary MacGregor's world-weary eyes as the door's rusty hinges screeched. Bare feet thumped against the floor, as though both Mary and the boy were bolting out into the yard.

"Yer honors! Yer honors! Praise St. Andrew ye've come!" her cries seeped through the floorboards, distant yet still audible. "Ye be just in time t' catch a brace o' thievin' scum!"

Fear drove deep into Brianna, and she heard Creigh's breath hiss between his teeth. A gravelly voice barked something she couldn't hear, and panic jolted through her. Had Mary MacGregor felt her debt had been paid by suffering Creigh's scathing tongue? Or did the woman plan to assure her safety, and that of her son, by proving her loyalty to the conquering army beyond a doubt—through gifting them with the fugitives they sought?

Brianna battled to push up on the wood panel, gain them at least a fighting chance, but Creigh's arms tightened around her, his body shifting to trap her against the dirt wall.

"Aye, sir colonel," Brianna heard Mary shrill. " 'Twas them for certain. A man, tall, braw as Finn McCool, wi' eyes that looked like silver, an' a girl wi' naught on but 'er chemise—the shameless trollop!"

There was the rumble of another voice, and bile rose in Brianna's throat. Even though she couldn't decipher the man's words, his face pressed in at her from the blackness— the drooping eyelid, the pockmarked jowls, slack, drooling lips. Ogden. Aye, terror had a name.

"Eh, your worship?" Mary's voice came again. "Oh, sure, an' 'e was wounded, devil take 'is thievin' soul! Was bleedin' fit t' die, 'e was. Hope he does, curse him. Stole my horse. The only thing me James left us when the angels took him. Which way? The bloody cutpurse rode off to the north. I heard him sayin' to his strumpet he was headin' for that blackguard Ormonde."

Brianna tried to breathe—couldn't—through the lump of thankfulness in her throat. Her whole body trembled with relief, even the crumbly earth pressed to her brow feeling good against her skin as she heard Ogden's horsemen thunder away.

She felt the silky warmth of Creigh's lips part against her neck, and knew he was smiling. "We've bested the bastard again, Tigress!" he whispered exultantly, kissing her soundly on the ear.

"I—I thought . . ." Brianna began unsteadily.

"I know." Creigh's fingertips smoothed over the inside of her wrist. "I was beginning to think we'd but trussed ourselves up for them myself." Despite the darkness, she could feel his rueful grin. "Truth, and I'd not have blamed poor Mistress MacGregor if she'd sent Ogden in here with chains, the way I behaved. Something about you makes me act like a beast, Brianna Devlin."

His voice dropped, sensual, husky, as she felt him nudge the curls at her nape aside with his nose, his lips drifting over the delicate hidden flesh in the softest of kisses. "Something," he murmured. Brianna closed her eyes,

107

drowning in the feel of his mouth upon her. "Mayhap, milady Tigress, 'tis that whenever I'm near you, you scratch or bite—"

Brianna jumped, banging her head on the floorboards as sharp teeth suddenly caught at her earlobe. But the light, cutting pressure of his teeth, the brush of his hot, wet tongue whirled dizzying sensations up from the pit of her stomach. Sensations that terrified her, hypnotized her. She arched her head back against Creigh's hard chest, a tiny moan breaching her lips.

He buried his answering groan in the soft lee of her shoulder, and Brianna could feel his sex stirring where it was cradled against her buttocks.

She stiffened, steeling herself for revulsion to eclipse her wonder at feeling his hardness against her. But before it could happen, she heard the rasp of the pallet being dragged across the floor above, heard Creigh breathe a curse.

"Yer lordship? Lady?" Mary's voice drifted through the door. "The soldiers be gone. I set Jemmie t' keep watch lest they come back."

The floor planks gave a grinding noise as she ripped up the panel, and Brianna blinked her eyes against the cottage light that suddenly seemed blinding. She pried her knees from where they had dug into the wall, then struggled to pull herself upright, and drag herself from the tiny space. But either being jammed into such cramped quarters, or the soul-stealing force of Creighton Wakefield's kisses, had robbed her muscles of their usual coordination. A hundred needles seemed to drive into her stiff limbs as Mary grasped her elbow, helping her out of the earthen pit.

Brianna stumbled, bumping against Mary's bony hip. "Milady," the woman asked worriedly, "be ye hale?" Brianna nodded, catching Creigh's grimace from the corner of her eye.

"Some of us are more 'hale' than others." She heard him grumble as he unfolded his long frame and stepped up to the floor above. She saw him surreptitiously adjust something in the region of his breeches, his lips twisting in a wry smile.

"And ye, yer lordship, yer wound . . . it be—"

"I vow, I forgot 'twas even there. Did I not, Tigress?" The devilish glint in his eyes danced to Brianna's face.

Her cheeks flamed. "I—he—uh, we . . ." Her gaze flashed to his mouth, expecting it to be twisted into an expression of smug satisfaction, but the beautifully wrought curve of his lips was shaded with a lambent desire that set her pulsebeat to tripping. She felt Mary watching her, waiting, and rushed on. "We—he was fine. Mistress MacGregor—Mary—we can't thank you enough for giving us shelter."

"Thank me? Bah!" Mary scoffed. "'Tis I should be blessin' ye and yer man. I'll do it every day o' me life." The woman turned to Creigh, and Brianna was surprised to see Mary's eyes fill with tears. "Aye, m'lord," she whispered. "Every day o' me life."

Brianna stared, confused, intrigued as Mary sank to her knees before him, lowering her brow to his dusty boottops. Creigh fumbled with the buckle of his baldrick, his gaze fastened on the floor, the cracked walls, anywhere but Mary MacGregor's face. "Please, goodwife, don't . . . don't do that." He almost seemed to squirm as he grasped the woman's wrist, drawing her up. "'Twas naught . . ."

"Naught?! Ye but saved my Jemmie's life! The lad came runnin' back here that night, full o' the tale o' yer courage. An' even though ye be a thievin' Englishman—beggin' yer lordship's pardon—I prayed that when the killin' was done in Drogheda-town, that ye, at least, would live."

"You saved the child's life?" Brianna asked, turning to Creigh. "But how? When?"

"Christ's blood! 'Twas but a small misunderstanding! Any man would have interfered."

"Nay, m'lord," Mary contradicted. "Few men the like o' yerself would bother to trifle with a peasant lad's woes." She turned to Brianna, unabashed tears trickling down the wrinkles toil and worry had carved in her cheeks. "They was goin' t' cut off me Jemmie's hand, thinkin' he was a-stealin'. Had his wrist t' the choppin' block, Jemmie says, an' sword drawn. But he—" she nodded toward a patently uncomfortable Creigh. Her voice quavered. "Yer man stopped 'em, thank God. *Thank God,*" Mary echoed in a whisper, her eyes clenching shut. "Jemmie be all I have left, now that me James is gone. If I'd lost me son, too . . ."

Sobs shook Mary's bowed shoulders. Brianna wrapped her arms around the other woman and raised her eyes to

Creigh's. As she drowned in belligerent, flashing silver, a strange feeling of joy, pride swelled within her, rippling through every nerve in her body, tangling there, in silk threads of confusion, and some other, terrifying emotion she dared not name.

"You saved the boy's life," she said quietly.

"'Od's wounds, they were going to cut off his hand!" Creigh bellowed, yanking open the lace about his throat. "What would you have had me do?" He glared at Brianna. *"Quit* gaping at me! And wipe that—that *damned* smile off your face!"

He stalked across the room to a tiny window and jerked the shutter open.

Unable to resist repaying him for the innumerable times he had made *her* squirm, Brianna smiled sweetly. "'Tis just that I never pictured the high and mighty Lord Creighton Wakefield as the patron saint of urchins." She stifled a giggle as his brows crashed together in a thunderous scowl.

"Well, you needs must restrain yourself and cannonize me later," he snapped, planting his fists on his hips. "The minute Ogden realizes we've outwitted him again, he'll be racing toward the coast, with whatever men Cromwell will spare him. And unless you relish the thought of an early death, milady, the two of us had best be halfway to Carikbrah by then."

The amusement that had bubbled in Brianna's breast vanished, her arm falling, numbly, from about Mary's shoulders. "You think they'll pursue us all the way to the sea?"

"Ogden would dive through the devil's own gates to gain what he wanted. And now, for some God-only-knows reason the bastard wants me. You heard him. Saw him. He'll not rest until he has my head upon a pike." Brianna felt a chill of foreboding whisper icy fingers down her spine, hideous, haunting images taunting her through a Druid's haze, taunting her as they had within the walls of Drogheda. She clenched her fists, willing the visions away, not wanting to see. But the mists would not be banished. Nor the fear. She started, suddenly aware that the room had fallen deathly quiet, even Mary's choked sobs stilled. Both the woman and Creigh were watching her. The sparkings of temper that had glinted in Creigh's silvery eyes gave way to exasperation.

"Come now, Tigress, I know you've been aching to sever various parts of my person ever since we met, but it becomes you not to stand there with that bloodthirsty glaze to your eyes."

"Don't!" Brianna burst out, her own throat tight. "Don't say—" She couldn't finish, hurt, dread roiling inside her. She wanted to fling herself into the warmth of his arms. Aye, and wanted to hate him, hate him so that the vision's whisperings wouldn't tear at her very soul.

"Bree?" Her name fell from his lips, questioning, confused as he crooked one bronzed finger under her chin, tipping her face up to meet his gaze. He peered into her eyes endless seconds, and 'twas as if he could taste her fear. "Don't concern yourself, Tigress," he said. "All will be well. At least," his mouth twisted in a self-deprecating grimace "once I gain control of my damnable temper." He brushed his thumb across Brianna's lower lip, and she clenched her teeth against the exquisite agony of Creigh's fingers on flesh soiled by Ogden's pawing hands, slavering mouth.

"There's little enough to fear from Ogden and his curs," Creigh said. "And with Mistress MacGregor's aid we'll be well away before they suspect we've eluded them." Bree pulled away from the warm roughness of Creigh's hand, suddenly furious that he dared stand there, the sunlight streaming in the window gilding the cleanly hewn planes of his face, the sensual wonder of a mouth carved to pleasure. He had no right to be so perfect, so near, taunting her with the promise of his lips and hands, when if he knew . . .

She turned toward him deliberately, hurting, wanting to hurt him back. "Tell me, *your lordship*," she bit out, "could you find no better sports in England than terrorizing your kerns?"

"Terrorizing?"

"Aye. It seems to me you've had much practice at it, the way you were able to make both Mary and I half expect your Sassenach brethren to be racing down upon the cottage."

"Milady, your lordship, nay!" Mary's worried voice was drowned out by Creigh's expletive.

He took a step toward Brianna, but she leveled him a

111

freezing glare. "Mayhap I should call young Jemmie in," she goaded. "'Twould be past amusing to see a child thus fear."

"Child? Fear?" Creigh growled. "Damn it, Bree—" He stopped, anger sparking like flint in his silvery eyes, but beneath their fire lay a hurt that pierced her, bone deep.

Brianna turned away from him, striding to the window.

"Yer lordship?"

She heard Mary MacGregor's quavery voice, and glanced out of the corner of her eye to see the woman lay her work-ravaged hand upon Creigh's sleeve and lift her earnest face up to his. "Ye can depend on us, Jemmie an' me, t' aid ye in whatever ye need."

Brianna felt Creigh regard her long moments from beneath hooded lids, then turn to the other woman. "God knows you've risked enough for us already, Mary," he said with a warm respect that tightened the knot of despair in Brianna's throat. "But if you would be willing to secure some supplies for our journey, horses, eatables, and the like, we could be on our way before we put you or your son in any more danger."

Brianna stared at Creigh's broad back, turned pointedly upon her, as he listed for Mary what they would need for their journey, but even the anger she had nurtured, clung to, could not ward off the panic that rose in her chest. For other voices were clamoring in her head, mocking voices, cruel voices, voices full of hopelessness, desolation.

She wanted Creighton Wakefield, savagely, desperately, wanted his lips crushing hers, the sweet, heavy weight of his body bearing her down.

There had been in his touch a hunger, the promise of a passion so fierce, she had wanted to hurl herself against its raging tides, let it take her. But even as Creigh's lips moved upon her flesh, Ogden's ghost had lain between them.

Brianna bit her lip, staring blindly out the tiny window. *Do you think Lord Creighton Wakefield would have you?* she berated herself. *If he knew what had bedded you first?*

Nay, not bedded, her mind screamed. *Raped. Ogden raped me. 'Twas his crime, not my own.*

But, as she let her eyes trail to where Creigh stood, his magnificent hair capturing all the light in the room, the bronzed perfection of his aristocratic features so carefully secreting away the gentleness, compassion that lurked within him, she knew that no man—aye, and especially no man as fiercely proud as Creighton Wakefield—would be able to forget the fact that Ogden had soiled her.

She wrapped her arms about her ribs, as if to shield herself from a blow, the clinking of coins being exchanged, the click of the latch as Mary MacGregor opened the oaken door filling Brianna with dread at being caged alone in this tiny room with a man she wanted with desperate fury.

"Milady?"

She turned at the sound of Mary's voice and found the woman's worried eyes upon her.

"There be berries in the crock over there, an' new cream risin' in the pans, if ye be hungry."

Bree nodded.

"An' if ye want to—to cover yerself, ye're welcome to don my mass dress on the peg, yon. Yer man, he bade me get you a new gown at market, but 'til I do . . ."

"He's not my man!" Brianna snapped, hating the bite to her voice.

"I—your pardon, milady, m'lord, tis just that I . . . you both seemed so . . ." the woman raised her hands palms up, her gaze shifting uncomfortably between Creigh and Brianna. Hot humiliation stung Brianna's cheeks.

"'Twas an honest mistake, goodwife," Creigh said smoothly. "After all, 'tis not every day you see a cavalier roving the countryside with a *lady* thus garbed."

Brianna's fingers clenched in the folds of her chemise. She glared at him, but he only gave her a slow, infuriating smile. "I, however, prefer my *affaires d'amour* with tongues less sharp," he offered. "And bodies a deal less . . . encumbered with dirt." She could feel Creigh's expectant gaze upon her, sense the roguish smile that had curved his lips fade as no cutting repartee followed. But the scathing reply that had been on Brianna's tongue seemed to burn her, her heart twisting at the meaning only she could glean from his words. She wheeled back to the window, clutching her arms in front of her breasts, feeling the scar carved there as if 'twere being branded into her skin.

Silence blanketed the room, endless, excruciating seconds. The weight of Creigh's gaze bored into her back. She heard the oaken door rasp upon its hinges, the aged floor-boards creak as Mary stepped out into the cottage yard and closed the portal behind her.

Boot heels thunked toward Brianna. Stopped an arm's length away. The presence of Creigh's broad shoulders seemed to smother her.

"Tigress," he began wearily, "whatever I said to offend you—"

She turned on him like a raging fury. "Offend me?" she hissed through gritted teeth. "You've done naught else since the moment we met! You've belittled me, tormented me, used me as the butt of your jests."

"Damn it, Bree—"

"But then a filthy Irish barbarian the likes of me is scarce worthy to kiss the seat of your breeches, is she, your worship? I but serve to empty your chamber pot, or to be pawed like a cursed whore!" Despair swelled in her chest, and she despised herself for the raw pain in her voice. "Mayhap I am a whore, because I wanted—"

"Sweet Jesu! I'd scarce label what we did mortal sin!" Creigh raked an impatient hand through his hair, his eyes rife with exasperation. "I kissed you once when I was senseless with fever and once in that blasted hole in the floor! I couldn't even reach your lips, for God's sake."

"Nay, but you could well 'reach' me with something else, could you not?" she flung back, her gaze flashing to the corded silk of his breech flap as though it bore the coils of a snake. Her eyes leapt back to his face.

Beneath his heavy-slashed brows, his hooded eyes glittered like sun striking ice. "Somehow, milady, I fail to recall you voicing any such *maidenly objections* at the time."

Brianna recoiled from the disdain in his voice, his words cutting deep. "Nay, your lordship," she raised her chin agonized inches, squeezing the words through a throat choked with misery. "I can assure you, I am far beyond *maidenly* anything." She wheeled away from him, aching for one sob to cleanse away her grief, sorrow. But the chains crushing her chest would allow her no such ease.

Two strong hands dug deep into her shoulders, her teeth jarring together as Creigh spun her around. "Brianna, what the hell—" She had but a heartbeat to register the fury in his eyes, the questing, and to see her own tormented face reflected in their silvery depths.

'Twas as if he battled himself. Surrendered. His mouth captured hers, and she fought it, raking at his jaw with her nails, twisting like a wild thing, wounded. But even so, he held her.

A tiny, hopeless sound snagged in Brianna's throat, and he took it into himself, crushing agony into sweetness. Before he had kissed her to infuriate, kissed her to tease, and kissed her in a hazy world where fever colored what was real. But there was no goading, no rakehell finesse in his mouth now as he took her lips with his. 'Twas as if he offered her something, some part of himself kept hidden beneath the cavalier facade, a part that needed desperately to give her comfort, and needed to take, take of something precious within her that she could not name.

His hands knotted deep in the thickness of her hair, his chest bearing her back, until her spine was pressed against the cottage wall, every sinew in Creigh's body molded into the curves of her own.

Hot, hard, his tongue probed the crease between her lips, and she opened to him, reveling in the wet, rough strokes, the feel of his hands moving upon her, so hungry, it seemed that this time 'twas she must be snared in fever's web.

Her nails dug deep into the steely muscles of his shoulders, slid down to tear at the stiff velvet of his doublet, her palms aching to caress the bronzed skin beneath. But the garment would not give way. Brianna gave a half-savage snarl, her fingers curling into the lace at the base of his throat. Her knuckles drove into the heat of his skin, the hot pulsing of his veins throbbing against her fingers.

"Creigh . . ." she pleaded. "Need to—to touch . . ." She felt the jolt of pleasure that shot through him, heard his ravenous growl. Then his fingers were between them, tearing her clenched fist from his doublet. There was the sound of fabric rending, the crush of his hand clutching hers. But in the seconds it took for Creigh to open his skin to her hand, Bree felt it—web-fine threads of doubt, fear, spinning out to ensnare her.

She gave a tiny, despairing cry of denial, her fingers cutting deep into the rippling muscles of Creigh's chest as he flattened her palm against his naked flesh. She felt him stiffen, his head arching back.

"*God!*" The word hissed between Creigh's clenched teeth as he dragged his mouth from hers. "Tigress, I—" She tore at him in a frenzy of need, fear, feeling even as she battled to clutch him closer, that the wonder that had sheltered her from shadings of horror was melting away, mocking her.

"Nay!" The word ripped from her throat, agonized, her hands balling into fists as icy dread engulfed her. She tried to tear away from Creigh, despising herself for the cowardice that drove her to flee his touch, but the hands, mouth that had been whirling her into magic clenched, iron-hard upon her fear-chilled skin, leaving naught but the harsh sound of Creigh's breath rasping in his chest, and the soul-deep terror that left her barren.

He stared down at her, eyes as fathomless as a winter sea.

"I'll kill him."

Cold as the clash of blade against blade, the words pierced Brianna.

"Kill . . . ?"

"The bastard who did this to you."

"What?" She tried to force confusion onto her face, to hide truth, but his silvery gaze seemed to delve to the core of her soul.

"*This,* Tigress," he said. One thumb skimmed over her mouth and she felt it trembling. "A moment ago when I held you, you were fire in my arms, fury. Wild as a wood-witch, and sweeter, sweeter than any woman I've yet tasted. But now . . ." His thumb traced her full lower lip. "Damn it, I want you to be shaking with need for me . . . want my hands, mouth . . . to drive you—" Thick lashes swept low over his eyes, his lips twisting in a grimace of both pain and pleasure. He sucked in a shuddering breath, opening his eyes, lowering them to her face.

"You're not hungry for me now, Bree. Not now. You're terrified."

Brianna tossed her head, struggling to effect a bravado she did not feel. "I've yet to cower from anything, least of all the touch of a man."

"A *man,*" Creigh snarled. "Naught but a monster could have brought you to this. Raped you." Creigh's hand flexed, and she could sense he was aching for the hilt of his sword.

"Tell me who this bastard is, and I swear I'll drive my dagger through his heart."

Brianna stared up at the perfect, aquiline features, the arrogant brow, the eyes, blazing with rage. There was no revulsion in the gaze fastened upon her, no disgust in the fingers still warm upon her arm, only hatred, black, deadly, for the one who had harmed her.

"I battle my own demons," she said quietly. "And when steel pierces his heart, 'twill be my hand that drives it." But even as she said the words, she felt a blade drive to the center of her own soul, lodge there. She gazed up into Creigh's face, in its magnificence, fury, and knew then that she loved him.

Chapter Nine

Creigh shoved at the wadded up doublet that served as his pillow, cursing groggily as he struggled to shift his clammy blankets into a position that would spare him the sensation of being crammed into an *Iron Maiden*. But despite the thick carpet of moss that Brianna—asleep in her blankets an arm's length away—obviously found soft as swansdown, he could gain no ease.

For five days now, it had seemed that some unseen torture master had been plying his trade upon Creigh's body, and worse, within his mind. Whether riding the endless miles across the Irish hills, attempting to sleep along the high-roads, or staring into the golden eyes of Brianna Devlin, he had felt the searing of something white-hot in his belly, the raging of a fury such as he had never known.

Someone had raped her.

Creigh flung one arm over eyes gritty from lack of sleep and fought the urge to drive his fist into the ground. He was no stranger to the brutality of men. From the time he had toddled about in the wake of his father, he had witnessed the treacheries of the court, the cruelties to Lindley, the careless injuries dealt to the peasantry by the cavaliers—aye, and had seen the peasantry strike back at those innocent of doing them harm.

Why, then, did the hauntings of this child-woman claw at the very heart of him? Make his whole body seethe with the need to bury his sword hilt-deep in the belly of the bastard who had savaged her?

Creigh's hands balled into fists, crushing the musty wool

folds of blanket beneath his fingers as the image of Brianna's face rose in his mind. Fiery as a captive goddess, she had faced him in the MacGregors' humble cottage, flinging his suspicion that she had been raped into his face like a warrior's gauntlet, expecting him, nay, daring him to turn from her in disgust. But when she had detected no censure in his eyes, the defiant lines of her face melted into a subtle beauty that robbed him of breath. Her voice rife with quiet strength as she whispered: *I battle my own demons.*

She had asked naught of him, only squared her slender shoulders to face the world alone. And with that one simple gesture Creigh had felt the shell of cynicism he had drawn about himself shatter.

He dragged his bleary gaze to where she now lay, burrowed 'neath her coverlet's concealing folds. Nay, even though she had refused his offer of aid, there had been in her eyes a pleading more real to him than the whinings of marchionesses and fine ladies, a cry to be freed that clutched his very soul. And he had wanted to wrench back the bands of fear that held her, wanted to show her the beauty that could be found in the act of love that, for her, had been corrupted into horror.

Yet not once in the days since they had ridden forth from the cottage yard had she allowed him to touch her, heart or mind. She had but watched him with eyes vulnerable as a doe poised to flee, keeping herself secreted away from him until he felt as if 'twas he who groped in the dark, clutching at something elusive as the dawn.

Something he desperately needed to catch . . . hold . . .

Creigh kicked savagely at the blankets tangled about his legs, cursing the ache that knotted his loins. 'Twas madness to need anyone in this world gone awry. Madness to think to hold even a woman's heart while England lay in Parliament's fist. And for a man bound on a quest to free not only a crown, but father and brother as well, it could well prove fatal to have his mind clouded with the silken webs of a woman.

Webs . . . Creigh swore, his eyes fastening on the blankets that hid every golden curl from view. Nay, Brianna Devlin would weave no spells to snare a man, she would but look up at him, with those melting gold eyes full of innocence, and . . .

"Damme!" Jamming one heel into the soft moss Creigh shoved himself upright, another oath tearing from his lips as his head cracked into the low-hanging bough of a strawberry tree.

He hurled his blankets away from him, and with them the last reinings of his temper. "Damme, Tigress, do you think to sleep your life away?" He dealt the mound of blankets a none-too-gentle buffet with his foot. "I'll never get off this godforsaken island if—"

The fury that had seemed his only shield froze in his chest, then vanished, dread stealing over him as he stared at the unmoving folds of wool, folds that had been too soft to hold Brianna's well-toned form.

"Tigress?" he snapped. A sudden, hated shaft of panic drove deep into Creigh's belly. "Tigress, damn you—" He reached down, snatching the slate-colored coverlet aside, but beneath it lay only a hollow in the sweet heather, the crushed blossoms still clinging to the warmth from her body. Creigh spun around, his eyes raking clumps of hawthorn, clusters of late summer blooms as he willed her to be somewhere in the tiny valley.

But nowhere was there so much as a glimpse of spun-gold curls, or forest-hued gown. There was only the wind ruffling the hillside's lacing of flowers, the burbling of the stream that lay just beyond the valley's crest, and the sound of . . . what was it? Sobbing?

"Brianna!" he bellowed the name, dashing to the top of the rise that sheltered the valley. "Bri—"

His muscles locked midstride, his cry dying on his lips. Relief and fury blazed within him, as he peered at the scene spilling out below. His fury melted into a shimmering wonder.

Bright ribbons of dawn rippled down the emerald hill to a glen splashed with such dazzling colors as never bedecked an artist's palette. Greens, mauves, blues from the shade of smoke upon the wind to the richest sapphire blended in a perfection that should well have awed him, but left him scarce touched as he stared at the vision that must surely be an Artemis lost upon her hunt. Yet the hand that this Artemis stretched out toward an ivory-colored roe offered no piercing arrow, but rather a sprig of tender grass. And even the deer seemed enchanted, for it reached out its velvety muzzle, cropping off a few of the green leaves before returning to its meadow.

Creigh's mouth fell open in astonishment, his loins tightening painfully as Brianna spun around, laughing in delight. Slender, lithe as a new-sprung willow, she danced in the stream's laughing waters, her tawny hair clinging in damp waves about her gold-brushed skin. Sparkling droplets of water bedewed the perfect curve of buttock, breast, the dusky-rose tips of her nipples that peeked through the shining curtain of her hair, tempting beyond all reason.

Creigh tried to tear himself away, feeling as if he were somehow breaching the tenuous thread of trust she had offered him—knowing she thought herself alone. But just as he started to turn she hesitated in her play. She paused but an instant, her face angling almost imperceptively toward the rise where he stood, then turned her rose-blushed cheeks away so quickly that he was certain he'd imagined it. Yet in that instant something indefinable held him there, as though a silken thread had spun out from her fingertips, binding him to the hillside.

Breath rasping in his throat, he watched as she splashed up graceful arches of water, darting beneath the silvery rainbows, her head thrown back, her tumbled hair baring breasts so ripe his palms burned to feel their soft, firm weight. His jaw clamped shut, his teeth clenching against the raging desire that tore at his vitals.

But the nymph in the waters had not done with her torment. She flung back the last tangled curls of her hair, her whole body gloriously revealed as she spun about in the wavelets.

Creigh's fists knotted at his sides, every muscle, sinew in his lean body straining toward her—wanting . . . needing to taste of the sweet sun-gold of her skin.

Then she turned, slowly, so slowly toward his place upon the hill, her innocent face with its courage, fire, turned up to the newborn sun as though she were some winsome wood-witch offering herself to the skies.

Creigh felt something deep in his chest rage, pound, burst. "Tigress." He said the name aloud, the sound of it, ragged even to his own ears. And the fragile trust, shy eagerness in her eyes as she lowered them to his robbed him of his soul.

As though drawn by a sorceress's charm, Creigh strode

121

down the hillside and into the stream. Chill, sweet the water rippled about his ankles, knees, the waves soaking the thighs of his breeches, but he cared not, felt nothing except the pull of Brianna Devlin's magic—the magic of her honesty, inner strength. But an arm's length away from her he stopped, needing to be certain that she knew what she was wooing with her eyes, her body, sensing the dread that lurked within her, shades of past horrors she was fighting to master. He said not a word, just drowned in her eyes endless seconds that stretched into eternity.

Then he felt it, the brush of her fingers, warm, supple against the plane of his chest. "Creigh . . ." the tiniest tremor stole into her voice, her eyes vulnerable, yet so achingly brave they tore at his heart. "I want you to love me."

A groan ripped from deep inside his chest, and Brianna felt it beneath her palm. Every muscle in his body drew whipcord taut.

"Tigress . . ." he grated. "You're certain?"

"I don't want to be afraid anymore, Creigh. Make me not afraid."

Brianna trembled, watching in wonder as his face tightened into an expression akin to pain, the arrogant curve of his lips lowering to hers with a tenderness that made her want to cry.

"I won't hurt you, Tigress," he murmured, tracing the curve of her cheek with his fingertips. "I swear to God I won't."

He drew her into his arms, gently, so gently the lean plane of his body scarce brushed the wet nakedness of hers. And then he was hurting her, healing her, molding his mouth to hers with such a loving persuasion that she felt as though he were cradling her in clouds of silk as silver as his eyes.

Her heart thundered, leapt in her breast, the slightest edgings of fear pressing there, like a still-sheathed dagger. But Creigh held it at bay, his fingers weaving magic into the satin fall of her hair.

She lifted trembling hands, running her fingertips across his lean cheeks, dark brows, delving back into the rosewood waves that tumbled in disarray about his forehead.

"You—you're so beautiful . . ." she murmured. "So . . ."

"Nay, Tigress," he whispered. "This is beautiful." Slowly,

122

he dipped up a handful of the sparkling stream, drizzling it in a glistening, mesmerizing waterfall over her breasts. She felt his eyes like the lick of a flame as their silvery light followed the wetness running down that lush curve, past the gentle rise of her stomach to where the droplets vanished in the dark-gold down at the apex of her thighs.

That place which had been torn, brutalized by another man a lifetime ago. Brianna shivered, hating the icy wisp of remembrance, fighting against it. She felt herself stiffening, felt Creigh's hands tighten on her shoulders.

"Bree, don't—don't let him hold you captive even now," Creigh's voice penetrated the shadows of pain. "Just let me—let me touch you."

Touch . . . Brianna had never known the feel of another human being could be so wondrous, so right as Creigh's hands eased down the curve of her shoulders, his thumbs brushing, just brushing the rounded sides of her breasts. He kissed her, his tongue, hot, wet, skimming the crease of her lips, probing, entering. And it seemed, as that warm roughness swept deep within her mouth, that he was plumbing the depths of her soul.

She wanted him to, this magnificent man with his aristocratic pride, had wanted to spark this shattering of self-control from the moment he had landed her on her rump in the midst of Drogheda's streets and dismissed her. Had wanted to feel his mouth hot, questing upon hers since he kissed her in the heat of fever. But the fever that Creigh loosed inside Brianna now was fiercer, by far than that which had torn at his body, for mingled within her were the white-hot searings of passion and the jagged blade of fear.

She kissed him back, wantonly, almost desperately, molding herself against him as if the very force of her love for this man could banish the ghosts that yet haunted her. And 'twas as if he took her pain into himself, to hold.

His hands moved over her body with a skill that left her gasping, his strong fingers cupping the slender curves of her naked hips, easing upward to nigh span her waist. Then the warm, calloused tips paused, lingering in the delicate cay beneath her breasts.

Brianna stilled, the thin lines of scarring a breath above his hands seeming to eat, acidlike at the glorious sensations that had been racing through her veins. "Nay!" she cried the word against his lips, her tongue daring, fierce as it learned the taste, textures that lie within his mouth. He kissed her, stroked her, held her, letting her tongue, hands move at will over his face, mouth, slide beneath the damp lawn of his shirt.

Suddenly he tore his mouth from hers, and she raised leaden lashes to see his eyes burning into the dainty circles of her nipples, the silvery light of his gaze dark, sweet, heavy upon her skin. He curled his fingers, brushing the dusky-rose crests with the backs of his knuckles in a caress as soft as butterflies' wings.

"I'm going to take you to the stream bank now, Tigress," he said thickly. "Love you."

She hesitated an instant, suddenly shy, and she was stunned that even a shadow of the untouched girl she had been yet remained. But as Creighton Wakefield swept her up in arms tensile, sinewy, 'twas as if the Celtic warrior of her childhood dreams had sprung from the dawn, spiriting her off to some secret, Druid glen. She closed her eyes, reveling in the hard muscles crushed hot against her stream-chilled skin, reveling in the reality of this man who far surpassed the weavings of her fantasies.

Wavelets splashed at her feet, the water clinging to them as Creigh carried her up, out of the sparkling wetness. And she felt clean, purged, as though his hands and the ice blue stream had washed away all horror.

She let it fall away, let herself fall free, with naught but Creigh's strong arms to guide her as he lay her back into a myriad of wildflowers.

Then his hands were upon her, charting every curve, hollow of her body, his lips, tongue taunting the delicate flesh of her throat. And she wanted him naked, wanted to feel every sinew of the body she had watched with such longing in the endless, aching eternity since they had ridden out of Mary MacGregor's dooryard.

"Creigh," she breathed. "I want—want to . . ."

"Anything, Tigress," he vowed against her skin. "Anything you want . . . only what you want."

His words were lost in a groan as Brianna's hands swept beneath the collar of his shirt, her fingers yanking at the last of the lacings that kept his bare flesh from her hands. He pulled away from her but long enough to tear the garment from his broad shoulders, cast it in a heap beside her own abandoned gown. Then he was beside her again, touching her, kissing her, the hair-roughened plane of his chest abrading her own soft skin.

"Tell me, love," he whispered harshly, "tell me what you dream of. Of me holding you? Kissing you? Do you burn for this?"

Brianna's breath caught in her throat as he dipped his head down, his parted lips skimming the taut peak of her nipple. A strangled cry breached her lips as his mouth opened over the hardened bud, his hot, rough tongue sweeping the point.

"Aye. There . . . oh, God, Creigh . . ." She drove her fingers back into the waves of his hair, knotting her hands in the silky thick mass as she clutched his mouth to her flesh. He drew her nipple deep, deep into the hot, wet haven of his mouth, spinning a hundred thousand sparks of agonizing pleasure spiraling into the pit of her stomach.

She arched her head back, driving it into the soft earth, her nails digging into the rock-hard muscles of his shoulders as his mouth trailed moist kisses across the valley between her breasts, then lower. The light stubbling of his jaw rasped against the soft swell of her stomach, his fingers painfully gentle as they drifted over the soft tuft of dark-gold curls at the joining of her thighs.

Brianna felt a wire-thin piercing of fear jab at her, but she clenched her teeth, forcing away the hideous memory of cruel, groping paws, filling herself, instead, with the feel of Creigh's fingers parting her, stroking her, loving her.

"Creigh," she cried out, writhing against the magic of his hands, wanting him, needing. But his hand kept up its ceaseless magic, his mouth upon her breasts, thighs, driving her past bearing. "Creigh, please—"

With a savage oath, he tore himself away, his eyes piercing hers like twin rapier points, his lips drawn in a grimace of near pain. "Bree—don't ask me to stop . . . Don't—"

But the cry that rose in her throat could scarce be mistaken for ought but a woman far gone in passion. A woman nigh desperate to join with a man. She clutched at his shoulders, taking half-savage bites at his collarbone, tasting the sweetness of the stream, the salt of his skin, the heat of his desire.

Creigh shot to his feet, his fingers tearing heedlessly at the fastenings of his breeches, ripping them from his lean hips, long, muscled thighs, kicking them free. The image of his perfectly honed body seared into Brianna's brain, the daunting breadth of shoulders, the mat of hair that spanned his chest, then arrowed in a narrow ribbon of dark brown silk across his flat stomach. Her eyes lowered to that part of him that sprang from the thick nest of dark curls 'twixt his thighs, but instead of the terror she had dreaded, she felt only a singing anticipation, and wonder.

He was the horned god of Druid days, fierce, proud, beautiful. And he wanted her.

She stretched up her arms to him, and he came to her, the loving of his hands spawning in her a need that drove her past the bounds of the valley in which she lay, past the chains of grief, memories.

Her name was like a litany on his lips, touching her everywhere, cocooning her in enchantment. And when he kissed her, there, upon that part of her still throbbing from his expert fingers, Brianna screamed, cried, clawed at his shoulders.

"Tigress," he rasped, tearing himself away, looming over her. "Tell me—tell me you're ready . . ."

Something akin to a sob ripped from her throat, her fingers clenching in the hard muscles of his arms. Creigh groaned, his mouth capturing hers, savage, sweet. His tongue plunged deep, withdrew, plunged deep again, mating wildly with hers. She felt the evidence of his desire hard against her thigh, felt him part her legs. Despite the beauty of the sensations he had wrought upon her, Brianna steeled her body for the tearing that would surely come now, the agony that had pierced her that other, horrible time. But oddly she craved it, craved the hard heat of him within her in spite of the roiling dread, the certainty of pain.

Her hips writhed against his, seeking, and she felt the shudder of response in Creigh's lean form. His fingers delved deep in the curls at her temples, his strong palms cupping her face.

"Tigress," he grated, his eyes capturing hers. "So beautiful, sweet. Let me gift you with wonder . . ."

A low cry ripped from Brianna's throat, her fingers digging into the hard-muscled curve of Creigh's buttocks.

She could feel his whole body shaking against hers, feel the rigid control he was attempting to hold over his own driving need. He probed the entrance to her womanhood, parting the petals as tenderly as if she were the most delicate satin rose.

Her senses whirled in a maelstrom of light, scent, jewel-toned colors as he arched his hips forward, coming into her by proud, precious inches. And there was no pain, no fear, only a haven of enchantment such as she'd never known.

"Tigress, did I—hurt . . ." The concern in his labored voice struck to the heart of her.

"Nay." She closed her eyes, marveling at the tears that stung beneath her lids. "Creigh . . . Creigh, please—"

His mouth slanted over hers in a hungry kiss, a groan tearing from low in his chest. Then his muscles bunched, and he moved within her, that part of him embedded deep seeming to reach for her very soul.

Something wild, primitive loosed inside Brianna, and she cried out in agonized pleasure, arching her hips to meet his smooth thrusts. Her tongue swept deep into Creigh's mouth, her nails raking the satiny nakedness of his back, shoulders, the driving, mind-shattering muscles of his buttocks. 'Twas wildfire, seastorm, and Brianna was his captive, but she sensed that beneath the straining muscles of Creigh's face, beneath the wire-taut sinews of his body, Creigh was captive too.

His gray eyes were alive with flame, his mouth contorted in a grimace of iron-willed control and exquisite pleasure. He drove himself deeper, harder, the rasp of his harsh breath against the delicate flesh of her throat fanning the desire that licked white hot through her veins.

She whimpered as Creigh's mouth left the cay of her shoulder, and she strained toward him, struggling to recapture his hot sweetness with her lips, but the rough, wet tip of his tongue trailed down her breast in a blazing path, hungry as it circled the delicate peach crest of her nipple, taunting, tormenting until she could bear it no longer.

She cupped the ripe mound in her hand, her other fingers knotting in the mass of waves at his nape, tugging his head down. His mouth opened over her nipple, drawing it deep, suckling it with a raging need that stole her breath. She clutched at him, clawed at him, a sob tearing from her throat. But even through the ecstasy that whirled her in its vortex, the tiniest stirrings of remembered fear, helplessness slashed at her joy.

"Tigress," Creigh rasped savagely against her flesh. "Tigress, don't!"

And then 'twas as if the world spun off its axis. Creigh's strong arms banded about her, the glorious, magical valley whirling in a montage of incredible color and scent as he rolled both himself and Brianna over upon the wildflowers. And 'twas his tousled, rosewood hair that lay pillowed in the heather, his broad shoulders crushing the sweet grasses while Brianna arched against him, the sun's warm caress upon her back.

His hard palms closed on the ridges of her hipbones, his eyes compelling, strong, fired with passion as they blazed into hers. "Take it, Tigress," he said fiercely. "All of it. Pleasure. Pain. 'Tis your right."

He moved not, his face taut with waiting, his hardness yet buried within her. Somewhere, midst what tiny fragments of sanity were left to her, Brianna marveled that this man had sensed her fears, that even now he was battling those demons as surely as she was. Despite the blaze of passion that shone upon his features, she knew that if she rolled away from him now, still prisoner of her fears, Creigh would but let her go.

Love swelled unbearably within her, a heady sense of freedom breaking over her fear, as she lost herself in the molten silver of his eyes. She arched her back and molded her soft curves against the lean, hard plane of his body, her hip-length curls slipping from her shoulders, to pool in a cascade of gold upon his chest. And then she dipped her head, her lips skimming the flat, dark circle of Creigh's nipple. His breath hissed between his teeth, his hands crushing her hips as her tongue darted out, skimming the hardened point.

"Tigress, sweet Christ," he hissed. "Sweet—" With a primal snarl he clutched her against him, his hips driving deep between her quivering thighs, his fingers crushing, bloodless, as he guided her hips to receive his thrusts.

Brianna moaned, cried, at the incredible sweetness of his mouth sweeping her breasts, his voice murmuring raspy words of praise, urging her to ever higher planes of magic. A rainbow seemed to spring forth within her womb, its colors blinding her, swirling her into a cerulean sky. She clawed at Creigh's sweat-damp skin, her teeth sharp upon his shoulder, the column of his neck as she grasped at the single, silver star that blazed at the rainbow's crest. But it danced just beyond her reach, elusive, mesmerizing.

She hovered there forever, upon the brink of something blade-sharp, white-hot. Exquisite.

"Let it . . . take you . . . let it!" Creigh's hands knotted in her hair, dragging her lips to his. His mouth mated with hers, primitive, wild, his sex driving so deep, it seemed to reach her very soul.

And then the rainbow burst.

A low scream tore from Brianna's throat, a thousand jewel-hued fragments catapulting her into shimmering silver. She felt Creigh thrust inside her, once, twice, his primal cry burying itself in her heart as he, too, captured splendor.

They clung together endless moments, stunned, spent, the only sound the thundering of their hearts, the harsh rasping of their breaths.

Creigh's hand was gentle in her hair, stroking the silky curls against her skin. "Bree." His hands urged her face from the muscled pillow of his chest, and the tenderness that melted within his eyes made Brianna's breast ache. "Did I . . . did I hurt you? Frighten you?"

She shook her head, unable to squeeze words past the knot of love in her throat.

"Wanted . . . wanted it to be so beautiful."

She reached out fingers that trembled, tracing the arrogant curve of his lips, the hard line of his clenched jaw. But there was strength in her voice, certainty, as she said, "I love you, Creighton Wakefield."

His dark-lashed eyes widened, flashing with some unreadable emotion before a guarded expression secreted it away. "Love?" he echoed, "Tigress, I—"

"Nay," she interrupted. "I know you love me not. I but wanted you to know what it—what this meant to me, after—after the other time . . ."

Creigh gazed up into the earnest gold of her eyes, her angel's face, vulnerable, strong. And the innocent beauty he found there robbed him of the blithe, witty words that had proved his shield against a dozen like declarations of love. For he knew, even within himself, that what had happened between he and Brianna Devlin was no casual romp 'twixt each other's legs, no mildly diverting method of whiling away the long hours of journeying.

She had gifted him with something ineffably precious, this child-woman, with her courage, and her terror. She had given him entrance to her darkest fears, had reached out her hand, and offered him trust. And she deserved more than sensual banter, careless platitudes cast at her feet with little thought, and less real feeling. She deserved . . .

Creigh's jaw clenched.

Self-loathing washed over him, mingled with a sharp tang of sorrow. "Tigress," he began slowly. "Finding pleasure in a man's arms has but little to do with love. Passion, desire, are far different from a blending of the hearts, and what you—we felt was no more than—"

"I know what I feel, Sassenach."

He glanced up sharply, expecting a glisten of tears in her eyes, or at least righteous anger, but instead the tiniest of smiles toyed with the corner of her kiss-swollen lips. Her eyes glowed with soft amusement.

"Come, my Lord Creighton, you needn't look so panicked. I'll not demand you salvage my honor and wed me. And I'll try not to cling to you more than half of the day."

A strange irritation pricked Creigh at her easy dismissal of the emotions she had claimed, then anger jabbed through him—astonishing in its power—at the thought that her talk of love might have been jest all along.

His hands closed on her arms, and he lifted her off him, plunking her onto the crushed flowers to one side.

" 'Tis an immense relief to know you'll not be choking me for at least part of the journey," he growled, levering himself to a sitting position. " 'Twill give me some peace from your attempts to make a fool of me."

"A fool?" The soft golden skin about her eyes crinkled in puzzlement.

"Aye," Creigh accused, snatching up his shirt. "Making me think, believe that I had made you love me, fearing how much I would hurt you, while in truth—"

Creigh cursed himself as he caught a glimpse of understanding in her eyes. Her fingers reached out, staying his hand as he attempted to jerk the damp lawn sleeve over his arm. He stared pointedly into the burbling waters of the stream.

"Creigh, my loving you—'tis no jest," she said softly. "When you—when you made love to me, 'twas more beautiful than ought I've ever known. Doyle . . . Doyle said—"

"Doyle?" Creigh bit out, the sound of another man's name on her lips filling him with fury.

"Aye, Doyle. My—my brother." Sorrow shadowed her face. " 'Twas he who found me after I was raped."

Creigh fought to keep his gaze fixed upon the dancing waves, but the still-raw pain in her tone and the fresh, tearing rage that she had been brutalized would not be banished. He looked into her face.

"Doyle said that—that what I had suffered had naught to do with the joinings of man and woman," she continued. "That comparing rape to—to loving was the same as linking the act of childbirth to that of murder." Her gaze dropped to a late-blooming gillyflower. She plucked it, her eyes heavy with grief as she peered into its velvety petals.

"I wanted to believe him, but I felt so—so soiled—as if no man would want to touch me. But you . . . ." Her voice was soft as she raised luminous eyes to his. "Creigh, you knew that I was—that I had been—" She pressed trembling lips to the delicate flower, and the quaver in her voice tore at Creigh like a knife. "But it mattered not," she breathed, wonderingly. "It mattered not . . . ."

Creigh stared into her face, some unnameable emotion stirring in the pit of his belly. "Bree—" His fingers slipped gently 'neath the curtain of her hair, his chest tight with agonizing tenderness. A fleeting, incongruous image of Michel Le Ferre's face flashed across Creigh's mind, the Frenchman's countenance etched with unaccustomned pain as he had stared at the miniature of Juliet. *Love* . . . the image seemed to whisper in Creigh's mind, *there be no space for love in a world gone mad. There is but a moment to catch, hold* . . .

Creigh gazed at Brianna, all innocence, fire. And he ached

to offer her a haven from the war that tore the world around them, ached to offer her love.

But he had only this dawn-blushed valley to give her, and the wooing of a body that burned for her touch.

His lips sought hers as he lay her gently back into the sun-warmed softness of the meadow grass, and the world spun away.

Chapter Ten

Carikbrah lay drowsing, its humble roofs and lowly spires blanketed in the cold mist that rolled in off the sea. Creigh drew his soaked doublet tighter about his chilled shoulders, his worried gaze straying yet again to where Brianna rode beside him.

The impish smile that had been his delight in the nights they had spent tumbled together in the wildwood had vanished, lines of exhaustion tugging at the corners of her mouth. Her hair was plastered against the sodden folds of the blankets he had insisted upon draping about her, and despite her stubborn insistence that she was not weary, her shoulders drooped 'neath the weight of the tiresome journey.

Two days the skies had given them no respite, the unceasing mist dampening both bodies and spirits, and yet, even as he swiped away the beads of wetness that clung to his face, Creigh cursed the quiet village that offered shelter, for 'twas also to see the parting that he had come to dread more than the fall of the headsman's axe. For this blow would sever all that he was, leaving him barren.

Brianna . . . His hands clenched upon the reins, his eyes sweeping the pale curve of her cheek. Was it truly but two weeks' time since she burst into his life, flashing her sword, daring him to tame her? Had it been only a matter of days that they had shared their bodies 'neath the dawn, 'neath the twilight, in woodland, sharp with the tang of pine? It seemed she had been at his side forever, goading him, tormenting

133

him, loving him with a fierceness that drove away the
realities of war, betrayal, death. But now . . .

He squinted his eyes toward the east, glimpsing, in the
distance, the dark silhouette of a ship at anchor in the
harbor.

In but a day's time he and Michel would set sail to the
only world Creigh had ever known; courts awash with satin,
jewels, treachery, and Brianna would again take up her
rapier, to battle at the sides of her beleaguered countrymen.

Creigh's jaw hardened at the vivid picture his mind
conjured at the thought—streets painted with the horror of
Drogheda, rapacious swords cleaving the firm, sweet flesh he
had caressed—and Brianna's eyes as a horde of Roundheads
fell upon her.

Yet, if he were to snatch her away from Ireland tomorrow,
take her with him to Charles's court at Jersey, would he not
be condemning her to but a death slower still? Wild, fey, one
with the moors and the mists, Brianna Devlin would waste
away like one of the creatures in Merton's menagerie, if
Creigh held her captive in a prison woven of golden threads.
In but a little time she would ache for the windswept glens of
her Ireland, for the freedom of dashing across the moors on
a half-wild stallion. The fierce pride that blazed in her eyes
would fade 'neath the cutting barbs of court beauties, and
she would long for honest, forthright anger she could battle
with her sword.

She would be labeled his mistress—and 'twould become a
game amongst the other women to see who bore charms
enough to topple her from his favor. And when he was
forced by duty to take to him a wife of wealth and noble
lineage, Brianna would be condemned to watching another
woman bear his name, and the Wakefield heirs that would
come of his body.

Creigh cursed savagely under his breath, raking back the
sticky waves of hair that clung to his face and neck. Christ,
half of the wenches in England would barter their soul to
Lucifer for the "honor" of being mistress to Lord Creighton
Wakefield. Why, then, did the thought of this Irish peasant
lass ensconced in rich apartments for his pleasure fill him
with naught but disgust?

Because Bree is so much more than any woman I've ever

known, Creigh whispered inside himself. *And that is why I needs must leave her.*

A fist seemed to clench in his belly, unreasonable fury sparking through him. He wanted the wound of their parting to be quick, clean. He wanted to hold it forever. . . .

He turned on her, his voice harsh even to his own ears. "Christ, is there not a single hostlery upon this whole infernal island? I thought you said this was a town!"

She angled toward him, the hooding of blanket slipping back to reveal dry humor 'neath the weariness that whitened her cheeks. "You're not in England, Sassenach," she said. "And I vow the fisher folk hereabouts have more pressing concerns than preparing a gold-encrusted bed—even for a lord."

"I'd settle for a blasted hole in the dirt right now, if it was dry," Creigh bit out.

Brianna laughed, and Creigh felt an irrational surge of rage, that she could make light so, when his own chest was torn with the knowledge he was about to leave her.

She tipped her head, flashing him a smile. "Would a ferret's lair do, your worship?"

Creigh glared.

"For your hole in the ground," Brianna clarified. "They would at least have a clump of hay for us to sleep upon, and if you're not too particular about your sheetings . . ."

"'Tis no time for jest, you little fool. I'm wet to my marrow, and if either of us escapes lung fever 'twill be a—" Creigh stopped, his teeth jarring together as his eyes swung along the path her finger was pointing. His lips set in a line of disgust as his gaze locked upon a building to his right. Dull, saffron-colored windows seemed to dare the unwary traveler to enter the hovel's crumbling walls, while a half-rotted sign dangled askew from a roof that threatened to collapse at any moment.

FERRET'S LAIR, once-scarlet lettering proclaimed, EATABLES, SPIRITS AND RIGHT MERRY COMPANY.

"I vow I've endured inns the like of this before," Creigh muttered. "The eatables most like will taste like charred saddle leather, the innkeeper will do his best to 'spirit' away what coins are left in my purse, and the 'merry company' will attempt to slit my throat while the rest make off with the horses."

"And I'd scarce blame them if they divested you of your tongue as well, it's waxed so sharp of late." A thread of infuriating tolerance ran through Brianna's voice.

"It seems we bear no choice, in any instance," Creigh groused. "'Tis nigh past midnight, and though God knows Michel would not be caught dead in a hovel the like of this, if he and I are to sail on the morrow, we'd do best to get some rest this night." He flung the words off as though he cared not, watching Brianna's face for her reaction. He wanted, perversely, for her to show at least some sign of being as miserable as he was over their impending farewell. But in the light from the glowing window, her soft lips merely pressed together, some emotion flashing like quicksilver across her features before she crushed it into a determined, yet wrenchingly melancholy smile.

"You needn't fear, my Lord Creighton," she said, lifting her face toward the whitecapped waves. "From the feel of the winds, the Lady of the Sea has fallen 'neath your charms as easily as one of your court belles. I vow you'll be back amongst your velvet bedclothes before a fortnight has passed."

A lump of molten lead seemed to lodge in Creigh's throat at her calm acknowledgment that he would soon be with other women, when the very thought of another man touching Brianna, even in love, filled him with a rage such as he'd never known. He hauled back on his mount's reins, gritting his teeth as he flung himself from the saddle.

"'Twill be passing heaven to escape the dirt, the rags, and the thrice-damned lowlings that litter these rat-infested dens," he snarled, his eyes flashing to Brianna's in challenge.

But instead of anger, he sparked naught but the slightest lift of her chin, her voice bland as she said: "No doubt 'twill be a great relief to be again amongst the cavaliers with their chivalry and impeccable manners."

The velvet-sheathed barb struck Creigh more deeply than shrewish screams could have, and in that instant he knew just how fiercely he would miss the proud tilt of that chin, the glow of strength in eyes the hue of a miser's treasure.

He would miss her with all that he was, because when he sailed for Jersey, he would be leaving his heart in the small palm of her sword-callused hand.

He loved her.

The horse's reins fell from numb fingers, trailing into the muck at his feet. Creigh knew a soaring wonder, and a bone-chilling despair. He, Lord Creighton Alexander Gareth Wakefield, loved this sharp-tongued, bedraggled peasant lass. Wanted her with him more than he had ever desired anything in his entire life. And, yet, even if he were to cast all his lands, all his wealth to the sea, he could never have her. Because there was one part of himself he could not sacrifice, even for Brianna.

Honor.

He clenched his fists, Charles Stuart's image rising in his memory. The dark, hooded eyes peered out at him with a trust rarely seen in that royal visage, and Creigh could still feel the clasp of Charles's hands upon his shoulders. *I place my hopes for England in your hands,* the exiled king had said. And in Charles's face, with its patience, humor, and tolerance, Creigh had seen the salvation of a nation torn the decade past by fanaticism and hatred. Since the day the axe had fallen at Whitehall, martyring Charles I, Creigh had hurled all he possessed into his boyhood friend's bid to regain the crown. For the merry prince, aye, but most of all for the torn, bleeding country Creigh loved.

No passion between man and woman could take precedence over the fate of an entire nation. Nor could this love, so new, wondrous, eclipse the unquestioning devotion of a lifetime, the loyalty of brothers who had clung together 'neath the tempests of the court. Creigh ground his fingers into his eyes. Even if he could discount his fealty to Charles, he could never forget gentle Lindley, yet imprisoned in the tower.

Creigh started, the slosh of small feet in the mire drawing him back to the present as he raised hopeless eyes to Brianna's. She had dismounted sometime when he had been lost in black reverie, and she stood, speaking softly in Gaelic to the scrawny grasshopper of a lad who was, no doubt, to tend to their horses.

Creigh stared at her, marking each droplet of mist that ran down her cheek, each tendril of hair that clung to her temple, her throat. He wanted to burn the image of her face into his mind, to take out and hold in the years that stretched, empty before him, wanted to banish her at once from his heart and mind, spare them both the agony that was to come.

Yet, even while she was yet by his side, to taste, touch, a white-hot blade seemed buried in the pit of his belly. And when, an hour later, he left her to search for Michel in the sleepy little town, he felt the first shadows of the pain he would know on the morrow when he stood aboard the deck of the *Valiant Hope* and watched her fade into his memory.

Brianna curled up on the wide windowsill, dangling her feet into the dawn breezes that drifted in cool waves over her still-damp skin. Her whole body ached. Even the steaming-hot bath Creigh had ordered for her before he had left to seek his friend had done naught to ease muscles cramped from days of hard riding and long bouts of a lovemaking that had grown more hungry and desperate with each vanishing hour.

The nights past they had slept naught but a few scattered hours, she and Creigh, only surrendering to slumber when both were too exhausted to fan yet again the passion flames that had engulfed them. Even then, their rest had been that of wood-creatures hunted, alert to every stirring of leaf or twig despite the fact that Creigh had long since judged Ogden and his minions far afield of their trail. Only now, sheltered within a town that was staunchly Royalist, had Brianna been able to ease the warrior-honed sharpness of her senses, and sink back, tired, sad, yet safe. A wry twist tipped up Brianna's lips. Creigh had called Carikbrah a town to wage battle, yet though the village folk might well love merry Charles, in truth they were more concerned with the harvest of the fishes that schooled off the rocky shores than their conquereror's crown.

She glanced back at the basin full of water still in the center of the room, its cracked brass belly drizzling gray streams of water across the canting floor. Aye, 'twas little wonder she had sunk into sleep, even against the dubious pillowing of the tub's dented rim.

She shook back the thick mass of her drying hair, turning her face again back into the sweet sea winds as the stench of sour ale that clung to the tiny inn room assailed her. It had been the stench that had driven her to force open the room's windows when she had awakened in the time-cooled waters of her bath. She had drawn on her chemise, and thrown wide the wooden shutters, fully intending to turn again to the basin, rinse out her travel-stained gown, but when she had seen the sea spilling out beneath the high window, the tang of salt air had beckoned her like the bittersweet strains of a ballad. A ballad about a hero sailing off to war, of great love lost . . .

Brianna's eyes slid closed, the corners of her mouth tipping up just a whisper. How Doyle would smile, if he could see her now, gazing out to sea, pensive as any of the heroines in the legends he loved so well. She could almost see his dark, earnest eyes, hear his voice cracking 'neath the weight of his newfound manhood the long-ago day she had discovered him wooing fair Moira O'Niall behind the cow byre. Bree had teased him unmercifully, tossing her tangled gold mane, making jest of the ballad's melancholy story in a high falsetto with a laughing Shane.

"Someday, you'll feel the cut of love's fangs upon your heart, you little harridan," Doyle had warned, "and I hope to God I'm there to watch you squirm!"

"I'll not lay about, wringing my hands for any man!" she had cried, planting grubby fists on her hips. "'Tis daft, the way your 'fair-haired damsels' screech their love to the mountaintops, and then lie about while their menfolk get killed. If *I* ever love, I'd like to see the bloody bastard blast me back to some sweet little cottage!"

Doyle had pressed his lips together, hard, battling a smile, but Bree had pulled a simpering face, mincing about him until his laughter had rung out, clear and deep. He had swooped her up in his strong arms, tossing her high in the air.

"What am I to do with you, moppet?" he had mourned, shaking his head.

"Teach me to fight," Bree had said with a fierceness that had stunned Doyle. "Then when my *Fotahd Cannan* goes to meet his death, I can battle there, beside him."

Brianna bit her lip, banishing the memory of that flower-spangled summer day back into the secret corners of her mind. That wild girl-child who had lugged about her brothers' swords, and romped across the heather playing at Finn McCool, had been soul-wrenchingly innocent, naïve. She had truly believed that naught could defeat her as long as she bore courage and daring. Shane and Doyle had weaned her on tales of miracles, wrought by stout hearts and brave deeds. And she had had little patience with the panderings of ballads that had made the other girls sniffle into their kerchiefs. But now, as she watched the sun steal across the horizon, she felt in her heart every aching strain of the bard's harp's music, each lilting, melancholy phrase wrapping crushing fingers about her heart.

The man she loved more than life was leaving on the tides that swept toward Jersey this day. And before the sun sank to its rest, she, like those ancient, immortalized women she had despised, would lay waiting for word that her lover lay dead.

Nay, not waiting, Bree upbraided herself. She would to war again, find Fergus and Daniel and join with them in the fray. Most like, she would never know if Creigh lay dead on some bloody field of honor, or rotted in some dank prison cell, his hands heavy with chains. She would never know if he lived a long, prosperous life, wed some gold-laden beauty and sired children with eyes the shades of storm.

Bree tried to swallow, a knot of pain rising in her throat. Aye, she prayed he lived to gift his wife with a score of babes, Brianna thought defiantly, hoped he would live endless days, blessed by the love of the woman destiny chose for him. From the first Bree had known that Lord Creighton Wakefield could ne'er be hers to hold—an English peer, pride of a noble lineage that stretched to Conquering William. She had waged a constant battle inside herself to keep at bay anger, rage at the fates that had cast them together, only to tear them apart.

Yet, now, the thought of him wrapped in the arms of some faceless beauty clawed at the very heart of her, and the acceptance of fortune's blows she had learned throughout a lifetime of hardship faded in unguarded moments into sharp despair.

"No one could love him as I do," she cried fiercely to the sea. "No one." But the waves answered not, merely tossed their sweet foam upon the crags that rimmed the shore.

Brianna's hands clenched into fists, as she glared at the waters, the sparkling waves oblivious to the miseries of the insignificant creatures that sailed upon their surface. A thousand years hence the waters would yet crash upon the same jagged stones, the winds would sweep in from the distant English coast. Yet she and Creigh . . . they held only this day in their hands.

Or have you even that much? a taunting voice whispered inside Bree. *Mayhap he stands even now upon a ship's deck, jesting and drinking wine with his cavalier friend, too caught up in his games of power to trouble himself with bidding a mere peasant wench farewell.*

"Aye, and mayhap he flew to England astride a swan!" Brianna berated herself, swinging down from the high sill. "'Od's blood, Brianna Devlin, you'll cease drowning in your own pity. He'd not just leave without telling you. I know he—"

Her feet thudded into the floor, the room echoing with her sudden silence as a sharp, sick feeling twisted her stomach. *You know?* the insidious voice mocked her. *What do you truly know of the man, Creighton Wakefield? The steel-honed perfection of his body? The way his eyes warm with laughter, darken with desire? He has shared naught of that secret self hidden inside him, shared no tales of his childhood, his hopes, dreams . . .*

Brianna hugged her arms against her breasts, wanting to block out the sounds of truth, but the nights she had spent drowsing beneath the stars in Creigh's arms rolled back in her mind, dancing like mimes, sly 'neath painted faces. She could see, hear herself spinning for him pictures of the Devlin cottage, of Doyle's futile attempts to mold her into a lady, of Shane's rakehell ways, hot temper.

Creigh had voiced heartiest sympathy for the beleaguered Doyle, had laughed aloud at the worst of the pranks she had played upon her brothers, and had held her gently as she again mourned their deaths. Yet he had mentioned naught of his own youth, nor of those shadowy, tormented people he had cried out for in his delirium. Someone called Lindley, a headsman—

And Juliet . . . the breeze seemed to whisper. Brianna wheeled, pacing across the room, her fingers twining in the lacings of her worn chemise. 'Twas as if the woman's very name was molded of gold-tissue, rich, yet incredibly delicate, lovely.

In all the days Brianna had shared with Creigh, she had locked doubts, fears away, consigning the mysterious Juliet to the same nether reaches as the horror of Brianna's own rape. But now, in the silence, confined in this tiny room with its cunning, creeping shadows, the shades that haunted Brianna's heart seemed loosed as well.

The nearer they had drawn to Carikbrah, the more surly Creigh had become, prey to long silences, broken only by harsh rejoinders. And when he had started out of the inn, to go in search of Michel, Creigh had turned upon her, snapping, angry, as she made to accompany him. She had seen him grit his teeth, battling for control of his temper. At last he had raked his fingers wearily through his hair, and said softly: *Bree, I need a breath alone.*

She had thought mayhap 'twas guilt that had driven him, some breach of his cavalier's code that forbade him deserting a mistress in a war-torn land. But perhaps 'twas a far different guilt—that of a man deep in love with his wife, a man who had been caught up in a whirlwind of war and impulsive passion and had strayed . . .

Brianna gripped the shutter's edge, the rough wood grating against her palm. "Have you flayed yourself enough, witling?" she grated to herself, "or do you intend to conjure up every calamity known to man? Perhaps you could have him trampled by a herd of wild horses, or skewered on the steeple of a church."

She stomped over to a crude bench, snatching up her crumpled gown and jerking it over her head with a force that popped stitches in the bodice. "Come, now, Bree," she said, "certainly you can find some other tragedy to befall him— or yourself. Ought, that is, except the possibility that the infernal man is but wandering about the village, lost."

She jammed her arms into the sleeves, stalking to the window to survey the town below through narrowed eyes. "It should be simple enough to rout one velvet-clad Sassenach aristocrat out of a village that most like spends feast days in homespun. If I start at the nearest alehouse . . ." She grimaced, remembering the countless times she'd found Shane slouched over a tankard. Her mouth set, hard, as she grasped the shutter's handle, swinging the wood panels closed. But before the honey-toned wood could block out the village below, she caught a glimpse of something far off on the street that wound its way along the harbor; something familiar, disturbing.

She shoved the shutter wide, startled at the sudden tightness in her chest as she searched the distant street. She had seen naught but a flash of scarlet in the midst of the dozen other colors that bedecked the village folk traveling the road, most like a fisherman's kerchief, knotted about his neck to keep the sea spray from his collar.

Bree fought to banish the stirrings of unease, pausing to take up Doyle's sword, bind its soft leather scabbard to her waist. Yet even after she had waded through the thick darkness that shrouded the inn's rickety stairs, and had stepped into the sunshine, the chill that had prickled her nape clung like breeze-borne cobwebs to her skin.

Her fingers touched the griffin head, as if to take strength from the symbol that had stood for Devlin courage for generations past. Then she hurried into the teeming street.

"A 'risticrat, lady? Be ye daft?"

Brianna gritted her teeth against the wizened old man's raspy voice, as his rotting gums gaped into a sly grin. "There been no Sassenach leeches slinkin' 'bout fer the crown here since old Crom ground Drogheda int' hell. They all be off combin' honest men's blood outa their perfumed wigs."

"This Sassenach wears naught but his own hair," Bree forced into her voice a patience worn thin through an hour of scouring Carikbrah's streets. "'Tis the color of polished wood, and falls just past his shoulders. Here." She tapped the side of her hand against her collar bone. "He rode in just last night, stayed at the Ferret's Lair for but a little—"

"The Lair, eh?" the old man chortled, hitching up his sagging trews with a crippled hand. "'Tis not the lodging I'd have judged a 'risticrat bastard'd take. But then fer a wench the likes of you . . . Tell me, love, did 'is lordship not think ye worth ought but a lump o' straw?"

"Straw?"

"Aye." His pale tongue slithered out, wetting his lips, his eyes sliding over Brianna's breasts in a way that made her skin crawl. "'Course, no doubt the Sassenach's pampered arse ne'er touched the bedding. But I wager he ground your backside int' the filth wi' a relish."

Bree felt hot anger stain her cheeks, anger and a sharp sensation of pain at the defiling of that which had been so beautiful. "'Tis none of your concern, old man. Just tell me if you've seen—"

"I seen naught, milady trollop, savin' the inside o' an ale mug this night. An' as fer yer high an' holy Sassenach, I'd hurl 'im t' Hades wi' the rest o' the fools that died fer the crown if I but had a hand t' do it with." The man thrust his arm into Brianna's face, his mangled hand dangling useless at the end of his ragged sleeve.

Bree shuddered, more from the hatred that glazed his beady eyes than from the hideous old scars. She turned away, starting back into the maze of streets, but a cry stopped her.

"Milady! Milady, pray wait."

Bree spun toward the sound, surprised to see a plump, fluttery woman darting toward her from the chandlery across the way. A white linen headdress bobbed above a brow smooth and pink as a babe's, the pale green eyes beneath crinkled in concern. Feet that seemed too tiny to carry the woman flashed out beneath spotless skirts as she hurried toward Brianna, a bunch of white wax candles clutched to her ample bosom.

"I couldn't help but hear you, milady, what with that horrid Kinnard MacMurrough shouting to raise the dead," the woman said. "And when I realized 'twas an Englishman you were seeking—a wealthy one at that—I thought, well, I . . . 'Tis not certain I am, but I saw a man the likes of the one you described enter Swan's Way just before dawn."

"Swan's Way? Where—"

"'Tis an inn, milady, but a little ways from here. Caters to ship's captains, and the rich merchants that sometimes sail these ports. The innkeeper, he charges so much, no rabble can stay there, and those who want to avoid the likes of MacMurrough are more than willing to pay."

A chill fury built inside Brianna at the thought of Creigh lounging in some well-appointed aleroom while she was tortured with worry. "And you saw a man—passing tall and dressed in velvet—entering this inn?" she asked.

"Aye. Saw him from my window, I did. It opens onto the street across from the Swan. See, I had spent the night on my knees, starin' at the heavens, givin' thanks to all the saints fer bringin' my lad back, alive. 'Twas a miracle, sure, that he survived the slaughterin' at—"

"Where?" Brianna grated from between clenched teeth.

"Drogheda-town," the woman answered, startled. "My Seamus, he—"

"Nay. The inn. How do I find the inn?" Bree demanded, smoldering.

"Why, 'tis but around this corner, next to the butchery, so the keeper can get fresh meat."

"'Tis an apt place indeed," Brianna said grimly. "Mayhap I'll borrow a well-honed cleaver."

"Milady?" The woman's brows lifted in puzzlement.

"I may well be doing some butchering of my own," Bree answered. She felt the woman's gaze, and that of the glowering old MacMurrough, upon her back as she stalked off down the street.

At the first glimpse of the sign that hung without the exclusive inn the fury that had been building inside her burst into flame. A golden-crowned swan sailed in pristine whiteness across a beautifully painted sapphire pond, calm, serene, yet with patrician arrogance that made Brianna want to hurl a clod of mud at the fowl's arching neck. Even the bright-polished windows seemed to lord over the muddy streets below them, displaying, through diamond panes, glossy tables already scrubbed free of last night's debris. Brianna's chin jutted upward, her eyes narrowing on a willow-thin wisp of a man who was sweeping a nonexistent pile of dust off of the doorstep.

The man's gaze caught hers, his mouth widening into an uncertain smile. "Milady, may I help you?"

"Help me?" Bree repeated, stalking toward him. "Aye. You can tell me if 'tis true that Lord Creighton Wakefield lodged here last night."

"Lord—Lord Creighton? He purchased my finest suite of rooms just at dawning. What—what business have you with—"

Bree loosed a string of curses that made the innkeeper go scarlet.

"Milady, I must ask you to cease at once," the man bristled. "His lordship was awake most of the night, and no doubt lies sleeping. If you disturb him——"

"Disturb him!" Brianna burst out. "I intend to do worlds more than disturb him!"

The innkeeper barred the door with his broom. "You'll do no such thing, madam." He drew himself up to his full five feet.

If she had not been so furious, Brianna would have collapsed on the man's polished floor, laughing, at the shock in the innkeeper's face when she tore the broom out of his hands.

She jabbed the oak handle at the man's spotless apron. "You'll tell me where that bloody Sassenach is this instant, or I'll——"

"You'd best surrender, Houlihan," a husky voice said from the stairs. "I can vow from past experience, she'd as soon slit your gullet as look at you."

Brianna's face jerked up to the crest of the carved newel-post, the mocking countenance that towered over the rail filling her with fury. "Wakefield, you thrice-cursed, bloody bastard!" she blazed, barging up the stairs. "So help me, I'll——"

The threat was crushed in her chest as iron-strong arms snatched her up, yanking her, hard against a chest clad in rose-colored satin. She squirmed and kicked, taking immense satisfaction in his grunt of pain as the point of her elbow found his belly. But he merely strode past the doorways that stood open into the hall, past the dozen curious faces that peered out at them from beneath starched nightcaps. When he reached the end of the corridor, he turned, and paused, giving the other inn guests a patronizing bow.

"A bit of a lovers' spat," he explained. "She's a wild thing, and she's not yet learned her place." Brianna sank her teeth into his shoulder, and the howl of pain that punctuated his words filled her with grim joy.

He swore, throwing her onto the bed in the center of the room. Bree fought to free herself of the tangle of down coverlets, bursting from their smothering folds just in time to see Creigh kick the carved cherry door shut and throw the bolt.

"By God's wounds, you drew blood, you little witch!" he blustered, glaring at the tiny, red-smeared stains her teeth had torn in his doublet. "The first set of fresh clothes I've had since our dousing in the Boyne, and you ruin them."

"Oh, forgive me, your worship! God forbid that *you* should have to endure such hardship as a stain on your silk when *I* have been so enjoying myself, tearing apart the town in search of your cursed Sassenach hide!"

"Bree . . ."

"I vow I had you dead in a ditch somewhere, or at the very least prisoner of a band of brigands, but now that I know you're safe, I'll not trouble you with my company any longer."

"Damn it, Bree, I was just leaving to find you." He grabbed her arms as she started for the door.

"Oh, of a certainty." She glared at him. "And I'm the queen of England."

"Look about you, you stubborn little fool. When I failed to find Michel, I wanted to make what time we have left together as beautiful as possible. I spent the whole night gathering—"

"Tankards of ale?" Brianna grated, "or lightskirts?"

"Skirts, aye, but not those of another woman. Look." He caught her chin in his hand, forcing her to turn toward a gold-framed mirror. Hanging from a hook at its crest was a waterfall of shimmering silk, woven as if of a maiden's dream.

Sea green overskirts drifted like the petals of a lily over pearl-hued satin, dainty, embroidered edgings draping back to frame coral rosettes of glistening taffeta. The delicately wrought bodice was a wondrous confection of exquisite lace caught at each shoulder by trailing gold ribbon. And the décolletage swept low in clouds of gauze that promised to caress the shoulders and breasts of any woman fortunate enough to don its delicate folds.

"I found it 'mongst the cargo of a frigate just arrived from Calais," Creigh's voice was warm in her ear, melting the edges of her wrath. "The captain had bought it for his daughter, but I convinced him she would as lief have a purse full of coin."

"'Tis—'tis for . . ."

"For you, love. You should have seen the poor seamstress

I dragged from her bed to alter it. Make it to fit a wood-witch, I told her, with a waist slender as a willow frond and hips that curve to fit my hands." His hard palms slipped down the hollow beneath her ribs, flaring outward as he fitted her back against his lean hips. "Don it for me, Tigress. Now."

The urgency of his voice, his burgeoning hardness beneath the curve of her buttocks stoked in Brianna far hotter blazings than anger. She turned her face up to his, hunger welling gold in her eyes as she kissed him. Her fingers, suddenly bold, fumbled with the fastenings of his clothes, wanting, needing to feel the rippling strength of his muscles, bared to her hands.

But he stopped her, his fingers gently circling her wrists, drawing her hands away from his skin. "Nay, Tigress, not like this. Not this time," he said with a heavy quiet that stole her breath. "I've been readying for this moment half the night. Let me . . ." The words drifted into silence, only the laboring of his breath betraying the depth of his need.

The sound of it, sight of his pulse throbbing lightning fast at the base of his throat filled Brianna with a desire so fierce her whole body shook with it. But she stood, frozen, drowning in the feel of Creigh's fingers as they slipped free the tiny hooks that held the green wool of her bodice closed at her throat, letting the garment fall into a pool at her feet.

She shut her eyes, steeling her body to keep from flinging herself, clawing against his chest, as he stripped away her chemise, and let it too fall away. She heard a muffled creak of a board beneath his boot, sensed the warm presence of his lean frame leaving her. She moaned in protest, her eyes opening as she heard the soft clink of crystal against wood.

His long fingers were curled about a tiny, glistening decanter, tipping its slender spout against his broad palm. A tingle went up Brianna's spine as the rich scent of jessamine blossoms permeated the air.

"Creigh . . ." her voice was strangled, pleading.

He came to her. "I know, Tigress," he said hoarsely. His hand reached out, and Brianna felt a cry tear from her throat as the heat of his calloused palm burned her naked breast. Oil, fragrant, hot from his skin, dewed her body with the subtle scent of flower-kissed meadows, and the headier scent of roughly leashed passion. She whimpered as Creigh's hands caressed her, smoothing the expensive oils over her buttocks, belly, even the soles of her feet, his lips daring breath-light kisses on the soft flesh behind her knee, the creamy skin of an inner thigh. Higher.

But though Brianna was nigh sobbing with longing, he held her at bay whenever she fought to clutch her to him, drive his passion out of control. An agonizing eternity later Creigh's hands left her. He rose from his knees, but instead of leading her to the lush bed with its drapings of scarlet, as she expected, he turned to the mirror, drawing from beneath the still-hanging gown undergarments so delicate they seemed spun of mist. He bound them about her with sky-shaded ribbons, his fingertips hot as they brushed her skin. Then he raised the green silk of the gown over her head, letting it drift down her body.

She felt Creigh's fingers tremble through the satin as he worked the last fastening of the gown, and she felt afraid of a sudden, certain that after all the effort he had gone to turn her into all that his lady should be, he would be disappointed when he discovered, that, even garbed in satins, she was no beauty. She stood, stiff, her hands clenched in fists at her sides, fighting the magic of his fingertips as they drifted over the bared curve of her shoulder.

"I wanted there to be starlight when I took you thus," his voice wooed her. "I wanted strains of music, drifting up from a gallery soft with candle-shine, and goblets, iced with the finest of wine. I wanted, just once, to make you mine, Tigress, as I would have had there never been a war."

Against her will, Brianna felt herself drawn by the throbbing longing in Creigh's voice, her gaze lifting to his dark-lashed eyes. She was stunned to see the stormy gray oddly misted.

"Dance with me, Tigress. Let me feed you sweet cakes dipped in honey. Let me weave flowers into your hair, take your body in tenderness and passion. For just this day, let us both dream that you are not just my lady, but my wife . . ."

Chapter Eleven

Moonlight melted in pools of silver upon the rumpled bed, gilding the rich-embroidered satins cast aside hours past. Creigh propped his jaw upon his naked arm, reveling in the soft stirring of Brianna's breath upon his chest. Resting quiet, thus she looked scarce a child, her gold-tipped lashes thick upon cheeks soft as the apple blossoms he had loved as a lad at Wrensong. Yet she had known more pain than most bear in a lifetime, suffered losses that had driven the strongest of men to seek death at the point of their own sword. How, then, could she still appear so innocent, untouched?

He gently brushed a wayward strand of hair away from lips reddened with his kisses. She sighed, snuggling closer, her hand, yet buried in his hair tightening reflexively, as if to hold him there. "Tigress, I love you," he mourned with aching softness. "There is so much I want to share with you. So many secrets within you I still need to learn."

He closed his eyes, brushing the soft well of her breast with his mouth gently, so as not to waken her. "I want to discover it all, Tigress," he whispered, his lips touching the scar that marred her soft flesh. "The tiniest sorrow, the greatest of joys."

"Ask, Sassenach."

Creigh's eyes flashed open at the soft, sleep-blurred voice, and his gaze was captured by warm gold. "Creigh," Brianna lifted her hand, laying her fingertips upon the curve of his lip. "We've not the time, you and I, to unfold each other's mysteries over a lifetime, as it should be. But I love you enough to give you all that I am, now, unafraid."

Creigh shut his eyes, tight, her trust a searing pain in his chest. Bending over her again, he touched his lips to the scar. He opened eyes heavy with silent questions.

Bree shifted on the pillows, curling her knees tight against her chest, drawing the gold curtain of her hair about her nakedness as if to shield herself. Some beast seemed to sink its talons in his chest, and he wanted to bid Brianna to stop, stay silent, wanted her to spill to him all of her pain.

But she merely lifted one silken gold strand of her hair, twining it about her fingers as she began in a hushed whisper.

"'Twas the night Shane died that I . . . I gained the scarring," she said. "And at the time, I wished only that the monster who wielded the knife had but the kindness to drive his blade into my heart."

"Tigress . . ."

"'Twould have been just for me to die." Her eyes blazed, wounded. "Far more just than for Shane to . . ." She swallowed, and Creigh felt the white-hot lump of her anguish in his own throat.

"'Twas my fault, Creigh. All that befell us that night. If I'd but crushed my cursed stubbornness, just once, if I'd but listened to Doyle. But, nay, both he and Shane had challenged my damnable pride, so I had to best them."

Creigh eased upright, gently stroking her hair. "Brianna, love, you don't—don't have to tell me . . ."

"They were off for Drogheda," she continued as if she hadn't heard him. "Shane and Doyle. Off to fight devil Cromwell. 'Twas to be a grand adventure, Shane claimed, battles rife with glory, courage, honor, all the magical, wondrous things men spin into legends. Danny—Danny and I wanted to go with them, fight. Daniel could use a pike better than either of them, and I was passing fair with a sword. We bundled up our things along with Shane's and Doyle's, readying to go. But when we broached the subject on the night before they were to leave, Doyle went iron-stiff, unbending. *You'll not set foot off this farm,* he said. *War, 'tis no place for babes.*"

She paused, and Creigh watched the quicksilver flashes of

pain cross her face. "If Doyle had but said: I love you, don't want you hurt . . . or insisted Danny and I were needed to bring in the season's crop. If he had said any of those things, mayhap I would have obeyed him. But I—I couldn't bear being dismissed as though I'd be worthless in the fray. So Danny and I followed them."

She shivered, and Creigh carefully drew the coverlet up about her shoulders. She scarce seemed aware he was yet in the room, scarce seemed aware of aught but her own torment.

"We were three days from Drogheda when Shane discovered us. I vow he wanted to box our ears, he was so angry. But for once he had to curb his temper because Doyle . . . I'd ne'er seen him in such a fury. Shane tried to intercede for us, calm him, but Doyle was beyond listening. He raged that my stubbornness had not only endangered myself, but Daniel as well—that war was blood and filth and agony, and now because of my idiocy both Danny and I might die."

"He must have loved you both very much," Creigh said.

"Always. In all things." Tears were in her voice, and they ripped at Creigh's heart. "Never once, in all the years he was forced to cast off the games of the other lads to play both Da and Ma to the rest of us, did he show anger, resentment. Not once did he raise his hand to strike us, even when we tormented him past bearing. But that day, on the road I swear, if Shane had not come between us, Doyle would have slapped me. And with good reason. I knew I'd been wrong, but even in the face of his fury I couldn't admit it. So I mocked him, goaded him, said *he* should go back home, sit at the fire with the old women."

"You were hurt. Scared." Creigh's tone was gentle as he could make it.

"I was a spoiled, selfish little shrew. Doyle . . . he bolted toward me, but Shane blocked his way, shouting at him, telling him to gain control before he did something we'd all regret. Doyle cursed then, and in his eyes I saw his love, his fear, and the feeling within him that I had betrayed him. I didn't even see him turn and bolt into the woods. I couldn't tear my gaze from the ground, I was so ashamed.

"Danny . . . he followed him, hoping to calm Doyle once the wrath was spent. And Shane and I, we waited by the road. I—I was trying so hard not to cry, I couldn't speak.

And Shane . . ." She gave a sick little laugh. "Doyle had always been our rock, strong, calm, always there to draw strength from. It gave the rest of us freedom to stomp about, rage, wail. Shane's temper was legend in three counties. He'd never before had to chain his fury in the midst of a crisis. An hour passed. Two. And with every second that slipped by Shane's face grew more strained, his knuckles whiter. I could feel it in him, the need for anything, anyone to loose his fury upon." Seconds passed, and her hands, wrenchingly small, trembled where they were tangled in her hair.

"'Twas then that the riders came," she continued. "Eight of them. Roundheads all. Mayhap they would have but ridden past, taking no more notice of us than of the sheep grazing the hills, if Shane had—had been able to still his tongue. But he was so angry . . .

"The Roundhead leader . . . he sneered as he neared me, barking out a bawdy jest to his men. For Shane 'twas like fire to tinder. He drew steel, lunging at the Roundhead in a fury. There were eight of them, Creigh, and we were but two. I—I didn't even get to my sword. The leader, he grabbed me . . . used me as a shield as his men fell on Shane. I screamed . . . screamed. But Doyle and Daniel . . . they didn't hear me."

A sob tore from her throat. Creigh's arms clutched her to him, holding her, wanting to take her pain.

"He killed two of the Roundheads before they cut him down from behind. And the leader . . . he said that since he'd paid such a price to gain his hold of me, he 'tended to get his coin's worth. Shane . . . Shane was still screaming when the leader forced himself inside me."

Creigh ground his teeth together. Tasted blood and hate.

"I—I carried a little dagger in my belt. When—when the murdering bastard lost himself in his thrusting I managed to pull the blade out. I slashed his face. Slashed it. And I was glad," she whispered brokenly. "He rolled off of me, then. Made his men hold me down while he—he took the dagger . . ."

"Bree. Bree don't . . ." Creigh's fingers clenched on her arm, bruising, aching to crush the throat of the man who had brutalized her.

She laughed a wild, terrifying laugh. "I thought he was

153

going to kill me. Wanted him to. But he—he held my breast, and cut . . . A cross, he said, to brand me as a harlot before God. *God*. The man had murdered Shane, raped me and . . . Oh, sweet Christ!"

Sobs ripped her chest, wracked her body, her fingers tearing at the strands of hair that were yet twisted round them. Creigh crushed her against him, hating himself for forcing her to live through the horror yet again, hating himself for being so helpless even now.

"All I . . . remember after that is crawling over to Shane, trying to stop the blood. His—his whole side lay open, and I . . . tried to stop the flow with my hands, but—but there was so much blood . . . so much. Doyle found us later. He—he never cried, Creigh, never blamed me. He washed the blood away from me, stitched the wound on my breast with a strand of my hair. And held me. Held me hours, days, I'm not certain how long. I don't—don't even know when he buried Shane, because he never left my side."

Creigh pressed his lips against her cheek, the salt of her tears burning his mouth. "Tigress . . . dear God, I'm sorry."

"He should have hated me, Creigh. Blamed me," she cried brokenly. "'Twas—'twas my fault."

"Nay, love. You bore no way of knowing. Doyle loved you."

"Aye. He died for loving me. When Drogheda fell he was trying to shield Danny and me. Trying to, and . . . a Roundhead, a cursed murdering Roundhead cut him down. 'Twas my fault, Creigh. My . . ."

She sobbed then, her small fists pounding on Creigh's chest in a grief so wrenching it tore her very soul. Creigh felt it, the guilt, love that had nigh destroyed her.

"Aye, Tigress, strike me," he said fiercely, his hands clenching on her hips, "let it free."

She cried until there were no more tears, and even the pain seemed drowned by the warmth of the arms surrounding her, the voice murmuring half-savage words of love against her hair.

And when at last, even the sobs were naught but a catching in her breast, she felt Creigh's hands cup her cheeks with such infinite tenderness her heart broke.

"I love you, Brianna Devlin," he said. "Carry that with you always."

"Creigh . . ." She skimmed her fingertips over his face, memorizing every plane, every line, curve bespeaking unbridled love.

"And I do understand what it is to blame yourself. Live with the knowledge that you might be responsible for wounding someone you love. I didn't tell you the whole truth, the whole reason for my being in Cromwell's army. I was Charles's eyes, true. But 'tis for the life of my own brother, Lindley, aye, and my father's as well, that I battle now."

Brianna watched torment tighten his jaw, and she expected the defenses he drew about his inner self to clamp shut. But he spoke, quiet, solemn, until she, too, loved the earnest, devout Lindley, felt anger, resentment bitter-sharp at the father who had sacrificed, not only his daughter into a marriage she loathed, but his simple, gentle son to the cruelties of the Tower.

"'Tis because of Lindley that Michel and I must reach London with all haste," Creigh finished at last. "The execution is set for but a few weeks hence. Lindley . . . I'll not let him die like that, Tigress. With a vulgar mob screeching for his head."

"And your father?" Bree ventured.

"I could let the *honorable* Duke of Blackthorne meet his death and shed not a tear," Creigh said, his eyes ice on the sea. "But he sired me, for what little that is worth. Even in my hate, I cannot leave my own father to die."

Brianna watched, quiet, seeing beneath the coldness in Creigh's face the warring of a world of hurt and pain. 'Twas as if, behind the bold, arrogant features of the cavalier, yet lurked those of the child he had been, confused, tortured with loyalties, longings he did not understand. Needing desperately the love of the father Creigh claimed he hated.

"Your mother . . ." Brianna said soothingly. "She must be sick with worry. No doubt she'll be in ecstasies when you all arrive safely home."

"She'll most like invite half of France to a celebration ball." Creigh shoved himself upright amongst the pillows, the lines of anguish in his face softening. "My lady mother . . . there is naught more important to her than the safety of those she loves. When I told her the plan Michel and I had concocted to affect the rescue of Lindley and Father, she didn't want me to go—sobbed that she couldn't risk another son in some wild scheme—even if it meant sacrificing those already in danger."

Brianna made a wry face. "I vow, if *I'd* been privy to your scheme, I'd have bolted both you and this Michel in the cellar until you came to your senses."

Creigh chuckled. "The Lady Esmeraude Wakefield is much more subtle than that. She whisked in reinforcements."

"Reinforcements?"

"Aye, of the only type she knew I could not resist. One ebony-eyed, dark-haired imp by the name of Juliet."

Brianna tried to swallow the lump of jealousy clogging her throat. But despite her best efforts she felt her lips snap into a taut line. "And if you could not resist this *Juliet,* Sassenach, why are you here?"

Creigh glanced at Brianna sharply, and 'twas as if she heard her own voice in echo, snipping at him like a shrewish fishwife. She saw his mouth dawn into a grin so triumphant she wanted to cram a cherry tart into his face.

"Juliet, much to my mother's dismay, saw the wisdom of our plan." Creigh grimaced. "Insanity seems to run in our family, and my *sister* got a heaping dose."

"Your *sister!*" Brianna burst out, thunking her fist against the broad chest that now rumbled with laughter. "You . . . you arrogant, incorrigible blackguard! I've been torturing myself for days that she was your cursed lover!"

Brianna struggled but a moment as Creigh tugged her into his chest, burying one large hand in the tumbled fall of her hair. "Ah, Tigress, you are such a joy!" he said, kissing her soundly. "Not one woman in a thousand would admit jealousy thus. But you hurl it out with all your other emotions, honest, free." His voice dropped, softened. "My Tigress, what will I do without you?"

Bree lowered her face into the warm, spice-scented curve of his shoulder, her eyes suddenly stinging with tears. "You'll do what your honor demands of you," she said against his skin. "And you'll best them, Creigh—the tower guards, Cromwell—I know you will."

The arms surrounding her tightened, and she felt a suspicious catching in Creigh's chest.

"Creigh," she began softly. "What—what if . . ." She paused, hating to give voice to her fears. "Your friend, Michel, he's overdue already. What if he never comes?"

"Then I'll to London alone. Even if the only way I can aid Lindley is to bury my own dagger in his heart."

Brianna felt something cold, terrifying clutch at her vitals. She started to speak, but he seemed to sense her fears.

His mouth tipped into a taut smile. "Don't fear, Tigress. Michel Le Ferre is scarce noted about Paris for his reliability. But in all the years of our friendship he has ne'er failed me. I've left word where he can find me in every cranny of this little town. Most like he'll be here soon."

Bree looked into Creigh's eyes. Nodded. "But if—if perchance something has happened, I'll come with you to England." She stopped Creigh's protest with her fingertips. "I'm good with a sword, and—"

She was surprised, warmed to see Creigh's lips widen in a genuine grin. "I've been on the receiving end of your thrusts and parries, milady," he said. "And I know well how you fare at fighting." He kissed her fingertips. His hand banded her wrist gently, drawing her fingers down to his flat belly. "I'd lief have you battling on my side any day, Tigress. But Michel will come. I know it."

He reached up, tracing the willful curve of her chin. "When 'tis over . . . all of it, and a crown again sits on Charles Stuart's head, I'll find you, Bree. And I vow to you, I'll see to it that you and your brother ne're want for anything as long as you live."

Bree buried her face against him, wanting to believe. "Creigh," she choked. "My gallant cavalier." He tipped her face up, kissing her with all the tenderness, longing she knew was in his heart. "I love you, Creigh. Love you . . ." She cried brokenly against his lips.

The sharp rap on the door was like a stake in Brianna's heart. Creigh started to rise, but she tightened her hand on his chest.

"M'lord? M'lady?"

An audible sigh slipped from Brianna's lips at the familiar sound of the innkeeper's voice, and she was surprised to feel Creigh's body sag back into the pillows in what seemed relief.

" 'Tis your dinner, m'lord, readied here on the tray," the voice piped up on the other side of the door. "If you could but undo the latch."

With a surge of joy that she and Creigh yet had but a little time, Brianna scrambled out of bed, sweeping on a lace-embroidered dressing gown Creigh had given her. She jerked the sash tight, hurrying over to open the door.

The small man was nigh doubled over under the weight of a silver tray, its surface all but hidden beneath enough food to satisfy half a regiment. " 'Tis sorry, I am, I be so late," the innkeeper apologized. "But Widow Loughlin's boy arrived home from Drogheda last eve, and he and his comrade have been in the ale room below, keepin' us all at the edge of our benches, a-listenin'."

Brianna watched the man slide the tray onto a beechwood table. "Drogheda," she said, trying to blot out the sounds of the revelry below as hope and fear battled within her. "They were soldiers?"

"Aye, an' looks to be they were the only two who 'scaped with their heads still connected to their bodies. Loughlin, he said—"

Brianna spun around, to where Creigh sat propped on the pillows. "This Loughlin . . . he might know something of the others I fought with. Rogan . . ."

"Rogan?" There was an edge to Creigh's voice.

"Aye. He was a friend, a much-loved friend. He was with Doyle when Danny and I last saw him, but we never found his—"

"Christ! Sweet Christ!" The cry from the hallway made Brianna jump aside, just in time to avoid the door as it crashed into the wall, a blurred figure in a ragged green jerkin bursting through the opening.

A sob of joy tore from her throat as familiar arms swept her up into a crushing embrace, whirling her about as though she weighed no more than a child's rag moppet.

"Bree! Oh Bree! I can scarce believe 'tis you!" The deep voice was gruff with emotion. "Love, I ne'er thought to see you again!" Brianna arched her head back, to peer into the haggard, yet rejoicing countenance of Rogan Niall.

She had but an instant to take in the half-healed scar at his temple, the violet circles of weariness about his eyes, before his mouth crushed down on hers. 'Twas the kiss of life from one she'd thought dead, and she stroked the shaggy russet hair, letting this man who had meant so much to both she and Doyle lose some measure of his pain within her.

But with every shift of his mouth upon hers, Brianna felt the burning of sea-gray eyes, savage upon her back. And when that arctic, aristocratic voice shattered the stunned quiet, she felt a bolt of fear jolt down her spine.

"'Tis a pity I failed to order plate for three, *my love,* but I didn't know you were expecting guests."

Brianna felt Rogan's arms go still about her, his eyes firing with shock. She broke from his grasp, spinning around to face Creigh. He stood, magnificent in fury, the satin breeches he must have drawn on in haste, clinging in rich lines to his powerful thighs.

"C-Creigh . . ."

Any explanation she had meant to make was shattered by Rogan. "Bree, who the devil is—"

"'Tis—'tis Lord Creighton Wakefield," she interrupted hastily. "He . . . I've been helping him to reach passage to England."

"Helping him?" Rogan's eyes swept the rumpled bed, her tumbled hair. "Whoring for him, you mean! Dear God, Bree—" The hurt in Rogan's face tore at her, but the look on Creigh's face wracked her far worse. Ice on steel. Chained torment.

"Rogan, he's an emissary for King Charles," Bree rushed on, heedless of Niall's cutting words, "and—"

"And you'll give the lady fair apologies, sir. Whatever hold you bear on her," Creigh's steely voice broke through her stammerings. "Or I'll divest your tongue of its cutting edge."

She ran the steps to Creigh's side, laying her hand on the iron-hard muscles of his forearm. "'Tis—'tis all right, Creigh. 'Tis but the shock of—"

Brianna stopped midsentence, bone-deep fear flowing icy-hot in her veins. She stared at Rogan's visage, the dark eyes wild with horror, disbelief as he stared into Creigh's face.

"Oh my God," Rogan whispered. "This—this man is no Royalist. He fought for Cromwell—"

"Nay, Rogan, he was but posing as a Roundhead until—"

"*Posing* as a Roundhead? And how many Irishmen did he cut down playing at soldier? One, at least, eh, sirrah?" Niall's gaze tore from Brianna's eyes to Creigh's, then locked again upon Brianna, his face contorting into a hideous mask of pain. "Sweet Christ, Bree . . ." he choked. "You've bedded your brother's murderer."

Chapter Twelve

Murderer?" Brianna gasped. "Rogan, 'tis mad. Creigh would never . . ."

"He murdered Doyle! I saw him drive his sword through . . . Oh God! You let him touch you!" He wheeled on Creigh, one shaking hand grasping the hilt of his sword. "Tell her, you murdering bastard! Tell her!"

"'Tis wearied you are. Distraught. 'Midst the hell of that day there's little chance you might have seen me, let alone held my image these weeks." Bree was surprised at the tinge of understanding in Creigh's tone, the commander, well used to soldiers exhausted in body and mind.

"The well, you lying bastard! 'Twas in a deserted lane, you murdered Doyle, by an old well. There were three of us, and your troops poured in and . . . Tell her! Tell—"

"A well?" Creigh's brow creased in a puzzled frown. "'Twas madness that day, but I vow I recall no . . ." His voice trailed off, the expression of confusion shifting to wariness, disbelief, and then to wrenching horror. A tremor wracked Creigh's body, and Brianna felt it, saw his fist knot, bloodless in the air. She dragged her gaze to his face—the face she had kissed, caressed, loved with every ounce of her being—and she felt excruciatingly ill.

"Tigress." His eyes locked with hers and in them she saw a reflection of her own hideous anguish. "Tigress, I—"

"Nay!" Huge talons ripped into Brianna's chest, crushing her. She tore away from him, bile choking her, a horror greater than any she'd ever known rending her very soul. "You—you killed him? Doyle . . ."

161

"Bree, I had no way of knowing." Creigh grabbed her arms. Her eyes, so tortured, shattered, pierced like a pike in his belly. "There were soldiers everywhere. Bree, listen to me . . ."

"Take your hands off of me, you murderer! Murderer!"

The deadly rasp of steel rang through the room, mingled with the innkeeper's cry of alarm. Creigh heard the blade hiss toward him, heard the ancient Gaelic battlecry that had struck terror into his troops at Drogheda. He hurled Brianna away from him, diving across the table to grasp the hilt of his own sword as Rogan charged.

Creigh's blade whipped free of his scabbard, arching upward just in time to deflect a blow that would have cleaved his skull. Rogan's blade skidded down, and Creigh felt a knifing pain as the point of the Irishman's sword bit his shoulder. He rolled out of Rogan's path, gaining his feet, his sword battle-ready.

"Nay! Nay, stop!" he heard Brianna shriek, but there was no time to spare her so much as a glance as the Irishman bolted toward him. Half-crazed, the man fought, grief, fury and aye, jealousy, suffusing his arms with nigh inhuman strength. But despite the death that glowed from Rogan's eyes, Creigh could not bring himself to drive his sword home. For in the man's visage he had also seen love for Brianna and her love for this, her brother's friend. And to rob his Tigress of yet another whom she cherished . . .

Creigh gritted his teeth, parrying the man's thrusts with arms that ached, watching, praying for an opening that would allow him to knock the weapon from the Irishman's big hands.

He could see Brianna struggling with the innkeeper, fighting to get to her own weapon, and fleetingly he wondered if she battled to halt the fight, or to slit his throat.

Lunging to the right, Creigh drove Rogan's blade down, saving the taut muscles of his silk-clad thigh from the edge of the other man's sword. At that instant Rogan stumbled, his foot snagging on the coverlet that trailed upon the floor. Lightning fast, Creigh's blade flashed out, sparks flying from grating steel as he pinned the sword to the floor. His knee slammed down on the flat of Rogan's blade. He heard the innkeeper cry out some warning, voice reed-thin, desperate.

But the words were lost in the horrible crack, as Rogan's sword snapped beneath Creigh's weight, clattering to the floor in two pieces.

There was a heartbeat of silence, broken by the sound of rushing feet in the corridor outside. And then there was laughter—demonic, familiar—icing Creigh's blood.

He wheeled, gripping his sword hilt in fingers gone numb. Framed by a terrifying backdrop of scarlet uniforms, Brianna stared at him, eyes glazed with the mindless terror of a savaged fawn, her hair yanked back by a meaty fist, exposing the slender column of her throat below. Horror, fear, helplessness swept through Creigh in a paralyzing wave as his gaze jerked upward, to the leering face, slack above Brianna's shoulder. Evil, triumphant, Saul Ogden sneered, his dagger pressed tight against Brianna's throat.

Creigh sensed Rogan tensing to spring, caught the Irishman with one hard hand. "Nay! They'll kill her."

"Astute, Creighton, my lad," Ogden gloated. "Most astute. But then you were always passing wise. And considerate. Aye, 'twas most considerate of you to spread the news of your whereabouts through the town."

Creigh cursed himself, cursed the folly that had lead him to thrust both himself and Brianna into such danger.

"Drop the sword, my traitorous lord," Ogden demanded, his lips widening in a predatory leer. "That is, if you care aught for your peasant whore's life."

Creigh gripped the hilt of his sword, rage ripping through him.

"Hurt her and I'll kill you, Ogden. I swear it, if 'tis with my dying breath."

"You'll do naught but kiss the headsman's blade, aristocrat scum!" Ogden hissed. "And your doxy, here, will share your traitor's bed. Drop the sword."

"Nay, Creigh, don't! The window . . . Break for the window!" Brianna's voice, desperate, thin with terror, lanced him more deeply than any sword could have, the sight of those eyes that had enchanted him with their courage, wounded, now, all but broken, filling him with killing fury. Creigh's jaw tightened, steel-hard, his fingers taut with the need to tear Ogden's defiling hands from Bree's delicate shoulders. Creigh glanced at the window to his back, open, promising freedom. Then he turned, eyes locking with the unchained evil in Ogden's gaze. Creigh's fingers loosened, the silence shattered by the falling of his sword.

The ship reeked of pitch and tar, the filth-stained planks of the hold, far beneath the waterline, closing in around Brianna until she felt as if she were imprisoned in the belly of some hideous beast. A beast conjured of nightmare, of her own tortured guilt.

Eyes gritty with exhaustion, wide with barely leashed fear, darted about the dank cell Ogden had shoved them into hours ago, the rolling of the sea as the ship cleaved the waves painting the shadowy walls in shapes of dragons, harpies, ancient Druid gods. Bree tore her eyes from the shadow demons, her gaze sweeping past the sleeping form of Rogan to lock upon Creigh's silhouette, blade-straight, wire-taut against a timber, despite the heavy chains that manacled his wrists and ankles.

In all the time since Ogden and his minions had barred the heavy trap door, imprisoning them, Creigh had not spoken. He had but stared straight ahead, silent, regal as a captive king. Why, then, could she sense his pain?

She wanted to hate him. Hurt him. Break the strength and pride bred in him through centuries of men born to rule. Wanted to shriek at him for hurling himself into the hands of an enemy when he might have escaped to fight another day. Aye, and she wanted to run to him, bury her face in his chest, seek sanctuary in the arms that had robbed Doyle of life.

She huddled into the filthy straw, the meager warmth of the green satin gown doing little to fend off the dampness that seeped into her very bones. 'Twas cruel, malicious, the destiny that had thrown them both into war. More cruel, still, that in a city full of death and destruction fate had cast Doyle and Creigh at the points of each other's swords. Faceless enemies, they had been, both battling for their lives 'midst a scene straight from hell. And one had had to die.

Brianna's fingers dug into the rushes strewn across the floor as she battled to banish the images that tormented her—Roundheads, blood-red in their casaques, silver weapons gleaming death, pouring through Drogheda's shattered walls. Doyle, beside the well, desperately trying to shield her and Daniel. She could feel Creigh's sword cut deep, hear Doyle's scream of agony. And yet, the thought of Creigh cut down by the griffin-head blade lanced through Bree as savagely as the image of her brother's death.

And she hated herself, because even now, if she were given the power to touch life to but one of the two men she loved, she knew not which one she would choose.

She closed her eyes, feeling hot tears burn beneath her lashes, and she wept, silently for Doyle's life, full of promise unrealized, and for Creigh, whose broad shoulders bore her loathing and her pain. Not once had he tried to defend himself, force her, a warrior, to face the hard truth that if he had not bested Doyle, his own life would have been forfeit.

A sob caught in her throat, and she raised her eyes to that arrogant face, carved now in pain. She could feel him strain toward her, then ruthlessly hold himself back, leashing the love he was certain she'd reject. Only the mist-gray of his eyes reached out to her, and the sorrow she saw within them burst the shell of agony within her, hurling the shards of hate, blame, and guilt from her breast.

"Creigh," she choked, raising trembling arms. "Creigh, please . . ."

Chains crashed across the floor, tearing at the rotted planking, the stinking green slime, as he flung himself toward her. She felt the cut of steel links upon her arm, breast, the tangling of her hair on the rough iron banding his wrists. But she knew no pain, only the strength of his body, beneath its covering of satin, only the rasp of his breath against her throat.

"Tigress," he said. "Forgive me, I—"

"'Tis naught—naught to forgive. There was nothing you could have done."

"I could have found a way to but wound him. From the time we broke through the walls I killed not a man. I wounded, aye, but only that, used my sword only enough to keep my own soul in my body. But at the well . . . Doyle warred like a madman. I tried to take his sword, knock him senseless with the flat of my blade, but he kept coming . . . coming. I was wheeling about, aiming for the hilt of his sword when he charged. I tried to leap out of the way, but 'twas too late. My blade . . . it caught him, and . . . Oh God, Tigress, I'm sorry."

Brianna lifted shaking fingers to his face, her fingertips gathering up the wetness of tears, and it humbled her, filled her with wonder, that this man, so strong, proud, could weep for her sorrows. "Doyle . . . Doyle would have loved you, had he known you," she said brokenly. "Oh, Creigh. Creigh . . ." She buried her face in the rosewood waves of his hair, clutching him close to her heart.

The tears came, then, cleansing her mind and her spirit, washing away guilt, grief. And when at last she lifted her face to Creigh's haggard countenance, she knew that if she lived a thousand years, there would be naught for her in life except this man, this moment, and a love so overwhelming, 'twas the essence of her very being.

A crash on the deck above made Brianna go rigid, the hated, mindless fear inspired by the Englishman that held them captive stealing through her veins. She felt Creigh's arms tighten about her, the chains binding him cutting deep into her flesh. "I won't let them hurt you, Tigress," he said. "I swear it."

He caught her chin in hands sticky with blood from the iron slicing his wrists, and she knew he saw the terror in her eyes. "Michel will come, Bree," he said fiercely. "By the time we reach England, he'll have sailed out of Carikbrah. And Ogden and his curs will be lucky to make the mouth of the Thames before the *Valiant Hope* catches them."

Bree tried to quell the doubts that raged in her mind, tried to banish the questions that screamed inside her. *Michel will come,* Creigh said. But what if this Michel lay dead on some highroad? What if he had been trapped between the crushing lines of Cromwell's armies?

She shuddered, the shadows on the walls shifting into malicious, slavering lips, a beefy hand clutching the hilt of a dagger. Cutting . . . cutting . . .

Her fingers dug deep into the hard muscles 'neath the silk of Creigh's warm skin, feeling the life in him, the strength.

A traitor's death, Ogden had vowed awaited them both: the fall of an axe cleaving Creigh's throat, the blood-crazed screams of a crowd of rabble as they lifted his severed head high.

Brianna's hands knotted in the cloth of his doublet. "Michel will come," she said fiercely. "He must." But even as she spoke, the groaning of the ship seemed to whisper secrets at the banshee's cold bidding.

The torch ripped a hole, jagged edged in the darkness, illuminating the trapdoor like the gateway to hell. Instinctively, Creigh drew Brianna closer, his mind, groggy from the endless days in the dank hold, snapping alert as his eyes were assaulted by the glaring light.

In the far corner he heard the sullen Rogan shifting upright, staring, no doubt at the opening above them. And in his arms he felt Brianna's sleep-lax body tense. But his gaze never left the face that peered down at them, painted in flame. Creigh had expected to see that face long since and had rejoiced when the boatswain that hurled them moldy bread once a day had divulged that the colonel was taken with a bout of the grippe.

But now, staring at Ogden's malicious eyes, Creigh sensed that the hours of reprieve would cost them double the Roundhead's ire now.

"My Lord Creighton," he sneered, "I regret to inform you that your time as the guest of the *Martyr's Glory* is nigh through. By morn you'll be arriving at your new quarters in London, so the crew and I wanted to make this last night aboard ship a most memorable one for you and your *esteemed* companions."

A rope ladder slithered down from the hole, snaking into the slime-coated rushes below. Creigh felt Brianna stiffen, her flesh clammy as Ogden continued. "'Tis most unfortunate I was incapacitated whilst you were here. Lord Cromwell gave strictest instructions that you were to be treated as befitted your rank. But alas, 'twas little I could do, lying at death's door, as I was. But now I vow to see you well tended."

"You needn't trouble yourself, Ogden," Creigh said. "We've been casting at dice most of the night, and were just after taking a nap."

The ropes of the ladder groaned beneath Ogden's bulk as he lowered himself through the portal. "A nap, my fine lord, or one of the bacchanalian rites you aristocrats take such delight in?" he snarled, reaching up to take the torch from a sailor's hand. "Mayhap you and the Irish brute were planning to share the wench? Wrap her in your chains . . ."

Rage tore through Creigh—raw, piercing, but he bit back the fury, knowing that to rise to Ogden's baiting, reveal how much Brianna meant to him, would be like dangling a wounded lamb before a jackal. He shifted his body with feigned boredom, the movement shielding Brianna from the Roundhead's gaze.

Creigh forced a lazy smile, his eyes tracking the bobbing of the torch as the Roundhead negotiated the ladder. "Ogden, only lowlings like you need to chain your doxies," he drawled. "If Rogan over there has a taste for the girl, he's welcome to her, but I favor my conquests a bit cleaner than this wench, and my sheetings a deal less populated with vermin."

Ogden's boots thumped onto the floor, the rope snapping free of his hands. He turned, jamming the torch into an iron ring. "Oh, aye, Wakefield, no doubt you pissed in satin privies at court, but things will be a world different now. In the Tower you can scream for eternity, and no one will hear but the rats."

"Even the rats will be better company than you offer at present," Creigh taunted with a yawn.

Ogden's face bulged in the torchlight, and Creigh was stunned to see the depth of hate that blazed in the man's slits of eyes. Creigh saw the blow coming, the crack of Ogden's meaty fist against his jaw spiking pain through his skull. His head snapped back, and he heard Brianna's strangled scream. But he didn't even raise his fists in defense, merely leveled narrowed eyes on the Roundhead, the chill of generations of nobles icing his gaze.

"Smirk, you filthy Wakefield bastard!" Ogden growled. "Trample any less highborn than you into the dung at your feet. But 'tis over for you and your family. Over. 'Tis time that you pay."

"Pay for what? For being fair stewards to our lands? For treating our kerns justly when others were cruel?"

"Justly?" Ogden jeered. "I but hope God treats you with the same mercy you claim. The same mercy shown—" The man spun around, and an odd feeling stirred in Creigh's stomach, as though he had been flung onto a stage at Drury Lane midst a performance half-gone.

His eyes narrowed, wary. "I've no intention of flinging myself upon the mercy of God any time soon, Colonel Ogden," he said. "But I assure you, when that time comes, I'll answer without fear for whatever sins I might have committed."

Ogden jerked the torch out of its holder, cold laughter upon his lips. "Oh, aye. 'Tis against your high-flung code of honor to show fear if the devil himself is at your door, is it not, my Lord Creighton? 'Twill be a pleasure, indeed, to see how long your cavalier's courage can hold once we reach the Tower's . . . er—entertainments."

Creigh felt Brianna tremble against him, tasted her terror like a tangible thing. He forced his lips into a half smile of dismissal. "I fear I'll have to disappoint you, colonel. By the time you reach London, you'll wax fortunate to keep your own neck from the torturer's grasp."

"How so?"

"For allowing three more valuable prisoners to slip from your fingers. No doubt Cromwell is still fuming at the escape of Le Marquis de Charteaux. And when Le Ferre snatches us from your grasp . . ." Creigh shrugged.

"Le Marquis." Ogden spat the name.

"Is most like closing upon this disgrace you call a ship even as we speak," Creigh said, leaning negligently upon one elbow. His hand stole surreptitiously to lay upon Brianna's icy knee, his fingers tightening in comfort. "Tell me, Ogden, how 'twill feel to have that dull mind of yours again outwitted by your betters?"

Creigh saw Ogden's fist clench, steeled himself for another blow. But the Roundhead's fist hung in the air, frozen long seconds before it dropped to the man's beefy side. Then Ogden laughed, just laughed, a hideous cold sound.

Creigh felt Brianna tremble behind him, felt an icy lump of dread form in his belly. The Roundhead thrust the torch up, into the waiting hands of one of his cohorts, the light dancing over a leer reeking of triumph.

The rope ladder strained beneath Ogden's weight as he pulled himself up the worn rungs. He was gone but a minute, the gaping hole spilling fiendish light into the hold.

169

Creigh heard the clumping of something heavy being dragged across the floor, heard it scrape the edge of the opening.

Then Ogden's face was framed in fire. "A gift, my Lord Creighton," he jeered, "from Lord Lieutenant Cromwell."

Creigh saw Ogden's hand grip the edges of a stained cloth sack, his other fingers ripping free the cord that bound it.

He heard Brianna shriek, Rogan gasp as the sack's contents plunged through the air, striking Creigh's thigh.

A terrible cry tore at Creigh's chest, trapped there by a horror that chained his very soul. He hurled the rotting, bloodcaked object from him, his stomach heaving at the sight of tangled blonde hair, once-handsome features bloated in death.

The severed head rolled across the rushes, flashing vacant eyes that had snapped with life, sparkled with amusement at Juliet's witty quips.

"Michel!" The name ripped deep within him, horrible, clawing. "Ogden, you bastard! You—" Molten fury surged through him, consuming him. He bolted to his feet, even the encumbrance of the chains doing little to check him as he clawed up the still-dangling ladder.

He lunged through the trapdoor, dodging a burly sailor as he hurled himself at Ogden. Fists locked together, Creigh swung the heavy chains like a knight's mace, the arching path of the iron links a deadly weapon. Ogden stumbled back, groping for the sword at his belt, but the shackles cracked into his face with a force that split skin, shattered cartilage, driving him back into a pile of cast-off weapons.

Ogden screamed with pain, the sight of his bloodied face filling Creigh with death-lust. Crazed with fury, grief, he smashed the chains down on the sprawled Roundhead, swung them, vicious at the sailors closing around him. He heard someone scramble up from the hold, heard Brianna cry out.

A sudden jolt of fear shot through him, mingling with the fury that had driven him past bearing. He glimpsed her running toward him, caught a flash of russet that was Rogan Niall breaking through the trapdoor behind her. There was a sickening sound of heavy boot connecting with Rogan's chest, a thud as he crashed down into the hold. Then a snarled laugh as a thickset sailor dove for Brianna. Creigh threw himself at the sailor, blind with rage, but before he could reach them, a babe-faced boatswain charged between them. With a scream of fury, Creigh tried to battle his way past the man, chains slashing, chest torn with anguish.

Out of the corner of his eye he caught the flash of something thick, dark hurtling down at him. He tried to lunge out of its path, but the chains caught on a rusted pike. He pitched forward, splintered wood scraping his jaw, chest. Agony exploded at the back of his head as something heavy struck flesh. Creigh rolled, instinct driving him to try to gain his feet. But the chains tangled about his ankles, trapping him, leaving him captive. The face of a rum-drunk sailor floated before him in a haze of pain, blotting out Brianna's tortured face. Creigh focused on the seaman's fist clamped about the handle of a huge cudgel.

There was a clatter of metal crashing together, a garbled, satanic voice. "Th' 'stick . . . gi' me the 'stick."

Creigh kicked desperately at the chains, as he saw Ogden's savage, bloody face above him, nose crushed, his jowl layed open by the shackles.

Doubling his fists, Creigh fought to drive them into the Roundhead's thigh, but two burly sailors grasped his wrists, crushing them to the deck.

"Kill y' . . . I'll kill y' bloody Wa'field ba'thtard."

Creigh heard Brianna scream, the sound of her terror echoing through the darkness. He battled the arms imprisoning him, battled the torment engulfing him as the cudgel crashed into his body. And then there was pain, naught but pain as Ogden drove the cudgel into his flesh.

He tried not to cry out, grinding his teeth until he tasted his own blood. But the pain tore at him like a wolf's fangs, rending his flesh. The filthy walls of the ship spun about him in macabre patterns, the torch at their apex.

The cudgel cracked into his skull, and the torch burst. Creigh screamed as the orange light exploded into a million glowing candles, bleeding silver. He shut his eyes, praying for oblivion, but even as unconsciousness warred to claim him, his tortured mind spun onward. It swept him relentlessly down to the center of the flame, searing his soul with the image of Juliet, her face bright with love, and Michel Le Ferre's vacant, death-glazed eyes.

Chapter Thirteen

Screams of agony, silenced centuries past, seemed to cling to the steel-gray waves of the Thames river, specters borne of mist clawing at the wooden sides of the wherry as it glided toward Traitor's Gate. Brianna shivered, cradling the yet unconscious Creigh closer against her as the grasping shadows of London's dread Tower captured the tiny boat in chill fingers, dragging it inexorably toward the huge iron-barred gate that had proved gateway to death for so many.

Doyle had oft spun tales of this daunting fortress, of Henry's Anne Boleyn falling 'neath a sword from Calais, and of her daughter, bold Elizabeth, who as a captive princess had sat upon the stones, refusing to enter the walls by the gate reserved for traitors to the crown. Yet amongst these exalted personages, hundreds of others had been swept by the tides of war, treason, and conspiracy through the great stone watergate below St. Thomas's Tower, and 'twas these, time's faceless victims, who cried out to Brianna now. For soon she, and the man she loved, would be one with them.

Her fingers tightened, drawing the sodden folds of her skirts about Creigh's broad shoulders in an attempt to shield him from the driving rain. Despite the weals that cut in angry violet slashes across his face and body, his features held a regal arrogance that defied the fortress before them, and challenged the commoners who had snatched up the power of the realm. Yet the Tower had betrayed before men of great courage, caring naught whose blood lay spilt upon its hill.

Bree glanced at Rogan, shrouded in shadow, his face etched with the silent expression of betrayal that had ne'er left his features since he had lost his sword in Carikbrah. He, too, would die, entrapped in events he knew naught of, cared naught about. He would die because he had borne the misfortune of loving her . . . and finding her.

She swallowed, her eyes burning with tears she refused to shed as she remembered Rogan's joy when he had burst into the inn room, sweeping her into his arms, kissing her. He had been alive with rejoicing, that part of him bitter from years of battling his father's misdeeds melting 'neath the light of the love Brianna could not return. It had been blow enough to find her in love with another, but for her to lie with the man who had murdered her own brother—Rogan's most cherished friend . . . Aye, and for her to dare love him yet, even knowing . . .

Bree's trembling fingers reached up to smooth away the rain-soaked waves of Creigh's hair, gently brushing the curling strands from an angry cut that arced across his brow.

Her throat constricted, and she glared at Rogan's sullen profile, silhouetted against the Tower's cold stone, then at the wherry's shadows dripping off of Saul Ogden's bulk far at the prow of the craft. Aye, she would battle them all to spare Creighton Wakefield one second's pain—battle this crucible of terror with its legacies in blood.

Creigh groaned, the thick rain-dewed lashes stirring on cheeks the color of ash. Bree bent low, praying for some sign that he was regaining his senses, but the blackened lids merely stilled again, the ragged breath catching in his chest. "Creigh," she prodded gently. "Creigh, love . . ."

She started at Rogan's snort of disgust, his eyes scornful as they raked her from the far end of the bench opposite her. "Mayhap you should give the murdering bastard a sugar teat and dry his cursed feet with your hair," he said under his breath.

"If my hair were dry enough to gain him comfort, I would cut it off to wrap around him," Brianna flung back.

"Aye, just as you cut off your feelings for Doyle? He gave his life to keep that blackguard you pillow in your lap from killing you and Daniel. *His life,* Bree. If Doyle were here he'd—"

"Don't dare to tell me what Doyle would do, what he'd

173

feel. Doyle hated war, wanted only to tend his fields and raise a cottage full of babes. If he had known Creigh—"

"But he ne'er will, will he, Bree, because Doyle died on the point of your cursed lord's blade. 'Od's blood, I—"

The guffaw of one of Ogden's guards cut off Rogan's words, and the foul colonel craned his thick neck back to jeer at the chained prisoners. "Jealous of his lordship's sword, Irish?" he taunted Rogan. "'Tis not blaming you I am, what with the pleasure the aristocrat scum must have taken tossing the wench about upon his staff."

"Damn you! Say a word about her and—" Rogan cursed savagely, lunging halfway from his seat before the chains that bound him caught in their anchoring iron ring. The force jerked him back hard against the wood bench, his shoulder striking the wherry's side. The boatswain chortled.

"'Tis well ye made 't leash the three o' 'em, Colonel Ogden, sar," he said. "They be like rabid curs, these Irish, wi' no common decency 'mong civ'lized folk. An' Lord Creighton—" the man barked a laugh. "'Twas passin' 'musing to see 'im brawl in the muck like the rest o' us poor sots, there aboard the *Martyr*."

Brianna's gaze shifted from the sailor, his grime-coated body reeking of ale, to Rogan—Rogan with his temper, and the inner wounds that ne'er healed. And despite his loathing of her, and the cruel words he hurled like Romany daggers, she felt the urge to ease his pain.

She reached a hand out, resting her fingertips, moth-light upon his shoulder. He flinched, as if she had dealt him a blow, but didn't knock her hand away. "Rogan," she said, her eyes boring into his stubborn-set jaw, willing him to look at her. "I love him."

The familiar, craggy features twisted, pained.

"'Tis naught you can do to change that," she said. "Naught anyone can do. But know that you lie in my heart, with Daniel, and Shane . . . and Doyle."

"Oh, aye. I lay with your brothers whilst Wakefield lies in your bed?"

She stiffened, her arms tightening instinctively about Creigh's shoulders. Her gaze dropped down to his mist-blurred features. "Aye. For as long as the fates allow it."

"Well, Brianna Devlin, the fates will allow you and your Sassenach lover precious little in the Tower's dungeons."

174

Brianna felt a chill creep down her spine, her eyes shifting to the looming walls.

"'Tis amazing they even allow us to travel upon the same boat as a high and holy English lord," Rogan snarled. "Think you they'll let the two of you set up housekeeping in some cozy little quarter? Most like they'll ensconce your Wakefield in a tapestry-lined apartment 'til his death-day, and Ogden will thrust the two of us into some rat hole gnawed 'neath the walls."

"Oh, aye. Ogden has shown already what high regard he has for Creigh's peerage," Brianna snapped. "He nigh cudgeled him to death."

"'Twould have saved the headsman his labors."

The words were bitter, cutting, and they drove deep into Brianna's terror. Her hand flashed out, unbidden, her open palm cracking hard into Rogan's cheek.

Rogan's hand snapped back as though he would strike her, but his fingers froze, midair, the force of his glare boring into her as the imprint of her hand reddened his skin. She thrust her chin out at him, defiant, furious, an odd feeling of loss assailing her. "Blast it, Rogan, I—"

The sound of grating iron, of water breaking over stone cut off her words. Their eyes leapt to the prow of the wherry. The bars of the huge gates slashed shadows across the boat, the great stone archway seeming to gape like a dragon's mouth, drawing the fragile craft into jaws of death. Brianna gritted her teeth, battling the nigh mindless fear that tore at her as the wherry was swallowed up by the stone, and she stared into the face of the horror that had broken so many before her.

Even the waters of the great river Thames were captive here. The waves that had tossed about the wherry outside the stone arch lay trapped, broken between the huge gate, and the inner walls of the fortress, while stone steps rose from the dark river's surface, leading those destined for the Tower's dark dungeons upward toward their living tombs.

Brianna trembled, felt Rogan's hand close over hers.

"Well, milady harlot, what think you of your new brothel?" Ogden's voice, grating, sadistic, swept away any comfort she had been able to draw from Rogan's strong fingers. Against her will, she raised her eyes to the Roundhead's

175

paunchy face, and was captured by a gaze glowing red as a dungeon rat's.

She struggled desperately not to reveal the true depth of the terror he inspired—this monster of a man who had so brutalized her, yet remembered her no more than a cruel lad would remember a fawn he had tortured.

"'Tis not . . . not half so fearful as you Sassenachs would have the world believe," Brianna forced herself to say, wresting her gaze from the clutch of those evil, evil eyes.

"Others more wise would argue with you, sweeting." Ogden heaved his legs over the wherry seat, and Brianna could feel him, hear him move toward her. "But then, you've yet to see the Tower's darker treasures."

As if on some silent command the boatswain caught Rogan's chains in his fist, just as Ogden's thick fingers reached toward her.

A scream welled in Brianna's throat, but terror silenced it in a grip so savage she could not move. Ne'er in her life had she faced aught with the crazed, childlike fear she knew as Ogden's flesh touched hers. She wanted to flee, scream, retreat into the darkness of madness, anything to escape the terror that engulfed her as Ogden's cold fingers slithered down the curve of her throat.

"Methinks, milady, that you know more fear than you admit," the Roundhead purred. "We must make certain you are made to acknowledge the demons inside you."

The small boat jarred against the stone steps, the aged wood scraping against the corner. Ogden ostensibly fought to regain his balance. His hand slipped low, his weight falling upon his hand as it grasped Brianna's breast in a cruel, twisting grip. Tears of pain stung Brianna's eyes, and she sank her teeth into her lip, battling her own scream. Ogden's face contorted in sadistic pleasure.

Then suddenly, the hand was yanked away, and Brianna saw surprise flash across Ogden's bloated features as he was jerked upright. All eyes in the boat leapt up to the stone landing, now obscured by six shadowy figures illuminated by a guttering flambeau, but their gaze was captured by the slender form of a young man at arms, the torchlight dancing off his oddly childlike features as he withdrew his hands from Ogden's beefy shoulders. Brianna heard the Round-head snarl, wheel in fury upon the lad who seemed scarce strong enough to have moved the colonel's great bulk at all, let alone withstand his wrath.

But the young soldier leveled eyes empty of fear at Ogden's rage-flushed face. "Colonel, sir, did you injure yourself?" he asked with a solicitousness betrayed only by the tightness about his finely cut mouth.

"Injure myself?" Ogden bellowed, clambering over the wherry's side to the slippery stone. "You nigh knocked me from the boat, you bloody fool!"

"A thousand pardons. I meant but to aid you, sir. 'Tis oft times rough to land here at the Gate, lest you have a wherryman skilled at his trade, and when I saw you start to . . . fall . . ."

Just the slightest hesitation in the man at arms's words made Brianna's eyes lock upon his face, and she sensed he knew Ogden's stumbling had been but a ruse to gain his cruel twisting of her breast. Fine, dark hair clung to a brow hinting at intelligence, framed a mouth sensitive despite the firmness the young soldier tried to school into it, while his eyes lay empty with a disillusionment at odds with the lad's childlike face.

She heard Ogden's breath hiss through his teeth, saw his ferretlike eyes dart up to the features lit by the struggling flame of the torch.

His gaze feasted greedily for a moment upon the young corporal's features, a sly grin snaking across his mouth. "Dunley," he muttered, eyes glittering with malicious pleasure. "Jules Dunley."

"Aye, colonel, sir," the young man answered. "Now if you'll allow my men and I to tend to the prisoners."

Brianna watched Ogden and the man called Dunley, sensing the silent challenging, vying for power between them that had naught to do with military rank.

Ogden chortled, a look of nigh ghoulish anticipation upon his features as he turned to the boatswain, tossing the enormous sailor a ring of iron keys. "Free their chains from the anchoring, Pickney," Ogden commanded. "Then you—you bear the prisoner yet senseless."

Brianna stared at Ogden, confusion and a creeping sensation of unease stealing over her as the Roundhead shifted to block the young corporal's view of the wherry. The chink of the locks being freed echoed through the stone enclosure, a

177

mocking, taunting sound, heralding naught but a captivity more dangerous than the one they were escaping.

Bree clung to Creigh's inert form as long as she could, wanting desperately to fight the boatswain as the jeering Pickney jammed his beefy arms between her and Creigh, jerking the unconscious lord out of her grasp. She stifled a cry, her own shackles slicing deep into her wrists as she tried to catch at Creigh, steady him when the sailor heaved him, facedown, onto one massive shoulder. Creigh's head snapped back, a groan tearing from his white lips as the hard curve of Pickney's shoulder drove into his battered stomach.

"Least he be not dead, Colonel Ogden, sar." The boatswain cackled and turned to Ogden. *"Yet."*

The sailor swung one thick leg over the side of the boat, gaining the landing with as much ease as if he bore naught heavier than the sea wind upon his back. One of Dunley's men extended a hand to aid Brianna in disembarking, but she scarce touched it. Rogan caught her elbow as she stumbled onto stone steps, her own hand reaching out to capture Creigh's limp one.

The boatswain glanced behind him, jerking Creigh away from her savagely. "Ye'll have t' wait 'til th' corporal, 'ere, 'scounces ye an' yer lover in yer cell, afore ye start playin' catchskirt, wench."

Despite the harsh words that had passed between them, Brianna felt Rogan's chain-bound arm tightened about her shoulders, in a gesture of fierce protection as Dunley's men closed ranks behind them, the spindly private bearing the torch leading the way up the rain-slickened stairs.

"You see how it is with harlots, Pickney?" Ogden said. "They but get one man free of their skirts, and they're grasping after another, eh, Corporal Dunley?"

The young soldier turned, and his eyes were gentle upon Brianna. "I know little of the fairer sex, but the lady scarce seems a lightskirt."

"Ever the gallant," Ogden sneered. "Aye, and the hero, as well. 'Twas the talk of Cromwell's camp—your courage during the sack of Drogheda, Corporal Dunley," Ogden sneered, casting a careless glance back at his charges as he started up the stone steps. "I vow 'twas a stroke of genius,

178

putting St. Peter's church to the flame. Nigh all the surviving Royalist garrison burned alive."

Brianna saw the man Ogden called Jules Dunley pale, his hand gripping the hilt of the sword at his side.

"'Twas not by my orders they died. I but followed command."

"Aye and ridded the city of yet another nest of traitorous vermin, eh, *corporal?* 'Tis no wonder Cromwell rewarded you with such a luxurious appointment as the Tower. After all, 'tis not every man who can stomach putting torch to human flesh, even if that flesh be fatted Royalist scum."

Brianna saw Dunley's gaze falter, his features taut with an inner anguish that made him seem suddenly unbearably old. Ogden's jagged-toothed leer closed in upon the flashings of emotion like a blooded wolf. "Is it true, *Corporal* Dunley, that you held a shield of women and children before you to gain entry to the church? 'Twas brilliant, sure, knowing the brainless Irish would ne'er fire upon their own loved ones."

Brianna's stomach churned at the image Ogden's words conjured, Rogan's oath choked as though he were suddenly, deathly ill. Dunley glared at Ogden, hate and anguish melding the lad's face into a mask of torment.

"Answer me, corporal," Ogden demanded. "Did you not best the Royalist bastards by hiding behind children?"

"I followed orders," Dunley said in a low voice. *"Orders,* Colonel Ogden, sir."

A cunning smile slipped over the Roundhead's lips. "Orders from your beloved commander?" he purred. "The right *honorable* Colonel Lord Wakefield?"

Brianna's gaze leapt to the young corporal's face, shock bolting through her at the mention of Creigh's name. She saw Dunley's face pale, a fleeting expression of pain and, aye, defiance flashing across his features. He stopped at the crest of the stairway, turned. "Colonel Ogden, sir, with all due respect, 'tis pouring down rain. No doubt you are hungry for the comforts of a fire, and—"

"The question, you cowardly witling!" Ogden roared, his meaty fist knotting in the folds of Dunley's mantle. Brianna saw the men behind Dunley bristle, felt their umbrage at the colonel's treatment of their superior. But Ogden took no note of their glowering faces. "Corporal Dunley, did you or did you not storm St. Peter's under the command of Colonel Lord Wakefield?"

"Nay," Dunley burst out. "He . . . 'Midst the battle I got separated from him and joined with the men of—"

"You got separated from him? Or did your exalted Colonel Lord Wakefield flee like the traitor he was?"

"Colonel Lord Wakefield was no traitor!"

Ogden's laughter filled the echoing cavern of stone.

Brianna stifled a cry as Ogden yanked free the chains binding Creigh, his hand knotting in the rosewood waves of his hair. "Allow me the pleasure of reuniting you with your beloved commander, Corporal Dunley," the colonel chortled.

Brianna broke away from the guard that fought to hold her, tried to stop Ogden, hold Creigh yet upon the boatswain's shoulder, but she was no match for the colonel's strength. Ogden's fist yanked back. Bree threw herself beneath Creigh, fighting to break the force of his fall, yet despite her efforts the foul colonel's hand sent Creigh's unconscious body cracking into the worn stone.

A groan of pain issued from Creigh's mouth as he sprawled at Dunley's feet. Brianna fought to clutch Creigh to her, a sob tearing from her throat, but before she could right herself, the young officer was kneeling beside him, a strange, haunted look stealing across his features as he stared into Creigh's brutalized face.

"There'll be no armorers to beg excuses from this time, boy." Ogden's smirk iced through Brianna, his face twisted as with some private jest. "The lord lieutenant 'tends to make it clear to the rest of the Royalist scum that England now lies in the hands of the godly."

"The *godly?*" Dunley cried, his face gray, tormented.

"Aye, good *corporal*. After all, 'tis *heroic deeds* the like of your own against Satan's vassals that have laid England in the palm of God's hand."

"I much doubt God would want it." The corporal's gaze flashed from Brianna to the bruised countenance of Creigh, and the boyish mouth hardened. "You've served your duty, Colonel Ogden," he said. "The prisoners are now in my charge."

"Oh, I beg to differ," the Roundhead challenged. He reached beneath this cloak, withdrawing a roll of paper.

"You see, 'tis most important to Cromwell, this disposing of one of Charles's more—er—enterprising supporters. I have volunteered to take quarters here in the Tower walls until Lord Creighton's head adorns London Bridge alongside that of his coconspirator, the traitorous Marquis de Charteaux."

Bile choked Brianna's throat, the grisly image of Michel Le Ferre's blood-encrusted curls shifting in her mind to the darker thick waves of Creigh's hair.

Dunley snatched the yellowed paper from Ogden's hand, his eyes scanning the rain-dappled page. Bree could see that he meant to protest, could sense in the young soldier a temptation to toss the ink-scrawled paper into the Thames flowing below them.

But at that moment the mists disclosed a man striding toward them, his somber raiment like that of one garbed for dying.

Face dour with command, the man swept the yellowed page from Dunley's fist, and his acrimonious features furrowed in approval. "Colonel Ogden, so you grace us yet again with vanquished enemies of Christ," the raspy voice intoned. "'Tis our pleasure to welcome the great Cromwell's emissary. The Tower and all its staff are at your disposal."

The triumph upon Ogden's pockmarked face filled Brianna with searing dread, as the colonel's tiny eyes, seething with hatred, shifted to Creigh.

"Sir," Dunley got to his feet, and Brianna detected a pleading in his voice. "Mayhap the colonel would lief have more comfortable lodgings . . ."

"I assure you, Corporal Dunley, there is nowhere I'd rather lodge at present," Ogden said. "'Twill give me the greatest of pleasure to watch the fierce rod of justice overtake the cursed clan of Wakefield at last."

The dour-faced officer grunted his agreement, his thin lips curling as he cast a disdainful glance at Creigh. "They be a stiff-necked lot, these king-lovers. But we shall break them, shall we not, good colonel?"

One black-clad arm draped in camaraderie about Ogden's shoulders.

"Oh, aye, sir, that we shall," Ogden chuckled.

His gaze traveled tauntingly to a nearby tower. He gave Dunley a smile of promise.

181

"That . . . that tower," Brianna ventured, her voice trembling. "What is it called?"

Dunley's eyes captured hers, their dark depths alive with torment. "'Tis the White Tower," he said quietly.

"The—the White Tower?" A thousand icy claws seemed to tear at Brianna's spine as Dunley tore his gaze away. He lifted Creigh from the rain-swept stones, carrying him gently as a grown child might carry an honored father. Brianna stared after them, scarce feeling the prodding of the guard at her rear.

The White Tower, her mind screamed, her eyes seeming mesmerized by its silhouette against the stormy sky. How oft she had heard Doyle tell of that tower of horror's legend, rich in the cruelest implements of torture the human mind could devise.

She ripped her gaze away from the dread edifice, her eyes sweeping to Creigh's dark head, now pillowed upon the young guard's shoulder. He was the Naisi of legend, Lancelot in chains. Battered as he was, he was yet the most beautiful man she had ever seen.

"Nay," she whispered fiercely, her gaze locking upon the tower's glowing window. "You'll not have him. You'll not." But even as Dunley led his little band deep into one of the other dark buildings, Brianna shuddered, unable to drive from her mind images of Creigh's face contorted in agony . . . images of steel crushing, ropes straining, white-hot pincers grasping at flesh.

The chink of a heavy key grating in a lock made her start to awareness, narrowly saving her from crashing into Rogan's stiff back.

The grizzled chin of a turnkey jutted from the dark, sinister doorway. "Yer palace awaits ye, yer lordship," the man cackled, heaving his weight against the heavy panel.

Dim light trickled out from the tiny room, oozing sluggishly over stones worn with centuries of prisoners' pacings. Shadows cowered from the rats in the corners, a thin slice of daylight taunting the cell's inmates with but a glimpse of life beyond their prison walls from the barred window high above the floor. Brianna heard something move deep in the inky shadows, saw a taper strike to life.

A face was haloed in the gold light of the flickering candle, the masculine features stricken, like that of a savaged lamb, yet laden with the same patient sorrow that had touched Brianna's very soul in old Elva MacFee's crude carving of Christ in Gethsemane.

With a grunted curse, the turnkey shoved past her, stalking toward the man. "Quit gapin', ye curst witling, lest ye want me to fetch Sayer Wells again." The grizzled gaoler dealt the gentle face a buffet with one fist. "Wake yer high 'an mighty Fa'r 'er I'll—"

"Hold, Blagden!"

Brianna was startled by the sharpness in Dunley's voice from without the doorway as the gentle man Blagden had struck retreated to the corner of the room. Yet she was startled still more by the sight of another figure rising up from amid the room's shadows.

"I am awake, Private Blagden," a voice taut with wariness, yet rich with the tone of command offered. "Whatever your business is, this time you deal with me." Brianna's gaze was captured by the tall form of a man, his ragged velvet oddly seeming robes of state as he stepped toward them.

Tangled dark hair, threaded through with silver, straggled about a countenance so haggard it seemed a raging sculptor had gouged out lines in an image that had not pleased him. Yet the features now lit by the torchbearer's flame were touched with beauty despite the weight of what Brianna judged as past fifty years.

"I'll deal wi' whome'er I choose, old man." The gaoler puffed his chest out belligerently. "Ye be not in yer palaces now."

"And you, Private Blagden, are not in some ha'penny alehouse," Dunley snapped. "Go fetch me some water, hot water, and—"

"Hot water, sir?" Blagden echoed, as though the man had asked for a unicorn's horn.

"Aye. And clothes, soft and clean."

Blagden scratched his thick chest, and Brianna nigh choked at the rising stench of his unwashed body. "'Tain't me job t' be caterin' to no 'ristocrats," he said in disgust. "They be far an' away too high an' holy fer me tastes already."

"That may well be, private. But it *is* your duty to follow my orders in all things," Dunley said. "And I am *ordering* you to get me hot water and soft clothes. Now." The young

183

corporal turned sideways, carefully easing himself and his burden through the doorway.

"What . . ." Blagden gaped at Creigh, and the turnkey's lip thrust out in indignation as Dunley strode into the cell. "Hold but a moment, corp'ral, sar," Blagden sputtered. "The lieutenant, 'e gave no orders fer the new prisoners to be lodgin' 'ere. I—"

"Oh my God. No."

The gaoler's grousing was cut off by a cry so quiet, yet so full of agony it silenced all in the tiny room. Brianna looked up to see the dark-haired inmate rush to Dunley's side. The prisoner's face twisted in an anguish that drained all life from his savaged visage, eyes the shade of a summer storm staring down at Creigh with such soul-wrenching emotion Bree felt it in the very core of her being.

"Damn you, you bastards, what have you done to him?" the man demanded, wheeling on Dunley in a killing fury. "What—"

One of Dunley's guards grabbed the inmate's arms, but the man yanked free, facing the corporal like a raging king.

Dunley gave a tiny shake of his head at the soldier. "Leave the duke free," he commanded. Leveling his quiet, unflinching gaze upon that tormented face, the young corporal said, "It happened aboard the ship that brought him here, your grace."

"Aboard the ship—?"

Brianna sensed the older man's disbelief, saw in him rage nigh ready to snap. She leapt between the two men, her hands held up in warning and plea.

"'Tis true, sir . . . I mean, your grace. I give you my word."

"Your word? Who in God's name . . ."

"She was with Lord Creighton upon the ship. She and this other Irishman," Dunley gestured to Rogan. "Near as I can tell, she and Colonel Lord Wakefield were . . . are . . ."

"I love him." Brianna lifted her chin, meeting the duke's piercing gaze. She saw something flicker deep in the duke's dark-ringed eyes, a kinship, shared so fleeting she nigh thought she had imagined it.

Then the duke turned away. Though Dunley's hands remained unerringly gentle as he bore Creigh to the pallet, the dark-haired man stepped in front of him. Arms obviously shrunken from long imprisonment slipped beneath Creigh's broad shoulders in a gesture wrenchingly protective, aiding Dunley as he eased Creigh onto the tangled coverlet.

Creigh moaned in pain as the two men shifted his bruised body to rest upon the softness of the pallet, his mouth moving as if in a plea for the pain to stop. "B-Bree . . ." Her name was but a breath, his swollen lips cracked, pale, but she rushed to his side, gently catching up one hand.

"Creigh, love. I'm here," she crooned, smoothing the tousled mane back from his brow.

"Michel . . . He's dead."

"I know, love."

"They—they killed . . ." His lashes stirred upon his cheeks, something akin to a sob raw in his chest. "Bree . . ." His voice was broken, tearing, as he battled to open his eyes, and she could see him struggling to steel himself against the waves of pain.

Brianna felt a sob constrict her throat, burning, aching, as Creigh's hand crushed hers. But before her own tears could fall, she felt upon her hand the hot wetness of another's sorrow.

She looked up into the face bending over them, the eyes so like Creigh's dark with grief.

"Creigh." Voice rough with emotion, tears coursing, unchecked down his cheeks, the dark-haired prisoner reached out a trembling hand, smoothing his fingertips across Creigh's brow. Brianna felt Creigh's grip suddenly still against her palm. His thick lashes dragged from bruised cheeks. She caught her breath as Creigh's gaze battled to focus, but instead of seeking her face, the dulled silver of his eyes struggled past her. They fixed but a moment upon the man leaning over him, and in the dark-fringed depths welled an inner anguish that pierced Brianna's heart.

"Creigh, lad," the older man whispered brokenly, touching his bruised cheek.

Brianna saw Creigh's mouth twist in longing, aye, and a wrenching hint of loss, his face death-pale as he whispered the word: "Father."

Chapter Fourteen

Brianna's gaze flashed back to the man standing beside her—that father Creigh had spoken of the long-ago eve he had at last opened his heart to her. The father who had been so cruel, heartless as to have sacrificed his daughter into marriage with a beast of a man in order to gain estates. The father who had cast a son, simple of mind, gentle of heart, into the hungry flames of his own ambition. The father who had exiled the child, Creigh, who had adored him, while keeping a favored son always at his side.

Yet as Brianna peered into the face of Galliard Wakefield, Duke of Blackthorne, she saw not the ruthless, grasping aristocrat she had pictured through Creigh's descriptions. Instead she saw Creigh's face, older, worn with time and trouble, yet still indomitable, proud and laced with the compassion that neither father nor son could conceal.

Bree sensed that despite the traits that bound them, and the blood ties that could not be denied, there lay between the two men a chasm of hurt and misunderstanding deeper than the moat that ringed the Tower fortress, a breach neither man dared bridge. And the certainty astonished her, pained her.

Scarcely hearing the sound of the lock rasping behind them, the sound of the guard's footsteps retreating down the corridor, she pulled her gaze away from Blackthorne's face, turning again to Creigh. But his eyes lay shut, the only visible sign that remained of his brief grasp at consciousness the haunting expression of loss that tinged his lips.

"Is . . . is he dead?"

Brianna spun around at the sound of a strange voice at her shoulder, and nigh crashed into the gnarled length of a crude walking stick. Eyes, the tender, innocent green of the first grasses of spring, touched hers.

"Nay! Nay, he lives," she said. "He—"

"He'll need his wounds cleansed," Blackthorne interrupted. "Lindley, the water . . ."

Brianna started as she heard the heedless ripping of Blackthorne's shirt as he caught it in two fists, rending the once fine material, heard the stumping of the man, Lindley's crutch, the strange, dragging sound of leather against stone as he made his way across the cell.

"There was little in the hold of the ship to work with," Brianna said softly. "But I tried to poultice the wounds as best I could."

Blackthorne's eyes caught hers for a moment, and there was a tenderness in his gaze that touched her. "'Tis certain I am that you did, daughter," he said.

She flushed. "Bree, sir. Brianna."

She heard a sloshing of water, then Rogan's soft curse as he relieved the crippled Lindley of the basin, and thumped it down beside the bed.

"If you can aid me at freeing Creigh of this filthy shirt," Blackthorne said, turning to soak the rag in soapy water.

Rogan snorted in disgust, glaring at Bree. "Ask her," he snapped. "She's gained practice enough."

Hot shame seared into Brianna's cheeks, then froze there. Her chin jutted defiantly, her hands going to the fastenings upon Creigh's chest, but there was no censure in the duke's gray eyes, nor in the soft green gaze of Creigh's beloved Lindley.

They seemed but to take her into their hearts, surrounding her with a comfort she had not felt since Ogden had burst upon she and Creigh in the inn. 'Twas madness, most like, that this feeling of well-being should steal over her in the cell that was likely but a resting point before the grave. But she clung to the precarious sense of security, taking up the bandages the irate Blagden hurled through the square of barring upon the door and wrapping the worst of the injuries Blackthorne's gentle hands uncovered upon Creigh's flesh.

Twice she nigh took the cloth from the duke's fingers, as she saw the gray eyes blur with tears over some vicious weal, but she sensed within Creigh's father an agony of inner wounds as savage as those marring Creigh's body, inner wounds that seemed eased only when the older man touched his son.

As the hours passed, Lindley and Rogan slept. The single taper in the room burned low, then guttered and went out. Brianna curled up close to Creigh's pallet, watching his face, holding his hand, and listening to the mighty Duke of Blackthorne weep.

Pain. He was drowning in it, buried 'neath a thousand iron blades, heavy, razor sharp. Creigh tried to move from beneath their crushing weight, but every time he shifted his body a freshly honed dagger seemed to drive into his flesh, lancing him with images of Michel's severed head rolling across the rushes, with the horrible sounds of Brianna's screams as Ogden's cudgel slammed into Creigh's flesh. Yet tormenting him deeper still was another image, one that twisted in his gut like the talons of some hideous harpy.

"Nay . . ." he groaned the word aloud, struggling to blot out the face that assailed him from all sides, glinting off the blades of his agony like images cast from shards of a shattered mirror. But the face would not be banished, nor the anguish it inspired.

His father . . .

Creigh flung one arm over his gritty eyes, the pain searing into his shoulder doing naught to dull the even sharper edge of agony that knifed through him as the Duke of Blackthorne's visage burned beneath his eyelids. And Creigh hated himself for the tears that stung his eyes, hated the child in him that yet clung to the gold-encrusted stirrup of his father's saddle, sobbing, begging the man he adored beyond all others not to abandon him upon a strange, distant estate.

Pleading with his father to love him . . .

Creigh felt a despised sob rise in his throat. He ground his head back into whatever held him, wanting to claw the image from his mind.

For the cruelest trick of all was the fact that the face of his father that lay yet tangled in his mind, had been a face etched deep with love.

Creigh twisted in his prison of pain, glad of an agony he

188

could battle with his will. Something to grapple with, confront, as he had ne'er done with his father. Anything to still the sobbings of the child within him, the lad still watching the tall, dark-haired duke disappear from his life. Disappear with Lindley riding at his side. Until maman ...

The image of his father shifted, drifting in a rose-colored haze into pale, curling hair, eyes the shade of obsidian, the hard color incongruously wet with tears. Creigh could nigh feel Esmeraude Wakefield's arms sweeping him up, her soft pink lips raining kisses upon his plump child's cheeks as she rescued him from the unseen chains at Wrensong.

Creigh knew again the desperation with which he had clung to his mother, terrified that, if his father could come to cast him off, his mother could as well. And from that moment on, Creigh could remember trying to please the beautiful court belle who had given him life, taking her sorrows, her disappointments as his own, battling all who showed her enmity—especially his own father.

Why then this haunting, this loving Blackthorne who gazed at him through this haze of agony with eyes that bore his own pain? Why this soul-wrenching sense of abandonment Creigh had not allowed himself to feel since that memory-blurred day at Wrensong?

"Creigh."

He heard a voice, fearful, hopeful, velvet with the lilt of the Irish hills whisper above him. The gentle tones made him want to flee from his mind-conjured torment into the haven the voice offered, made him want to lose himself in the tumbled gold of his Tigress's fragrant hair.

"Bree." His lips felt stiff, split, his tongue seeming thick with waddings of foul-tasting wool. And in the perfect row of his teeth, he could feel three roots loosened in his gums. He forced his lids open, needing to see that she was safe, near, needing her to heal him.

The light of the new day that conquered the narrow window slanted across the pallet upon which he lay, piercing 'neath his lids with a brightness that nigh blinded him. Yet in the midst of that sun's glare, he could make out spun gold, framing a face far too pale, deep violet shadows smudged beneath fatigue-reddened eyes that peered down at him, rejoicing.

"Brianna," he whispered. "Bree, love."

She laughed, cried, her arms closing about him in an embrace leashed only by her care not to jar his wounds.

"Hurts," he said, his mouth twisting wryly.

"*You* hurt?" Brianna exclaimed with a sparkling grin. "You've nigh crushed my fingers these three days past, Colonel Lord Wakefield. I vow I may ne'er wield a rapier again!"

"Healthier."

"What?"

"Healthier," Creigh managed. "Save me . . . from . . . blasted Irish . . . temper."

Brianna's clear laughter rang out, and Creigh wanted to capture the sound, hold it like a talisman to drive away the echoes of the child's sobbing in his mind. But she left him bereft, as she spun around calling out to someone he could not see. He reached out his hand, wanting to stay her, but the supple strength of her small fingers were swept away from him, replaced by a hand sinewy, large, its knuckles prominent with age.

"Praise God," a voice breathed above him. "Oh, dear God, thank you."

Creigh's muscles stilled, froze, his relief at finding Brianna alive, at being alive himself suddenly chilling into a dread that coursed through him like slivers of ice. He battled the glare of the sunlight, shoving himself up on elbows that felt as though they'd been crushed in a vise.

"Where . . . Who?" The words died upon his lips, the hand, clasped in that of another, suddenly seeming to be plunged in the searing oil of his own worst torment. "Nay!"

He thrust his foot against the pallet, jamming his body upright as he stared unbelievingly into Galliard Wakefield's sea-gray eyes—eyes wary, guarded, despite the circlings of weariness ringed around them—eyes that held no hint of the love Creigh's imaginings had painted there.

A curse tore from Creigh's throat as he yanked his hand savagely from his father's grasp, battered lips twisting in a mask of fury, hate.

"You!" Creigh snarled. "You thrice-cursed . . ."

"Creigh!"

Galliard's face was blocked out by Brianna's tousled gold curls, her brow furrowed over eyes dark with confusion, censure. "He's been keeping vigil three days . . . watching . . ."

"Watching to see . . . if yet another of his cursed pawns lay dead?" Creigh grated, anger firing life into his aching limbs. "Bastard . . . you . . . Where—where's Lindley? *Lindley!*"

Creigh fought to sweep the room with a gaze yet unfocused, the corners of the blurred gray stone seeming to flare into blinding colors as he struggled to stand. He felt Brianna's hand band his arm, resist him as he tried to force himself to his feet. Saw Blackthorne's face, oddly stricken.

"Nay, Creigh," she said. "Lindley's here. Safe. Blast it, lay down before you do yourself harm."

"Damn it, woman, I—"

"'Tis all right, Creigh. I'm here," the sound of Lindley's gentle voice made tears sting the corners of Creigh's eyes. He yanked free of Brianna's grasp, staggering to feet that could scarce support him.

"Lin—Lindley," he said, his voice catching in his throat as he defined pale brown curls, spring-shaded eyes set against the dark stone. "Thank the saints you—"

Creigh started to stumble toward him, wanting to clasp Lindley's slender arms, feel the life in him, but Creigh had scarce managed to stumble to the center of the room, when the sunlight struck Lindley's oddly stooped figure.

Creigh froze, unable to move muscles that screamed in pain, denial as he stared in horror at Lindley's right leg. The limb that had once been slender, straight, was bent at a sickening angle, its length shorter than his other leg, as if it had been crushed. A crudely sewn leather sheath curved about the savaged limb, as if some loving hand had sought to shield it.

"Nay! What—what—" Creigh staggered toward Lindley, eyes wild with rage, his stomach churning, heaving. "What has that bastard cost you?"

He saw Brianna rushing toward him, even the red-haired Rogan crossing the room in long strides, but Creigh turned on his father, the talons of pain that tore through his chest, scarce equaling those that ripped into his mind.

"What—what did they do to him? You cursed—"

"Nay, Creigh!" He barely heard Lindley's distressed cry,

the clumping of the gnarled wood of his brother's walking against the floor.

"They tortured him! Tortured . . ." Creigh staggered toward his father, his fist doubled, his whole being aching to strike. "You let them—"

"Nay, Creigh! Stop!"

Pain knifed through him, nigh driving him to his knees as Brianna's hand caught his arm, but he shook her off, half-wild with rage.

"How could you, you bastard? Let them—let them hurt him!" Creigh saw Blackthorne's face wax gray, his eyes hot with a sickness that would have silenced Creigh had he seen it in any other. But Blackthorne's stoic silence but served to stoke the fury that was driving strength into Creigh's limbs, rapier-sharp words from his lips. Hate drove deep.

"What ails you, Father? Couldn't you even . . . be man enough to suffer for your own idiocy?"

"Curse it, Creigh, *stop!*"

The furious cry struck Creigh like a blow, stunning him more certainly than the most brutal arc of Ogden's cudgel. He turned, staring into Lindley's face. The gentle planes were taut with anger, the eyes that had ne're even sparked with irritation hollow, now, with the horrible pain of a child.

"'Twas not Father's fault. He tried to—"

Creigh gave a harsh laugh of disbelief, turning away, but Lindley caught his arm in crushing fingers, forcing Creigh to face him.

"Damn it, Creigh, you're not the only one who can be dealt unconscious by a blow from a cudgel," Lindley said. "There were four of them, and Father—"

"You'd not be caged here in the first place if 'twere not for *Father's* idiot scheme! First he throws Jolie to that cur Bouret, condemns her to a life that's hell at that monster's hands, and now you—"

"I'd give my leg a hundred times if 'twould serve our father's cause."

The conviction in Lindley's voice poured like acid over Creigh's anger, the very fact that Galliard Wakefield had not only crippled the gentle man, but duped him as well spurring Creigh to fury.

"Lindley, think you he cared aught for you? Aught even

for martyred King Charles? 'Twas but for glory he dragged you here, risked your capture. Naught but his own grasping for power."

"If you'd but open your eyes you'd know that naught moves him but love and loyalty and an honor of spirit greater than any man."

"Spirit? Greed!" Creigh shouted. "'Tis naught but—"

"*Love*, Creigh!" Lindley flung back, his face a mask of hurt. "Cling to the scarf maman drew about your eyes years ago. Play at hoodman blind! Wander about in the dark doing her bidding, refusing to see—"

"Leave maman out of this!" Creigh grated. "She has naught to do with your being locked in the Tower, with the brutes that crippled you!"

"Nay," Lindley cried. "*Maman* was too taken with her crippling of you."

The words seemed to shatter all sound within the tiny room, the walls that had witnessed so many sorrows, torments, seeming to grasp at yet another inmate's pain. Creigh stared at Lindley's flushed face—that face in which he had ne'er seen aught but unquestioning love, and he hated Galliard Wakefield with a depth that terrified him.

He felt a hand, soft upon his elbow, heard the whispering of Brianna's hair as it slipped across her shoulder. "Have you both said enough," she asked quietly, "or have you more stakes to drive into each other's hearts?"

"Damn it, 'tis none of your affair!" Creigh snapped, but the rest of his tirade fell silent as the rasping of the lock being opened sounded in the room.

Instinctively, Creigh stumbled before Lindley and Bree, in the gesture he had used so oft before to shield those weaker than he, yet even before the door swung open a twisting of irony pulled at his lips. 'Twould scarce take a peacock feather to topple him to the stones now, even if a babe were to wield it.

Despite the wounding to his pride, he was grateful when Brianna's arm slipped beneath his, shoring up his suddenly unsteady legs.

His eyes narrowed upon the heavy panel, its hinges shrieking in protest as it was shoved wide.

Creigh heard Brianna's breath catch in her throat, her fingers digging deep into his arm, yet he felt no pain, only

193

fear, primal, raw—for her, for Lindley, aye, and for his father. Creigh forced his battered body to straighten, his eyes blazing challenge as he met the sadistic gaze of Saul Ogden.

But suddenly broad, velvet-clad shoulders blocked Creigh from the Roundhead's view, Galliard Wakefield drawing himself into his most regal bearing.

"If you have any business here, 'tis me you'll have to deal with," the duke warned.

Ogden's chuckle trickled ice down Creigh's spine. "Always the high and the holy, eh, Blackthorne?" the Roundhead chortled. "Well, today, Dame Torture bears a taste for younger flesh."

Creigh felt Lindley's terror leap, wild through the room, felt Brianna against him, fragile despite her inner strength.

"Ogden, your quarrel is with me," Creigh said levelly, his eyes narrowing, goading.

"Aye, that's true, Wakefield, but betimes, for noble witlings like you, 'tis greater torture to listen to another's screams than to bear your own pain."

"Curse it, Ogden, I—"

"Chain him," Ogden barked at the burly guards behind him. "And bind his whore."

Creigh lunged at the Roundhead, every muscle in his body tearing in pain, but four hulking guards were upon him before he could reach the smirking Ogden.

Heavy iron cut deep into Creigh's wrists, ankles as the four guards fought to quell his struggles. He could hear his own shouts of anger, see Rogan, Blackthorne, even Lindley trying to shield Bree. But before the guards could harm any of the three, Brianna dodged in front of them, offering herself like a martyr at the stake, Creigh thought with a sick twist in the pit of his stomach.

"I'll . . . I'll go with you. Just don't . . . don't hurt them . . ." Her plea clawed at Creigh's very soul. His eyes locked with hers, endless seconds fraught with desperation.

"Hurt *them*, sweeting?" the Roundhead's glee echoed through the room. "Oh, nay. I'll not hurt *them*, I vow. But you . . ."

Fury surged through Creigh as Ogden's defiling hand threaded through Brianna's hair, and the Tower's very stones seemed to cower from his cruel laughter.

Chapter Fifteen

A score of torches blazed within iron sconces, lining the walls like greedy spectators at some grisly pagan rite. Brianna stared, as if mesmerized, at the writhing flames reflected upon sharp pincers, thick ropes, taunting her from bands of iron designed to crush bones, aye, and spirits. Each glowing tongue of fire seemed to claw at the sweat-dulled metal and pitted stone as though lost in its own private torment . . . A torment she soon would share.

She turned her gaze to Creigh, battling, still, against the men that held him, as they yanked his shackled arms high, securing the chains to a hook set high in the stone wall. Thrice as they had made their way down into the dread White Tower, the guards had slammed Creigh with their pikestaffs, fighting to beat him into submission. And thrice he had broken from their grasp, warring not, Bree sensed, to gain freedom, but rather to gain the use of some weapon just long enough to pierce her heart.

I'll drive my own dagger into Lindley's chest before I allow him to endure that hell . . . she could hear Creigh say on that distant day in Ireland. And now, as the White Tower's dread chamber swallowed them, Brianna could see the same desperation wrack his face.

She tore her gaze away, unable to bear the agony she saw there, unwilling to torment him further by allowing him to witness the terror that crushed her in its fist. But no matter where her eyes darted in the torchlit room, terror tightened its grip, for even the walls dripped with the sinews of torture.

She heard Ogden's boot heels upon the stone as he strode over to where Creigh hung, chained. The Roundhead grasped the iron links above Creigh's wrists, yanking down on them to test their strength. A satisfied chuckle rumbled in his thick chest as he picked up a gruesome pair of tongs, fingering their sharp points.

"Ofttimes the keepers of the Tower bring their tools of justice to the prisoners' rooms, rather than dragging the guilty here," Ogden observed with a frightening detachment. "They say 'tis passing wearisome to drag a man broken upon the rack up countless flights of stairs, back to his cell. And they bear my heartiest sympathy. But when Private Blagden was so good as to introduce me to good Sayer Wells, Master Sayer and I had a difficult time deciding which of these delights your sins warranted, eh, sir?"

Ogden grinned at a huge sweat-grimed man with arms twice the size of any others in the room, and a face blank, stoic as an image carved in stone. "So we chose to risk the inconvenience of transporting you after . . ."

The man, Wells, scrubbed his palms on his stained leather apron. "'Tis no account to me where you choose to carry out your business," he said, turning to stoke a fire that blazed in a stone pit in the room's center. "I but ply my trade, as my fa'r did before me, an' my gaffer afore that. But me daughter, she be celebratin' her saint's day this eve, so 'twould please me to get on with the questionin', if yer colonelship pleases."

Brianna felt a quaver work through her, her terror made greater by the knowledge that throughout the city of London, aye, and in Ireland, too, others were gathered about family and friends, toasting their saint's days, eating little cakes, or tearing the ribbons off of tiny boxes.

She stared, sickened at Sayer Wells's broad face, wanting to scream at the irony that in but a few hours time, she would lay broken, or dead, and this man . . . this torture master, would be hanging an apron stained with her blood upon a wooden peg to saunter off to a revel.

Her gaze darted to Ogden as the Roundhead unfastened the flowing black mantle about his shoulders, looping its gold cord about an iron spike. He gave the master torturer a conspiratorial grin. "I much doubt this will take a great deal of your time," he said.

"That depends upon which one be ye plannin' t' work upon first," the man said, his eyes shifting from Creigh to Brianna with less interest than a butcher would take in selecting an animal for slaughter. "The woman . . . she be passin' small fer the implements we've got here. 'Twould take scarce a twist, I vow, t' break 'er, hellcat though she seems. But 'is lordship, there, well, 'tis policy from way back that we torture no nobles. Least not an' that we let 'em live t' blather about." Sayer shrugged. "Not that I be over partic'lar. I put one to the *boot* but a month past, an' I'd scarce started the crushin' when 'e fainted dead away."

Brianna heard Creigh's sickened curse, felt a twisting in her own stomach at the thought of Lindley's gentle face contorted in agony, thanked God that he had been granted the blessed release of unconsciousness.

Ogden smirked. "No doubt you had to apply a keg-full of vinegar to the wretch to make him face his punishment like a man. They be a weak-bellied lot, these aristocrat dogs," he jeered, casting Creigh a contemptuous glance. "And the Wakefields be the worst cowards of the lot. Women-killers and witlings. But 'twill be the whore we'll wreak God's justice upon first, good Sayer. No doubt she'll wax more entertaining than his lordship."

Brianna caught a glimpse of Creigh's face, his eyes burning with fury, desperation. "Test *my* courage, Ogden, if you dare," he goaded the Roundhead, "or do you fear to match your lowly peasant skills against the bravery of a man with the blood of kings in his veins?"

"All in good time, my Lord Creighton," Ogden sneered, "all in good time. But for now let us see how well your renowned Wakefield courage holds when you see your harlot's flesh burn, blood flow, when you see her bones yanked from their sockets upon the rack. Or, mayhap we'll test the boot again, and see if she bears it with more heart than your witling brother."

Creigh's hands tore savagely at the chains, his face a horrible mask of helplessness, rage, and terror . . . raw . . . primal, as he swore at Ogden, battled to goad the Roundhead into turning his wrath upon himself. Brianna's eyes darted to the door, catching the eye of a passing yeoman of the guard for but an instant, the face registering in her mind as vaguely familiar . . . streaked as it had been with rain the night they had landed at Traitor's Gate.

"Plotting escape?"

Brianna started as Ogden's breath slithered down her neck, and she could feel the Roundhead's lascivious gaze devouring the swell of her breasts. "There is nowhere for you to run to now, Satan's whore. Except back to your dark master."

Brianna fought the nigh crazed terror that ripped through her, as Ogden's hands locked about the chains linking her wrists—the hideous instruments of torture, Creigh's tormented eyes, and the Roundhead Colonel's slack, avid lips blending into a scene from her own most devastating nightmare. She felt a scream rise within her, quelled it, as Ogden slowly pulled her arms over her head, his eyes devouring every curve of flesh that thrust against the thin fabric of her bodice. He dragged her feet off the stones, the iron bands encircling her wrists cutting savagely into her flesh as he suspended her from some anchoring driven high in the wall opposite Creigh.

She caught the tormented gray of Creigh's eyes, saw his mouth twist with anguish, rage. And in that moment she knew that she would gladly endure whatever Ogden and his sadistic torture master might deal her, if only it would keep Creigh safe. Calling upon a depth of courage she had not known she possessed, she set her lips in a determined line. *Nay ... he'll not break me, this bloodthirsty Sassenach bastard,* she vowed silently. *I'll die as a Devlin, with courage and honor, and he'll not use my agony to savage Creigh further ...*

Her hands struggled to close about the chains above her, support her weight, the links driving deep into her palm. And the stubborn Devlin chin Creigh had teased her about on sunlit meadow days tipped up in defiance of the Roundhead before her, and his gallery of horrors. "As I said the day you brought us here, 'tis not half so daunting as you Sassenachs would have the world believe."

Ogden's pleasure sound rumbled in his throat as he paced around her, eyes cunning, probing every inch of her skin. "So you plan to make this easy upon your aristocrat lover, eh, Madame Harlot," he purred with an uncanny perception

198

that chilled Brianna's blood. "Thrust your chin out, spit defiance. But I vow once you dance with the Tower's dread demons, even the mighty Creighton Wakefield will cease to matter."

Ogden turned, thrusting the pincers deep into the flame, his hand caressing the handles before letting it go. "Ready the gauntlets, good Sayer," he commanded with a sneer. "'Twill be justice indeed that the whore's hands that pleasured my Lord Wakefield will ne'er be fit to touch another man."

Brianna felt her blood ice, stories of the device that slowly crushed the hands roiling in her mind. She could nigh feel the cold kiss of iron upon her flesh, the metal crushing her fingers, the blood bursting her skin, leaving naught but useless stumps.

She looked across the blazing fire pit at Creigh, her own heart tearing as he sawed the flesh of his hands against the rough iron manacles in a futile attempt to break free.

"Balking at giving up your revelings in this whore's bed, Wakefield?" Ogden chortled. "Well, mayhap we'll give you but one more glimpse of her whole . . . unscarred."

Brianna battled a scream, as Ogden's hands closed upon the low décolletage of her gown, his big fingers digging cruelly into her flesh as he grasped the delicate swathing of lace. The fabric gave with a horrible sound, the heat from the fire blasting her bared skin, searing her breast and the mark it bore.

She saw the Roundhead's slitted eyes fasten greedily upon her naked flesh, then saw his eyes widen, his mouth gaping open in slavering astonishment as his gaze took in the fragile, white mound, the rose-tipped nipple, and the scars carved deep beneath it.

"You!" Ogden said, his fingers reaching up to touch the scar slashing his own cheek. "You!" His eyes flashed up to hers, the sly depths writhing with hatred and sharp anticipation as he stared into her face. Bree's teeth dug deep into the inner flesh of her mouth, her own blood filling her with the taste of terror.

She could hear Creigh's shoutings, yet 'twas as if he had been cast into a far-off cave, his words blurred in the agony of fear that tore at her.

"Here be the *gauntlets,* colonel, sir," Sayer Wells's voice rasped in her ear, the shining metal instruments just visible above Ogden's broad shoulder.

The Roundhead turned slowly. "The gauntlets," he repeated, his face taking on a look of exquisite pleasure. He reached out his hands, taking the metal objects from the surprised Sayer's hand.

"I fear our dealings this eve shall take longer than I had anticipated," Ogden said, fingering the brutal metal glove.

"But . . . but 'tis my daughter's saint's day. I vowed to my good-wife that I'd be at table early enough to share bread with the family, colonel, sir, you—"

"Oh, nay, nay, good Sayer," Ogden interrupted hastily. "I'd not consider robbing you of your revels this eve. Get you gone, and drown yourself in your ale and the company of your loved ones."

Brianna saw the torturer's brow wrinkle in confusion, one brawny paw reaching up to scratch his receding chin. "But . . . but the questionin'. Ye—"

Ogden waved his hand in dismissal, a grin splitting his face. "I'll deal with these prisoners myself. 'Twill be more than a pleasure, I assure you, to work not only God's justice this eve, but a vengeance of my own."

Sayer's lips compressed in indecision, his arms crossing upon his leather-covered belly. "'Tis an art, torture is," he argued. "Not just somethin' any Tamkin Blind from the streets can turn a hand to when they have a yearnin'."

Ogden's ingratiating smile made Brianna's stomach churn. "I doubt not 'tis a skill gifted you by the angels, Master Wells. But with these two spawns of Satan at last in my grasp, I doubt not that God will guide my hand upon the tools of judgment until I work them nigh as truly as you."

Sayer grunted, scrubbing the sweat from his brow with the back of his hirsute arm. "I suppose I could leave young Wat wi' you," he said grudgingly, jerking his head in the direction of a scrawny, evil-eyed lad amongst the guards. "He be small yet for working the last turns on the rack, but a right canny apprentice, he be, good at applyin' vinegar when the pris'ners think to escape by faintin'."

"Many thanks for the most generous offer," Ogden said, rubbing one finger over the curved metal in his hand. "But this night I intend to revel in God's just pain with as much relish as you shall know at your celebration. And I intend to be most selfish in my pleasures. To share them with no one."

Ogden met Sayer's gaze with his own, and slipped a heavy coin pouch from the thick band of his sash. "For your kindness," Ogden said, slipping it into the other man's hand. "And in payment for the use of your most valued tools."

The torturer stared at the pouch emblazoned with Ogden's colors long moments before his fingers closed around it. He groped at his waist, pulling free a heavy metal ring weighted with keys. "To their shackles," Sayer offered. "And their cells. Return whatever is left o' the two of 'em there when yer done."

Ogden nodded, securing the keys at his waist.

Sayer jerked his head toward the door, signaling his men to file out. "In case you need aid, I'll leave Wat at the corridor's end. He'll be most pleased to instruct you in the finer points of applying the scavenger's daughter."

Brianna shuddered as the boy, Wat, lingered, framed in the stone doorway, his pale eyes boring into her nakedness.

"I doubt I'll have need of aught this night," Ogden smirked. "Within this room lies everything I could desire."

Brianna's hands knotted where they held the chain, her eyes avoiding the anguished ones of Creigh. Her whole body burned with shame, fury that he should see her so, stripped and helpless, her mind recoiling from the knowledge that soon he would know that the lips, breasts he had healed with his loving had again been defiled by his most hated enemy.

Brianna shut her eyes, listening to the fading of footsteps in the echoing passage, hearing silence fall onto the room like siftings of earth upon a grave.

A hand crawling across her naked skin made her eyes flash open, and she bit her lip as Ogden's fingers tightened cruelly in her hair.

"Tell him, whore," Ogden hissed, his breath wet against her. "Did you tell him how you spread your legs for me? Let me pierce you upon the road like the foulest of animals?"

"I—"

"Did the high and holy Lord Creighton Wakefield know that he was delving into another man's leavings?"

"Nay!" Creigh's denial seemed torn from his very soul. "'Twas . . . 'twas you! You who raped her . . . cut her . . .

I'll kill you! Damn you, I swear somehow I'll—" Creigh's fury dragged Brianna's gaze to his face, a face more anguished than she had ever seen it, even when he had first looked upon Lindley's crushed leg.

Gray eyes spitting fury, mouth twisted into a savage snarl, Creigh tore at the chains with a force that must surely rip even tempered iron from the walls. But the chains that had witnessed uncounted horrors held firm.

Brianna felt tears sear her eyes at his torment, sensing how his helplessness devastated him—this man who in all his life had met no crisis he could not overcome through honor and courage.

"Aye, Wakefield," Ogden chortled. "I cut her, the Irish harlot. Carved the mark of God upon her flesh so that any bewitched by her devil's spells would know what she was and run in fear of the wrath of His angels."

"You raped her, you bastard! Forced her!" Creigh raged. "How think you your vengeful God will judge that?"

Brianna saw Ogden's eyes narrow, a look of guileful deceit coming over his face. "'Twas necessary to teach the whore the wages of her sins. She lured me . . . lured many with her siren's ways."

"She was a virgin when you raped her!"

"You were fool enough to believe that?" Ogden jeered. "Look at her, Wakefield. Look!" Bree winced as Ogden shredded the remaining cloth that covered her, casting it upon the chill stones. "She bears a body formed to drag a man to sin."

"Nay, Ogden. She bears strength and innocence you'd not understand if 'twas ground into your lying face!"

"Mayhap 'tis true," Ogden conceded, his hand caressing the metal instrument in his hand. "But 'twill not be the mettle of my courage we test here this night. 'Twill be that of the woman." A glaze settled over Ogden's ferret eyes. "A Wakefield woman."

"Bree is no Wakefield!" Creigh challenged, and she could see his hands knot with desperation. "She's naught but a simple Irish lass who had the misfortune to be thrown in my path. If you thirst for Wakefield blood, Ogden—the *aristocrat* blood you claim that you loathe—draw *mine*. Bury your hands in blood with the taint of nobility within it. But leave the girl alone. She's innocent, Ogden. Innocent."

"Innocent?" Ogden bellowed, wheeling on Creigh, his mouth contorting over rotted teeth. "What matters innocence to a cursed Wakefield? You gnash your teeth over this . . . this Irish slut who played your whore, but where was the bloody Wakefield honor the eve one of your house murdered a woman—a midwife whose crime was naught but easing a babe into the world? A woman with eight babes of her own and a husband off battling in the name of Blackthorne. Where was your family honor then, *Lord Creighton?*" Ogden spat, jabbing the metal gauntlet inches from Creigh's face. "Where was the mercy that turned eight children out onto the highroads to starve?"

Brianna stared, stunned, her wits battling to take in Ogden's ravings, to glean some sense from the tirade that both confused and terrified her. She looked up at Creigh, praying to find some understanding, some answer in his countenance. But the gray eyes fastened upon Ogden's dull red face were dark with puzzlement, as though he were struggling desperately to grasp something he understood not at all.

"A midwife?" Creigh repeated. "Dead at a Wakefield's birthing? 'Tis . . . 'tis impossible. Old Madog, the seeress vows she pulled us all into the world, screaming—"

"Screaming? Mayhap, 'twas of God's torment, for the hand that slayed—"

Ogden wheeled, hurling the gauntlet of torture into the wall. The clatter of metal against stone raked Brianna's nerves, and she shivered as he turned, his eyes spitting death at the chained Creigh. "'Tis but justice that those you turned out to starve should profit by your blood and that of your idiot brother, and sire. 'Twill take some small pleasure from your downfall—my not being able to plunge a knife into your coward's belly—but the headsman's axe will serve . . . 'twill deal you death, and gain my master . . ."

"Master?" Creigh echoed, Ogden's implications dragging an icy blade of dread down his spine. His dark brows slashed low above his eyes. "Ogden, what in God's name—"

"Aye, in God's name," the Roundhead said, his eyes staring deep into the pit of fire before him. "'Tis in God's name that I take this, your whore. In God's name I bring the mighty house of Wakefield to its knees. And in God's name I avenge that woman's long-cold grave."

"What woman, Ogden?" Creigh cried. "Damn you—"

Brianna felt horror, terror break in waves over her skin as Ogden's fingers hooked around the long handles of the pincers plunged 'mongst the coals earlier. The white-hot claws pulled from the center of the huge, flaming brands, sharp-filed points gouging holes in Brianna's courage. Despite her vow to be brave, she felt the first tearings of desperation in her own flesh—desperation and fear as Ogden's eyes fastened upon the delicate pink tip of her breast, his ghoulish intention clear.

She ripped at her own manacles, grinding her hands down into the metal rings in an effort to escape their ruthless grasp. They cut into the joint beneath her thumb, paring away the flesh of her hand as she twisted, fought against the rough iron.

Ogden laughed, a demented, evil sound. "Tell me, Wakefield, did you take pleasure in these," he purred, his thick finger snapping hard into the tender flesh. "Did you kiss them, Wakefield? Suckle? How will they feel upon your tongue once they are cleansed with Milady Justice's sweet fire?"

Brianna felt the heat of the pincers upon her arm, the glowing tips but inches from the outer curve of the breast which had known the sharp point of Ogden's dagger.

And 'twas as if the Roundhead's leering face, slack lips were a vision born of hell. She battled within herself to leash her terror, battled to hold the courage that had been hers to call upon from the time she'd left the cradle. But the fierce warrior within her was trapped, imprisoned now beneath the stark terror of a child. And no power of reason could stay her from crying out to the one person whose strength she needed more than any other.

"Creigh!" She screamed his name, sobbed it as she felt the first kiss of the white-hot iron searing into her flesh, but 'twas as if the pain, mingled with Creigh's cry of rage, desperation, fused life into her numbed limbs. Her feet slammed into Ogden's belly, chest, as she fought against the manacles. The pincers glanced off the curve of her breast as she battled, searing the soft underside of her arm. But Brianna could scarce feel the iron burning into her flesh. She felt naught, knew naught but Saul Ogden's paunchy belly

204

beneath her heels and the terror that robbed her of all reason.

"Bree! Sweet God, Ogden, hold!" She shut her eyes, her ears to Creigh's screams, losing his cries in the sharp echoes of her own as she kicked, clawing at the chains, the stone wall. Her foot slammed outward, connecting with something oddly hard amidst Ogden's soft body.

The Roundhead's bellowed curse tore her eyes open, the sound of the pincers clattering to the floor jarring through her whole body. She stared, disbelieving at the huge Roundhead, doubled over upon the stone floor, his huge paws clasped over his groin. The still-glowing pincers lay but an arm's length from Creigh's chained feet, the hot iron blackening the stones upon which they lay. But 'twas Creigh's face that held her gaze, his eyes flashing, desperately trying to penetrate her fear, convey some message as Ogden pushed himself to his knees.

She saw Creigh's stormy silver gaze lock on the wall above her, frustration twisting his lips. His mouth moved, forming a silent word. *Hands.*

The word struck Brianna like an axe blade, her gaze shooting up to the shackles that bound her wrists above her. But 'twas not her wrists the manacles grasped now. 'Twas the bony joints that linked her thumb and smallest finger to her hands. The thin covering of skin had ripped away, the manacles crushing the slender bones together.

"Bitch!"

She heard Ogden's snarl as he pushed himself up from the stones. "Bitch! I'll—"

"You'll do what, Ogden? Let her drive whatever manhood you do possess back into your body?" Creigh's taunting laugh echoed against the arched ceiling, and Brianna sensed he was trying to gain her time, draw the Roundhead's wrath down upon himself. "Even locking her in chains a lowling the likes of you bears not the power to best my lady," Creigh goaded. "But then 'tis small wonder. I vow there's little courage taught wallowing 'mongst the swine."

Brianna saw Ogden's face wash scarlet, the muscles in his huge arms bunching in angry knots as he gained his feet. The Roundhead wheeled on Creigh, eyes red, savage. "Nay, Wakefield," he hissed, sweeping up the pincers. "There be

205

little courage. But there be other lessons taught upon the highroads—at the sword points of cutthroats, and brigands with naught more entertaining to pass their time than tormenting wayfarers cast before them."

Brianna tore at her hands, grinding them savagely within their circlets of iron, tearing flesh, crushing bone against bone, feeling her own blood run warm, wet, down her bare arms as the Roundhead stalked toward Creigh. Ogden yanked the handles of the pincers apart, baring the instrument's sharp-pointed jaws, its teeth designed solely for the tearing of human flesh. He jammed the instrument deep into the fire-pit's leaping flames.

"Know you what I learned one night," Ogden grated, staring at the heating iron, twisting it, turning it in the heart of the blaze. ". . . one night after they'd tired of placing coals upon my belly? I learned how a blade could rob a lad of his manhood . . . how it could cut . . . bleed . . . He . . . he was tied next to me and his blood . . . it soaked the grass, pooling 'neath me."

Brianna could feel Creigh's horror, her own, even in her fear the scene Ogden's words painted wrenching her stomach.

"But these . . ." Ogden's fingers caressed the pincers, to voice tainted with a distant, grating tinge that bordered on insanity. "These would sear the flesh even as they cut . . . tore . . . would they not, Lord Creighton? They would burn the skin so that you would live . . . live as no man . . . gelded."

Brianna's eyes locked upon Creigh's face, the arrogant features suddenly deathly still, his eyes hooded. She could sense the raw fear ripping through him, a fear far greater than that of facing torture, death. Brianna wanted to scream, cry, but her own throat was strangled with the thought of Creigh—bold, gentle, all that was best in a man, torn by the pincers' sharp teeth.

She yanked on her hands, pain driving deep into the savaged flesh, tearing, rending as she saw Ogden lower the pincers now inches from Creigh's taut belly.

The Roundhead's eyes narrowed on Creigh's, and Brianna could see Ogden lick his wet lips.

"Ogden." Creigh's voice was low, the muscles in his jaw standing out sharp against his skin. "Do it," he said, meeting the Roundhead's gaze with rigid calm that terrified Brianna more than rage. "Take whatever twisted revenge you desire upon my body, and I vow I'll not so much as scream. But Brianna . . . let her free."

Ogden's mouth stretched into an eager sneer. "Let her go? To spread the news of your torture to all of London? To carry the tale back to your whoring king? Oh, nay, Wakefield, I think not."

"Then let her death be swift," Creigh hesitated, and Bree could detect a plea in his voice that crushed her heart. "Let it be . . . painless."

Ogden laughed . . . laughed, the hideous sound echoing off of the stone, swelling in the arches of the roof above them, dripping like blood over the wooden bars and wheels of the rack. "By the time the devil carries her to hell she'll embrace him like a lover," Ogden vowed. "And you, my lord Creighton, will ne'er embrace anything again."

Ogden yanked wide the handles of the pincers, their sharp points closing the slight distance between the glowing iron and Creigh's taut stomach. With one desperate, tearing jerk, Brianna ripped her hands downward, the rings of iron cutting deep into her flesh, then suddenly the manacles flew upward, her hands tearing free of their clasp.

With a sob of fear, fury, she stumbled toward Ogden's broad back, her eyes searching desperately for some weapon to use against him. Her whole body was alive with terror as she heard the hiss of white-hot iron, smelled the stench of burning cloth. Her eyes locked upon the fire pit, its thick logs orange with flame. Tears blinding her eyes, she grasped the heavy end of one log, not feeling her hands blister, burn. She raised the brand high, cracking it, with strength borne of horror in a glowing arc upon Ogden's head.

The Roundhead screamed, one huge hand clawing at the back of his head, his hair singed, scalp splitting. He hurled the pincers away, charging Brianna like a maddened bear. Terror, stark, paralyzing ripped through her, freezing her limbs in cold horror.

"Bree!" Creigh's scream pierced the haze of fear enveloping her just as Ogden's meaty fist swung toward her. Half screaming, half sobbing, she threw the brand back again, driving it into the scarred, evil face with all of her might. Stunned surprise, sharp pain twisted Ogden's hideous fea-

207

tures, but the force of his charge drove his thick body into hers, crashing her to the ground. Brianna screamed as his hand grasped at the tangled mass of her hair, his weight landing atop her. The brand flew from her fingers, skidding across the floor in a rain of orange sparks.

She fought, kicked at the hulking body bearing her down, clawing in crazed terror at the flesh that seemed oddly quiescent upon her.

"Bree!" She heard Creigh's sharp voice as if 'twas far away. "Brianna . . . he's unconscious! Tigress!"

She shoved at Ogden's shoulder, his bulk at last sagging off of her, rolling onto the stone floor. Bree scrambled away from him, shaking, sobbing, huddled against the wall like a terrified child.

"C-Creigh are you . . . did he hurt . . ." Bree looked at Creigh, a sob catching in her throat as her eyes locked on the seared, blackened wound marring his belly.

"Tigress, 'tis all right—but a little burn. You struck him before he could do more." Creigh's voice was the lifeline she clung to, its tone strong, clear, rife with love. "Get the keys, Tigress, Ogden's keys."

Brianna stared at the Roundhead, laying, still, his slack lips gaping like a broken purse string, his eyes rolled back in his head. "C-Creigh," she quavered, unable to tear her eyes from Ogden's evil face. "C . . . Creigh, I can't—"

"Bree!" Fierce, savage, yet quiet, Creigh's voice drove through the terror that threatened to rob her of her sanity. "We have to make our way out of here. Find Lindley . . . the others before someone comes. Get the key!" She reached out a hand, tentative, shaking, then yanked it back, clutching it against her churning stomach.

"Brianna, you can do it, love," Creigh urged. "Just reach out. Take it." Slowly, terror crashing over her in drowning waves, Brianna inched her fingers toward the ring that dangled from Ogden's sash.

"Do it, Bree! You're nigh there," Creigh urged and she clung to the strength of his voice in this world gone mad.

Her hand closed over cold iron, and stifling a sob, she ripped the ring of keys from the swath of silk about Ogden's waist. Eyes nigh blind with tears of fear, relief, she scrambled over to Creigh, unlocking shackles, releasing chains with terror-numbed fingers. The instant his manacles fell away, Creigh swept her hard against him, his hands delving into her hair, his lips taking her face as she sobbed into his chest. "Hush, love, hush," he whispered fiercely against her skin. "My bold, my brave, sweet Tigress."

Brianna clung to the hard heat of him, feeling his life pulse through her—the supple, sleek sinews, satiny bronzed skin. He seemed to draw the fear from her, take it into himself as he held her, whispering his love.

Suddenly he went silent, his hands freezing, his breath hissing softly between his teeth. Brianna went cold in his arms, listening. 'Twas but a ghost of a sound, far off in the stone corridor, a scraping that might be the wisp of a tapestry caressing the stone, or the scurryings of a dungeon rat across the floor. But Brianna sensed, knew instinctively that 'twas no red-eyed vermin, no chill draft that whispered within the walls.

With the stealth of a jungle cat, Creigh eased his arms from Brianna's waist, padding over to Ogden's yet senseless bulk. There was the faintest rasp of a sword being drawn from its scabbard, and Brianna felt its cold hilt being pressed into her palm.

She saw Creigh turn, his eyes sweeping the room, searching. Hastily he grabbed Ogden's mantle, yet hanging upon the iron spike, and bile filled her throat. "Nay." She backed away. Her arm clasped against her bare skin as if to shield herself from some mystical, supernatural evil that clung to the brocade folds. "C-Creigh, I—"

"There is naught else." An edge cut into Creigh's whisper, and she glanced at her gown upon the floor, shredded beyond hope. "Damn it, Bree, there's no time . . ."

Brianna shuddered as he swirled the garment about her, the folds that now covered her nakedness seemed crawling with thousands of tiny white-bellied creatures, their bodies death-cold with her own fear.

She clenched her teeth, struggling to keep from screaming at the horrible sensation. Her eyes followed Creigh as he slipped to the wall, taking up a pike that leaned in one shadowed corner.

Beckoning her to follow, he went to the open door, cautiously peering into the dark corridor beyond. *Quiet . . . 'tis too quiet,* Brianna thought fearfully, gripping the sword. Her eyes met Creigh's for but an instant, then the sound

209

came again, clearer, more frightening. Boot heels. Brianna's gaze swept out into the passage, her hand clenching on the sword. 'Twas the sound of boot heels cracking into stone.

She started to speak, tell Creigh, but his hand grasped hers with a force that showed he, too, knew they were in danger.

"Guards," he whispered, "coming this way. There's a tiny room but a little way from here. 'Tis our only hope."

Brianna glanced back at the torture chamber as Creigh pulled her out into the corridor. If the guards should chance to look in—if they were Sayer Wells's men—she and Creigh would be discovered. And if they were discovered . . . Brianna shuddered, the gruesome instruments of agony, the fire, Ogden's contorted face searing into her mind. 'Twould be the devil's price they'd pay at the Roundhead's savage hands.

She struggled to blot the thought from her mind, the prospect of facing Ogden yet again too horrible to even give voice to. Her heart thundered against her breasts, her stomach roiling as Creigh dragged her swiftly, silently into the darkness.

A darkness that seemed rife with specters, spirits as she ran. Bree shut her eyes against them, trying to drive away the laughing countenance of Anne Boleyn, the image of the gentle Lady Jane Grey and others . . . so many others . . .

"'Tis but around this corner."

Bree caught Creigh's hissed whisper, nigh inaudible through the sound of the fast-gaining guards.

The shadowy stonework seemed to widen, a small door standing out against the stone. Creigh's fingers tightened about hers, as she stumbled toward the room's haven.

But the fleeting sense of relief she had gained was swept ruthlessly away. A scream ripped her throat as she felt something within the room grab her, the sound of her terror crushed into her mouth by a hard hand as she was yanked into the swallowing darkness.

Chapter Sixteen

Rage struck Creigh like a fist to his belly as he heard Brianna's muffled scream, saw the shadowy arms clutch her struggling body. The sword he had given her struck the floor, the hollow clatter sounding like a knell of death as she fought, clawed at the face yet concealed in the meager light of a taper.

Creigh charged into the room, the pikestaff in his hands poised to deal death—to her captor, aye, yet if escape proved hopeless, death to the woman he loved. With all the strength he possessed, he slammed the thick end of the pike into his adversary, unwilling to risk using the weapon's sharp blade lest he accidentally strike Bree. Pain shot up Creigh's own bruised arms, driving deep into his shoulders. But with a grunt of pain, the shadow-shrouded figure rolled away from her, one flailing arm crashing against a small wood table, sending two pewter goblets plunging to the floor with a deafening crack.

Creigh shoved Brianna behind him, drawing back the deadly weapon in his hands, certain, now, of discovery, certain of death, but a voice broke the silence, its melancholy tones oddly familiar, staying Creigh's hand as it made to drive the gleaming weapon into the uniformed chest.

"'Tis me, Lord Creighton," the fallen man breathed, not moving, not lifting so much as a hand to shield himself. "Me, Jules."

"Dunley? Nay . . . you can't . . . Ireland. You were with Cromwell." Creigh's knuckles whitened upon the smooth ash of the pike, sick despair gripping his chest as he pictured the boyish face of his young aide-de-camp, knowing in that instant that 'twas indeed Jules. Knowing, too, that he would have to kill him.

"They shipped me back here after Drogheda," Jules whispered, his mouth twisting bitterly. "With all honor. Saying I . . . I was not fit to do combat. 'Tis a story that would take half the night, sir, but—"

A savage oath tore from Creigh's lips as a shout of alarm rang out from the direction of the torture chamber, the sound of men, thundering down the corridor heralding the discovery of their escape. His hands knotted on the pike-staff, his eyes fastening upon Brianna.

But Jules struggled to his feet. "Nay, sir. Trust me," the youth whispered, clasping Creigh's arm. "Your lady—she must be silent, or I vow there'll be naught I can do to aid you."

"Aid me? For God's sake, 'tis your duty to see us back in chains." Creigh's eyes raked the serious face, the determined chin, the uniform of the honored yeoman gaoler whose sole purpose was to monitor the prisoners. He clutched the pike, a sick feeling jabbing deep in his vitals as images of Brianna, Lindley, his father flashed through his mind. "Christ," he hissed, turning the pike's point down toward Dunley's belly. "I daren't risk—"

"Sir, you daren't *not* risk," Jules whispered fiercely. Creigh clenched his teeth at the lad's words, the sound of the thundering boot heels driving onward down the corridor filling the stone walls, piercing the barred windows, the confines of the small room.

Daren't not risk . . . the boy's words beat within Creigh's mind, offering a fragile thread of hope, a thread that might snap into betrayal.

"Creigh, trust him."

He turned, stunned at the sudden strength in Brianna's still quavery voice, the trust infused in her quiet plea.

"Damn it, Bree, what if—"

"I'll not fail you, sir," the young man's voice brought heatings of shame to Creigh's lean cheeks. Then Jules stepped out the door. The light cast from the torches of the running guards washed over the lad's features—features wrenchingly changed from those of the green youth Creigh had ordered about, harried, and aye, come to love like a younger brother in the ranks of the Roundhead army.

Creigh drew Brianna deeper into the veilings of shadows, shocked at the aura of command with which Jules faced the men bolting toward him. Five of them, Creigh counted, burly men with broad, swordsman's shoulders. Men who, despite his skill with a blade, would no doubt subdue him in the end. His hand tightened over Brianna's leaping heart, the feel of it piercing his palm like an iron spike.

"Steadman, Thornley," Jules barked. "What is amiss?"

"Sir, 'tis the room in the cellar," the first man rasped. "The one they use for torture. A prisoner—I know not who—must have made his escape. Colonel Ogden lies unconscious and—"

"A prisoner?" Creigh stared at Dunley through the doorway, astonished at the puzzled expression the lad was able to call to his face. "I knew of no orders for an interrogation this night."

"But there were signs of a struggle . . . a fire lit, chains, aye, and the shackles were wet with fresh blood. I think—I fear 'twas Colonel Lord Wakefield and the woman, for 'twas her gown that lay torn upon the stones."

"Wakefield? 'Tis absurd. Lord Creighton is of noble blood. No order would be given to put him to the rack. And the peasant girl—there would be naught to gain from questioning her under torture's lash."

"I . . . I fear 'twas som-mat of a grudge, sar, 'twixt Colonel Ogden an' those two," piped a man with an accent thick as Yorkshire butter. "I saw 'im whisperin' wi' Sayer Wells at eventide an'—"

"Well, no matter who eluded us, we'd best make haste to secure the building. They could be halfway to the Thames by now."

"Sar, we heard a crashin' sound down here," the Yorkshireman offered. "Mayhap they bolted this way."

"I fear not, Rankin. I've been here nigh an hour, and the only sound I heard was my own blasted fumblings with a candlestick."

Creigh studied the faces of Dunley's command, saw the pain in the lad's earnest eyes. Jules looked away, as if unable to bear meeting their gaze.

"Thornley, you take two men and search the area to the

south," he said. "Steadman and the rest delve into the area 'bout the chamber where you found Colonel Ogden. I'll hie to Wakefield's cell to see if our esteemed guest is yet in his chains."

Creigh watched the group of soldiers, half expecting them to question their young officer, argue. But they merely nodded, with faces full of respect and eagerness for the hunt, then they spun and dashed off. Creigh felt Brianna sag, limp against him, felt his own heart give a leap of relief as he heard the men retreating to whence they had come.

Dunley stood out in the passage long moments, a look of self-loathing crossing his features as he watched his men rush off on their fool's errands. 'Twas breach of trust, Creigh knew, as foreign to the honest youth as the lies Dunley had told to save Creigh from Ogden's plottings at Drogheda. And as Jules swept back into the room, grabbing up the guttering taper, Creigh felt an urge to lay a bracing hand upon the lad's shoulders as he had so oft before. But there was a new stiffness to their narrow breadth that kept Creigh's hand at his side.

"You bear our gratitude," he said softly. "Again I owe you my life."

The solemn eyes met Creigh's. "'Tis far too early to be congratulating ourselves. Hasten." Dunley grasped the pewter base of the taper. Peering out into the corridor, he motioned Creigh and Bree into the wide passage. Candlelight flickered over Brianna's face, and Creigh ached at the sight of it, wraithlike, terrified, still drained of all color. He grasped her hand in his own, wishing he could draw her into his arms, hold her. But Dunley was hurrying down the corridor, his eyes searching the silent passages.

"A boat awaits you below the Cradle Tower," he flung over his shoulder. "If we can but reach it before—"

"Nay."

Dunley turned, stared as Creigh stopped at the mouth of an echoing stairway. "For God's sake, my lord—"

"My father and brother, I'll not leave without them. If Ogden yet lives Christ alone knows what the bastard would do to them."

"But 'twill be nigh impossible to gain their cell and reach the Cradle Tower before the alarm is raised. 'Tis a miracle we've gone this far without—"

"They broke my brother upon the *boot,* Jules. Crippled him."

"I . . . I know." Dunley turned away, and in his eyes Creigh saw the same crushing horror as that of the damned plunging into hell.

"They'll ne'er touch him again. Not while I live." Creigh reached out one hand, taking the taper from Jules's stiff fingers. "There is a passage Charles and I romped about once as lads. 'Tis at the head of these stairs, and it leads—"

An echoing of voices approaching from the other direction stilled Creigh's words. He jerked his head toward the stairway, beckoning the others to follow, but young Dunley had already grasped Brianna's elbow through the billowing mantle, hastening her up the stone steps.

Even in their dire straits, Creigh could hear Jules's whispered chidings. "Have a care, milady . . . 'tis passing steep."

Creigh glanced over his shoulder, seeing the grave nod of encouragement Dunley gave her, seeing Brianna's own lips curve up in but a fleeting hint of her old, bold smile. And he wanted again to gift the young officer with his thanks.

But all thought of even the vaguest of smiles was lost again as they hastened away from the nearing voices, and wound upward, ever upward through corridors—dark, echoing, each shadow whispering of danger. A danger that now held Jules in its treacherous grasp as well, Creigh thought grimly.

When at last they crested the final staircase, Creigh held up a hand to stop them, and peered cautiously through the stone archway. The Wakefield cell was lost in night's blackness, only the weak glow from the meager fire within shining through the small barred window in the door. But even that dismal light was able to pick out a slumped figure outside of the cell, his greasy dark head bobbed over to one side, snores issuing from a wide, sagging mouth.

Creigh sensed Brianna shuddering, heard Dunley's whisper.

"'Tis naught to fear. 'Tis but a guard named Blagden, a poor guard at best," Jules said, taking the taper from Creigh's fingers. "'Twill take me but a moment to rid us of him."

The archway dipped into midnight blackness again, as Dunley carried the candle down the corridor, his stride that

215

of an angry commander, firm, threatening. Creigh watched as the lad's foot shot out, nudging the snoring guard.

"Private Blagden!" Sharp, cutting, his voice sent the sleeping soldier scuttling to his feet, his filthy hand reaching for his sword. But as soon as the small, bloodshot eyes focused upon Dunley, Blagden dropped the ill-kept weapon back into its scabbard as though the sword's hilt were aflame.

"C-Corporal Dunley, sar," the man stammered, "I . . . I but sat down for a moment t' check the leather in my boot. 'Twas a stone caught within, an'—"

"Well, your searching for this stone must have proved passing wearisome, Private Blagden, as afterwards you obviously felt disposed to indulge in a nap."

"N-nay, sar, I—"

"'Tis no small matter, falling asleep while on watch. And you may be certain that the lieutenant will be informed of your neglect of duty."

"B-but Corporal Dunley, sar. The lieutenant . . . he said the last time—"

"That you would be relieved of your position," Jules finished. "'Twill be a vast improvement in the security of the Tower to have you removed from its gates."

"S-Sar . . ."

"While you were lying at your ease a prisoner escaped the White Tower," Dunley said coldly.

"A . . . a prisoner," Blagden stammered.

"Aye. 'Twas but by the grace of God 'tis not one of the Wakefields hieing for the ha'penny road, the way you were neglecting your watch. Now, report to your lodgings and remain there to await your official dismissal."

The look the private shot Dunley was a mixture of hatred and panic. Creigh half expected the surly man to draw sword upon Jules, so furious was the glint in Blagden's eyes. But the stocky guard merely pursed his thin lips into a line rife with menace. "As ye command, *Corporal Dunley*," he spat. "But ye've not heard the last o' Ebeneezer Blagden, sar. Not by a quoit's throw."

Creigh saw Jules level Blagden an indifferent glance, the lad's control worthy of a far more seasoned officer. But it seemed at that moment Jules realized he had made a grave

216

tactical error. Instead of turning and retreating down the empty passage, Private Blagden pushed past him, stalking toward the staircase above which Brianna and Creigh hid.

Creigh's breath caught in his throat, his fist tightening about the pikestaff as Jules's voice rang clear. "Blagden! Halt!" he ordered, attempting to step in front of the man.

But Blagden barged on with an angered growl. "Ye be not me master now, *Corporal* Dun—'Od's wounds!"

Creigh cursed silently, savagely, as tiny, red eyes fastened upon the sheltering archway. Blagden's lips twisted into a sneer as his gaze raked Brianna's still-quavering form, Creigh's unmistakable features highlighted in the glow from Dunley's taper.

"Me neglectin' me duty, was it," Blagden challenged, his eyes narrowed, sly as he reached for his sword. "'Twas you playing at traitor this night, me fine corporal!" But the gloating tone in the private's voice died, his eyes widening in sudden fear as the metallic hiss of Dunley's blade rasping from its scabbard filled the narrow corridor. Creigh lunged into the light of Jules's now-abandoned candle, pikestaff in hand, as Blagden's scream of alarm split the air.

Stomach crashing to his boots, Creigh gauged an opening in the private's ill-practiced defenses. His arms flashed back, then drove forward. The feel of flesh splitting beneath the blade reverberated up Creigh's bruised arms, Blagden's cries of pain mingling in the echoing archways with his screams of warning.

The dull thud of the soldier's body striking the floor was lost in Creigh's hissed demand for the cell-key, the rasp of iron in the recalcitrant lock. The heavy door slammed against the wall, the light from within the cell spilling out onto the stones now wet with a spreading pool of Blagden's blood.

"Sweet Jesus!" Rogan Niall's stunned curse cut the air.

Creigh wheeled to see the Irishman's disbelieving face framed in the doorway, Lindley, his mouth wide with surprise, his father's haggard countenance—

But then their faces were blotted out as Brianna rushed past him into the room.

Creigh sensed she was heading for Lindley, saw her reach out to aid his crippled brother as he struggled up from his

217

pallet, but Rogan's big arms swept out, catching her against a wide-muscled chest. "Bree . . . oh, God, Bree, I thought . . . Sorry . . . I'm so—"

The rage that had been roiling within Creigh burst in a flood of fire at the sight of another man's—any man's arms about her, a rage borne of feeling death's skeletal fingers coil about his throat and being powerless to tear them away, rage borne of watching, helpless, as Saul Ogden tormented Brianna. Unbidden, one hand flashed out, grasping the Irishman's shirt, hurling him against the wall.

"Don't touch her," he hissed through gritted teeth. "Damn you, don't you ever touch her."

"Creigh!" Brianna's voice at his shoulder made him spin around, to see her golden eyes snapping with a hint of their old fire. "What in God's name—"

But he whirled away from her accusing face, from the sounds of the burly Irishman clambering to his feet. Grasping Lindley about the waist, he guided him toward the door. "Hasten," he snarled, "or the whole cursed garrison will be upon us."

He heard Rogan's muttered curses, felt the weight of Brianna's reproach, his father's silent disapproval, but he merely thrust his chin out like a belligerent lad, leading them at a killing pace down corridors echoing with the distant shouts of soldiers.

When at last the little party spilled into the velvet shrouding of night, Creigh sucked in deep breaths of air scented with sweet grass, moonlight, and freedom, his eyes ever seeking the tawny gold of Brianna's curls where she ran, flanked by Dunley and Rogan.

The open green spread before them, wide, dangerous in its path toward the Cradle Tower. As they bolted across the broad expanse, Creigh tightened his grasp on Lindley and struggled to brace his own aching muscles, battered still from the cudgeling on the ship, savaged further at Ogden's hands. But his ribs felt like fire, his exhausted arms nigh weak as a babe's.

They had almost reached the daunting outer wall when Creigh felt the burden of Lindley ease, the warmth of another arm brushing the exhausted limb he had wrapped about his brother. Creigh turned glaring eyes upon the figure opposite him, the moonlight limning the harsh planes of

Galliard Wakefield's face. Hate welled inside Creigh, fierce, raw, mingling with a wrenching inner pain.

"I can carry him," Creigh grated, wanting to dash away Blackthorne's hand.

"He's my son."

The words, dead-quiet, slammed into Creigh's senses like a blow, and he was stunned to feel the heat of bitter tears prickling his eyes. He gave a snort of laughter, wanting the sound of it to rake his father. "Aye, and at your hands they robbed him of his leg."

Creigh heard Brianna's gasp behind him, felt Blackthorne's arm go rigid against Lindley's back. But Rogan Niall's stifled cry dashed away all thought of verbal sparrings.

"St. Savior, look!"

Creigh wheeled at the sound, seeing moonlight glancing off a dozen raised pikes, the nightwind rippling a dozen flowing capes as a bevy of soldiers thundered across the green.

He caught Lindley about the waist, glad, suddenly, of the added support of Blackthorne's arms as they made a mad dash toward the tower that promised escape. Yet even as they crested the walls high above the Thames, it seemed that freedom might elude their grasp. The thick rope Jules had rigged earlier dangled down to a waiting boat, the craft small, yet appearing swift as sea winds. But before Creigh could reach the length of hemp, the sound of the approaching soldiers was drowned out by a gruff, stunned curse.

Creigh caught a fleeting glimpse of a stained leather apron and hairy bare buttocks as Sayer Wells shoved himself from the shadows, extricating himself from the plump thighs of a sour-faced scullery wench. Steel flashed out, the torture master's hand astonishingly quick as his sword sliced the night.

Creigh glimpsed Blackthorne's face, heard Lindley's desperate cry. He raised the pike, meaning in that instant to shove Lindley away, but with a strength Creigh could scarce believe, his crippled brother wrenched himself from Creigh's supporting arms, hurling his own body in front of that of his father.

Horror clogging his throat, Creigh dove for Lindley in a desperate attempt to save him from Wells's sword, but the lame man crashed into the torturer's hulking form, the impact of Creigh's body driving both men hard against the edge of the wall. Creigh saw them teeter upon the stone rim, slip.

A hideous scream split the air, tearing Creigh's heart from his body as he fought to grasp at Lindley. The slender, warm hand clutched his but an instant, Lindley's eyes wide, terrified, catching his. Creigh screamed, fighting desperately to clutch at the hand with his other sweat-damp fist for what seemed an eternity, but the fingers snapped free of his clawing grip.

"Nay!" Creigh lunged toward the wall's edge, his hands clutching at air as the gut-wrenching thud of bodies crashing to the ground far below twisted a knife in his soul. Tears, searing hot, agonizing, blazed down Creigh's cheeks, his gaze locking on the body of his gentle brother, bent, twisted upon the earth like that of puppet whose strings had snapped.

An irrational surge of fury, protectiveness drove through his grief-maddened mind as the cluster of tower guards slammed to a halt, stopping just a heartbeat away from the two fallen men. With a sob, Creigh shoved past his father and Brianna, bolting toward the staircase that led down to the tower yard. Brianna's tormented cry clutched at him, yet he cared not, knew naught but the need to shield Lindley even in death.

His teeth jarred together, head snapped back as a hard hand clenched round his arm. "Nay, Wakefield," Rogan Niall commanded. "There's naught you can do for him."

"Damn you, let me go!" Creigh tried to tear his arm from the Irishman's grip, but Rogan held firm, Jules catching at Creigh's other arm, shoving him toward the rope.

"Creigh . . . Creigh, nay—" Brianna sobbed, her fingers clasping the thin lawn of his shirt, her eyes pleading, wounded.

"Damn it, let me—"

"*Creigh*, he's dead."

Creigh's head jerked up at the sound of Galliard Wakefield's sharp voice, and eyes the storm-gray of seas clashed with those the shade of jagged stone.

"Aye, Father, dead because you—"

"Blast it, Wakefield, do you mean to get Bree killed too?"

Rogan Niall's accusing growl penetrated the haze of grief, fury that choked Creigh. His eyes raised to Brianna's face, pale, tear-streaked . . . beloved.

He felt his sorrow crushing his chest, driving him deep into a grief greater than any he'd ever known, but that fragile, tormented countenance turned up to his forced him to rein his inner anguish, go to her.

"Creigh," she choked, "I—"

"Hasten, Bree," his voice sounded hollow, hard even to his own ears, the sound of the guards resuming the chase drumming in his brain. He helped her grasp the rope's hempen length, watched her lower herself down the outer wall. But even after Blackthorne, Dunley, and Rogan had slid down to the small craft, and Creigh's own aching body was huddled on the boat's hard wooden seat, 'twas not the bite of the coarse hemp he felt on his rope-burned palms, but rather the heat of Lindley's fingers in his, and the hideous sensation of them ripping free as he plunged to his death.

Chapter Seventeen

Creigh shifted his shoulder away from the rough boarding of the ancient hay cart, the flesh hidden beneath his soiled doublet feeling as though a thousand insects with tiny pincers were eating their way into his body. He shut his eyes, forcing his mind to again conquer the gnawing, burning sensation, wishing he could blot out the groaning, rattling of the cart as certainly as his warrior's will could master the pain within his shoulder. But the ceaseless noise hammered on at Creigh's wire-taut nerves until his whole being ached to tear the ill-crafted wheels from their rims, ached to do something . . . anything to rip free the agony strangling his soul.

He fastened dry, gritty eyes upon the sleeping form of Brianna, curled in a ball at the end of the cart, Rogan's arm cradling her against him, as if to protect her from the most savage wounds she had endured this night—those dealt by the grief-honed edge of Creigh's tongue.

His jaw clenched at the memory of her tear-bright eyes, her hands, so gentle as she sought to comfort him. He had wanted to bury himself in her loving, sob out the agony that clawed in his chest. But he had struck her hands away from him, snarled at her to leave him in peace. Still she had huddled near him, desolate, until the big Irishman had drawn her away.

Creigh tore his gaze from her tousled gold hair, the dawn-hazed countryside shifting into the soft, vulnerable curves of her face. Nay, he'd not wanted her soothings, not wanted soft words, or tears, or mourning. He had wanted to feel Lindley's hand within his one more time, wanted but one more chance to cling to the fragile thread of his brother's life.

The cart jarred over a stone, cracking Creigh's shoulder against the wooden sides. His fists knotted, ached, pain from where Ogden's cudgel had burst open the skin what seemed a lifetime ago shooting up his arm. Hours it had been since the wagon had shed the streets of London, endless miles in which each lurch of the wheels had driven lances of guilt deeper into Creigh's heart until now it seemed 'twas Lindley's voice haunting him on the wind, the beloved tones harsh with accusation.

You let me die . . . the voice seemed to whisper.

"Nay," Creigh choked back the anguished denial, not wanting his pain revealed to the man who sat opposite him, empty gray eyes staring out into the first ribbons of dawning. Aye, and yet needing so desperately for one glance, one tear to prove that Blackthorne mourned Lindley's death, too. Creigh wanted to scream at his father, pierce the steely mask that was the Duke of Blackthorne's face . . . wanted to feel those hated arms around him, comforting.

But Blackthorne, silent, still, merely stared out into the rolling English hills.

Wishing, most like, that 'twas you who had fallen . . . a demon shrilled in Creigh's mind. *That you lay on the Tower's ground, broken, dead, instead of the son he favored. The son that ne'er left his side . . .*

Creigh shut his eyes against the image of Lindley's bright head, set against the sleek black coat of their father's stallion the day Galliard Wakefield had abandoned Creigh at Wrensong. There had been in Lindley's face a sorrow, as if, in his simplicity, he could feel Creigh's pain, and also in the depths of those gentle eyes there had been understanding, a wisdom far surpassing his four-and-ten years.

Creigh felt a sob claw at his chest, but he quelled it ruthlessly, gritting his teeth against the horrible grief. What had Lindley been thinking then?

And what roiling thoughts had been flashing through Lindley's mind as he had felt Creigh's damp palm upon his, felt himself slipping . . .

A shudder wracked Creigh's body, the autumn winds feeling suddenly chill. He dug his fingers deep into the flesh of his own crossed arms, trying to still his trembling. 'Twas fever again, trying to gain its fierce hold upon him, Creigh thought grimly. He could feel it seeping through his veins, turning him from chill, to burning, robbing him of the strength he so desperately needed to assure the escape of the exhausted party of fugitives. But no matter how its searings tore at him, Creigh knew he must not, dared not succumb to the malaise, for Brianna's sake. His eyes shifted yet again to her sorrowful, sleeping face. Despite the fact that he'd been naught but a beast to her since they had escaped the Tower, he knew she'd ne'er consent to leave him behind.

Creigh's mouth compressed into a white line. If she knew what he suffered, most like she'd bring the whole cursed cart slamming to a halt, and have the Duke of Blackthorne himself out grubbing herbs for her possets and philters. And if she did that . . . Creigh's gaze turned to the rutted dirt road ribboning out behind them. 'Twas but through the whims of Dame Forturne they had eluded capture thus far. If their progress was slowed even but a little, it could well prove the death of them all.

"Lord Creighton." Jules Dunley's quiet voice made Creigh look up, meeting the young corporal's gaze.

"'Tis sorry I am to disturb you, knowing . . . knowing the grief you must be feeling," Dunley said. "But in but an hour's time we'll reach Ralston House, and the next leg of the journey."

Creigh gave a curt nod, wanting nothing more than for Jules to retire again to the far end of the cart, taking with him his sorrowful eyes and his pity.

"I sent a rider off the day you were brought to the Tower to a man I know yet bears loyalty to Charles—one Crandall Ralston, a simple country squire. He promised to have a fishing craft awaiting off the coast to take you to Jersey."

Creigh battled the returning chill, clenching his teeth to keep them from chattering. "My thanks." Hard, biting, the words had more the sound of a curse than of gratitude. Creigh glimpsed Blackthorne's head jerking toward him, but he stared straight ahead, defying his father to voice disapproval.

"And as for the Irishman, and your lady . . ." Dunley's voice trailed off, and Creigh's eyes snapped up to meet his level gaze. "Ralston and I . . . we agreed t'would be less conspicuous if you traveled alone. That you would bear more chance of gaining freedom without—"

"Without?" Creigh sensed the direction Dunley's concern was leading, and he felt himself bristle, glare. But the lad's eyes never faltered.

"When we reach Ralston House, I will be making my way west, to a hidden cottage, deep in the country. Horses lay ready at Ralston House to carry Mistress Devlin and the Irishman with me, and from the cottage to a ship bound for Ireland."

Narrowing his eyes, Creigh growled, "You and this Ralston take upon yourself a great deal, Corporal Dunley."

"Aye, sir. Because we bear a great risk."

"Damn it, I—"

"Creigh!" Blackthorne's voice cut in. "This man has risked his life to gain your freedom. You'll not rail at him as though he were your cursed servant!"

"Oh, I'll not, eh, father?" Creigh challenged. "Well, if you wish to be spared of my *railings,* you'd best heed this warning. There will be not another word about anyone hieing off to some ship bound for Ireland . . . nay, even if the devil himself nips at our heels."

"Sir, I—" Jules's protest was lost in Galliard Wakefield's angry curse.

"Damn it, Creigh, think!" Blackthorne said. "Not only of yourself, but of the girl. Surely you can't mean to thrust her into Charles's court!"

"What matters it to you, old man? Worried that I'll breed your cursed Wakefield heirs in the womb of a peasant wench?" Creigh snarled the words, glorying in the snapping of anger in his father's eyes.

"'Twould please you no end to believe that, would it not?" Blackthorne grated. "But in truth naught would make me prouder than holding in my arms a grandchild bred of her body."

Creigh gave a bitter laugh, turning away, but Blackthorne barged on.

"She bears more courage than any woman I've e'er known. Aye, and more pride. But even if she had saved Charles from the headsman's axe herself, the king's court would hold naught for her but misery. She'd be despised, Creigh."

"She'd be 'neath my protection." The sound of his own fears voiced by Blackthorne filled Creigh with dread. "None would dare speak against her."

"Oh, aye, they'd dare. They'd dare when you were off fighting with Charles. They'd dare when your back was turned. But 'tis more than that, Creigh. If you drag your Brianna back to France, you'll be hurling her into danger nigh as great as that she just endured."

"I doubt not Brianna can parry the court belles' spiteful tongues."

"But can she parry a murderer's dagger? A glass full of poisoned wine?"

Creigh's eyes flashed to Blackthorne's, the duke's cryptic words closing like icy fingers about his throat. "You speak in riddles, old man."

"Then 'tis a riddle we needs must solve, lest all with the name of Wakefield are cast into the grave, aye, and mayhap the king as well. 'Twas no accident that Lindley and I fell into Roundhead hands. No accident that you, too, were captured."

"Don't try to blame your failings on phantoms. 'Twas your own cursed carelessness that gained you the Tower, led to Lindley's death."

Creigh saw the gray planes of Blackthorne's face tighten, the thin lips pale. "We were betrayed, Creigh, by someone deep within Charles's confidence."

Creigh felt a prickling at the base of his spine, some memory stirring of Ogden's leering face. The odious Roundhead had claimed a master, some force behind his crude power . . . a force driven by hatred of those bearing the Wakefield name. Creigh had dismissed it as madness, ravings, but if 'twas true . . .

Creigh shook free of the shadings of fear, forcing his lips into a nasty smile. "Even if there *is* a traitor lurking about the court," he sneered, "I much doubt that he will trouble himself with a simple Irish lass. But regardless it matters not."

"Creighton, I—"

"Mark me, *Father,*" Creigh warned, a killing edge to his voice. "If either you, my lord duke, or you, Jules Dunley, breathes another word of this cursed plot to exile Bree to

Ireland, you'll answer to the point of my sword. Aye, and I care not whether you profess to be my sire or my friend."

Creigh fixed them each a level stare, then turned his gaze back to the horizon. Yet their words clung to him, Ogden's sneers clamoring in his head, haunting him with the possibility that he was leading Bree yet again into a web of death.

It was three days later that the blazings of fever overtook him, and the billowed sails of the brig *Nora Lee* whirled him not only onto the churning waters of the English Channel, but also into a nightmare world of bodies broken on the Tower yard, of murderers, poisons and Saul Ogden's knowing leer.

Chapter Eighteen

C*hateau aux Marées Vengeresses,* the drayman had called it, *Castle by the Vengeful Sea.* But though the forbidding stone walls, squat round towers that clung to the cliffs that bordered the Isle of Jersey seemed more menacing, sinister than any tempest could be, Brianna cared not, vowing that she'd take Creigh to shelter in hell, if 'twould not jar the wound that held him poised on the knife-edge of death. Blackthorne, he had nigh vowed so as well, his face so grim Bree thought even if they met with the devil old Lucifer would bow to his will.

The crack of Blackthorne's boot into the thick oaken door sent the panel slamming into the chamber's walls, the very stones of Messire Mauricheau Bouret's daunting stronghold seeming to quake with the depths of Creigh's father's fear. Brianna ran beside him, her eyes ever fastened upon the burden he carried. Creigh hung in his father's arms, limp, flushed with fever, the tangled rosewood waves of his hair spilling across his father's travel-stained doublet as the light from three dozen candles struck his haggard face.

"Y-your Grace," the baldpated majordomo blustered as Blackthorne stalked past him. "This . . . 'tis Lady Esmeraude's chamber. Lady Juliet . . . she gave it to—"

"Jolie will give not a tinker's damn if we rob her of this chamber for a year," Blackthorne snapped, "as long as Creigh draws ease. And Lady Esmeraude can sleep upon the straw with the stable boys, much as I care. Ready that cursed bed, or plague take you, I'll break your thick skull beneath my fist!"

Brianna dodged past Blackthorne and the astonished retainer, yanking the stiff, embroidered bed curtains wide, their huge satin petals opening to reveal the cloth-of-gold coverlet as if 'twere the heart of some magnificent flower. Ripping back the bedclothes, Brianna turned, aiding the duke as he bent to lower Creigh's lifeless body to the swansdown feathertick.

"Your Grace, I beg you to wait with this madness at least until my Lady Esmeraude and my Lady Juliet return from the Lockebourough estate," the majordomo burst out, his nostrils flaring. "'Tis all well and good to bring Lord Creighton here, but—but to give a ruffian such as that—that wild Irish Rogan the run of the castle, and to allow such as this woman within the walls . . . Messire Mauricheau would hardly approve of such as she within his walls during his absence."

"His back, Your Grace," Brianna cried sharply. "Have a care." The words, sharper than Brianna intended, drew a gasp of outrage from the long-nosed servant, yet did naught to spawn resentment or anger on the mighty Blackthorne's face. The duke but gave her a grateful nod, gentle as a woman as he eased Creigh down onto the silken sheetings. Carefully, he turned Creigh so that he lay like a child, belly down upon the bed, one cheek deep within the softness of a plump, embroidered pillow.

"Master Beadle." Blackthorne slipped his arms from beneath Creigh, and turned to face the majordomo, eyes bearing the full weight of ancestors bred from the time of Conquering William. "I have little time for your arrogant ways, and less for your master's. I have charged Rogan Niall to gather what supplies we will need to race a message to King Charles. And this woman, Mistress Brianna—you will treat her with the respect due my Lord Creighton's lady."

Brianna felt Beadle's owlish eyes fasten upon her, widening until she half expected him to collapse into apoplexies. "L-Lord Creighton's lady . . ."

"Aye," Blackthorne said in iron-stiff tones. "And until I return from an errand I needs must tend to, Milady Brianna shall be my voice, my command. Ought she needs, wishes for, is to be delivered to her as though I personally had ordered it."

Brianna knelt upon the high bed, hastening to rid Creigh of garments soiled with the race to Chateau aux Marées.

"But—but Your Grace," the majordomo blustered, scurrying to Brianna's side as she drew Creigh's tattered breeches down his long-muscled legs. "She . . . milady mustn't . . ."

"There is naught beneath those rags milady has not already seen," Blackthorne said, taking the breeches from Bree's hand, and casting them onto a chair.

Brianna felt a flush heat her cheeks, then vanish as the duke continued. "She has tended my Lord Creighton from the moment he fell ill. And I wax full certain that she is the only reason he yet clings to life."

Brianna felt Blackthorne's eyes gentle upon her, an instant before they hardened again upon the prim-faced Beadle. "If you or any other within this castle hinder her in any way, you shall be treated as though you defied the Duke of Blackthorne."

"But . . . but 'tis Messire Mauricheau's estate. He—"

"He too will do Brianna's bidding as though he were a scullery lad, or by God, he'll answer to me. I'll not lose Creigh, damn you! I'll not lose another son!"

Brianna felt Blackthorne's torment in her own soul, saw the overbright glistening of wetness in his weary eyes. Her hands stilled in their awkward task of divesting Creigh of his doublet. She reached out, laying her hand upon the arm of his father.

"Your Grace," she said with a briskness, designed to brace Blackthorne in his sorrow. "We'll need cool water to help bring down his fever, and broth . . . if we could but get some sustenance down his throat, help him gain strength to fight."

Blackthorne turned grateful eyes to her, laying one hard hand upon hers, squeezing. And his voice, when he turned back to the servant, was firm, confident. "You heard milady," he snapped out. "Hasten, or I'll see to it that my daughter relieves you of your position."

"You greatly overestimate Lady Juliet's power upon this estate." The majordomo, nigh purple with indignation, drew himself to his full five feet. "I'll see you the items you request," he said stiffly, "but when Messire Mauricheau arrives, I wager 'twill not be I who faces his displeasure."

The bitter twist to Blackthorne's mouth was an exact replica of Creigh's nastiest grin. "I'll risk my son-in-law's wrath, Beadle. Aye, in fact I may well welcome it."

Brianna stared after the small man as he stormed out the doorway, his whole body fairly quivering with suppressed outrage. Beadle turned for an instant, and an uneasy feeling stole over her as the majordomo's eyes narrowed upon her in loathing, shifting then to Blackthorne in what seemed frustration, aye, and an odd expression of anticipation.

"Go, Beadle," Blackthorne roared, "or I'll not be responsible for the consequences."

Brianna saw the majordomo's lip curl in checked fury, then he spun away, vanishing down the brightly lit corridor.

"Plague take them . . . Bouret . . . Beadle . . . plague take the lot of them," Brianna heard Blackthorne mutter. She noted the arrogant tip of his chin, the look of supreme confidence, power she had oft seen on the face of his son. Somehow the strength of it aided her as she shook away vague stirrings of dread she did not understand.

Hastily, she set herself once more to the difficult task of drawing the ragged velvet over Creigh's injured shoulder. He groaned into the pillow, his muscles twitching as if he were trying to shift away from the hands that were causing him pain. But there was little strength in the supple warrior's body in which Bree had known such pleasure. She bit her lower lip to quell the unbidden stinging of the tears that threatened to surface.

Blackthorne's shadow fell across Creigh's face, and Brianna glanced up to see the duke's mouth tighten as he gazed down at his son. "Curse them, curse them all. Naught matters but Creigh," he said, compressing his lips into a line white with anguish. He brushed his knuckles over his son's fire-hot cheek. "Damn it, child, it hurts him so fiercely."

Unshed tears knotted in Brianna's throat, and she raised her eyes to Blackthorne's but a moment, wishing she bore the power to banish the torment she saw in the face of this man she had once thought to despise, yet now looked upon with the deepest affection. "'Tis true, he bears pain, Your Grace," she managed, stripping away Creigh's fine lawn shirt to bare a back once powerful, now savaged by Ogden's cudgel and raging infection. "But he lives . . . he yet lives."

Aye, Brianna thought inwardly, *when he could well lay,*

231

even now, within the grave. She reached out a hand, testing the dry, blaze-hot skin of Creigh's back, wincing at the feel of it, stretched taut, swollen, teeming, still with deadly fever. The fever that had robbed Creigh of reality, turning the voyage to France's blue-hazed coast into the stuff of nightmares.

Yet it could have been worse . . . far worse, Brianna thought with a shudder. *If he'd not fallen off his horse before they had sailed . . .*

"Why, Brianna?"

She heard Blackthorne's tortured voice. "Why did he not tell us that he was wounded . . . in such pain? By God, I care naught if the whole Roundhead army was closing in about us, I would have forced him to stop, seek ease."

"That is why he kept it hidden," Brianna said softly. She shut her eyes, remembering Creigh's ramrod-stiff shoulders, his face, cold, rigid as an iron mask as the party of fugitives rode for the harbor carved into Ralston's land. She had thought 'twas his grief over Lindley's death that had made him ride far ahead, allowing no one close to him that whole endless flight to the coast. But it had been the wound that he had held secreted beneath the folds of his doublet. The wound that might cost them the precious time needed to gain their escape.

As he had the night they had escaped Drogheda, he had held firm to his resolve to keep his own injuries hidden, though even still, Brianna knew not how. Yet two miles from where the *Nora Lee* lay anchored, his weakened body had betrayed him. He had slid from the back of Ralston's gelding at full gallop, his shoulder slamming hard against the unyielding earth.

Even now Brianna's stomach churned at the memory of the cloth of his doublet, soaked through with blood and putrification. She had cut the garment from his body, baring one of the marks that yet remained from Ogden's cudgel. But instead of the fading half-healed lines that crisscrossed most of the bronzed skin, the weal that slashed from the base of his neck to the outer curve of his ribs had turned into a wound seething with infection. An infection that had spread through the entire sheath of muscle drawn over the ridge of his shoulder bone. Had the fall not burst the wound open, allowing the poisons to drain, Creigh surely would have died.

"He's worse, is he not? You—you but fear to tell me." Blackthorne's words spun her back to the grand chamber at Chateau aux Marées, and she looked up to see the duke's lined face close above her.

Brianna ran her fingertips over the angry flesh yet visible around the poultice she had bound over Creigh's wound hours ago, aboard ship. "It takes a bit for the herbs to draw out the poison," she offered with more confidence than she felt. She smoothed the spotless coverlets over Creigh, the silken white pooling at the base of his spine. "If we can but break his fever . . . he is a fighter, this son of yours," she said, battling to curve her lips into a confident smile.

"And you, Brianna child?"

Bree felt the warmth of Galliard Wakefield's fingers beneath her chin. He tipped her face up, peering down with eyes sorrowful as mist upon the sea, eyes with the same depth of honor, compassion that shone in his son's. "What is it you fight for?"

Brianna turned away, unable to meet the gaze that was soft with understanding and sympathy. 'Twas as though he saw the love she bore Creigh, yet knew, as did she, that it could be naught but a memory if Creigh lived to return to his king and his court. Brianna's gaze fell to Creigh's face, the beautifully honed planes defined, harsh against the pillows. "If love holds power at all with the angels, Creigh will live," Brianna said.

Blackthorne cleared his throat, smoothing the tangled hair back from his son's temple. "I loathe the thought of leaving him now, Brianna, even for the little time it will take me to send word to King Charles. But something is afoot— some treason that threatens to undo us all. And unless Rogan and I reach the king in time . . . unless Charles makes haste, all the information Creigh gleaned while in Ireland, all his suffering, Michel's, Lindley's death, 'twill have been for nothing."

Bree nodded, glancing at the door as a tiny sparrow of a serving maid fluttered in, bearing in her plump arms a gem-encrusted tray that held all she had requested. "Make haste to return," Brianna said, an odd catch in her throat. "I know . . . know he senses you are near." Blackthorne winced at her words, his face unutterably weary.

"Your Grace . . . he . . . he needs you so much," Brianna said, wanting, more than anything, to find a way to bridge the years of mistrust, anguish between father and son. "More than even he knows."

Blackthorne swallowed hard, shoulders stooped with years of command, squaring. "I love him, child."

His words, wrenchingly simple, yet rife with longing, tore at Brianna's heart as she watched Galliard Wakefield stride from the room.

Hot . . . so hot . . . Brianna struggled to open her eyes, feeling as if she were afloat upon a sea of flame. She dragged her face from where it lay pillowed in the shallow dip at the base of Creigh's spine. The cloth that she had been smoothing across his fevered flesh in an effort to cool him hung limp in her hand, heated by his skin until it felt hot as a kettle just drawn from the fire. And the room itself seemed hotter still, the roaring blaze in the magnificently carved fireplace and the scores of lit tapers spilling from huge silver sconces painting the opulent room in shades of flame.

With a pungent curse, Brianna sat bolt upright, her fingers testing the height of Creigh's fever, even as her eyes swept the room in disbelief and fury. Sweet Lord, when she had drifted asleep it had been cool, soothing, but now . . .

Bree bolted up from the feathertick, and dashed over to the window casements, high above the floor. Dragging a heavy table beneath it, she clambered atop its walnut surface, still having to stretch up on tiptoe to reach the iron latch that held the mullioned glass panes. She yanked on the stubborn oiled iron, banging her fingers on the recalcitrant latch. But finally it snapped free, and she shoved the window wide, a great gust of cool sea air driving back the oppressive heat.

Scrambling back down to the floor, she swept up a candlesnuffer that lay upon the mantle, extinguishing all but three of the candles with a force that drove the softened tallow down to the silver bases that held them. Then, scooping up the pitcher of once-cool water that the maidservant had brought in upon the tray, she cast the now-hot wetness over the blaze upon the ornate hearth. The flames hissed their protest, flinging dizzying waves of steam from the depths of the fireplace, but the dousing seemed to help at least some, taming the roaring beast into some semblance of a normal blaze.

Brianna stood in the center of the chamber, looking about her in complete confusion. God's blood, who had dragged in all those candles? Built the fire while she slept? She had been exhausted, true, yet the weeks since Drogheda, fleeing through the Leinster countryside, imprisoned in the hold of Ogden's ship, all had fostered within her the need for but little rest. Survival had depended upon waxing alert even in sleep, and she had felt secure in the knowledge that her warrior's senses lay always at the ready. Yet she had heard nothing. No one.

Even still, what could have possessed someone to turn the room of a man wracked with fever into an inferno that would rival the dark king's lair?

"Hot . . ."

The moan from the bed made Brianna whirl about. Creigh's flushed face shifted weakly against the pillow, one hand flopping awkwardly toward his jaw, as if to brush away the heat that burned him.

"Creigh?" Brianna said, rushing to the bedside.

"Hot . . ." Creigh's lips struggled to form the word. "Michel . . . always said . . . end . . . in hell."

Despite herself, Brianna felt a smile tug at her lips. She folded the damp coverlets away from his broiling skin, leaving him bared, yet hopefully far cooler. "Nay, love, 'tis naught so permanent. 'Tis but a bedchamber at your sister's castle that some overzealous—" and stupid, Brianna added mentally—"servant overheated. 'Twill be cool soon. I promise."

"Promise, Bree . . ."

"Aye," she reached up, smoothing away the tangled curls that tumbled over his sweat-beaded forehead.

"Promise . . . won't leave me."

"Nay, I—I won't leave you." Brianna's throat ached at his whispered plea.

"Lindley . . . I—I let him fall."

"Nay, Creigh, you tried to hold him, did all you could."

235

"Could—couldn't hold on . . ."

Brianna felt tears knot in her chest as she watched Creigh's face go taut with grief. "I know."

"Trusted . . . trusted me, Bree. Tried . . ."

She leaned over to catch the tortured words, her fingers threading through his fire-hot ones, tightening into a straining fist, as if to will her own strength into him. "Lindley knew that, Creigh. He loved you. Loved you so much."

Creigh's mouth twisted, bitter against the soft pillow. "Father doesn't. Hates . . ."

The raw anguish in Creigh's face, mingled with the memory of Blackthorne's tormented eyes, twisted deep in Brianna's soul. Skirts tangling about her thighs, she curled close to Creigh, her arms about his naked body, her lips pressing tear-damp kisses to his hot cheeks. "Nay, love. I vow to you, your father . . . he loves you, more than you know."

"Nay, Bree, he—"

The sound of the door slamming open drowned out Creigh's voice. Brianna started, turning toward the door, expecting, hoping 'twas Blackthorne returning from his errand. But instead of the duke, two women swept into the room, one, a vision in emerald satin, her gown a-glitter with gems as hard as her eyes, the other, a shy, graceful doe of a girl.

"Sweet God, Juliet, is the cursed knave mad?" the pale-haired woman hissed, her gaze sweeping the opened windows, Creigh's lean, naked body, before alighting upon Brianna in onyx fury. "Who are you, girl, and who, by George's Cross, allowed you in here?"

Brianna struggled upright, kicking down her skirts as she hastily whipped the sheet up to cover Creigh's nakedness. A self-conscious hand whisked the hair that straggled like rain-wet hay about her cheeks, her other fingers fumbling with a lacing upon the bodice that stuck in sweaty patches to her breasts. "I . . . my name is Brianna Devlin," she said, her gaze shifting from the woman whose face seemed all ice and angles, to the soft, quivering lips of the dark-haired girl. "I—"

"I give not a damn who you are, you little strumpet!" the woman hissed. "You'll away from here at once, or I'll summon the servants to drag you away!"

236

"Maman, don't . . ." the girl, Juliet's voice was soft, pleading, yet threaded through with the tiniest shading of fear.

Brianna stood stiffly, meeting the older woman's affronted glare with one unyielding as stone. "I fear you'll be much disappointed if you attempt to have me evicted. 'Tis at the Duke of Blackthorne's bidding that I tend my Lord Creighton."

"Blackthorne!" The woman spat. "I might well have known he would charge Creigh's care to such as you! But Chateau aux Marées is my daughter's castle, and I vow that your precious duke has but little power here."

"Maman!" the dark-eyed girl raised a reproachful face to her mother, gathering up her pale pink skirts and whisking past the furious older woman to Creigh's side. "You . . . you must forgive the Lady Esmeraude. She has been most distraught since—since word of Creigh's condition reached us."

One of the girl's delicate hands took up Creigh's limp one, the other brushing Brianna's 'neath the veiling of her skirts, as if she bore not the courage to openly defy her mother, yet wanted to offer support.

But Esmeraude Wakefield scarce paused at all, her voice, dripping hatred, filling the room. "Tell me, mistress, when the duke bid you care for Lord Creighton, did he order you to wind yourself about *my son* like a serpent?"

Through the heating flush of Brianna's cheeks, the humiliation, shock of having a stranger burst in upon what had been a moment full of sharing pain, aching love, the label *serpent* seemed to bore into her mind. The jewel-toned gown, glittering jet eyes of the woman—Duchess of Blackthorne—giving Bree a sense of danger, despite the undeniable beauty of the pale-haired woman before her. The woman . . . Creigh's much-loved mother.

Brianna struggled to regain control of her snapping temper, imagining how the scene upon the great tester bed must have appeared to the distraught woman. Smoothing her hand over the silken sheetings now veiling Creigh's legs, she said, "It seems while I slept for a bit, someone got carried away at stoking the fire. Creigh was so hot that I—"

"That you stripped away his clothing and plastered yourself upon him?"

237

Brianna's fists knotted in her ragged skirts, but she forced her voice to remain calm, continuing as though the woman had not spoken. "—that I drew back the coverlets to cool his fever. I but soothed him as he mourned . . ." Bree hesitated. "Mourned the deaths of his brother and his friend."

Impatience curled the duchess's pink lips, then vanished so quickly Brianna scarce believed she had seen it at all.

"'Tis like Creigh to lament the failings of others," she said. "But my son has no further need of the *comfort* of an unkempt peasant urchin, as he now has his family about him."

"Bree . . ."

The duchess's gaze darted past Brianna to the pillow, and as the black eyes fastened upon Creigh's face, Bree was astonished to see a fierce, nigh feral protectiveness snap within them. "Creigh?" the woman's cry rasped across Brianna's nerves as the duchess flitted across to the bed, nigh shoving Juliet out of the way as she descended upon Creigh in a whirlwind of billowing satin. "Nothing shall hurt you now! Maman will take care of—"

"Bree . . . where's Bree?"

Brianna heard Creigh's strained voice, saw his hand fighting through the jeweled cloth, reaching out. "Tigress . . ."

The duchess's breath hissed through her perfect teeth, Juliet Bouret's eyes flashing to Brianna's face in astonishment, and some other emotion Bree could not name, but Brianna bore no patience for any but Creigh. She rounded the bed, caring not what the duchess thought of her as she again sat upon the coverlets. "I'm here, Creigh. All is well," she said, taking his hand in hers. "And look, love, 'tis Juliet and your lady mother come to see you."

"Tigress . . . promised . . . wouldn't leave me." Creigh's lashes trembled on flushed cheeks. "Lindley . . . can still feel . . . hand . . . see falling."

"Creighton, 'tis not your fault!" the duchess's sharp voice cut in, one beringed hand clutching Creigh's bare arm. "'Twas but God's blessing Lindley did not drag you over the wall as well."

Brianna looked up sharply at the hard tones in Creigh's mother's voice, the sound incongruous with that of a mother grieving for a dead son.

Creigh groaned, and shifted his head toward Brianna, his gray eyes slitting open a whisper as he searched for her. "Bree . . ." he whispered. "Hold . . . hold me."

Brianna raised her eyes to Creigh's mother, feeling, despite the woman's biting insults, a stirring of sympathy for this woman who had lost one son and no doubt felt rejected by the other. But what compassion Bree could muster vanished as she looked into Esmeraude Wakefield's eyes. The delicate oval of the Duchess of Blackthorne's face was dark with a fury that sent a quiver of unease down Brianna's spine, unease mingled with an odd, crawling feeling in the pit of her stomach. As if . . . if Creigh's mother held a jealousy bred of the body, not of the blood.

"Witch!" the duchess gasped. "Dear God, you've bewitched him!"

Brianna paled at Lady Esmeraude's words, remembering, as a child, hearing of those accused of dabbling in devil-arts facing the justice of the flaming stake. 'Twas no idle accusation, but a threat chillingly real.

"Maman, don't be absurd!" Juliet cried.

Brianna's chin tipped up, her gaze, calm, unflinching, meeting that of Creigh's mother, yet 'twas as if those onyx eyes beckoned her to tread upon pools of dark ice, smooth upon the surface, yet treacherous beneath.

"'Tis but the fever speaking," Brianna said levelly. "I vow sometimes he yet thinks himself to be at the Tower."

"The Tower?" the duchess sneered. "Nay, milady strumpet, you need not spin your wiles for me. I know much about a woman's chains, woven to ensnare a man, and have seen a hundred far comelier than you try and fail to trap my son. Once Creighton awakes—has those of his station about him—you, with your rat-snarled hair and plain face, shall be worth naught but his scorn."

"Esmeraude!"

A bitter curse broke from within the doorway, all three women slewing around to see Rogan's russet head and a travel-wearied Blackthorne framed within the arch, his mud-spotted boots, branch-torn mantle yet smelling of the wild sea winds, his eyes clashing like the tempests that tore at the rocky coasts.

Juliet stiffened, the duchess's lips curling in hate, and Brianna felt a chill sweep over her skin, as though from an opened tomb. *"Oui,* husband, 'tis I," Esmeraude said. "Arrived, it appears, just in time to save Creighton from your fumblings."

"In time to choke the lad with your cursed power-greedy hands, more like."

Brianna was stunned at the depth of enmity that raged in Blackthorne's eyes.

"Go, woman, mourn for the son who already lays buried, instead of murdering Creigh as well with your blasted interference."

"You dare to speak of murder to *me?"* Esmeraude sneered. "'Twas you who cast Lindley from the Tower wall, surely as if you threw him from the stones yourself."

Brianna heard Rogan's disbelieving gasp, saw Juliet Bouret's eyes swim with tears, Blackthorne's face go gray. Unable to stop herself, she slid from the bed, hastening to the duke's side.

"'Twas none of His Grace's doing!" Bree cried, but it seemed Creigh's father was beyond hearing her, seeing ought but the face of his wife, subtle evil wreathed in a nimbus of pale gold. Brianna wanted this man for whom she now cherished deepest affection to fly at the woman who was his wife, to cut the sharp words from her tongue with a scathing defense of his own innocence. But he only stared at Lady Esmeraude, endless silent seconds, his face pale with a defeat Brianna did not understand.

"How," he whispered. "How did you . . ."

"How did I discover the culmination of your grand farce? I bear my ways, *husband,"* Lady Esmeraude said with a coldness that made Brianna's eyes lock upon her, searching for any hint of emotion beneath the delicate curves of her face. But the half-smile that curved the duchess's lips made Brianna think unaccountably of a glutted snake, its belly distended with a rabbit's babe. Creigh stirred against the pillows. Bree started to go to him, stopped, feeling that same odd panic that drove the mate of a wounded falcon to feign injury, drawing down predators upon itself.

"Cease this warring, both of you," Bree said, her eyes flashing from Esmeraude to Blackthorne. "Or at the least leave the chamber so Creigh can rest."

"I take no orders from a peasant slut," Esmeraude

sneered, "I who answer to none but the queen herself."

"The *dowager* queen." Blackthorne's voice held an edging of steel, and Brianna saw the duchess's iron-hard mouth twitch, as though her husband had at last dealt her a verbal blow.

Esmeraude tossed her moon-silk curls, her nostrils flaring in disdain. "A woman's power comes through her sons, and Henrietta-Maria yet holds her Charles's ear."

"And she may well hold his head, severed from his body if she fails to cease her foolish meddling! Power means naught, woman, when your child lies dead. Lindley—"

Esmeraude Wakefield's harsh laugh cut through Blackthorne's words. "Instead of hiding your head, sniveling over Lindley, *Your Grace,* you should be on your knees thanking God that for the first time in over fifty years the House of Blackthorne shall bear an heir who is a whole man—a man in body and spirit."

An iron-toed boot seemed to slam into Brianna's stomach at the duchess's words, Lindley's gentle, pale face rising in her memory with images of both Creigh and Blackthorne's grief. She heard Juliet Bouret gasp, her face crumpling as a sob choked her.

"How . . . how could you, maman? Father? How . . . with Lindley dead . . . and Creigh lying here—and—and Michel . . ." Raw, tearing pain savaged the delicate curves of Juliet's face.

Brianna felt an urge to reach out to the dark-haired waif, take her in her arms, rock her like a sobbing child, but Juliet caught up the billows of her skirts, fleeing past Rogan in a cloud of pink satin and wracking sobs.

Blackthorne stared after her, the jaw so like Creigh's clenching.

"See what you've accomplished now," Esmeraude taunted. "The poor maid was nigh devastated with grief anyway when she received the news of her precious Michel. And now, she's off to weep again. Who knows, she might well be carrying Messire Mauricheau's babe by now, and I vow the knight will not take it kindly if she miscarries of his heir."

"Get out." The duke's voice was low, deadly, more dangerous than Brianna had ever heard it, yet holding an edge of pain so deep she could feel it within her own heart.

241

"Go," the duke said, "or I vow I'll kill you where you stand."

Lady Esmeraude tossed her head, a laugh like the sea breaking over jagged shells rippling from her throat. "Very well, I'll go, Galliard. Revel in your paltry power over our son while you yet hold it. As soon as Creighton awakens, you will again hold naught but his contempt." Esmeraude started toward the doorway, drawing back her skirts as she swept past Brianna and Blackthorne, as if she feared to soil herself. She stepped into the corridor, turned, onyx eyes narrowed to slits. "But mark me, Galliard, both you and your peasant minions," Esmeraude hissed low. "If my Creighton dies . . . if he dies, hell will not be deep enough for you to hide in."

Rogan's hand cupped Brianna's shoulder, yet despite its warmth an odd quiver of fear and dread iced through her, chilling her further still as Blackthorne's voice fell in lifeless tones in the silence. "As long as you burn there beside me, my lady," he said, "hell will be the greatest pleasure I've ever known."

Brianna looked down at Creigh, issue of their bodies, torn by their hate, and wondered if he would ever escape the prison they'd cast about him.

Chapter Nineteen

The night stole across Chateau aux Marées like a thief, unfurling its black cloak to savage the gnarled trees with swords of tempered wind. Brianna peered up at the open window high above, letting the breezes that fled from the darkness wash across her face, wishing that she could feel something, anything to rid her of the numbness that weighed her body and soul.

But the hours of vigil that had melted three times from dawn to dusk had drained away what strength she still possessed, stealing away the last threadings of hope.

He was going to die.

Bree shut her eyes, fighting to block out the image that haunted her yet from the embroidered pillow but an arm's length away—handsome, patrician features drained of even the flushings of fever, the hair, so wild and glorious that even the wind seemed unable to resist running fingers of mist through its waves, now lay limp, dulled, and his back barely stirred with the laborings of his lungs to draw breath.

The festering flesh beneath the poultices she had changed throughout the weary days had at last begun to heal, the poisons draining from Creigh's body, leaving the skin pale, but healing. But 'twas as if he bore no will to live, had not the strength to pull himself from the despair that had driven him past bearing.

Brianna heard a shifting at the bedside, and turned to see Galliard Wakefield's head bent low over his son, the once proud countenance of the Duke of Blackthorne that of a general, defeated. *He knows,* Bree thought dully, too tired to drag her eyes from Blackthorne's face. Some selfish part deep inside her was glad. Glad to be spared the pain of having to voice aloud that Creigh lay dying. Yet despite the cruelties of Lady Esmeraude, and after having witnessed the love Juliet Bouret bore her brother, Bree thought 'twas only right that they be summoned to the chamber now.

Forcing herself to move, she walked to the side of the bed, laying one hand upon Blackthorne's shoulder. "Sir," her voice was thick with tears. "'Tis . . . 'tis time. Creigh's sister and mother . . ."

"Nay!"

Blackthorne dashed her hand away, anguished gray eyes piercing her with sorrow, and helpless fury. "I'll not let her soil even his dying! I'll—"

Bree clasped the duke's gnarled hand, tears squeezing from beneath her lids as she looked past him to where Creigh lay. Suddenly she froze, staring at Creigh's ash-gray lips. They moved.

Brianna's breath snagged in her throat, her heart ceased beating. "Sir . . . sir, he . . . Creigh . . ."

But Blackthorne's face had taken on a fierce glow, his eyes locking upon his son. "Creigh!" his voice was commanding, unyielding, brooking naught but response from the one his order was directed to, yet laden with a love that was nigh a palpable thing. "Creigh lad!"

Creigh's lips parted, forming a word Bree couldn't interpret, the startlingly dark lashes against his pale cheeks quivering as he tried again.

"Father . . ."

Brianna felt the tiniest springing of hope within her breast, saw Blackthorne's exhausted face alight. "Aye, lad, 'tis me," the duke managed, "Creigh, son . . ."

The muscles in Creigh's face strained, taut beneath their nigh-translucent skin, his hand clenching into the softness of his pillow as if—as if he battled to cling to something precious.

"Nay!" he groaned again, "nay, Father, don't!"

"What lad? I—"

"Promise . . . Don't—don't leave me."

Brianna knelt beside the bed, skimming a hand over Creigh's brow. "He'll not leave you, love. Your da and I, we're right here."

"Nay! Horses . . ." Creigh's hands grasped at the pillow, his fingers digging deep, shaking, his face contorted in a heart-wrenching mixture of fear, hurt, and confusion. "Scared . . . I'm . . . scared, Father. Don't!"

Bree pulled his head against her breasts, holding him, stroking his tangled locks. "'Tis all right, love," she whispered brokenly. "Don't," she swallowed hard. "Don't be frightened."

"Want . . . want Father!" Creigh cried, struggling weakly in her arms. "Father! Promise . . . promise I'll be good. Best—best at whole . . . whole court. Father, promise . . ." Brianna's gaze caught Blackthorne's tormented face.

His voice was gruff with emotion as he reached out to touch Creigh's hair. "You were always the finest son a man could ever wish for, lad. Always."

"Riding . . . riding away. Can't catch . . . Papa! Papa! Don't . . . don't leave me here." Child's sobs, all the more horrible because they came from a man, ripped through Creigh's body, tears streaming down cheeks rigid with such inner torment, it broke Brianna's heart.

"Wrensong."

She heard Blackthorne's agonized whisper. "Dear God, the lad is reliving Wrensong. Bree, child, please—"

Brianna felt Blackthorne's arms ease between her and Creigh, the big man lifting his son gently as though Creigh were yet ten years old, cradling him against his chest. "All is well, Creigh, lad," the duke soothed brokenly. "Papa . . . Papa is here. I'll not leave you."

"Scared, Papa. Love me. So . . . scared."

Brianna's fingers clenched in the folds of her gown, tears streaming unabashedly down her face as she watched them—father, son, both drowning in seas of anguish bred long ago. Bred, Bree sensed, through a pair of fragile white hands, cunning onyx eyes, and a mouth as sweet as a fallen angel's.

But as the hours passed, 'twas as if the love Creigh and his father had once borne each other yet retained some mystical power, the tears that mingled upon their cheeks somehow inducing Creigh to cling to life.

Nigh dawn, Juliet Bouret, her dark-circled eyes reddened with weeping, slipped into the room, curling at her father's feet to lean one pale cheek against Creigh's leg. She clung to her brother, silent, her lashes drifting shut, lips forming some prayer she alone could hear.

Brianna retreated to a dim corner of the room, feeling, of a sudden, the outsider, lost in the elegant surroundings, a street waif pressing her nose against the mullioned glass windows of a crowned prince's domain.

'Twas as if even Creigh's beloved features had shifted beneath the drapings of gold cloth, set amongst furniture so magnificent the small prie-dieu in the corner was most like more costly than the entire Devlin farm.

Here was where he belonged, surrounded by laces more precious than jewels, petted and adored by the most influential people in what remained of the English Royalists. Heir to the legacy of what remained one of the most powerful families in the aristocracy. While she . . . she no more had a place in this world than the scullery maid who darted about with soot smudged upon her freckled nose.

Bree gripped the lion's head arms of the chair, wanting—needing—desperately to go to Creigh, knowing that Blackthorne would welcome her, that there would be no censure in Juliet's sweet face. But she could not. She but watched Creigh, silent, rejoicing as a hint of bronze again tinted his skin, his mouth regaining its firmness, the stubborn arrogance she had come to adore, while the shallow rattle that had been in his lungs faded into sighs, heavy with weariness.

Silent as she had come, Juliet Bouret departed, pausing only to brush a single kiss across her father's weathered cheek.

As the girl swept from the chamber, Brianna saw Blackthorne's craggy features contort. He buried his face in the coverlet bound about his son, his broad shoulders shaking. Brianna thought Galliard Wakefield had forgotten she yet existed, but as Creigh stirred, a moan coming from his parched lips, Blackthorne raised his head, silver eyes full of gratitude. "He's going to live, Bree, child," the duke choked. "Sweet God, he's going to . . ."

Brianna rose from the chair, going to Blackthorne, daring to rest her fingers upon Creigh's chest. "Aye," she whispered. "He's breathing naturally. No trace of fever." She shut her eyes, tears searing her cheeks. "'Twill—'twill mean so much to him. Knowing that 'twas you who stayed . . ."

Blackthorne's features seemed suddenly horribly old as his gaze turned down to Creigh's still face. "Nay, Brianna," the duke whispered. "'Tis too late for us, Creigh and me. Esmeraude has assured that. If she were to be sucked into Hades on the morrow 'twould make no change between us." Galliard stopped, rising reluctantly, easing Creigh onto the rumpled feather tick. "But for you . . . there is yet some chance." Blackthorne turned, catching up Brianna's hands in a crushing, pleading grasp. "Don't let her drag Creigh into the abyss with her, Brianna Devlin. Hold him. Aid him where I cannot."

The duke released her, then leaned down, pressing his lips to Creigh's brow for a long, aching moment. "Take care of him for me, child," he bid her. Then Blackthorne turned, striding from the echoing chamber.

"'Od's blood, Tigress, I swear to you, I could take on the whole of Cromwell's army with this shoulder of mine, if you'd but let me free of this cursed bed!" Creigh's grousing filled the sunlit chamber. "Four days it's been since I awoke, and the wound is fit as 'twill ever be. Unless I start testing it by hefting my sword, the muscle may scar, and I'll ne'er be able to wield a blade again. How like you the prospect of bearing that calamity upon your conscience?"

"My conscience is quite burdened enough as it is, thank you, my lord Creighton. One more sin such as that will make but little difference to St. Peter," Brianna flung over one shoulder, reveling in the sound of Creigh's fit of temper. "If you'll recall, sir," she teased, spinning about with a chessboard in tow, "when you decided you were passing hale yesterday and attempted to rise from your bed, it took three servants and me to drag you from where you'd collapsed upon the floor to the bed that—even as stubborn a wretch as yourself—must agree you abandoned too soon."

Creigh glowered at the chessboard as she settled it upon the bed beside him, the bronze tinting his fever-sharpened features filling Brianna with a sunny temperament that even his foul humor failed to dampen. "'Twas the cursed carpet," Creigh growled. "If you and that blasted Juliet had not left it twisted up like a bloody mass of tree roots, I'd have been just fine."

"Oh, aye, fine," Brianna agreed with a sage wag of her

head. "You looked passing fine when your face turned the color of old tallow, and you pitched into a dead faint."

"Damn it, Bree, I didn't faint, I . . ." Despite the embarrassment in his face, Bree caught the hint of laughter in Creigh's eyes. She raised one brow. He grimaced. "I merely decided to examine the pattern of the carpet at closer range."

Laughter bubbled in Brianna's throat, the feel of it upon her tongue beautiful after so long a drought of joy.

"I'll have you know 'twas a pattern worked during the time of Queen Elizabeth," Creigh defended, "a most rare— oh, plague take you and your blasted chessboard, you saucy little witch!" Creigh jerked up one coverlet-veiled knee, sending the inlaid game board and its exquisitely wrought armies scattering to the floor.

Brianna grabbed instinctively for the gilt edge of the chessboard, but before she could reach it, Creigh's hand shot out, gripping her arm. She squealed with laughter, overjoyed at the astonishing strength again within that sinewy grasp. He pulled her off balance, sending her sprawling across the great tester bed, the gown Juliet had loaned her flying about her in waves of biscuit-colored taffeta. She made a halfhearted attempt to wriggle away, but Creigh rolled her beneath him in a tangle of coverlets and long-muscled limbs.

Bree looked up into his laughing gray eyes, their silvery light washing over her in glorious waves. "Creigh . . ." she protested, shoving against his chest, "'tis too soon for you to be . . ."

"And what do you expect, milady?" he asked archly. "Since you'll not allow me to practice with my sword, I needs must find other ways of testing my prowess."

"Your *prowess* is just fine, you arrogant Sassenach—"

"Arrogant, *aching* Sassenach, milady," Creigh cut in, and Brianna felt a tautening in the pit of her stomach at the fire in his eyes, that turned his teasing gaze to molten silver. His hands cupped her face, the faintly calloused palms curving about her cheeks, delving into the soft masses of her plaited hair as Creigh lowered his lips, tasting the tip of her nose. Bree's breath caught, ragged in her breast, the feel of his warm, moist, vibrantly alive mouth upon her skin filling her with roiling happiness as he nipped at her jawline, chin.

"Creigh—Creigh, you mustn't . . ."

A satisfied growl rumbled in his chest as his mouth trailed down her throat, pressing hot kisses to the pulsing artery that bore her life's blood, blood now singing with passion. Bree whimpered as he molded her, coverlets and all, beneath him, the hardening heat of his body permeating even the thick wad of satin-cased down between them. "Mustn't, wood-witch?" he said against her skin. "You leave me no other choice."

Brianna felt herself surrendering, past caring that he was yet weak, past caring that the door to the chamber stood open to any who chanced past. 'Twas but heaven to feel Creigh's strong arms again about her, feel him weave the magic of his loving in this elegant room which had begun to feel more a prison to her than London's Tower.

She arched her head back, shivering with pleasure as Creigh's lips charted the sensitive flesh exposed by the low neckline, his tongue darting out to moisten the heated curve of her breast, taunting the swelling nipple that strained against the fine cloth. Brianna felt the heat of his breath penetrate the layers of taffeta, the sharp edges of his teeth rasp against the hardened bud through its covering of cloth.

His fingers worked the fastenings of the stomacher that bound the front of the gown together, the kiss of the cool air upon her skin sending tremors of pleasure through her body. A moan started deep in the pit of her stomach, his hot caresses drawing it out until it broke from her lips in a pleasured groan. And she ached for the mouth that swept closer, closer to her aching nipple to take it into the hot wetness of his suckling. "Creigh," she breathed. "I—"

All of a sudden, the heated pleasure that had been sluicing through her stopped, as the wondrous feel of his kisses was abruptly withdrawn. Bree opened passion-drugged eyes, and the cocksure grin that stretched Creigh's mouth doused her flaming desire like a tub-full of new-fallen snow.

She narrowed her eyes, glaring at him as he feigned a yawn, pillowing his head upon the breasts that yet burned for his kisses. "And what, pray tell, ails you of a sudden, Lord Creighton?" she bit out.

"'Tis but that you were right, love. I yet suffer the effects of my wounds more deeply than I'd imagined. Perhaps we might attempt our 'swordplay' another day—Oww!"

249

His teasing was cut short by a pillow being slammed into his face with all the force Brianna could muster. He rolled to his back, laughing, trying to pull her with him, but she got free, sitting upright in a flurry of billowing taffeta and rosy, kiss-blushed flesh.

"Creighton Wakefield, you can bloody well attempt your *swordplay* upon some other poor unfortunate from now on," Bree blazed, tugging the edges of her bodice together over her breasts. "For I'll damn well not—" Her tirade died in her throat, her eyes locking upon the opened door. Hot blood flooded her cheeks, turning even her breasts crimson as she stared into the wide eyes of Esmeraude Wakefield.

With a gasp, Brianna fumbled with her bodice, struggling to shield her bared breasts from Creigh's mother's keen gaze, but Creigh met Lady Esmeraude's stare without having so much as the decency to flush, his skilled fingers taking over the refastening of Bree's recalcitrant garment.

"Welcome, my lady," Creigh grinned. "I was just giving Brianna a lesson in defending her virtue here amongst the cavalier court."

Brianna expected cold fury from the woman now sweeping into the room, or at the very least, bitter dislike, but Esmeraude Wakefield turned upon her a smile devastatingly rich in tolerance. "My son should be well versed in those techniques, Brianna dear," Esmeraude trilled. "These worry lines in my face will attest to the fact that he's well-practiced in affairs of the like." She reached out a white hand, tapping Creigh with the end of the fan she carried. "But you, sir, should have a trice more respect for the maiden who saved your life."

Brianna stared, astounded, unable to fathom this smiling Lady Esmeraude, with her ready laughter, and eyes that sparkled, just a shade away from holding real warmth.

"I bear Brianna the greatest of respect, maman, I assure you," Creigh said, catching his mother's hand and carrying it to his lips. "If I did not, this compassionate healer you see before you would most like slit my throat with her rapier. She nigh did, you know, during the siege of Drogheda."

"Then we owe her for your life twice over, do we not?" Esmeraude turned toward the still-flushed Brianna. "We must make certain all her efforts on your behalf prove worth her while."

Creigh's booming laugh rang out, but Brianna felt some of the humiliation racing through her ease as his hand clasped her wrist, drawing her close. Creigh's eyes held Brianna's long seconds, his voice softening as he said, "I fully intend to display to her my undying gratitude." He smiled. "For however long it might take to do so."

In spite of the warmth that spread through her at his earnest words, Brianna caught a glimpse of Esmeraude's face out of the corner of her eye. The porcelain curves were yet smooth, smiling, only the lashless onyx eyes betraying the duchess's agitation.

"'Tis most . . . most generous of you," Esmeraude said, "but I'm certain Mistress Devlin will understand that you bear many responsibilities in your rank. As the rightful heir Wakefield, you—" As if the duchess herself caught the hint of satisfaction in her voice, Lady Esmeraude quickly cracked her voice into a tiny, pathetic sob. She turned away, dabbing a lace-edged handkerchief to her eyes.

"Maman." Creigh's voice was laden with love and concern, and Brianna felt a deep stirring of dislike as she saw Lady Esmeraude clasp his hand.

"Nay, Creighton, 'tis all right. Even in the face of the tragedy of dear Lindley's death, a mother must be strong." The duchess sniffled. "'Tis for you and Juliet that I must—must bury my grief."

Brianna's fingers twisted in the folds of taffeta, her eyes searching the duchess's face, but Esmeraude Wakefield was the picture of self-sacrifice and motherly devotion, and Creigh looked back at her with the eyes of a son who would do anything to spare her pain.

A sharp surge of anger speared through Bree at the sight of Creigh's mouth tightening in sorrow over the brother he truly loved, the memory of Esmeraude Wakefield's casual dismissal of Lindley's death rasping across Brianna's temper.

Bree bit the inside of her lip to stay the reproving words that sprang to her tongue, but as Esmeraude effected a mien of motherly courage, Brianna had an urge to slap her beautiful face.

"Nay, Creighton, my heart's treasure, there is naught I can do now for Lindley, but I fully intend to devote myself to seeing you totally recovered."

"My thanks, lady mother," Creigh said. "I appreciate your offer, truly I do. But there is naught I could ask for in a nursemaid that my Tigress does not provide." Creigh caught Brianna's stiff fingers, and Bree swallowed the lump of anger in her throat.

Esmeraude's smile grew strained. "Well," she said with a forced laugh. "'Tis obvious I am to be of no use to you in the sickroom. But, even the most *devoted* of nursemaids must take respite sometimes, Creighton. Though you deem me not necessary to dispense your physics, I vow I could at least sit here beside you, and entertain you while this poor child takes a bit of fresh air. She's pale as a shade and hasn't seen the sunshine since the day you arrived."

"'Tis all right, my lady," Brianna objected, "I've no wish to—"

"Damn it, Bree, she's right." Creigh's voice made Brianna's gaze jump to his contrite face. "I'm a selfish beast not to have noticed it sooner. You've been locked up in this blasted room for days, scarce eating, not sleeping. 'Tis a wonder you've not taken sick yourself."

"Creigh, I—"

"My daughter, Lady Juliet, tours the gardens every day at this hour," Esmeraude interrupted smoothly. "I'm certain she would be pleased to show you the ... amusements about Chateau aux Marées."

Brianna's chin set, stubborn, some part deep inside her sensing that 'twas dangerous to abandon Creigh to his sweetly smiling mother. But Creigh's eyes turned suddenly wistful, his voice insufferably sad.

"No doubt it has been a long time since Jolie had anyone of her own age to gallivant about with. Your wit might help her, Tigress, ease her sorrows as you have my own."

Brianna's jaw clenched at the knowledge that, though she could have withstood any form of pressure, or wheedling from Esmeraude Wakefield, a single pensive look from Creigh had shattered her resolve.

"How do I find the gardens?" Bree conceded defeat.

"Why, Beadle will be most pleased to show you," Esmeraude scarce raised her voice.

"Then where may I find Beadle?" Bree started as someone stepped up behind her. She wheeled, nigh bumping into the smirking majordomo.

"If milady will follow me," the man's lips curled in a subservient smile.

Creigh lifted one strong hand, blowing her a kiss. Bree gritted her teeth, turning to follow the majordomo's stiff shoulders down the narrow passage. But with every step she took she sank deeper into the sensation that she was abandoning an unsuspecting victim to a cunning, pale spider.

When Beadle and she had nigh reached the huge, heavy doors leading out to the castle grounds, the servant paused, taking up a loose wrap of amber-colored velvet and offering it to her. "'Tis most important to my lady Esmeraude that your stay at Chateau aux Marées be a . . . comfortable one. 'Twould be a shame indeed for any . . . er, inconvenience to befall the woman who saved my lord Creighton's life."

Brianna looked up sharply, catching in the servant's tone some subtle hint of sarcasm, a cynicism that seemed to bind into the folds of the rich velvet wishes that were far from kindly. She took the garment from his hands with a strange reluctance, shivering as she remembered tales she had heard of Catherine de Medici, that paragon of all scheming mothers, working her deadly poisons into a pair of gloves.

Banishing such musings as folly, Brianna resolutely thrust her arms into the fur-trimmed sleeves, the soft folds falling about her body in an elegant caress.

"Chateau aux Marées holds many most intriguing curiosities, milady," Beadle offered silkily. "Take your fill of them."

"Curiosities?"

"Aye. Messire Mauricheau's menagerie is the most envied in all of England. Even now he is off attempting to secure yet another nest of adders for what he terms his 'pit of death.'"

"How charming." Brianna met the little man's eager gaze steadily, refusing to let him see how much his words had unsettled her. "I shall have to explore this collection of horrors as soon as I find the Lady Juliet."

Beadle smiled. "You'll be able to witness its full glory once my master arrives home. There is a northland bear he's been preparing for a baiting these many months—a fearsome beast with blood-colored fangs and claws that have already torn the flesh from his first keeper."

Bree couldn't stem the shudder that worked its way down

253

her spine. "I am most certain the man Messire Mauricheau has installed in poor Dunstan's stead would be pleased to aquaint you with his charges." Beadle's eyes narrowed to gloating, eager slits; one twig-thin hand reached out, opening the great door. He pointed across the cloud-shadowed yard to where the silhouette of a black-stone building lurked against the castle's curtain walls. Brianna felt suddenly cold, shadings of feelings, unseen menace brushing her with bloodless wings. "The beasts, they prowl within," Beadle said, the expectant smirk on his face goading Brianna to force her lips into a grimace of dismissal.

"Nay, Master Beadle, they prey without the walls," she said, "I've ne'er yet met the animal whose fangs and claws could compare with the cruelty of man." She took small pleasure in the majordomo's souring expression. "Now, if you would direct me to the garden?"

"It lies but a little way down this path," the servant said, pointing toward a badly overgrown trail that wound through framing hedges of untrimmed yew. "Lady Juliet, she favors grubbing among the roses, but I fear 'twill do her little good. It seems some malaise has struck at the roots, and they are withering."

Brianna gave the man a wary nod, sensing some undercurrent, some hidden meaning that had naught to do with Creigh's sister's passion for flowers. But she did not remain in the grand hall, questioning the aggravating man further. The interior of Chateau aux Marées seemed suddenly oppressive, the opulent leather wall coverings, heavily carved chairs, tables, seeming but a sham veiling away secrets so dark that to discover them could prove one's undoing.

Brianna shoved away the unsettling feelings, stepping out into the storm-shrouded courtyard and hurried in the direction Beadle had indicated.

She had wandered for nigh a quarter of an hour, with no sign of Creigh's sister, when, through the tangle of hawthorn and yew, she heard the muffled sound of weeping.

Pushing aside a twisted clump of brush, Brianna eased herself through the gap it made in the hedging, stepping into the one part of the castle garden that seemed to bear light. But if light could be measured in the joy to be found in someone's face, the tear-streaked countenance of Juliet turned the small, immaculately tended corner of these gardens into the most dismal on the whole estate. Juliet knelt upon the freshly spaded earth, crumbling the dirt clods with her small hands. Her skirts were crumpled about her legs, great patches of earth clinging to stockings of the finest silk and pink satin slippers molded for dancing. And her cheeks, robbed of their natural rosiness, were streaked with dirt and tears as she dug about five badly ailing rose trees with what seemed nigh desperation.

"My lady?" Brianna said softly, stopping just within the circle of meager sunlight that was able to penetrate the encroaching clouds. "Is aught amiss?"

Juliet spun around, all but upsetting herself into the thorny plants as she swiped at her streaming eyes with one mulberry-colored sleeve. The girl flushed guiltily, and Brianna could see her try to force her baby-soft lips into some semblance of a smile.

"Miss . . . Mistress Devlin . . ." she said, scrambling to her feet. "I . . . 'tis but . . . but one of those vagaries maman is always telling me brides are prey to." Juliet's gaze fastened upon her own dirt-crusted fingernails. "These roses . . . they were a gift . . . a wedding gift from someone who . . . died." The word fell from lips that the child could not keep from trembling. Brianna saw a single, silvery tear well at the corner of Juliet's eye, saw it roll slowly down her cheek. "Maman . . . she says 'tis foolish to set such store by a few paltry cuttings, and I know most would think her right, but . . . but these are all I have left of him, and—"

Brianna ached for the girl as Juliet covered her face with her hands, unable to stem the sobs that shook her slender form. "I'm sorry . . . I can't . . . can't help . . ." Instinctively, Brianna went to her, drawing her down onto a chipped marble bench that flanked a gnarled oak. She took Juliet into her arms, gently, comfortingly, sharing the girl's rending pain.

"Michel," Bree said softly, sensing Juliet's need to free the grief she had so long kept locked deep inside, knowing from the deaths of Shane and Doyle that the one thing Creigh's sister needed above all others was to talk of this man she had loved, to know he was not forgotten. "They were a gift from Michel Le Ferre?"

"You . . . how . . . do you . . . did you know him?" Juliet

lifted her face from Brianna's shoulder, her fawnlike eyes swimming with tears.

"Nay, I never met him." Bree crushed the only image that would ever remain for her of the marquis's face—that of its handsome planes contorted in a hideous mask of death. "But Creigh . . . my Lord Creighton told me much about him."

"Michel and Creigh . . . from the time they were babes suckling at the same wet nurse, they were inseparable." Juliet's face took on a lost, empty expression. "I . . . I was too small to remember, but Lindley claimed that once, when Creigh was three, he managed to escape from their nurse and tumble from a castle window two floors high. Michel didn't even look to see where Creigh had gone. He but clambered over the sill and dove headlong after."

"Did they . . . were they hurt?" Brianna winced at the thought of the two children plunging from so high, despite the fact that they obviously had both come through their adventure safely.

"The poor nurse nigh went into apoplexies—what with her two noble charges supposedly crushed on the stones below, but when she reached the courtyard, they were both giggling atop a huge pile of whortleberry bushes the gardeners had uprooted, and sat popping the berries into each other's mouths as though 'twas the grandest jest anyone had e'er played."

"I can imagine they were both well pleased with themselves." Brianna smiled at the scene Juliet's words had painted, and a tremulous half-smile tugged at the corners of the other girl's mouth.

"Aye," Juliet said, "but I fear maman was not amused. She drove the woman from the estate like the furies, Lindley said. And though I didn't see it, I can well imagine the poor nurse woman fleeing before maman's wrath."

Juliet stared at the withering roses long moments, the hint of a smile that had clung about her lips fading. "It was ever that way with Michel and Creigh from that time on. It mattered not who cast themselves into peril first, the other merely plunged after. I cannot tell you the number of irate husbands demanding the satisfaction of a duel Papa fended off betwixt the two of them, creditors banging upon the door whom neither had a care to pay, and the mistresses . . ."

Juliet's words stabbed jealousy through Brianna, but the girl appeared so forlorn, Bree hid her pain. "I'm well acquainted with your brother's penchant for hurling himself into hopeless scrapes."

"Aye. From what I remember, you just pulled him out of his latest." The girl smiled softly, a real smile this time, despite its dewing of tears. "Thank you, Mistress Devlin. If . . . if I had lost them all—Michel, Lindley and . . . and Creigh, I know not how I would have borne living."

"'Twas not I who saved your brother. My possets might have taken the edge from his fever, but 'twas your father and you who made him cling to life." Brianna fished a plain linen kerchief from her pocket, turning up Juliet's chin, and wiping her eyes as though she were yet in short skirts. "There is naught I can do to restore your Michel to you, but I bear a way with growing things; mayhap I can yet save your roses."

"Oh, Bri—I mean, Mistress Devlin, do you truly think you could?"

"Upon a single condition. That you cease calling me Mistress Devlin." Bree pulled a face as she swept up her skirts and knelt down upon the chill autumn earth mounded about the flowering shrubs. "I've ne'er been aught but plain Brianna, and 'twould please me greatly to think of you not as the lady of the estate but rather as a friend."

"Then you call me Juliet as well." Dark eyes turned wistful, warm. "'Twould be wondrous good to have a friend here, at Chateau aux Marées."

Brianna looked into the other girl's face, its open, loving eyes, sweetly rounded cheeks, the lips that seemed molded for smiling, and her astonishment was genuine as she said, "I'm certain you bear dozens who love you."

"At court. There were eight of us that Creigh and Michel called 'the beehive' because they claimed we were always buzzing at each other. But one by one we all were wed and dragged off to the corners of the earth."

Brianna took up the tiny spade Juliet had been digging with, and began working in the loosening dirt. "Creigh and Michel must have tormented you past bearing," she said. "I, too, was raised in a bevy of brothers. Half the time I adored them; the rest of the time I was bent on seeing their backsides brought to a willow switch for abusing me."

Juliet sighed. "With me, I fear, 'twas that I adored overmuch. From the time I toddled about with my fingers in my mouth, I worshiped Michel Le Ferre. I would stitch for him Christmas gifts that were scarce recognizable, treasure any word he happened to fling my way, cherish the trifles he'd cast to me with no more thought than if I'd been his own little sister. 'Twas only after he and Creigh returned from the wars that Michel saw me as aught else. I was able to soothe him after Nasby, and he felt he could shed his cavalier façade in my presence, acknowledge his anger and frustration, for I was naught but little Jolie. But somehow, someway, during that time when his soul was healing from its first taste of defeat, he came to love me."

Brianna's hands paused over the roots, and she raised her eyes to Juliet's rich, glowing ones. "Why, then . . . if your families were so close in both rank and loyalties, if Michel was Creigh's most cherished friend, and if you loved him, did your parents not leap at the chance to see you wed so happily?"

"I know not. A month after Creigh and Michel returned to Charles's side, I was forced to marry Messire Mauricheau."

"How? How could they force you when you loved—" Brianna stopped, appalled at herself for prying into a subject that could bring the girl naught but pain.

"I received a letter from Father saying Michel had eloped with Isabella St. Croix, and I . . . I was to marry a man named Sir Mauricheau Bouret with all haste."

Brianna raised her eyes to Juliet's face, not wanting to force confidences the girl did not feel comfortable sharing. Yet there was about Juliet Wakefield's eyes so much trust, loving, that Bree found it hard to believe she had but taken to heart the letter exposing Michel's supposed betrayal and had plunged into marriage with another man. Silently, Brianna moved to the second rose tree and began digging afresh.

Juliet's eyes were locked on her hands, her fragile fingers twisting at the gold boar's head bedecking her betrothal ring. "I was far from certain of Michel's love, then, and had known him to be immersed in a grand passion with the lady but a season past. I'd seen him free himself of so many—far prettier, more witty than I. I thought . . ." she shrugged, blinking the tears from her eyes. "What had he to do with an innocent the like of me, Brianna, when all the court's most desirable beauties were his for the taking?

"With Michel . . . Michel wed, I cared not what became of me. I vowed I would take whatever husband my father had chosen for me, try to take some small joy in the children that I might have. But when Mauricheau arrived, a priest in tow, I panicked, terrified."

"Because you did not love him?"

"Nay, 'twas more than that. There is about Messire Mauricheau an evil that clings about his features like the devil's robes. I could sense it, feel it . . . like the shadows that fall just before a tempest. I ran to maman, pleaded with her to help me escape him. She . . . she vowed she would. Took the letter I had drafted begging Creigh to intercede with father. Maman wrote one of her own as well. But the messengers had scarce sailed for England when maman received a final letter with the ducal seal saying that I would wed Messire Mauricheau Bouret without delay, or father would disown me, cast me into the streets without so much as a farthing."

Brianna scarce noticed her grubby hands, limp upon the velvet wrap, so caught was she by Juliet's tale. "And you . . . you believed . . ."

"'Tis a father's right, Brianna, to dispose of the burden of a daughter as best he can. I had nothing of my own, bore no future except the one he made for me." Juliet toyed with a ribbon that ornamented her gown, dragging the wisp of pink silk through the dirt. "The day after I was wed a gift arrived from Michel," she said softly, her fingers brushing the leaves before her in a tender caress. "These rose trees. And tucked within their branches was a message promising that before they put forth buds again I would be his wife."

Brianna shook her head, hardly able to fathom the chain of ironies that had imprisoned Juliet at Chateau aux Marées. "Creigh . . . Creigh told me some of your story, about how your father thrust you into this marriage. And about how the duke had abandoned Creigh himself, as a child. I . . . I hated the duke before I had ever met him, judged him harsh, cruel, unloving. But once I grew to know him . . ." Brianna chafed the dirt from her thumbnail. "'Tis so . . . so difficult to reconcile the hard, cold man in those

259

tales with the Blackthorne who . . . who so loved Lindley, wept over Creigh when he lay nigh death."

" 'Tis not so uncommon, what happened to me," Juliet said, resignation tinged with bitterness in her tone. "Most parents in the nobility would have had me betrothed from the cradle to some boy-child or some old man I'd never seen. But Father . . . he never did so. Mayhap 'twas but that he ne'er found a suitor that satisfied him. Or mayhap with all that was going on about the court he had no time to spare over something so trivial as the future of a mere daughter."

"Doyle—my brother—always said that if 'twas not for women patching things together, God would've sent another flood to cleanse the earth, promises to Noah be damned."

Juliet's mouth curved in a sweet smile. "I wager your brother is not too popular when he puts forth that view."

"Sometimes I vow he but said it to throw my other brother Shane into furies. Most of my childhood they spent at baiting each other—that is, when they weren't making my life miserable." Bree stood up stiffly. "Nay," she said, a bittersweet tugging within her heart. "That's not true. Doyle and Shane and Daniel, they made my life overflowing with love, and joy, and a teasing that warmed me to my soul, made me feel safe. So safe."

"Your brothers . . . when you return to Ireland, will they be waiting?"

"Doyle and Shane, nay. They died 'midst the fighting. But Daniel . . . I know not. I pray so with every breath I draw."

Brianna was astonished that she could now give the girl, visibly stricken with guilt over bringing up her brothers' deaths, a reassuring smile. "Your roses, too, will be just fine in a week's time," Brianna said, laying the spade in Juliet's palm. "Go to the butchery and have them grind for you the bones left after they prepare meat. Sprinkle it through the dirt, then cover the roots of the plants with a thick mulching of dried leaves and moss to protect them as winter strikes."

Juliet Bouret's dark eyes shone with tears of gratitude and a deep, abiding sadness. "I'll send you a blossom, dried to rose dust when the spring comes, if the messenger has to travel all of Ireland."

The feeling of warmth, sharing, that had been flowing through Brianna chilled. 'Twas true, by the time Juliet's beloved roses burst into bloom, no doubt Bree would again be upon Ireland's distant shores, with naught of Creigh except memories of the days they had raced, wild across the countryside. And Creigh . . . by then he would again be embroiled in the battle for a crown, his body dripping in velvets and power, but his heart . . . aye, his heart mayhap would be as empty as Juliet's, as Brianna's own, unless . . .

She looked up from the unkempt garden, seeing, over the tangle of trees and vines, the ancient stone turrets of Chateau aux Marées piercing the dark clouds like a sorcerer's gnarled hands. Hands spinning webs of mystery, deceit, and treachery that Bree sensed were slowly winding their strangling hands about not only Juliet's life, but Creigh's as well. The muffled roar of some wild, caged thing tore at the quiet from the sinister silhouette of Mauricheau Bouret's menagerie.

Brianna shuddered, feeling deep within that part of herself still haunted by Druids and senses unseen some force, evil, threatening peering out at them with eyes the hue of blood.

She linked her arm through Juliet's more fragile one, the urge to protect, defend, surging through her. But 'twas as if she could hear it, there within the silence, the honing of invisible talons, blade-sharp, as some unseen menace awaited its prey.

Chapter Twenty

Creigh leaned upon his pillows, peering past his mother's ribbon-dressed curls to revel in the stubborn set to Brianna's shoulders as she exited the chamber. She looked as if she would take the greatest of pleasure in squashing the hovering Beadle like the annoying pest that he was, and, Creigh could have sworn, would also have loved to take a bite out of his own resolve to send her out a-sunning. But, despite her tempers, he was certain 'twould do his wild witch worlds of good to romp amongst the flowers. And Juliet . . . his memory twisted, bittersweet, at the image of dark, haunted eyes, a mouth quivering with sorrow. Aye, mayhap Bree could gift Jolie with some of her own strength.

He pulled his gaze from the doorway as the footsteps—Bree's militant, Beadle's creeping—faded into silence.

"So, maman," he said, turning mischievous eyes upon Lady Esmeraude, "what think you of my lady?"

"L-lady . . ." His mother's babe-smooth cheeks dimpled in arresting innocence. "She is . . . er . . . quite original. Most charming in her own way, of course," Esmeraude added in a rush, "but then, my pet, your women always are."

Creigh laughed aloud. "Even you must admit that Bree can scarcely be cast in amongst the other ladies I've wooed, maman. I've seen her battle brave as any man calamities that would have made even you faint dead in horror."

"'Tis most . . . most admirable, I'm sure, Creighton," his mother said, one beringed hand fluttering through the air. "Especially to find courage buried within one of the girl's station. But despite the gratitude I bear the child, I have more pressing matters to discuss with you at present. Matters respecting the roilings that have been overtaking the court."

Creigh suppressed a smile, the corners of his eyes crinkling in amusement. "And what pressing matters might those be, my lady Esmeraude? Did the Viscountess of Wartlesea fall asleep in her syllabub yet again? Or, horror of horrors, did Lucy Waters's gloves not match the most recent gown our leige Charles secured for her?"

Esmeraude gave his knuckles a rap with the folded fan, compressing her lips into an expression of patent irritation. "You know full well I have no time for that sort of nonsense. Leave nipping at the heels of those frivolous tarts to the witlings whose heads are worth naught but to hold up their ribbons. I am weighed with far greater cares."

Creigh levered himself higher up amongst the pillows, leaning back with an indulgent smile. "Well, then, my dearest lady mother, you must share your concerns with me directly, before you become wrinkled and gray with worry. 'Twould be a passing shame for ought to dampen the sparkle in your eyes."

Esmeraude simpered, and Creigh nigh laughed aloud again at the sight of her blushing like a miss scarce out of the nursery. "You, Creighton Wakefield, are the most impertinent of men. If I have become a dried up old crone, 'tis your doing, what with your brainless schemes worrying me half to the grave. But you can repay me in full for every wrinkle, every silvering hair."

"It seems but just, if I have wreaked the havoc you claim," Creigh said. "And what, pray tell, is the payment you demand? Am I to wait upon you at an upcoming ball? Aid you in selecting ribbons at your hatmakers? Or is it some bauble you desire, that Father is too penurious to secure for you?"

"Nay."

Creigh felt an unaccustomed stirring of caution steal over him at the glint in his mother's narrowing eyes. "Then what . . . ?"

"Beg King Charles for the hand of Princess Henriette-Anne."

"Charles's little Minette?" Creigh echoed, stunned. "Even if the child were not but five years old, the dowager queen would never consent. And with the state Charles's purse is in at present, even my friendship with him would not permit him to give to me in marriage his favorite sister. If anything, he should be scrambling to find the child a husband with a treasury as rich as the princess's royal bloodlines, so that he can fund yet another attempt to retake English soil."

"You greatly underestimate your power with the king," Lady Esmeraude said, leaning forward upon the seat of the embroidered chair. "You are now rightful heir to the Dukedom of Blackthorne, have risked yourself in the name of Charles's crown, as well as proved your loyalty by nigh emptying your private coffers for his benefit. His Majesty owes you, Creighton, owes you power, position, and what better way to maintain your place at his side than to fuse the Wakefield fortunes to that of the Stuart royal house through marriage?"

"Maman." Creigh ran his fingers through his hair, the rollicking mood that had brightened the morning dampening. "I can hardly go to Charles and say, 'Excuse me, your majesty, but I'm here to collect upon your debts. One princess in payment, if you please.' "

"Certainly not," Esmeraude said, her fingertips plucking at a rosette upon her gown. "You could tell Charles that you were enchanted with his sister, that despite her youth, the promise of her beauty—"

"And her crown," Creigh added wryly.

"—is all that you could wish for in a wife," Esmeraude continued, dismissing his sarcastic aside. "You could claim that you . . ."

"Love her?" Creigh felt within himself a strange kind of clinging sensation, as if his mouth were dusted with grit from a long, tedious ride. "Come, Mother. Unlike some of the court's own, I bear no taste for babes scarce from their swaddlings, and Charles well knows it."

"Creighton, listen to me," Esmeraude's pouting lips pressed into a line of fierce determination. "The maid will grow into a woman soon enough. God knows, you've had no difficulty finding beauties willing to bed you thus far. While you wait for your princess to ripen, discreetly take your fill of all the court has to offer. Of all men ruled by their loins,

Charles will understand. But 'tis vital, Creighton, that you grasp this chance you bear to raise the house of Wakefield higher than any other in the land save that of the king."

Creigh looked into his mother's determined face, the face that had borne so many disappointments, sorrows. How oft he had listened to her bewail the weakness of Blackthorne, the laziness that made Galliard Wakefield dismiss family duty, honor so that he could grub about playing country gentleman upon estates white with roaming sheep, mansions gray with boredom. And all his life, Creigh had vowed within himself that he would see his beloved mother raised to the heights she so longed for, that he would provide her with all she had missed through his father's thoughtlessness.

Creigh's gaze dropped from that expectant, pale face, his fingers lifting one of the chessmen that had tumbled upon the coverlet while he and Brianna had been tussling. He turned the small piece of marble in his hand, watching the sunlight glance off its carved planes. *A pawn,* he thought idly, laying it, again beside him. "Maman," he began, choosing his words as carefully as possible in an effort not to hurt her. "I know you've struggled mightily on my behalf, and most truly, I am grateful for all you have given me—love, support, defending me when, as a child, I was yet too weak to battle for myself. And laughter . . . so much laughter." Creigh paused, taking up his mother's strangely stiff hand.

"A season ago, I would have leapt at the chance to ally myself to Charles by blood. 'Twould have mattered naught that I would have to wait for a child bride to grow into womanhood. 'Tis nigh expected in marriages of the reigning house. And to be bound to a bride with whom I might someday share naught but affection, mayhap respect— 'twould have been all I had e'er hoped to hold. But now . . ." Creigh swallowed, a lump of emotion knotting in his throat. "Maman, I have found that there is so much more to life: love."

"Creighton." Lady Esmeraude's voice was thin, her cheeks whitening perceptibly. "You . . . you surely can't mean . . . mean that this . . . this girl . . . this Irish peasant . . ."

"Aye, I do. Peasant she may be, yet Bree has the courage of a king, and a heart rife with compassion, both tempered together into the finest of women."

The slender hand within his went ice cold, and it pained him to see the mask of disbelief that swept across his mother's features. "She—she will bring you naught but the disdain of your peers . . . even as a mistress, she is hardly acceptable. All we have worked for, Creigh, devoted our lives to—"

"I know, and I am truly sorry to disappoint you. But ever since I was a lad, I've known that within it all—your striving, your defiance of father—it has been a quest for my happiness that drove you. Know this above all things: Brianna Devlin makes me happy. She brings me more joy than I've e'er known."

"Creighton . . ." Esmeraude began in a tight, pleading voice, her fingers clenching about his. The sharp-edged nails dug into his hand. "The girl is not even overcomely. She—she's nigh muscled as a man, and her features . . . they're sharply drawn. In but a few years she'll be scarce fit to look upon, let alone cherish a tendre for. You cannot . . . must not hurl away all that we've labored for these many years. Not when at last 'tis within our grasp."

"I love her, maman. Naught else matters."

"Love her?" his mother echoed. "What . . . what is love but some fantasy the minstrels sing about? I . . . I have been in love at least a dozen times, but the fire, it always fades, Creigh. I swear to you—"

"Not the flame my Tigress spawns." Creigh caught both his mother's hands in his, wanted her to feel, share the love that he held. "Accept her, maman, for me, and please, please forgive me if I have caused you pain. But I want—need to keep her beside me."

"Chateau Le Ferre, then. Install her at Chateau Le Ferre. You could tryst with her there 'til you've taken your fill of this madness."

"Nay, I want her not as mistress. I . . ." Creigh's voice caught in his throat, his eyes stinging with emotion. "I want her as my wife."

"But . . . but Creighton . . . I—" Esmeraude started to protest, but her gaze caught Creigh's. The dark eyes that had

266

always turned upon him with such warmth seemed suddenly chill, the depths opaque as a silvered glass.

"I will have her, maman, though the devil himself bars the way."

Esmeraude's gaze fell to the embroidered sheetings. "Very well, then," she surrendered. "I've ne'er been apt at tilting with devils. If . . . if this Brianna is what you truly want, you know you can . . . can trust me. Have I not always done everything in my power to bring about what . . . what is best for you?"

Creigh tried to smile at his mother's concession, but for the first time since she had entered the room, he saw that the duchess was not meeting his eyes.

Brianna dodged in front of the giggling lady Juliet, the two of them nigh upsetting a round-eyed chambermaid as they bolted up the wide stone steps three at a time. A garland of autumn flowers rippled behind them like a jewel-hued bunch of ribbons, its breeze-kissed freshness driving back the shadows that had clung to their spirits in the garden a week past. Stockings knit of the finest silk flashed beneath mud-spattered cloak hems, the bright cherry velvet secured beneath both dainty chins not half so cheery as the roses the wind had bussed into their cheeks.

"'Tis unjust!" Juliet gasped through her laughter, stumbling up the last stair. "You ran me into poor Charity a-purpose!"

"You needn't blame me for your own clumsiness!" Brianna flung back at her, ribs aching with merriment as she slammed open Creigh's bedchamber door. "Especially after the trick you played me upon horseback!" She burst into the room, her once severely plaited hair wild, gloriously aflame with bright leaves tangled in the harvest-gold tresses, mischief bubbling inside her with the unabashed joy of a crystal-water spring.

"Creighton Wakefield, rouse yourself this instant!" Brianna cried, yanking the flower garland free of Juliet's hand and hurling it at the man propped in one of the large, carved chairs cast in the room's late afternoon shadows. "I demand this rogue sister of yours be brought to justice at once!"

Creigh's hand flashed up, catching the blossom chain with a laugh, his flashing white teeth visible in the dim light. "Sweet Christ, if 'tis not the Roundheads after wounding me, 'tis my own women!"

"'Tis your blackguard sister that bears chastising, you great oaf," Bree said, scarce noticing the rumble of amusement from a velvet-draped corner. "*Take stallion Mercury, Juliet said. He runs swift as his name*— Well I vow you'd best rechristen him Sir Slackpace, or the Romans or whoever Mercury was god to will be raining lightning bolts upon the lot of you."

"At least 'twill save us from your breakneck riding, Brianna Devlin! She all but spilled me into a streambed!"

"'Tis just like a Sassenach," Bree teased, plopping down onto Creigh's lap, her skirts flying up her dirt-speckled stockings. "Yowling when they fail to—"

The comfortable banter was interrupted by Juliet's squeak of dismay, and Brianna looked up into her friend's face, stunned to see the sweet, pink lips puckered as though she had swallowed a keg of sour ale.

Bree burst out in another peal of irrepressible merriment, tears trickling from the corners of her eyes as she clutched her aching side. "Sweet heaven, Jolie, you needn't look so cross-eyed; 'twas but one race across the . . ."

The words had scarce breached Brianna's lips when she felt Juliet's fist knot in the skirt of her riding habit, jerking the fabric until Brianna nigh spilled from Creigh's lap onto the carpet.

Bree yelped a surprised curse, regaining her balance just in time to see Juliet sweep down into the deepest of curtsies, her cheeks scarlet. "God's blood, what ails y—"

Brianna's breath whistled through her teeth as she sucked in a sharp breath, a tall regal figure stepping out from the veiling of a flowing velvet wall hanging. Deep purple mourning draped shoulders dauntingly broad, while rich black hair flowed in a perfect foil to a countenance whose undeniable sensuality and subtle shadings of cynicism was softened by a pair of the merriest brown eyes Brianna had ever seen.

"And so, milady," the man's deep voice commanded, "pray enlighten me upon how we *Sassenachs* yowl. 'Twill be of greatest use to their erstwhile king."

"P-please, Your Majesty, Brianna . . . er . . . Mistress Devlin meant it but in jest," Juliet stammered, pleading. "She . . . she knew not who you were."

Who he was? Brianna peered up at the stranger's arresting face, and her stomach flipped over. King . . . Majesty . . . her mind struggled to grasp the knowledge. Oh, sweet Lord, and she had been railing about Sassenachs!

Clutching hanks of her gown in sweaty palms, Brianna dropped into a curtsy with the grace of a felled oak. "Y-your Majesty," she squeezed through her throat. "I . . ."

Creigh's hand, warm, firm, scooped up her suddenly icy one, and she could feel his smile, despite the fact that her eyes were now fastened upon the English monarch's lace-edged boothose.

"Saints save us, Charles, 'tis the first time since these two hoydens were cast together that they've been struck speechless. Mayhap once we set in motion the plans we've discussed, you can drop by the estates upon occasion to give my poor ears a rest."

Brianna's gaze leapt up to Creigh's, her tongue burning to snap out a sharp rejoinder, but despite the warmth in Charles Stuart's face, she could not forget that she now knelt in the presence of the rightful king of one of the most powerful nations in the world.

"What think you, James?" Charles laid one royal finger aside his full-curved lips. "Shall we make it a royal prerogative to ease my Lord Creighton's battered eardrums upon occasion?" Brianna glanced over to where another man stood, younger than Charles, a pale copy of the king's royal magnificence.

The black-robed man's lips tilted in a somber smile. "My Lord Creighton has proved himself most loyal to your interests, brother, from the time Halliwell Burchard threatened to thrust your billet into the flames."

Brianna's gaze flashed in confusion from Creigh's heartily amused face to Charles Stuart's as the king broke into a gale of laughter. "I vow I'd forgot that, James. But loyalty such as that needs must be rewarded." One dark hand waved at both Brianna and Juliet, bidding them to rise as Charles said in a conspiratorial voice, "'Twas the despair of my poor nurses, my billet was. Naught but a length of wood. Yet I had to have it in my royal bed when I was a lad, or God himself could not cajole me to sleep."

Charles reached out, ruffling Juliet's dark curls with affection. "You were yet a babe then, little sunshine," he said, "and look at you now, a woman grown."

"Aye, Your Majesty."

A pensive, and, Brianna sensed, unaccustomed moodiness stole over the king's saturnine features as he peered into Juliet's innocent face. "Those were the most cherished of times, were they not, little Jolie? When we thought all the world was the clashing of wooden swords, and played at quests of the legendary Arthur the king."

Charles smoothed his fingertips over the silky wing of black that swept across his curling upper lip. "Aye, 'twas the most treasured of ages. And you, Mistress Devlin," he said, turning the full weight of those dark, royal eyes upon her, "whilst we were mumming at Lancelot, and sweeping about the gallery with our dancing masters, and practicing at the pavane, what was our golden Irish warrior maid about?"

"Cracking the skulls of any poor lads that were so foolish as to try to steal a kiss, no doubt." Creigh rolled his eyes heavenward.

"Is this true, milady?" the king asked.

"Well, ofttimes, Your Majesty," Brianna replied, a sudden imp of mischief piqued by Charles's own merry spirit. "But most of the time I spent at growing cabbages."

"I vow 'tis time we remedy that," Charles said, his eyes twinkling. "My Lady Juliet, in your husband's absence, I beg your hospitality. In honor of the return of our most cherished and loyal friend, Lord Creighton Wakefield, and Mistress Brianna Devlin, his lady, I would like to hold a ball here at Chateau aux Marées with all who shine within the court here at Jersey present to do them honor."

"Y-your majesty," Juliet stammered. "I . . . I am certain my husband will be most honored."

"But the celebration shall be held here contingent upon only one condition." Charles's brows drew down in mock severity. "Both of you beauties, Lady Juliet and Mistress Devlin, must promise me one dance."

Brianna saw Juliet's cheeks dimple prettily, but felt her own burning with an abrupt stab of nerves. "But—'tis exceeding kind, but I know naught of dancing."

"Then you shall have the finest teacher in all Christendom," Creigh said, flashing Charles a pleased grin. "His Majesty is as nimble upon his feet as he is in wooing the ladies, and in that he is legend."

"'Tis . . . 'tis all very well," Brianna replied, more shaken than she cared admit. "But I fear if His Majesty dances with me, he might ne'er dance again, considering how badly I'll tread upon his feet."

"Why then, Mistress Devlin, we can observe firsthand . . . how did you term it . . . the way we Sassenachs yowl."

Bree had the good grace to go crimson. Charles Stuart stretched out one large, swarthy hand, tipping up her chin, his eyes tracing the curves of her face with the air of a connoisseur tasting wine. "I understand now, more certainly, the importance of the private matter we discussed here this day, my Lord Creighton," Charles said cryptically. "If you are certain 'tis what you want, I will do my best to see it comes to pass."

Brianna's confused gaze caught Creigh's, but the handsome features were blank, noncommittal.

"Aye, Your Majesty," he said. "'Tis the only thing I want."

Brianna's brow wrinkled, puzzlement and astonishment chasing about within her as she watched the king of England nod solemnly, as he and his dark-robed brother exited the chamber.

"Brianna!" Juliet's squeal of excitement pierced her musings. "Can you fathom it? You are to be taken into the king's own court. He is going to dance with you . . . with both of us, and—a gown, Creigh, she must have the most magnificent gown in the whole assembly!" Juliet whisked to her brother, gifting him with an exuberant hug. "Sapphire velvet, it must be, yards and yards of it . . . and lace."

Eyes, incredibly hot, despite their sea-gray hue, held Brianna's. "There is naught but one type of *lacing* I have any care to talk about at the moment," Creigh said in a husky voice, his arm curving out to pull Brianna full against him as he arched one brow.

"The most delicate white webbing—"

"Nay, *un*lacing Brianna's gown."

Brianna banged her fist into his chest, reprimanding him,

but Juliet only blushed, scurrying toward the yet open doorway.

"Jolie!" Creigh called, and Juliet spun about. "I give you full license with my purse and my lady. Hurl whatever coin you must to what dressmakers you can find hereabouts and concoct for my Tigress the most glorious gown e'er seen by a man."

Juliet's smile lit her whole face.

"I will, Creigh, I promise you," she cried, excited as a child. "I vow when Brianna enters the hall, you'll ne'er have seen her so beautiful!"

Brianna turned her eyes back to Creigh, his face bending close to her own as he watched his sister disappear, pulling the door shut behind her.

He feigned a sigh, looking down at Brianna with mock sorrow. "You know, 'tis an impossible task my sister undertakes."

"Impossible?" Brianna echoed, self-doubts she'd never experienced before chasing like mice about her brain. "Creigh . . . 'tis mad . . . the king . . . all his cavaliers. I'm no fine English lady! I'll break their toes with my shoe heels, trip over the other dancer's hems . . . at the very least I'll douse the whole front of my gown with dark wine. I'll shame you, and—"

"Brianna, you could never shame me," he said cupping her face in his hands. "'Tis not the night of the celebration that concerns me, love," Creigh's voice was low, his breath hot against the tender skin at the base of her throat. "'Tis poor Juliet's vow that she will make you more beautiful than I've e'er seen you. For I've held you garbed in naught but a wreathing of meadow grass and wildflowers," he said kissing the delicate ridge of her collar bone. "And the sight of you there, all golden, and ripe, and needing me, will ne'er be eclipsed in my heart, Tigress, no matter if Jolie spins your gown with the angels."

Brianna's lips parted, seeking Creigh's fire-hot ones in a fierce, questing kiss, yet 'twas still a while before even his blazing passion could quash the uncertainties that gnawed yet within her.

She belonged not in this whirlwind of intrigue and perfumed wigs, knew not how to survive amongst verbal daggers dipped in a poison far more dangerous than that of the honest thrust of a rapier. And the most lethal weapon of all, Brianna knew, rested in the hands of the one woman she could ne'er banish from Creigh's life.

She closed her eyes, remembering Esmeraude Wakefield's resentful face when she had seen Brianna but admitted to the same room as her son. What depth of hatred would be fired within the duchess, Bree wondered, when Creigh's mother saw the simple peasant she despised whirling about the great hall of Chateau aux Marées, not only upon the arm of Lady Esmeraude's son but on that of her king as well?

Chapter Twenty-one

Creigh's brows furrowed over eyes, narrowed, oddly watchful as he reread the daintily penned script, his finger worrying the edge of the missive Beadle had placed into his hands moments ago. He had received a thousand like messages over the years since his lady mother had taken him from Wrensong—rollicking notes full of court gossip and declarations of the undying love the duchess bore him. Always before the flowery words had given him a feeling of warmth, soothing that secret, hidden part of him that even now burned with the pain of his father's rejection.

Yet for some reason Creigh could not understand, the elaborate endearments written upon the pages now made him feel distinctly uncomfortable, as though he were smothered in oversweet perfumes. And rather than pleasing him, the sweetly worded request at the letter's end made him feel like a high-strung stallion in the midst of a brace of cannons ready to explode.

The touch of a hand upon his freshly donned doublet made him mentally shake himself free of the disturbing sensation. He lifted his gaze to Brianna's softly gold face.

"Receiving love messages from your adoring entourage of belles already, my Lord Creighton?" she teased, nipping at the tip of his earlobe. "You've scarce left your bedchamber, yet already it seems they are ready to storm the doors."

Creigh slanted her a loving glance, taking joy in the innocence of eyes never schooled in secreting emotions, and mouth full capable of trembling with compassion or shaking the very battlements with unbridled fury. "And if this is a

letter from one of my innumerable *affaires d'amour,* milady
Tigress?" he said, brushing her pert nose with his fingertip.
"Will you call the doxy out and demand satisfaction at the
point of your sword?"

Brianna dimpled, twin imps dancing in her amber eyes.
"Most fortunately for you, my lord, whilst my brothers were
most diligent in teaching me the finer points of deflecting an
enemy's blade, they were less able to chain me to the cottage
and teach me to read. Doyle, he learned a little from the
wandering friars that would pass across our land, but Shane,
Daniel, and I would bolt for the hills every time we saw a
brown-stuff robe winding up from the valley."

Creigh chuckled, delighted at the image his mind conjured of a tawny-tressed hoyden dashing, long-legged, strong
through the grasses as she eluded a dour-faced priest.
"Michel and I did much the same," Creigh said, a familiar
stab of loss piercing his lightsome mood. Brianna's lips,
moist, velvet-warm, brushed his in a soft, sweet kiss, and he
felt the edges of his sorrow melt 'neath the warmth in her
eyes.

"Well, my lord, even if 'tis a love missive, you needn't
look so grim," she said, her fingers threading back through
his shoulder-length mane. "I'd not waste my time preying
upon your fragile Sassenach women. I'd merely come after
you, and likely bind you to my bed until you begged for
mercy."

"Your word of honor as a soldier, milady?" Creigh
wriggled his brows archly.

"You can depend upon it, sir."

She closed what little space remained between their
bodies, the scent of her hair, sea winds with a dash of
sunshine, filling his senses. His head dipped down, tasting of
her unspoiled lips, her innocence, beauty. The knot of desire
that had been a nigh constant ache in his loins these days
past pulled excruciatingly tight. His hands slid down the
curve of her back, palms cupping the firm curve of her
derriere, pulling her against the evidence of his raging need.

"So, my lord, you mean to confess?"

"Confess?" Creigh repeated, closing his eyes against the
exquisite pleasure of her soft, feminine valley cradling his
sex even through the layers of cloth that were between them.
"I vow I'd confess to anything, as long as you imprisoned

me inside you, but alas, this message is only from my mother."

He felt the pliant body in his arms stiffen against him, though Bree's fingers still kept up their erotic stroking on his nape. "Well, mayhap we should practice placing you in captivity in any case. After all, 'tis nigh patent that a prime cavalier the likes of you will be harassed by the ladies at some point. We may as well—"

"Naught would please me better, Tigress," Creigh sighed, reluctantly drawing her arms from about his neck. "Unfortunately, the main purpose of my lady mother's letter has naught to do with me. Rather, 'tis an invitation requesting that you join her in her apartments."

"I? Wait upon Lady Esmeraude?" Brianna's mouth, so eager moments before, tautened, and Creigh was disturbingly aware that for the first time since he'd known her, Bree was struggling to veil her true emotions behind a calm façade. "Why, by the saints, would your mother want to pass time with me? She can scarcely stand—I mean, with the date of King Charles's ball approaching, she hardly has time to waste—"

"In her message she said she desired to come to know you better, to give you fair thanks for all that you've done for me."

Brianna's fingers fell away from his skin, and Creigh felt of a sudden bereft of more than just her touch. There was something indefinable about her hands that disturbed him greatly, the ever capable fingers agitated, nervous as a fumbling nursery-room waif's. He fought an urge to clasp his hands about her arms, command her to tell him what secret was hidden away in the depths of her amber eyes.

Bree's spine seemed suddenly stiff, as though she had braced herself for an expected blow, her chin tilting up in that stubborn defiance he knew so well. "Well, then," she said, her palms smoothing the brown folds of the plain muslin gown she favored above all of those Juliet had secured for her. "If the duchess has summoned me, I've little choice but to obey."

Creigh loosed a laugh, its tone forced even to his own hearing. "Bree, attending my mother is scarce facing a hangman's noose. Who's to say, even now she might be

276

grandmother to a babe just sprung within your womb." He had meant to tease her, cajole her into the saucy smile he loved so well, but her mouth only pressed tighter, what little pink had tinted her cheekbones paling to ivory. One slender hand strayed to the gentle rise of her stomach, and Creigh cursed himself for having thoughtlessly cast yet another worry upon her.

His own hand slid down, flattening over the warm sheath of flesh over her womb. "'Twould please me greatly, Bree, watching my son thrive within you."

"And a daughter?"

Creigh started at Bree's harsh challenge as she dashed his hand away, her eyes suddenly savage fire.

"What would you do if I bore a girl-child? Bury her off on some insignificant estate? Ignore her 'til you are ready to sell her into marriage? Nay, she'd be worth even less of your love, your precious aristocrat's time than your favorite stallion, for she'd not only be a worthless girl, she'd be bastard-born as well."

"Brianna, for God's sake!" Creigh bristled, frowning. "'Twould matter not to me if you bore me a castle-full of daughters! Think you I would condemn any child that you bore me—a child of *my* body—to what Jolie has endured?"

He saw Brianna flush, her glare falter. She spun about, and Creigh saw beneath her anger a hinting of shame. Creigh sighed. "Christ's blood, if suffering my mother's company is so distasteful to you, decline her invitation. Tell her I've had a relapse, or that the castle wall has fallen in, barring the door. Or let me go to her and explain you do not feel at ease enough yet to—"

"Oh, nay, my lord, I'll not give my Lady Esmeraude that satisfaction," Brianna snapped. Creigh reached out a hand to stop her, the expression upon her face filling him with dread. Vulnerable, yet brave, she looked like a child confronting terrors in the darkness. Bree pulled free, her back in its plain sheathing of brown muslin straight as that of an embattled general being cast into the midst of a war. She spun on her heel, her tresses, their curling, unruly locks tugging free of the coronet of plaits she had worked into the thick masses early that morning, wisping about her face in disarray.

Creigh peered after her as she marched down the corridor toward the distant wing where his mother now kept her household, and couldn't decide whether he wished most to strangle the stubborn girl, or make love to her until she spilled out to him whatever caused her so much distress. She had turned on him, words scratching, clawing, yet he had sensed that 'twas not her fears at his treatment of any child they might have that had spurred her to anger. It had been something else . . . far deeper.

His mother? Nay, 'twas absurd, that Brianna, who had faced Cromwell's army with impunity, should wax ill-ease merely at being received by Lady Esmeraude. After all, his lady mother had vowed to him . . .

Creigh stepped to the rosewood gaming table that stood in the corner of the room, taking up one of the chessmen from the board perched upon its glossy surface. Fingering the silver-helmed knight, in its enameled crusader's garb, Creigh let his gaze stray to the chair upon which Esmeraude Wakefield had seen the shattering of her plans. But instead of picturing her enchanting smile, or turning over in his mind the witty rejoinders she was so adept at casting out, 'twas her eyes he imagined, dark, lashless, shifting away from his own gaze as she chided him to trust her.

Brianna strode resolutely down the tapestry-hung corridor, the walls of the most ancient segment of the castle—built, Juliet claimed, when the Normans had owned both the small isle's properties and loyalties—giving way to the more modern additions constructed by Mauricheau Bouret's ancestors three generations ago.

'Twas astonishing the Lady Esmeraude had not been housed from the first here, amongst the finest Chateau aux Marées had to offer, Bree thought with an unaccustomed sting of bitterness. Her eyes took in the ornate stonework and rich French carvings that increased in both number and beauty as the part of the castle, in which Juliet, Creigh, and the rest of the little party had been lodged, disappeared into chambers groomed nigh worthy of a king.

Yet perhaps it had been the absence of the master of Chateau aux Marées—that and the dreadful prospect of being forced to breathe the same air as peasants—that had driven Creigh's mother to risk Mauricheau Bouret's wrath, and put to use the apartments Juliet's dread husband usually occupied.

But why, if she could not even bear residing in the same wing of the castle as her son's peasant mistress, would the Duchess of Blackthorne summon you to her chambers? Brianna narrowed her eyes, peering down the hallway to where candlelight spilled out from an arched door. Nay, 'twas most certainly not to express gratitude to the woman, Bree knew, the duchess viewed as her most threatening rival.

The sound of a minstrel, singing a French *chanson* of love in the most dulcet of tones, drifted from within the chamber, the scent of roast fowl and honey mingling in the air with the bittersweet tones of his musette. And Bree had a fleeting image of the man, suspended in a golden cage like a nightingale, captive for the duchess's pleasure.

Suddenly aware she had hesitated outside of the chamber, Brianna forced her slippered feet to the threshold, just as tinkling feminine laughter drifted from the brightly lit room. Bree froze, her gaze sweeping walls decked with garlands of flowers, the remains of an elaborate repast spread about a vast table set with a dozen soiled silver plates. She started to back away, certain there was some mistake, but the sound of voices from about the huge silk-work arras that sectioned off the far end of the room made her pause.

Bree grimaced, recognizing the scene depicted upon the silks—The Scarlet Nuptials: Henry of Navarre wedding Princess Marguerite de Valois whilst a benign Catherine de Medici looked on. Brianna shuddered involuntarily, remembering the tale of how but five days after the marriage, upon St. Bartholemew's day, Paris's Huguenots had been slaughtered . . .

"Look you, Alys, at *la comtesse*'s eyes," the complacent, feline voice snapped Bree's attention from the tapestry. "I vow, we'd best collect all the kerchiefs in the room for her before she drowns us in her sentimental mewlings."

"Please yourself, then, Lanette, making jest of my weeping," another sniffled. "But 'twas most monstrous tragic, the poor maid, casting herself from the castle ramparts for loss of her beloved knight. And Monsieur Verney, he bears the voice of an angel."

"And the face of a toad," came the first woman's reply. "What think you, my Lady Esmeraude, was it not but just that the little harlot was destined for the grave, slavering over one so high above her station?"

"One could hardly expect a knight to mourn over a mere milkmaid," Esmeraude Wakefield said in bored accents. "I doubt the immortalized Messire Guilliame even noticed the chit was missing until the estate's cows burst their udders." The other women dissolved into fits of nasty giggles.

Brianna bit the inside of her lip, the intention of Esmeraude Wakefield's *invitation* now springwater clear. No doubt the duchess hoped Bree would overhear the cutting remarks and flee in tears, but Devlins were tempered of finer steel than that. Bree straightened her spine, stepping into the room with a smile pasted upon her face. "Good evening, Your Grace," she said with acid sweetness.

"Brianna?" Esmeraude spun around, a study in shock and breathless embarrassment as she pressed her palms to the bosom of her gown, the scarlet shot silk catching the light from the glowing candles. "Why, my dear . . . I . . . we were not expecting you."

Brianna's smile nigh cracked her lips. "Odd," she said, "I would think 'twould be passing difficult not to expect someone you had personally summoned to your chambers."

"I? Summon you? I don't recall . . ." the duchess's face crinkled in puzzlement, her gaze sweeping from the top of Brianna's unruly hair, to the disheveled hem of the simple gown, and the aristocratic upper lip curled in an air of amusement. Brianna heard a muffled titter from a brown-curled beauty gowned in pink, the more malicious, cutting purr of disdain from a black-haired girl, whose slanted eyes reminded Bree of a cat about to snap the neck of a mouse.

Lady Esmeraude lifted her hands, as if in surrender to some distasteful task. "Well, my dear, it seems you are here in any case, and the ladies and I have done with our entertainment for the evening. Monsieur Verney just finished regaling us of a most tragic tale, and I vow the ladies are most anxious to away to their own rooms and sob into their pillows."

The cat-woman's lips stretched over tiny white teeth. "I vow I'll off to sob for Messire Guilliame's poor horse . . .

280

imagine a blooded stallion having to carry a lowling the like of the doxy in the song. 'Twould be most humilating, even for a horse, think you not, Mistress Devlin?"

Brianna turned brittle eyes upon the woman, suspicion confirmed that 'twas for her benefit Lady Esmeraude had staged this charade. "I've ne'er met a mount yet who cared aught for the rider upon its back, save whether its hands were skilled upon the reins."

The woman laughed, one perfectly manicured fingernail reaching out to gingerly touch the wilted lace that clung to Brianna's bodice. "And I, Mistress Devlin, have ne'er known a man who cared aught for a woman save how large her family's holdings were, and how well she is able to use her hands to bring him pleasure. But certainly our most ill-fortuned Messire Guilliame would prefer the soft, scented fingers of a lady to the hoary, calloused palms of a laboring wench, think you not? I know from . . . er . . . intimate experience that my Lord Creighton puts great store in the softness of a woman's hands."

The cat eyes narrowed in satisfaction, and Bree had a sudden urge to scratch them from the woman's flawless face. But she merely swept her gaze in a dismissing glance across the woman's low brow, saying, "That must be true, my lady, for, being as you say you entertain intimate knowledge of his preferences, 'twould seem my Lord Creighton prefers women with soft brains as well."

A gasp of startled laughter to Brianna's side made her turn to see a spritely young miss with a mass of auburn hair and eyes reddened from weeping stifling a giggle with her fingertips. "Lanette, I vow she's marked you well," the girl squeezed out through her mirth.

"Alimagne!" Esmeraude's voice cut, sharp, through the girl's laughter, and the bowed lips snapped together, crushing the merry sound. The woman, Lanette, glared through slitted lids at the russet-curled maid as a bevy of other bright-gowned beauties rose from embroidered chairs and scattered cushions and began drifting toward the door.

A nose pinched with years of sniffing in disdain poked into the air, as Lanette gathered up her satin gown, pausing in front of Brianna. "You may be certain, Mistress Devlin," she said in a low voice, "that all within this room are well versed in his lordship's appetites . . . and, I vow to you, will continue to be."

With a disgruntled flourish the girl swept up her gown, flouncing from the chamber, the others floating after, casting Bree amused glances, as though she were a curiosity in Messire Maricheau's menagerie.

When the honey-voiced Monsieur Verney trailed after the last as they vanished through the door, the Lady Esmeraude glided to the portal, shutting the heavy panel with a conspiratorial smile. "You must forgive Lanette," she said, one ruby-laden hand drifting to Brianna's muslin-clad arm. "She and my son have been most involved, and she waxes frightful jealous whenever another lady shares his attentions—however briefly. I fear she has oft witnessed Creighton's wanderings, and dreads his tiring of her, as he has of all the others." The duchess heaved a gusty sigh. "I must confess, 'twill be a pity, though, when he does set the girl aside, for though bastard-born, Lanette has taken her—er—training in the households of some of the finest in the French aristocracy. I vow she bears as much elegance and grace as if she were a princess of the blood."

Brianna's chin jutted upward, and she met Creigh's mother's gaze levelly.

"Oh, child," the duchess rushed on, "I meant no slander to your own position. You are quite—unique—I vow, an entity unto yourself." Bree saw the woman's nostrils flare slightly. "'Tis but that with King Charles arriving in two days, and with him the court . . ." Esmeraude swept to a small table, pouring out wine the hue of blood. "In truth a girl the like of you . . . bred somewhere in the wilderness, can scarce hope to deal in the niceties of royal society."

"The king seems to disagree. He invited me to—"

"Invited *Lady Juliet,* as I understand it," Esmeraude corrected. "Come now, dear, considering my son's passing interest in you, he could hardly do aught but include you as well. Most like you were looking at him wistfully, and Charles . . . from the time he was a lad he's ne'er been able to deny aught to a woman."

Brianna turned, pretending to examine most closely the thick gold fringe at the bottom of a squat stool, the slight gaining of confidence she had been cherishing since she had

282

spoken with Charles Stuart waning. "'Tis a dangerous trait in a king," she said.

"Nay, my pet. 'Tis but a harmless one that all the cavaliers indulge in. I promise you 'twill be but little time before Creighton immerses himself in it again as well—the most favored gaming of his cavalier friends—that of seeing which among them is most able to . . . how shall I phrase it . . . gather the most *enchanting* blooms about them."

Brianna gritted her teeth, struggling not to allow the duchess to see how deeply her verbal thrust had struck, but visions of the pampered, patrician belles who had just glided from the room goaded her, their faces like those of painted angels, their gowns clinging to bodies ripe, lush, temptresses in satin. Temptresses who belonged in Creigh's world of grand estates, who knew how to sweep about vast ballrooms and bandy power as if 'twere but a game of quoits.

Brianna flinched at the cool, smooth feel of a silvered goblet being forced between her fingers, and she looked up to see but a fleeting expression of watchfulness in Creigh's mother's eyes before the duchess hastily banished it, replacing it with one of such tender concern, Bree had to choke back the bile that rose in her throat.

"Brianna, my dear child, you look dreadful pale. Come sit with me for a little, talk."

"Talk? When you ordered me to come, I—"

"*Ordered* is far too harsh a word, sweeting," Esmeraude denied, perching upon a brocaded chair seat and patting the place beside her. "I had fully intended for my guests to have departed before you arrived, but the Comtesse de Alimagne is most sentimental, and she begged so many ballads from my musician that the entertainment waxed overlong." Esmeraude reached out, taking Brianna's hand in chill, thin fingers. "I pleaded that you come to me, as I have a most urgent matter to discuss with you. A matter that we must resolve for your own well-being."

Brianna's lips twisted, wry. "Your concern for me is most . . . unexpected."

"You are in love with my son, are you not?"

Brianna started at the blunt question, keen, obsidian eyes piercing hers.

"Aye, 'tis as I feared," the duchess said, shaking her pale

curls. "Ah, child, my very heart breaks for you, but surely, even you can see the impossibility of such a liaison? Creighton is now heir to the dukedom of Blackthorne, a man of much power in England, and in these treacherous times, 'tis vital that he make a marriage that will secure his place, not only in Charles's exiled court, but in that of France as well. Even if . . ." Esmeraude gave a soft, sorrowful sigh. "Even if my son were capable of cherishing some deep emotional tie with a woman—and I, as his mother, truly doubt that he is—'twould not be a simple lass such as you that could hold him."

Brianna touched the wine glass to her lips, the liquid within bitter, biting. "I have never thought to hold Creigh," she admitted, swallowing the tears that prickled at the back of her throat.

"There, and I thought not," Esmeraude Wakefield said, patting Bree's hand. " 'Tis a most astute child you are, and most brave. That is why I am certain you will accept this gift from me—recompense for your . . . er . . . services to my son, and will hasten to do what is best for you both."

Brianna heard an ominous jingle of gold, silver, saw the duchess's slender hand take up a soft leathern pouch from beside the wine tray.

"C-coin?" Brianna said, outrage beginning to seethe within her. "You seek to pay me as though I were his whore?"

" 'Tis but a trifle," Esmeraude said. "Consider it a reward for the hours you spent nursing him in his fever."

"And in his bed?" Bree snapped, bolting to her feet. "Tell me, your grace, what think you Creigh would say if he knew of the offer you now make me?"

Esmeraude's mouth curled in a smile, her white hands caressing the stem of her own wine goblet. " 'Twould please you if I begged you not to tell him, to expose me, would it not? And to think that, if you carried tales back to Creighton, he would rise to your defense like some embattled knight defending his lady fair?"

"I cast not my battles upon another's shoulders."

"Most admirable, Brianna, pet," Esmeraude sneered. "Especially since 'twould be pointless in any account." The duchess chuckled. "Mark me, Brianna, you are not the first so unwise as to fall beneath Creighton's considerable charms, and you'll not be the last to capture his fancy. You were no more to him than a diversion whilst he was stranded in a savage land, and now that he is home, among those who are his equals, 'tis but a matter of time until he finds a way to pension you off, as surely as he has countless others. 'Tis a most generous offer I make you, girl, enough coin to secure you comforts such as you never imagined for as long as you live. Take it."

"Nay." Brianna pushed herself to her feet, meeting Esmeraude Wakefield's gaze with unfaltering eyes. "It may well be that your son chooses to find pleasure in another, Your Grace, or that he dismisses me in favor of some high-placed marriage. But it matters naught. I would sooner die than take money for what I gave in love."

Esmeraude Wakefield's mouth opened, shut, the lips compressing into a hard, pale line. "There is a saying I heard once as a child, Mistress Devlin," the duchess said in a low, voice, its tones rife with hidden menace. "Have a care what you wish for, for it may be granted you." The white, seemingly fragile hand clenched upon the stem of the wine goblet as though 'twere the slender hilt of a Spaniard's stiletto, onyx eyes taking in the pure, obstinate curve of chin, fullness of lips so red, they filled Esmeraude with a raking jealousy the depth of which she had ne'er experienced before.

"And when I was a lass, I was taught something far different," the girl said, arching her neck regally. "I was taught that threats are a coward's means of securing what should be gained by courage."

"Courage!" Esmeraude snorted, rage boiling within her veins at the peasant chit's lofty tone. "What can a lowling cur's brat know of aught but crawling 'mongst the dung? I vow to you, *mistress harlot,* you shall regret—"

"I regret naught, your grace, except that Creigh, Juliet, aye, all but your husband seem blind to what you really are. But even a wolf must shed its sheep's clothing when closing for the kill. And you, milady, will be forced to do so as well."

Esmeraude's breath swelled angry-hot in her lungs, her chest threatening to burst with her fury. "How dare you!" One ringed hand slashed out, and the duchess gloried in the feel of her palms cracking into Brianna's face. She scrutinized the girl with a grim eagerness, expecting fear, sobbing.

But instead of the quailing the duchess's rare fits of unbridled temper had always before inspired, the peasant wench's too-pointed features merely tightened into a mask of distaste, as though Brianna Devlin were queen instead of naught but Creigh Wakefield's latest whore. Esmeraude wanted to scratch the gold-tinted skin until it ran with blood, wanted to rip at the girl's tawny hair until it lay in hanks upon the floor, but something in the chit's face stopped her—an inner resolve the strength of which Esmeraude Wakefield had ne'er encountered in another of her sex, yet one she well recognized, as she, too, possessed it.

"We have not finished between us, you and me," the duchess hissed in frustration. "Mark me, mistress harlot."

The girl met her threat without betraying even a whisper of unease. "At your pleasure, your grace," she said. Lifting the hem of her crude muslin gown, the despicable wretch turned, making not so much as a curtsy as she exited the room.

Esmeraude Wakefield's whole body quivered with outrage. So the peasant slut thought to match wits with a noblewoman? Esmeraude's lips curled in a sneer. Well, Mistress Devlin would find out exactly how idle the Duchess of Blackthorne's *coward's threats* could be. Slamming her silver goblet onto the tray, she stalked into the corridor, shoving open the door to a small antechamber. "Beadle!" she snapped into the darkened room in which she had directed the little man to await her command. "Get yourself to my chambers, you cursed witling! I have need of you with all haste."

Scarce pausing to see if the valet had followed, she returned to her own withdrawing room, stalking across to the small cherrywood escritoire that stood upon double-twist legs in the corner. She heard Beadle's feet scurrying after her as she took up a newly made quill, jabbing it deep in an ink pot, snatching a sheet of paper from the drawer.

Mauricheau, return at once, she penned in furious strokes across the shroud-pale sheet. *'Tis time the huntress sought her prey.*

Dashing sand across the script, she swept it up in one trembling fist, wheeling to glare at the breathless Beadle. "Summon your master's beast-keeper from the menagerie at once, you fool."

"B-beast-keeper? But Messire Mauricheau ordered the man ne'er to be seen within the keep's walls . . . he was to remain in the menagerie until my master had use for—"

"I bear a use for the slavering knave! This missive must reach Messire Mauricheau in Morlaix before the morrow or all is lost."

"Morlaix? But . . . but Your Grace . . ."

"Summon him!" Esmeraude shrilled, jamming the letter into Beadle's thin face. "'Tis time our pure Messire Mauricheau joined the rest of us in dipping his hands in blood."

Chapter Twenty-two

Faith, Bree," Juliet Bouret teased, "'tis only the final fitting for a gown! I give you my word you'll live through the ordeal. Will she not, Mademoiselle Longet?" She flashed a dimpled grin of amusement toward the stout little dressmaker as she swept up a length of sapphire velvet. Juliet examined the material that draped about Brianna, dark eyes benignly critical as she tested the fit of the newly sewn garment about her friend's narrow waist.

"I'd sooner face a horde of Roundhead pikemen any day," Brianna said through gritted teeth, wincing as another one of *Mademoiselle*'s sharp pins anchored itself, not only to the cloth, but to a bit of tender skin as well. "I can scarce breathe, let alone move in this cursed thing."

"Well, with the king's fete but one day away, we've scarce time to make you another one." Juliet laughed. "When my brother sweeps you out onto the floor to dance, you'll forget how uncomfortable you are, and glide about as though you were robed in clouds. Every cavalier in Jersey will take one look upon you and feel like Messire Cupid has driven his arrow through their hearts. And brother Creigh . . . he'll be hard put to defend his prize. Why His Majesty himself is nigh legend for his love of the ladies. Who knows what heights you might reach?"

Remembering the cruel barbs and scorn-filled glances delivered 'Lord Creighton's peasant wench' by the beauties in Lady Esmeraude's chamber, Brianna gave Jolie a quelling glare, but the girl was not chastened in the least. She merely tugged the décolletage of Brianna's gown the lower, exposing more creamy flesh above the gossamer icing of exquisite lace. Despite herself, Bree felt her stiff lips pull into a shading of a smile.

The frightened fawn of a lass who had first greeted Bree at Chateau aux Marées two weeks past was now more oft a curly-topped sprite, who danced about the room sprinkling bright jests, taking a special delight in tormenting not only Brianna and Creigh, but the stern-faced Rogan as well. At first, Bree had waited with bated breath, half expecting the surly Irishman to rake Juliet with the harsh edge of his tongue, but he merely looked upon her with a mixture of grudging tolerance and amazement, his glowering gaze following the dark curls whenever Juliet was in the room.

Bree turned slowly upon the seamstress's command, the cut of the sleeve seeming in question at the moment, from the dissatisfied mutterings of the other two women, but Bree's thoughts remained, bittersweet, loving, upon the bright-faced Juliet.

'Twas as if the child indeed had hurled herself into the philosophies of her brother's cronies, living each day as if she were to be gifted with no others. Only when someone— most often the ubiquitous Beadle or the sullen Lady Esmeraude—mentioned Messire Mauricheau or Michel Le Ferre, did the animation fade from Juliet's dark eyes, to be replaced with a hollow, burning hopelessness that drove all the joy from the room.

"Milady, please!" Mademoiselle Longet's voice cut into her thoughts. "Let your shoulders lay easily beneath the velvet. If you square them as though you wear my Lord Creighton's cuirass, you'll look like a squire got up in his mother's gown."

"I would feel far more comfortable in Creigh's armor," Bree snapped. "'Twould most like bear far less weight." She caught the surprised glances between the two women who had been so kind to her, and sighed, irritated at herself for her show of temper. Shifting her stiff shoulder muscles beneath the heavy weighting of rich fabric, lace, and jewels the seamstress's nimble fingers had worked into the cloth of the magnificent dress, Bree said softly, "'Tis sorry I am, both of you. I know not how you can bear me at present, surly as I am."

"'Tis but nervousness over your first ball," Juliet said,

patting Bree's hand. "Before I was presented to His Majesty, I wretched in the chamberpot for an hour."

"You . . . but you and King Charles seemed so . . . so close. I—"

"I claimed 'twas nervousness. Creigh insisted 'twas that I ate half a piggin of dates drowned in honey that morn."

Mademoiselle Longet guffawed, but Bree couldn't coax even a hint of a smile. Juliet's gentle fingers gave her a firm squeeze. "Don't fear, Bree," she said. "Even without this gown you'd be the most beautiful, bravest lady in the hall." The genuine love in the girl's face tore at Brianna's heart. "All anyone present will need to do is to look in my brother's eyes to know you belong always at his side."

Brianna turned her eyes to the polished metal mirror, Juliet's innocent faith stinging her lids with tears. The woman peering back at Bree from the framing of the mirror was a stranger, even her amber eyes unfamiliar as they faltered, uncertain, above the sapphire velvet creation. Yet even the wonder of jewels, laces reflected back from the mirror decking the chamber wall, could not banish the creeping sensation of unease, anticipation that raked across Bree's nerves with the insistence of rats in an *oubliette*.

If Creigh were to set her whole person ablaze with gems and cloth of gold, 'twould never change what lay beneath the trappings of wealth and importance. Always she would remain simple Brianna Devlin—a sharp-tongued hoyden, better versed in cracking the bones of cavaliers than in dancing with them. And Esmeraude Wakefield . . .

Brianna stiffened. Aye, well she knew that the duchess had all but declared her enmity openly, sparing only Creigh from the hate that burned in her lashless onyx eyes each time she was forced to look upon Bree. Yet the most disturbing thing of all was the expression upon the duchess's face whenever Bree caught her gaze, a look that bespoke a triumph already gained, as though she knew something . . .

"God's teeth!" Brianna yelped, yanking away from the seamstress's awkward hands as a pin point dug deep into the tender flesh beneath her ribs. She muttered a spate of curses in Gaelic that set both the cheery-faced Longet and Juliet into peals of mirth. Bree clenched her teeth, wanting to scream at them both that 'twas no jesting matter, this ball that Bree knew now held both promise and threat. That 'twas most like as Esmeraude Wakefield claimed, the beginning of Creigh's inevitable withdrawal back into the world he knew and loved, and for Brianna, 'twould be a night fraught with awkwardness, with social stumblings she knew not how to avoid. Stumblings that would drive the impeccably mannered Creigh from her side all the faster. But despite the uncertainties that roiled within her, she could not bear to chase the light from Juliet's eager face.

"There now, Lady Juliet, is she not *enchantante*?"

The seamstress's high-pitched chatter yanked Bree inexorably from her troubled thoughts back onto the short, carved pedestal upon which she stood. Bree's eyes focused upon Juliet's merry red lips. "'Tis more than enchanting!" The girl clapped her hands like a joyous child, spinning about in ecstasy. "Oh, mademoiselle, 'tis perfection!"

Juliet gave a little hop of joy, then swept into a deep curtsy, batting her thick lashes in a way immediately identifiable as that of the romantical Comtesse de Alimagne. "Oh, my *dearest* Mistress Devlin," Jolie crooned in a sickeningly sweet voice. "You *must* confess to me how you managed to tear down a piece of the sky. I declare you look like a veritable *angel.*"

Brianna rolled her eyes, her lips compressing in irritation, but Jolie caught at her hands, dragging her, gown and all, from the pedestal. Bree swallowed a curse, battling to remain standing as she stumbled across the carpet, certain that if she were to fall, she would crash to the floor like an axed tree, so stiff were the binding folds of pearl-encrusted velvet. But somehow the smaller Juliet managed to brace her until she could get her blue-green slippers beneath her.

"Whist now, Bree, 'tis time you learned to walk gowned as Creighton Wakefield's lady."

"I shall be overfortunate to be able to move at all. God's blood, 'tis no wonder I always beat you at racing. Beneath all these layers your poor mare is weighted as though she bore three riders instead of one!"

Juliet giggled, delving into the pocket of her gown to retrieve a sea-blue satin fan edged in tiny, luminescent pearls. "I shall remember that excuse the next time you defeat me," she said. "Now, attention, please, Mademoiselle Devlin." Brianna felt the edge of the fan thrust into her fingers, while Juliet snapped open a second, delicately painted one. "You shall poise the fan thusly," she directed, bringing the dainty scalloped edge a mere breath from her full lips, only her pert nose and sparkling eyes above its veiling. "This way, your cavalier will never be quite certain as to whether or not he is truly amusing you. 'Tis funny indeed, watching them try to make you break into a giggle. While—Rogan! I . . . I mean, Monsieur Niall . . ."

Bree started at Juliet's pleased cry, turning to see the big Irishman stalk into the room, his brows, always in a constant glower, now slashed so low over his eyes, that Brianna felt a chill of dread course through her. She started toward him, but he strode past her without sparing her so much as a glance, approaching Juliet with an expression Bree fully expected would send the child into a dead faint.

"My lady, he is arrived."

"Arrived?" Juliet gasped in dismay. "But His Majesty is not scheduled to come until morn. The apartments he and his retinue are to occupy aren't half ready, and—"

"'Tis not King Charles."

Bree saw Juliet's brow crinkle in confusion as her dark eyes met Rogan's, then her face paled in a stirring of fear. "If . . . if 'tis not the king, then who . . ."

"Messire Mauricheau. 'Tis not my place, I know, but I was on my way here when I saw the horses. I thought to warn you."

Brianna reached out a hand to catch Juliet's slender one, the look on the girl's face that of a reprieved prisoner being suddenly led to the gallows.

"Th-thank you, Rogan," Juliet managed, her voice reedy thin, as she attempted to straighten her thin shoulders. "You . . . you will excuse me . . . Mademoiselle Longet, Bree, I . . . I needs must wait upon my . . . husband . . ."

"That would prove most wise, madame *wife.*"

The door Rogan had entered so quietly now slammed against the inner wall with a force that scattered what small remnant of composure Juliet Wakefield had clung to. Bree glimpsed Mademoiselle Longet nigh leaping through her lace fallen ruff in shock, saw Juliet flinching in fear. Then Creigh's sister yanked across her features a mask of obedience beneath an overbright smile as she faced the man framed within the portal's huge stone columns.

"M-Mauricheau," she stammered, taking a step toward

292

him, stopping. "'Tis a most . . . most unexpected pleasure to see you home again."

"That is apparent." With a nasty laugh, the man stepped into the room. Bree's eyes flashed over the despicable Messire Mauricheau Bouret in one loathing-filled instant— He reminded her of a wolfhound she had seen once, interbred, Shane had judged, until the breed's noted courage and gentleness had been twisted into savagery, the ruthless beast ready to tear out its own master's throat. Bronzed skin was tight over Bouret's sharp-edged bones, his eyes, opaque, bearing no honest hue beneath their lids. His mouth, full with blatant sensuality, held not the gentle promise of good humor the king's had, rather, was edged with a ruthlessness that both repulsed and attracted.

"M-my lord husband, I . . ." Juliet's hands fluttered toward mademoiselle's sewing tools yet strewn across a table. "I was but helping Creigh's lady, Brianna, to—"

"Garb herself as the *whore* she is?"

Bree saw Rogan's hand knot into a heavy fist, heard Juliet's cry of dismay as the girl reached out one hand, staying Rogan's arm. "Mauricheau," Juliet said, the struggling for courage upon her countenance twisting at Bree's heart. "Creigh is my brother and Brianna . . ."

"Brother?" Bouret spat. "The cursed fool is heir to a duke! He should pay heed to regaining Blackthorne, instead of casting his attention upon rag wenches and ruffians the like of these." Scathing eyes swept Brianna and Rogan. "And now I am forced to abandon a most vital journey to discover *my wife* galivanting about with these barbarian Irish, embracing them as though they were royalty crowned. Praise God someone had the wit to summon me before you shamed this household."

"I have done naught to shame you." Juliet's eyes were wide, but Bree saw her meet her husband's gaze with what courage she could muster. "I—I swear it." Mauricheau Bouret's eyes narrowed, his sharp-drawn features stretching taut in a kind of sadistic eagerness that made Brianna's skin crawl.

"Swear it, my pet? We Bourets well know how to wrench truths from the lips of liars."

Bree heard Rogan's muttered curse, saw the big Irishman start toward the knight, his mouth harsh with fury, but

Brianna stepped in front of him, her voice the essence of reason.

"Messire Mauricheau, Juliet but agreed to aid me upon her brother's request. I—"

"Juliet!" the man spat, his ruby-weighted fist shot out, grabbing his wife's slender arm in a crushing grip. "So you are on such intimate terms with these Irish savages that they address you—wife of Messire Mauricheau Bouret—as though you, too, were a charwoman?"

The knight's tensile arm yanked her forward, then abruptly released her, pitching Juliet into the edge of the door. Her face cracked against the wooden panel, a cry of pain tearing from her throat. Brianna heard Mademoiselle Longet gasp from where the seamstress cowered in the corner, saw Rogan dive toward Juliet with a curse. Bree, too, flew to give her aid, but before either could reach Creigh's sister, she shoved herself upright, pressing one shaking hand to her bruising cheek.

"Nay! 'Tis . . . 'tis all right, all of you. I . . . I but tripped over my gown."

"Jolie, I—" Bree's gasped words stilled in her throat with one look at Rogan Niall's face. The green eyes blazed Celtic fire, the hand that had dealt a hundred enemies death clutched, white-knuckled upon the hilt of his sword. The plea Brianna had seen in Juliet's face took on a new, more desperate meaning.

"Rogan, nay," Bree hissed under her breath, her hand locking iron hard about his wrist. "You'll do her naught but harm." She could feel the tendons beneath her fingers, the legendary Niall fury pulsing there, all but out of control.

Messire Mauricheau reached for his own rapier, his fingers caressing its emerald-studded hilt. "You have a wish to test your skill against a *chevalier* crofter?" the knight purred. "Mayhap there is more of a reason to slit your throat than purely for my amusement." He glanced back at his wife.

Juliet tugged on her husband's arm, trying to urge him from the room. "Please, Mauricheau, 'tis my error, not theirs. I . . . I should have known 'twould displease you for me to . . . to seek them out."

"*Oui, mon amour,* you should have known." Mauricheau's slitted eyes fixed upon Juliet, malicious as a mad dog's. "We will make full certain that you remember to consider my wishes in the future."

Indignation, anger, and frustration warred inside of Brianna as the Frenchman's thin hand knotted in the curls at Juliet's nape, propelling her before him as he stalked through the door. Juliet glanced back but an instant, her gaze locking with that of Rogan, and Bree felt the tension in the big Irishman tighten further, his muscles iron-hard knots, before his shoulders then slumped in an odd sense of defeat.

"Damme!"

Bree jumped as Niall drove his fist into the stone pillar, battering his knuckles on the carved head of a lion.

"Monsieur Niall, si'l vous plaît," Mademoiselle Longet said, scurrying from the shadows. "'Tis most difficult, I know, to see—see my lady Juliet treated thus. But there is nothing any can do to aid her now. She is Messire Mauricheau's wife, devil take him, and . . ."

"And because Lady Juliet's father forced Bouret's ring upon her, I can do naught but let the cursed bastard drag her away, beat her if he desires it," Rogan bit out savagely. "Leave, woman. Now," Rogan spat at the seamstress. She scuttled from the room, scarce taking time to sweep the tools of her trade into a split-oak basket. She had barely fled through the door when the hilt of Rogan's sword clanked back against the scabbard. He spun to face Brianna. "Juliet Wakefield is less to Bouret than the stones he walks on."

"Think you I don't know that?" Bree cried. "Think you I'd not aid her if I could?"

"'Tis too late for her. Aid yourself, for God's sake. Sail home with me, Bree. Rid yourself of this damned Sassenach lord who drags you through the castle as his harlot!"

Brianna winced at the word, her jaw clenching, hands knotting in the folds of sapphire velvet. "I'm no harlot!"

"Nay? All from the lowest spit boy to the king of England know you bed in Lord Creighton's chamber. What think you they label you, knowing an Irish barbarian can ne'er share Lord Creighton's name?"

"'Tis none of their concern," Bree cried, battling the welling of hurt that rose from the lash of Rogan's words. "His . . . His Majesty was most kind—"

Rogan gave a snort of laughter. "Aye, I'll wager. They say

295

Charles bears an appetite for women greater even than his hunger for a crown." Rogan's big, square hands reached out, catching Brianna's arms, forcing her to look at him. "I know you think me but jealous, knowing that I loved you. But I speak as a brother, now, one who is fearful of your fate."

Bree tried to tear away, but he held her, crushing the scattering of pearls upon her sleeves into the soft flesh of her arms. "Bree, do you mean to endure the snide cruelties of bastards the like of Bouret for the rest of your life? Most likely Messire Mauricheau is even now in his chambers doing God knows what to his wife for even daring to speak to peasants low as we. What think you he and his kind would do to a child—*your child*—if you and Creigh Wakefield should conceive one?"

Brianna's fingers tightened protectively over her stomach, her eyes snapping fire. "'Twould be 'neath Creigh's protection. None would dare—"

"He could do naught to shield it from the whisperings, Bree. These stiff-necked lordlings be full masters at casting sly glances, stifled smirks, double-edged words that cut deep as any blade. And a child . . . it tortures him, tears . . ." Rogan's voice was thick with pain and he dashed a hand across his eyes. "List' to me once in your thrice-stubborn life— I know what 'tis to be outcast, hated for that which was none of my doing. I've felt it all my life the legacy left me by my father."

"Rogan—"

"Nay, and the worst of it is that 'twas true, what they labeled him. He *was* traitor, did betray the women and babes at Gobbin's Cliff. I knew, Bree, but there was naught I could do but deny it, even to myself. I had to fight it, him . . . Christ, I've been battling since I was but a lad."

"'Twill be different for my child . . . I'll make it so . . ." Brianna wanted to hate him for painting so clearly the agonies he had suffered, hate him for showing her the torment any child born of the love she held for Creighton Wakefield would suffer as well. Her chest seemed crushed with the pain of it, the certainty that even if, by some miracle, Creigh did choose to keep her beside him, she would be condemning her own babe to a youth of scorn and hate. How could she watch a child suffer, cause its pain when she had been gifted with a childhood idyllic in its magic?

The blue velvet that had once shone so beautiful seemed to weight her shoulders with all the anguish, cruelty Creigh's world could cast upon her.

She felt Rogan's eyes boring into her face, willing her to meet his gaze, and Bree wanted to scream at him, drive him from the room so that the tears searing the backs of her eyes could burst free.

"Bree, I but say this because I love—"

"I don't want your love!" she cried, pulling from his grasp. "I never wanted your love. Only his . . ."

Creigh . . .

Her eyes blurred, and she could picture his rosewood mane, his eyes storm-dark with passion as he bent to kiss her. And she wanted to weep in his arms, spill out the agonies that raked within her, but she knew that 'twas the one thing she could ne'er do.

"I give you only the love Doyle held for you now, and Daniel," Rogan's quiet tones broke into her pain. "'Tis because of that I came to the chamber in the first place. 'Twas but chance that crossed my paths with that of Messire Mauricheau."

Bree's hands clenched in the hated velvet gown, the pearls biting into her palms. "I vow you've done your *brotherly* duty and warned me of the error of my ways. Now go, leave me in peace."

"Aye, as soon as I give you the news I came here to deliver. 'Tis about Daniel."

A shaft of raw terror bit through Brianna's inner torment, and she despised herself at the realization of how seldom her brother had entered her thoughts of late, swallowed up as they were by her own anguish. She wheeled, reaching out, grasping Rogan, as though for support. "Is he . . . he's safe, Rogan? Oh, God, let him be . . ."

"Aye. He's tending the cabbage crop in Connaught, on Fergus MacDermot's farm. Fergus vows the boy is out of danger's path, and hale. When spring comes, if—if you still be here, Fergus's ma will send Daniel over upon a ship to join you."

"If . . ." Brianna's fingers slid of their own volition down her ribs to the slight swell of her yet smooth stomach. 'Twas two times the moon had reached its zenith since she had been troubled with her woman's flow. It had been but a relief to her, being free of it as she and Creigh had dashed across the countryside, escaped from London's Tower. And not once, while she had nursed him had she even questioned the flow's absence. But now . . .

She swallowed, feeling suddenly ill. What if, in truth, she did hold Creigh's babe within her womb? Dared she stay with him, binding him to her with a child that would but prove a burden to him once he decided to free himself of her? And even if he did not cast her aside, even if his love held true despite Esmeraude's predictions, and Creigh's obligation to provide the dukedom of Blackthorne with a noble-born heir, what future did a child of her body bear? That of a bastard, outcast.

Though she herself would be willing to endure any hardship to remain at Creigh's side, how could she condemn her own babes, and those of proud Creighton Wakefield, to the cruelties Bouret and his cronies would heap upon it?

She raised her eyes, her gaze meeting Rogan's, and she hated him for the pity she saw there. "Get out," she said dully.

"Bree . . ."

"Get out!"

There was the quiet sound of Rogan's boots upon the thin carpet as he made his way from the room. Brianna stared after him, feeling more lost, alone, than e'er before in her life. She ran her fingertips over her stomach, the slight protrusion filling her with savage protectiveness, fierce needs that raged in her body, and in her heart.

Rogan paused at the door, spoke. "I do love you, Bree," he said thickly, "as though you are as much mine as you are Doyle's and Daniel's. If you e'er have need of me . . ."

"I need nothing. No one." Brianna's chin jutted stubbornly in the air. She stood, silent, staring at nothing. The door shut slowly.

Bree clenched her teeth against the misery that welled within her, driving the hot salt of tears into her eyes. She looked at her reflection in the polished silver mirror, the rich promise of the gown's beauty now dull as an old woman's eyes. 'Twas to have been a night of magic, Creigh had vowed, woven of love, and candles, and a hundred hidden touches, but now . . . now 'twould be naught but farewell, one last night of branding Creigh's face, touch into her heart before she plunged into an agony of loss such as she had never known.

Bree looked down, her heart twisting at the sight of the heel of her slipper crushing the sea-blue fan Juliet had held up so laughingly a lifetime ago. But upon the pearl-rimmed edge, 'twas not tiny, pale jewels she saw, but rather the tossing of foam upon cerulean waves, bearing her and her child back to Ireland, and a life barren of the man Brianna loved beyond all reason.

Chapter Twenty-three

The great hall of Chateau aux Marées glittered like a miser's treasure-box, the jewel-hued gowns that flowed about the ladies and the flashing satins bedecking King Charles's gallant cavaliers filling the enormous room to bursting. Brianna struggled to keep her velvet slippers gliding across the huge expanse of floor in time to the lilting music, her eyes fastened numbly upon the other dancers, as the graceful necklet of bright-faced belles dipped and swayed with their complementing chain of beaus to the strains of a pavane.

'Twas the dance Creigh had taught her a lifetime ago, humming in an off-key baritone as he had swept her about the inn room at Swan's Way during a night born of magic. But now, instead of an indulgent grin, his mouth was tight with irritation. And even the touch of his sword-toughened palm could not guide her in the intricate figures as unseen slippers darted out, catching at her toes until she seemed to crash about, awkward as a newborn filly amongst a clustering of airy butterflies.

She gritted her teeth beneath the smile pinned to her lips, fighting to seem oblivious to the eyes fastened upon her from all across the room. The single person in the whole great hall who did not seem engrossed with the amusement of watching her fumblings was Creigh, who, heedless of her misery, flashed increasingly thunderous glances at the arched doorway as each late-arriving guest drifted in.

'Twas small matter enough, the tardiness of some of those honored with invitations, Brianna thought mutinously, when the host himself had not deigned to grace the gathering with his presence. The king's towering frame was nowhere to be seen amongst these, his favorites, and the thought that at least the merry Charles was not witnessing her humiliation gave her but meager comfort.

Bree dared a glance at Creigh, his brows crashed low over his eyes, aggravation, frustration in every line in his taut face. Could he truly not see how unhappy she was? Or was her clumsiness that which had brought the hardness that played about his mouth? Brianna bit the inside of her underlip, trying to force away the pain the thought spawned as a lump that felt distressingly like tears squeezed in her throat.

Yet, still, the tears threatened to burst free as Brianna felt Juliet's sympathetic gaze again upon her, glimpsed Galliard Wakefield, standing beside his daughter, tight-lipped, casting fuming glares toward where Lady Esmeraude sat with Messire Mauricheau and Lanette Perrin, enthroned amongst a group of smirking courtiers.

Yet more upsetting even than Messire Bouret's malicious sneer was the expression upon Rogan's face, one of grim satisfaction, laced with the chafings of impatience as his gaze strayed to where the sea winds swept against the narrow, mullioned glass windows.

A dull knife twisted in Brianna's heart as her eyes were unwillingly drawn to follow Rogan's gaze. Beyond the castle walls she could nigh picture the churning English Channel hurling itself against the cliffs that plunged from the island's rim into the water's night-glossed depths. And in her mind she could see the ship that lay at anchor upon those midnight waves, waiting. No doubt Creigh would be well pleased to rid himself of her now—now that they had both seen how ill-fitted she was to be at his side . . .

A sharp stab of despair plunged deep in the pit of her stomach, her teeth jarring together as a scarlet satin shoe thunked into her ankle. Creigh's gaze jerked from the door, his hand flashing out to grab hers a full count before they were to have met in the dance, steadying her as a sly-faced miss flung Bree a simpering grin.

Brianna wanted to whirl upon the girl, challenge her openly, giving way to the plain Devlin fury fast building beneath the princesslike façade. But for the first time in her

301

life, Bree felt awkward, inadequate, her usual defenses clumsy as a broken blade against the subtle barbs of those around her.

Creigh's hand squeezed hers as they met again in the dance, and she fought desperately to hide the roiling hurt she was feeling as he leaned close. She sensed that he was trying to leash his aggravation, fasten upon her at least a pretense of the attentiveness he seemed unable to gift her with.

"Remember, Tigress?" he asked, even his stiff smile doing naught to dim the raw masculine splendor of his lean body resplendent in slashed midnight velvet, his shoulders a-glitter with silvery panes of satin. "I'd give half my wealth if we could again be alone as we were in Ireland." The hard line of his jaw eased but a whisper, and Bree caught the barest hint of a weary sigh. "Aye," he said, his gaze flicking over the other dancers' heads to that infernal door. "'Twould be heaven if I could but sweep you, naked, into my bed, this gown that makes you look an angel crumpled upon the floor."

"'Twould be a hideous waste, after you poured so much coin into it," Brianna squeezed out icily, hating the edge that cut into her voice. "But then, I suppose 'twould have been passing humiliating if your aristocrat comrades had seen your latest mistress decked in sword and buckler."

She felt Creigh stiffen, the comforting warmth of his breath upon her skin disappearing as he drew away, his own flawlessly graceful corded silk shoes nigh missing a step as he moved them across the floor. "Damn it, Tigress, you're the most comely lady in the whole castle, and I've told you so a score of times already," he said in a voice too quiet for the other dancers to hear. "I would care naught if you chose to bear your dagger between your teeth, if you'd but cease trying to drive it between my ribs at every turn." His eyes skimmed her face, and she could see him attempt to leash his own ill humor. His voice gentled, and Bree wanted to clap her hands over her ears to stifle the wondrous, caring tones. "I well know you're nervous. 'Tis but natural, what with facing the court for the first time."

"I care not what these perfumed peacocks think of me!" Brianna snapped, balking in the midst of a graceful sweeping circle. Creigh's hand upon her waist tightened, all but dragging her through the rest of the figure.

"Oh, aye," he said between clenched teeth. "That must be why you've been battering all who come within reach of that cursed tongue of yours. Trust me, Bree, in time you'll become accustomed to all this."

"Accustomed to people making jest of me? I think not. Only the king's request that I be present saved me from being hurled bodily into the courtyard like an urchin come begging. And I half expected Messire Mauricheau to drive me from the room at the point of his sword."

Bree saw Creigh's jaw clench, his lips a thin white line. "Did the cursed bastard say ought to you? I vow I'll break my blade across his skull if—"

"Don't trouble yourself. Messire Mauricheau would sooner deign to converse with a stable boy," Brianna said as the dancers joined their partners, sweeping in graceful, dipping pairs down the polished stone floor. "I'd not be worth the breath he'd have to spend to cast an insult."

"If 'twill make you feel better, I'm full certain Bouret would as soon cast half this room to his cursed mad bears, if he could. And I well know little that would give me as much pleasure as dealing the arrogant cur a taste of my blade."

"And Mademoiselle Perrin? Will you strike her down as well? She has spent every second since she first laid eyes upon me smirking and tittering to any who will listen."

"I give not a damn what Lanette Perrin babbles to others as mindless as herself, and for God's sake, I thought you were one woman who would refuse to fall into the web of gossip she spins. What care you if Lanette and her kind wag their bitter tongues? 'Tis but in jealousy toward the love we hold—"

Brianna stifled a sick laugh, forcing her burning eyes to remain dry as she swept up the skirt of her gown, turning slowly in a move of the dance. "From what my Lady Esmeraude confided, Lanette has much to be jealous of, as that lady, too, once shared your favors."

Bree winced at Creigh's hissed curse, his face beneath the dashing plumes of his ebony velvet hat darkening with emotions Brianna could scarce read. "I never claimed to be a monk, Bree, in all the years before I found you."

The words struck deep, and Brianna clenched her teeth against the hurt they loosed within her as she parted from Creigh, and dipped, turned with the string of dancers. 'Twas as if, in hurting so horribly herself, she felt some irrational need to wound the man returning now to her side, a need to strike away the fierce passion that lit his eyes whenever he beheld her, to hurl his concern into his face, so that it would not bind her heart to his the more tightly.

"No doubt there are Wakefield bastards strung from one end of England to the other," she said, her own womb feeling heavy, burning beneath the velvet of her gown as he again took her hand.

"Oh, aye, I've peopled a whole estate with them back in Norfolk," Creigh snapped, his voice piercing a lull in the music. "That's why I dragged you here all the way from Ireland. Breeding stock to add to the brood. With you in my stables, mayhap I can move on to populating Sussex next year."

A gangly maid with a gown the same jaundiced shade as her face jabbed at the ribs of her partner and nodded toward Creigh, snickering behind her hand. Bree's jaw set hard, and she wanted to wheel on the girl, strike the smirk from her face, but in truth, her anger at the girl was naught compared with the fury she felt toward herself at throwing Creigh up for the chit's ridicule. The absurdity, cruelty of the accusations Bree had flung at Creigh made her conscience squirm. Her gaze flashed up to his, the patterns of the dance forgotten, only his practiced hand keeping her from crashing into the Comtesse de Alimagne and her escort.

Yet all she could see were Creigh's eyes, gray, turbulent as a storm-tossed sea, the depth of pain, confusion within them drawing tears to her lashes. "Christ, Bree," he grated under his breath, "what the devil has possessed you? Every time I touch you, you cringe, or turn to do some other vitally important task like refastening shoe rosettes, or dusting your fingernails with an oiled cloth. What in God's name have I done?"

"Nothing," the denial burst out too quickly, and she yanked her gaze away from him, in an effort to hide the truth she knew was all too clearly written in her eyes. That she would soon be leaving him . . .

She could feel his gaze piercing the veiling of intricately

arranged ringlets that shadowed her face. "If 'twas not I, then who, Tigress? Did my mother . . . Juliet . . . anyone . . . say something to upset you? Ever since yesterday you've acted as though 'twould please you to cast me to the bottom of the sea. When all I want . . ." his tone dropped low, aching, "all I want is to keep you always beside me."

Brianna's throat constricted at his emotion-roughened voice, the sound of it touching her very soul, but at that instant her gaze snagged the slanted, catlike eyes of Lanette Perrin as she whispered something to Messire Mauricheau. The Frenchman's thin lips curled in a malicious sneer, his nostrils pinched white as his eyes flicked over Brianna. Cold disdain seemed to strip from her the glittering pearls, rich velvet until she felt again a rag-clad waif, with mud caked about her bare feet.

'Twas as if she were not even worthy of the man's hatred, as if she were naught but vermin to be crushed beneath his heel and flung out into the dungheap before she contaminated his castle's sacred halls. Brianna battled the urge to smooth her hands over her stomach, protecting from the knight's raking scorn the life she was now nigh certain it sheltered.

"Tigress, did you hear me?" Creigh's voice, sober, insistent drew her gaze away from the Frenchman and the smirking Lanette. Brianna caught a flash of cream satin as La Comtesse de Alimagne swept through the shadows, her hands smoothing over the doublet of a comely, gilt-haired man as they slipped toward the door leading from the castle.

She turned her gaze back to Creigh, suddenly aware that he had guided her to a halt, maneuvering them somehow out of the circling figures, into the shadowy corner de Alimagne and her lover had just left. Shame stung Bree as she felt knowing eyes upon her, trying to penetrate the thick darkness that had shielded countless cavaliers as they had hied off their mistresses to dabble wine between their breasts and false love words across their lips. Her cheeks burned as she pictured the lurid scenes splashed across the imaginations of all who so despised her, and she wanted naught but to be riding wild across an Irish moor, to be free of this castle with its sinister whisperings, and the piercing, hate-filled stares of those who dwelled within.

Creigh's rough fingertips swept up, tracing the shape of her face, lips, his body pressing close against her in the secreting dimness. "Bree, whatever troubles you, let me heal it," he said, his voice harsh, intense. "Whatever the offense—by me or by others. I want naught but to hold you here, beside me. Always."

"Like some cursed curiosity in Messire Mauricheau's menagerie?" Brianna cried, wanting to wound before she flung herself into his arms, needing to drive away the love and pain that shaded his beloved face. "Or do you merely plan to drag me about in golden chains, for your own amusement, your personal Irish barbarian to display to your high-and-holy friends?"

"Damn it, Bree, I want you for my—" His words ripped into a savage curse. Eyes dark, furious bored into hers, and Brianna cringed at the rock-hard set of Creigh's jaw. His piercing gaze yanked away from her face, sweeping the room in a bitter, cynical circle. "Oh, aye," he gritted. "Now I understand."

"Understand?"

"'Tis these . . . what did you term them? Perfumed peacocks you fear—sanctimonious fools the like of Lanette and Mauricheau and the rest."

"Nay, I—"

His eyes swept in a path across her features, and the disappointment, disillusionment she saw there crushed a sob in her breast.

"Don't trouble yourself with explaining, Tigress, or fight to hold what is yours by right," he said. "Let them turn you to flee." He paused, and Bree thought he had ne'er looked so soul-wrenchingly handsome. "Strange," he continued at last, "I never judged you for a coward."

Brianna started to protest, stopped as he spun away from her, his whipcord lean body rigid beneath its icing of midnight and silver. She wanted to dash after him as he stalked through the milling crowd, cry out, pleading for him to return. But she sank her teeth into her lip, tasting the salt of her own bitter tears as she watched Lady Esmeraude tap the loathsome Lanette upon the shoulder with her fan, whispering something to the girl. With a toss of her beribboned curls, Perrin gave a delighted laugh, disentangling herself from Messire Mauricheau's attentions to wind through the crowd in the direction of the door through which Creigh was fast disappearing.

Bree tried to steel herself against the pain, vowing to herself that 'twas what she had wanted—to fire his anger, to make the breach easier when she left with Rogan to sail back to Eire. But seeing Creigh stalk away from her, blending into the jeweled noblemen and women who were his peers, filled her with an anguish that threatened to rob her of all reason. And watching the clinging Lanette slither after him sent jealousy ripping through her with a force that nigh drove her to cast caution to the winds, and yank the scheming witch back into the great hall by hanks of her ribbon-decked hair. If not for the babe . . .

She curled her toes in their slippers, forcing her feet to remain rooted to the stone floor. She, she was strong, well able to parry the verbal swords any here might fling at her, but the child she and Creigh had conceived had naught but she to stand between its fragile life and the brutal disdain of all who swept about this room. And she'd not allow it, bastard-born, to grow to adulthood as the spawn of a mistress and a nobleman who, in time, would care naught for either of them.

Yet it hurt. God, it hurt, knowing she would ne'er see Creigh's face again, ne'er touch his lips, the hard-honed perfection of his body. She had thought to share with him just one last night, to revel in the joining of their bodies, to burn the feel, taste of him into her heart to remember for all eternity. But now, she knew that to touch him once more would be to hurl their babe's life to the winds, for if she again delved her hands into that glorious dark hair, felt his lips upon her breasts, belly, she would ne'er hold the strength to leave him.

The concerned face of Juliet as she whisked about the floor upon the arm of her father blurred before Brianna's eyes. The tears she had held in check seared her lids, overflowing the thick, gold-tipped lashes to flood her cheeks.

She dragged her gaze away from her friend's worried face, and that of Blackthorne's puzzled, concerned one. But the whole ballroom seemed suddenly agonizingly silent as the last strains of the dance faded, all eyes shifting from the door where Creigh had vanished, to Brianna, abandoned, humiliated by her own tears. She glimpsed Rogan crossing the room toward her, his face drawn in a belligerent scowl that dared any to make jest of her, but she could bear to face no one with the evidence of her anguish on her cheeks, especially Rogan Niall. She turned, full intending to run from the room, but as she made to escape through a small arched exit, she slammed headlong into a broad, satin-clad chest.

Gaze darting upward, she gaped in horror as she met the dark, compassionate eyes of Charles Stuart. The king's full mouth curved in a smile of understanding.

"Y-your Majesty," Bree stammered, seeing, through tear-blurred eyes, Rogan's glowering face but a dozen steps from where she stood. "I plead for your pardon. 'Tis just . . . I . . . I am taken with a headache and was just returning to my bedchamber."

"Even an aching brow must buckle 'neath a monarch's will, milady. You promised you would honor me with a dance, the day we met in Lord Creighton's chambers."

"I . . . I am honored, but . . . but I . . ." Shame fired her cheeks, humiliation welling in a choked sob within her as she saw the king's knowing gaze sweep her face. She could imagine with horrible clarity how she must appear with her sniffling, reddened nose, her tear-filled eyes, trembling lips. But Charles merely smiled at her, as though he failed to notice she was but a heartbeat from weeping like a babe.

"Come, milady, I vow both you and Lord Wakefield bear reason enough to wax irritated with me. But you, at least, must allow me to atone for my tardiness somehow," Charles said in a voice gentled by woe, the deep tones bearing a kindness, humor that put even the lowliest at ease. "If you care not to dance, mayhap you would favor me with a few moments in your company. Your king would take great pleasure in hearing from your lips how you managed to enchant his most trusted courtier."

Scarce hesitating for a response, he turned, tossing a grin over his shoulder to where the musicians stood, their instruments poised for his pleasure. "Strike up another pavane to keep my ladies occupied," the king ordered. "I would favor the loveliest flower in all Ireland with some time alone with her *Sassenach* king."

Brianna felt the flush deepen in her cheeks as Charles's hand, cool, dry, touched hers, drawing her toward the massive enameled chair about which he was to hold court. The sea of disapproving faces that had dismissed her in scorn moments before now parted as if by some unspoken command, the patent disdain shifting into raw shock and uncertainty as a hush blanketed the whole room.

The first notes of a violin hung sweetly in the air for a moment, then swelled into a frolicksome tune that seemed formed solely to force one's feet to tap in time to its music. Dully, Brianna watched the glittering courtiers again take the floor. Aching, hollow with the impending loss of Creigh, she could muster none of the fear she knew should be gripping her at speaking intimately with the king. Charles's easy humor dashed away what small threadings of nervousness still lurked beneath her pain.

"And so, milady, tell me," Charles said, sinking into the chair and indicating the seat beside him. "Did my Lord Creighton also bear an aching head?"

"Majesty?"

"He seemed to quit the hall in a most unseemly haste."

"I . . . 'twas but a disagreement we had, over . . ."

"A disagreement?" The king chuckled. "I've ne'er known Creighton Wakefield to care enough for the favors of any lady to suffer bouts of temper—from her, or from himself. It bodes well for you, child, his stalking off to sulk."

Brianna looked down at her hands, twined upon her lap. "I fear . . . my Lord Creighton and I have spent most of our time since meeting battling each other."

"Creigh told me a sampling of your adventures, and I vow, if 't had been any other of my men, I would have termed it falsehood. But Creigh . . ." Charles's merry eyes warmed her. "I doubt him not, nor do I doubt that the two of you will solve your differences before the rest of us strike our pillows this night. Creigh is an exceedingly wise man, smart enough so as not to allow a lady of your mettle slip from his grasp."

"I . . . I think Creigh would be most pleased to be relieved of my company at present," Brianna said.

"As his king, and, more as his friend, I think not. He has cast out far more in your behalf than you even know. More than I ever thought possible in a man of Creigh's ilk."

"I . . . I don't understand."

"The first day I saw you, when Creigh was scarce up from

his sickbed, he had summoned me, not only to impart information concerning the campaign in your homeland, but also to ask of me a boon."

"A . . . a boon?"

"Aye. Every day I am plied with at least a dozen requests of some kind, pleas for titles, lands I no longer bear the power to give, and the fates alone know what else. 'Tis one of the burdens of being king, my father once said, and 'tis naught but to be borne, despite how deeply it chafes at times. But there are those men—rare, a breed unto themselves—who seek not what the crown's power can give them. They seek only to serve, to hold loyal, and gird England with justice and strength. Creighton Wakefield is one of those men. He has ne'er, in all the years since we were lads together, asked one favor, not so much as a shilling from the royal purse."

The king chose a golden-skinned pear from a silver dish to his right. "But that day, in his bedchamber, Creigh chained his pride and asked something of me. He vowed that you held his heart and asked that I ease your way into the circle of stiff-necked nobles that surround us."

Brianna stared at the king, astounded, and the merry, dark eyes twinkled back at her as he sank his teeth into the piece of fruit. "Creigh asked you to . . . to accept me?"

"Aye. 'Twas my intent to escort you into the hall as though you were a princess born, lavish you with so much royal attention that none would dare turn their eyes your way with aught but goodwill. But, unfortunately, there were matters of the crown that I had to tend to that took longer than I would have wished." He leaned toward her, with a wry grin. "I know many of my courtiers would scarce believe it, but there are *duties* to being a king . . . even an exiled one."

Brianna felt her lips, trembling with misery but moments before, part into an answering smile.

Charles reached out one dark finger, smoothing back a strand of golden hair that clung to her brow. "Before you and little Jolie came barging into the room, I thought Creigh's wound had affected his mind—so odd was it, his desiring an Irish urchin to stand beside him, but after meeting you, speaking with you, I vow, I think Creighton Wakefield might well be the wisest man in all Europe!"

310

Brianna felt the pain, misery within her swell, bursting into glittering joy too great to hold. Creigh had not only wanted her to tumble within his bed, that proud, honorable man had humbled himself to go to his king, ask that Charles Stuart exercise his great power to shield her from the disdain of the exiled court.

Bree felt tears of love burn in her breast at the memory of Creigh's scorn for those grasping fortune seekers who constantly plied Charles for favors. Yet, Creigh had loved her so deeply, he had been willing to breach his rigid code of honor to gain her ease. She raised eyes, wet with tears and gratitude, to the English monarch's.

"Y-your Majesty . . . I . . . I thank you . . . for all that you've shared with me this night and all you have done to aid my lord and me."

"Royal favor can blot out many stains, milady, be they real or imagined." Charles reached out, taking her hand in his strong, dark fingers. "I am but pleased that for once the request borne us has naught to do with lands, or monies, or ill-deserved honors, but rather with the joinings of the heart."

Brianna clasped his hand, bending to press her lips in a kiss of gratitude upon his ringed fingers. The king smiled, and beneath the façade of royalty, she could see gallant Charles Stuart, the man.

"Real love is a rare thing indeed, in our world," he said softly. "My parents, they held it, before my father was killed, but . . ." Charles's face took on a shading of melancholy and grief, then he banished it. "Cherish your 'Sassenach lord,' Milady Tigress," he said. "We command it."

Brianna flushed, suddenly shy at the king's easy usage of the pet name Creigh had gifted her with. Her lips widened into a smile.

"Aye," the king confirmed. "He told us that, too. Now, despite the fact that I wax so charming a cavalier, methinks there is someone whose company you would sooner seek out than your king's. And it appears that, lest you wish to be slain by the daggers of jealousy being hurled at you from yon lady—" the royal gaze flicked to the door where a sulky Lanette was reentering the room—"you had best away to find him at once."

Brianna laughed aloud, bounding to her feet with a joyful

311

little hop. Then she sobered, her face, bright with loyalty as she regarded the king. "Your Majesty, may God bless your kindness always and return to you your rightful crown."

"So your countrymen can again try to knock it from my head in yet another bid for their freedom?" Charles said dryly. "Go now, child. 'Tis a wondrous new experience to Lord Creighton, this burden of sulking. I wager even now he's had his fill of it."

Brianna flashed him a broad grin, dipping into a spritely curtsy before she wheeled, nigh tumbling off the small dais. Charles reached out quickly, attempting to catch her to help her maintain her balance, but before the king's hand could stay her, another hand, that of the Comte de Alimagne, shot out, curving beneath her elbow.

"Have a care, milady." The florid face beamed with kindness. "My wife, La Comtesse, vows these gowns were designed solely to make the ladies sprawl upon their faces." Brianna smiled uncertainly, scarce believing the bland acceptance that had replaced the hostility in most of the faces around her.

Bree was surprised to see La Comtesse's face pop up over the shoulder of her portly husband, but instead of the giggling dismissal Brianna had been treated to in my Lady Esmeraude's chambers, the crimson lips flashed a bright smile, La Comtesse seeming to enjoy mightily the sensation Charles's open acceptance of Brianna had caused amongst the guests.

The woman bent close, her rose taffeta brushing in a rustling path against Brianna's gown. "If you seek Creigh," she whispered, "look within Messire Mauricheau's menagerie. I was taking a bit of air with the Viscount de Laney, and I saw his lordship hie off in that direction, though I vow, even to escape Mademoiselle Perrin, I'd not seek out those dreary walls, what with the raging of that poor bear Messire Mauricheau is readying for the morrow's baiting." La Comtesse gave an elaborate shudder.

"Mistress Devlin will have naught to concern herself with at the bear pits," Rogan's voice, sharp with impatience, cut in, his hand curving about Brianna's elbow. "We have a most pressing engagement to attend to, milady, do we not?"

"Nay, Rogan, I attend naught this night but my lord."

"Your what? Damnation, Bree, you can't—"

"Aye, Rogan, I can, and I care naught if the horned god himself bars the way." She turned her face up to his and saw his eyes widen, chill as his gaze swept her features.

"Bree!"

She turned, paying no heed to his protest, scooping up her skirts, battling the desire to heft them to her knees, and bolt across the room shouting out her joy. As she rushed toward the doorway, she caught a glimpse of Juliet's face, the girl's smile sweet with triumph beside the pleased one of her father, the bruise caused by Messire Mauricheau's anger scarce visible despite the bright light of the candles.

Even the fury that whitened the Lady Esmeraude's lips as Brianna passed her could not dull Bree's spirits, and she returned Messire Mauricheau's outraged glare with an expression that matched his own arrogant pride.

'Twas but a few who yet waxed sullen, and it seemed nigh all she passed either gave her shy, chastened smiles, or averted their eyes in shame for their earlier behavior. Beneficent as a new-made queen, Bree smiled back at them, nigh skipping through the door, where Beadle stood, his eyes nigh bulging from their pockets of flesh.

As if anticipating her exiting the hall, a young footman, bedecked in livery bearing the raging boar of the Bourets, awaited her at the door that led out of the building, his gangly form all but obscured by the wrap Bree had been given days ago. But Bree dismissed him with a wave of her hand, not wanting to hesitate even a breath before going to Creigh, the chill night air that whistled about the castle holding no power against her happiness.

"If 'tis my Lord Creighton you seek, he ofttimes revels in the curiosities in Messire Mauricheau's cages," Beadle said with an odd eagerness in his pinched face as he opened the heavy door. "The new keeper—"

"So La Comtesse said," Brianna interrupted, too full of her own happiness to note the surprise that flashed across the servant's face. Beadle's thin lips formed a circle, his brows crashing together above his nose.

"La . . . La Comtesse? She said Lord Creighton was . . ."

"Aye," Brianna flung over her shoulder as she skipped through the archway. She turned to glance at Beadle, something in the man's tone striking her as strange, but the valet was already scurrying toward the ballroom, his thin frame lost among the bright-robed figures of his master's guests.

Bree shrugged, gathering up her skirts, dashing out into the moonlit castle yard. Mist clung to the jagged rows of gnarled trees, shrubs, the darkening of a threatening storm tangling upon the high curtain walls that guarded Chateau aux Marées. Brianna scarce noticed the sky's dark menace, her feet light, fleet suddenly despite the weighting of her heavy gown. She hastened through the garden, past the pooling shadows of Michel Le Ferre's roses, past the stone bench and the thorn-trees that raked slashes in the night.

Even the daunting outline of Messire Mauricheau's 'chamber of horrors' held no whisperings of fear for her this night. The weak light creeping from beneath the crack where the door skimmed the menagerie's floor merely beckoned her, now, with the promise of Creigh's arms, the haven of his love.

Brianna's fingers caught the cold iron of the door latch, and she shoved the portal wide, rushing through it. Even the muffled snarlings, whinings of Messire Mauricheau's pathetic captives had not the power to bridle her soaring joy, the building that had held for her shadings of foreboding, whispered evils now promising to shelter her love. A laugh bubbled in her throat as she saw upon the stones the elegant midnight velvet of Creigh's hat, the dashing silver plumes ignominiously trailing in the dust. Had he then lost his temper so thoroughly he cast the cavalier's most cherished garment upon the ground like a fractious lad? Or had he merely been in such haste to escape Lanette Perrin's attentions that he had scarce realized he had lost it?

She swept it up, pressing it to her, but instead of the feeling of joy that had surrounded her since the king's kind words, a sudden cold unease gripped her. Wet . . . the hat was wet with . . . She pulled her hand away, horror rising in her throat as her fingers came away from the velvet, stained crimson with blood.

"Creigh?!" she cried his name, her eyes fighting vainly to penetrate the shadowy dimness that veiled the room. Then fear exploded deep in the pit of her stomach, the sound of the heavy door crashing shut behind her sending spikes of alarm through her body. She wheeled, her heart slamming in her breast, as a man . . . Bouret's bear keeper . . . turned, a pike glowing evilly in his hands.

Bree's breath caught jagged-edged in her throat, a scream tearing inside her as her gaze locked upon the man silhouetted against the dark wood panel. She groped instinctively for her sword, a nigh crazed terror gripping her as she found not so much as a jeweled dagger at the waist of her shot-gold stomacher. But even if she'd wielded the finest rapier yet tempered, Bree knew that the horror choking her would yet have slashed deep, for still she would lie battling a monster born of her most hideous nightmare.

She stared, mesmerized, terrified, unable to believe 'twas aught but some demon's conjuring before her eyes. But the light from the single flambeau jammed into a wall sconce would not allow her to banish her horror as the flame's reflections danced devil's patterns across the evil countenance before her. Ogden . . . the name raked raw terror through her, screaming inside her mind. Nay . . . 'twas impossible . . .

"I be no specter, milady," the Roundhead purred, his malicious, evil eyes devouring her with the triumphant hunger of a thousand lords of darkness. "But you and your lord soon will be. Come. 'Tis time to tilt with the devil."

Chapter Twenty-four

Brianna's fingers clenched, fear warring with hysteria as she felt naught but the sticky wetness of Creigh's blood yet upon her fingers. Nails gouging deep into her palm, she let her sword hand fall, useless, to her side, lashing her panic into what she prayed would pass for courage as she met the glare of the man she feared more than Satan himself.

Ogden's lips slithered back from his rotting teeth, and Brianna felt nausea, swift, sharp wrench her stomach as he paced, circling her to perch a meaty hip upon the low ledge of one of Messire Mauricheau's horror pits. "Why so pale, milady?" the Roundhead purred. "Did my Lord Creighton forget to weave into your harlot's garb a baldrick and scabbard?"

Bree wanted to scream, to draw aid from someone, anyone, but even if aught of the fete's guests were in Juliet's garden, the thick wooden door, massive stone walls would quell her cries as certainly as though she screamed from the depths of a grave. Her chin jutted up, jaw clenched tight. "What business have you here, at Chateau aux Marées? And what have you done to Creigh?"

The snarl of some unseen animal sounded from the far side of the room, the creature's bestial misery mingling in sharp accord with Ogden's evil chortle. "Creigh?" The Roundhead smirked. "Let us just say that the high-and-mighty Creighton Wakefield now knows how it feels to crawl in the dung with the rest of us." Shifting his huge bulk to one side with a greedy leer, Ogden turned, jabbing the eerily gleaming point of his pike deep into the thick shadows beside what Brianna judged to be one of the pits in which Bouret's beasts were imprisoned.

Paralyzed with dread, sick with imaginings of what she would find, Brianna squinted against the poolings of darkness, fighting to penetrate the blanketing shadows. The flambeau's weak light trickled like blood across a pile of reeking, rancid meat, the heavy links of a mound of discarded chains, to what she had feared . . . known . . . would lie there. In a crumpled heap amid the filth and rusted iron, she could just make out one black-clad broad shoulder, the arrogant line of Creigh's jaw, cast at an odd angle.

Sweet God, he can't be dead . . . A voice inside Brianna screamed. *God, don't let him be dead!*

"Curse you, Ogden! If you've hurt him, I'll—" She bolted toward Creigh, intending to rip the pike from the gloating Ogden's hands, charge past him if ten thousand demons barred her way, but she froze before she'd taken three steps, instinctive wariness bred of hours of battle staying her as the room jolted again into painfully clear focus. The stone walls with their tiers of iron-barred cages seemed to reach out stealthy arms, turning the innocuous corner where Creigh lay into a deadly trap, a trap in whose jaws she would bear no chance to outwit the human animal now stalking both her and Creigh with more cunning, evil, than any beast of the wild.

"And so, the little warrior yet bears her battle sense," Ogden said, a satisfied growl rumbling in his thick chest. "'Twill but make this, our *final* clash, the more interesting."

Malicious eyes seemed to feast upon her helplessness, never wavering from where she stood as he took up another torch, touching it to the flame that tipped the one already in a sconce. Bree blinked against the flare of light as the flambeau burst into a hellish orange glow.

"Too bright, milady?" Ogden asked. "'Tis but a shade of what you'll suffer once you're cast into eternal flames. But first, 'tis most vital that you can see what lurks within these walls, that you witness every twist of agony on your lover's face, see your own flesh split, tear."

The Roundhead shoved the torch's end into the iron holder beside him, watching her, eager with bloodlust, greedy for terror. But as her gaze flashed over his massive shoulder to see Creigh more clearly, 'twas relief she felt, relief and a sharp sense of resolve as she took in the gash across his brow, the silver panes of his doublet stirring with his breath, his lips twitch as though fighting his pain. Alive . . . he was alive.

Aye, and if she bought his life with her own blood, he'd remain so.

She dragged her gaze away from Creigh, fastening it again upon Ogden. 'Twas as if fingers of his own twisted hatred had carved at the planes of the Roundhead's face, the evil visage that had struck a nigh supernatural terror through her in the Tower shrinking like the flesh of a corpse, leaving the evil, aye, yet shading it with madness. A madness that could be turned against him if she could but prey upon the Roundhead's sick fanaticism, get him to lose himself in his ravings until she could reach one of the countless lengths of chain and shackles that lay strewn about the room . . .

Affecting an air of icy calm, she demanded, "You are ever concerned with *God's* justice. Just what justice do you think your employer, Messire Mauricheau, will deal you, when he witnesses you've harmed his brother-in-law?" She glimpsed a long length of chain fastened to a spike imbedded in the pit's narrow ledge, the thick hook affixed to the binding's other end glinting in the torchlight, so near, yet impossibly far from her grasp.

"Messire Mauricheau?"

Bree jerked her gaze from the iron links at Ogden's laugh, praying that she had not betrayed her sighting of the weapon to the Roundhead. But Ogden scarce seemed to notice, the sound of his chortling crawling across her skin. "My master will deal me the justice of the purse he promised me Christmas last—" Ogden said. "Reward for freeing the House of Blackthorne of its wealth of Wakefield heirs."

"Mauricheau?" Bree scoffed, easing a step nearer the chain. "Why would a French *chevalier* pay one the likes of you to murder his own brother-in-law?" she demanded, not believing Ogden as she eased a step nearer the length of chain. "Why would he want Creigh dead?"

"A single life is worth but little, when set against the worth of a dukedom."

"Dukedom? But at Christmas last, Creigh wasn't heir," Bree challenged, trying to grasp the tangled motives that drove the Roundhead. "Galliard Wakefield still held the title, and Lindley was next in— Oh, merciful God, nay." The last words squeezed from a throat strangled with disbelief as Ogden's mouth gaped into a triumphant jeer. The weapon, still far outside of her reach, was forgotten as she stumbled back a step, fighting the urge to retch. *It was a fool's plan,* she could hear Creigh grit out. *They were captured before they even reached the city . . .*

"Lindley . . . Blackthorne . . . you—"

"Aided the sword of God's justice." Ogden ran one grimy hand down the pike's thick staff, licking saliva from the corners of his wet lips. "'Twas easy enough to expose their witling plan to free tyrant Charles. We even knew where the two fools were to stop to change to fresh horses on the road to London. 'Twas but a matter of informing the proper authorities."

"How . . . how did you know? Did Charles—"

"Deign to tell Messire Mauricheau?" Ogden cackled. "Oh nay, milady. My master bears not enough appetite for feasting and whores to be 'mongst Charles's favorites. Bouret be a godly man despite his Royalist taintings. One who well understands the need to wreak vengeance upon Satan's vassals . . . drown them in flame . . ." Bree saw his eyes roll in his skull, white-ringed . . . vacant, the scar she had slashed in his cheek dull scarlet against his pallor. Praying for her opening, she started toward the chain, stopped as she saw the veilings of insanity shrouding his eyes lessen, the malicious gaze snapping back to her unnervingly clear. "'Twas another who betrayed them— someone deep in the king's confidence, who knew all even before Wakefield's ship set sail. I well wish I knew the person by name, that I might cast them my thanks. 'Twas a triumph, grand, their capture." He licked slavering lips. "Easy as drowning a babe. And I . . . I won the undying gratitude of Cromwell, and all with any power in the new regime."

Brianna heard a faint stirring upon the pile of chains, the sound of it snapping her from the webbings of nausea Ogden's revelations had spurred in her. She fixed her attention yet again upon the hope of freedom that lay tangled upon the pit's narrow ledge. If she could but reach it . . . if Creigh would awake . . . Hope surged through her, but she forced her gaze not to waver from Ogden's leering face, knowing that if—please, God, *when*—Creigh regained consciousness, aided her in battling the Roundhead, their greatest weapon would be surprise.

She groped for something to say, anything to help rouse Creigh, to keep the odious colonel's attention from the shadow-shrouded figure upon the stone floor.

"So you planned Creigh's murder even then?"

"The bastard was but to die at a cursed Irishman's sword, fallen in the siege of Drogheda with all honors. His maman and weakling sister were to have wept over his hero's grave. And the most grief-stricken mourner of all was to have been my master. Then, once Galliard Wakefield and his idiot son lay dead, Messire Mauricheau would have been saddled with the wearisome duty of taking up the title of Blackthorne, with all its vast power and wealth."

Bree turned, moving in what she prayed seemed but pointless pacing to the Roundhead, in truth hoping that she could gradually edge close enough to sweep up the chain and shackles without Ogden's being aware of her plan. "Why then . . . why didn't you kill him when the fighting began?" Bree asked, desperately willing Creigh to shake off the bindings of unconsciousness. "Why did you wait, drag him to the Tower?"

"The aristocrat cur was 'ceedingly loath to die. He was passing cautious. He inspired even in the Roundhead troops he was bound to betray a devil-spawned loyalty that made it impossible to reach him. And when the night turned to killing, and naught would've noticed one more corpse bloodying the ground, 'twas too late . . . he had already made his escape."

The Roundhead's thick hands knotted upon the pikestaff, turning the lethal weapon in the flame's flickering glow. "But this time . . . *this* time there'll be no escape for the high-and-holy lord."

Something in the Roundhead's voice stilled Brianna's pacing, hypnotized her with the fascination of watching a serpent's head weave before striking. "This time," Ogden snarled, "your cursed Lord Creighton will know torment without end—more than just the clinging of filth upon his flesh, the bite of chains, cut of the blade. He'll know agony sharp as the grief his cursed family bound me with, the same agony my mother suffered 'neath the poison the Duchess of Blackthorne forced down her throat."

"The duchess . . ."

"Aye . . . poisoned humble Mag Ogden for delivering a child, bastard-born, a crime the Wakefield witch would murder for, rather than see either herself or her spawn cast to the scorn of their aristocrat peers."

"What . . . what are you saying? That Creigh—"

"It matters not who the child is. All those unfortunate enough as to have been trapped in that viper woman's belly will be dragged through the flames of God's vengeance. And then, when the last Wakefield spawn burns in hell, I'll take the cursed duchess, kill her slowly, oh, aye, so slowly in my mother's name."

Brianna's heart thundered in her chest, the reason for the nigh-mad hatred that etched the Roundhead's face whenever he looked upon Creigh starkly clear.

She heard again echoings of Ogden's threats, the tale he had told when they had been bound in the Tower of his own torment on the open high roads as a lad. 'Twas madness, this hatred that warped the evil Roundhead, madness borne of a string of horrors that had naught to do with Creigh Wakefield, the man, but rather with fates snarled, twisted, in Esmeraude Wakefield's scheming hands.

Brianna clenched her fists, crushing the fear that tore at her as her gaze shifted to the man she loved—loved enough to battle her own worst terrors—aye, tilt with the devil, as Ogden had said. A deadly calm settled over her like a warrior's mantle, strength, lightning reflexes schooled in a hundred spring-bathed Irish dawns flowing hot through her veins.

Bree tensed her body, fighting to gauge the unaccustomed weight of the heavy gown, the distance from where she stood to the flame-glossed iron links. But as if he sensed her goal, Ogden stepped between her and the dubious weapon, barring her way with his porcine body.

Frustration tore through Brianna, and she felt a fierce need to fight to grab the pike from the Roundhead's hands, despite the fact that, bound as she was in the velvet gown, she knew her chances of wresting the weapon from Ogden were next to naught. She steeled herself against the impulse, battling for control . . . the control that would save her from hurling her chance for freedom away through a rash, reckless move, the control that would gird her strength when Ogden's hate, madness stripped him of his reason.

She watched him, wary, alert, every muscle in her fine-honed, supple body at the ready. Red, glittering eyes narrowed, greedy for blood, as the Roundhead took a step back toward the nearest waist-high rim of stone bounding one of the dozen separate circles in the center of the vast room.

"Have you heard aught of my master's passion, since lodging at the chateau, harlot? A bear goaded to a fighting frenzy is a fearful creature indeed. It can sever an arm with its teeth, rip a man's belly open with blade-sharp claws, spilling his life onto the stones."

Brianna shuddered involuntarily, feeling icy fingers creep 'neath the edges of her courage. She forced her eyes back to Creigh, drawing strength, hope from his beloved features, quelling the restirrings of fear.

Ogden grinned ghoulishly. "Anticipating your visit, I've not fed Messire Mauricheau's little pet here for days. And as my master commanded, I've kept the beast in fighting frenzy, schooling it in pain with the point of my pike." Ogden gestured to the pit's rim. "Come, whore. Look." Bree glanced from the Roundhead's blood-crazed eyes, toward the pike in his hand. If she could just get close enough . . . Slowly, Bree stepped toward the stone ledge, taking care to stay out of the Roundhead's reach.

Black as the river Styx the darkness swirled deep within, only the glowing red eyes and flashing, deadly teeth of the bear visible in the darkness. She stared at it in macabre fascination, mesmerized by the sound of the beast's chains dragging across the floor, the flashing of razor-sharp teeth, white even through the blackness.

She bit back a startled cry as Ogden's weapon jabbed down, and despite her resolve, leapt back from the pit's rim as the tormented beast she could scarce see screamed in savage pain. There was a clanking of chains from the depths of the pit, a grating of claws, nigh crazed snarling as the beast fought to escape its prison. Ogden chuckled, bringing the pike blade over the pit's ledge, its point glistening with fresh blood.

"You see, milady." Ogden reached out the weapon, slowly turning the blade inches from Brianna's face. "The bear lies hungry for any flesh . . . be it slaughtered swine, live hound, or *human.*"

Bree flinched as she felt the flat of the pike blade touch her cheek, the iron slick, smelling of blood, death.

"And how will your master explain it—both Creigh and I dead?" Brianna challenged, chill, calm. She drew away from the pike blade, turning with a slow deliberation that could not be mistaken for fear. A sharp-edged stone from the filthy menagerie floor cut deep into the tender flesh of her instep, the grit that had gained the inside of her slipper grinding into the side of her foot. Dirt . . . Bree's gaze flashed from the filth-covered floor to Ogden's slitted eyes. If she could but scoop up a handful of dirt, fling it in the Roundhead's eyes, then mayhap . . . mayhap she could wrest the pike away from him before . . .

"'Twill be passing lucky if there's enough of either you or your aristocrat lover to be recognizable as human once the bear sets to devour you."

Bree's gaze snapped up from the floor, to see Ogden's mouth gape into a greedy smile, his crazed laugh crawling across her flesh. "I'll perforce have to carry the sad tidings to King Charles and his guests, that whilst I was off in the garderobe, you toppled into the pit. I was but reentering the menagerie when I saw Lord Creighton courageously fling himself over the wall in an attempt to wrest you from the beast's jaws."

"They'll not believe it." The words were dead calm, even to her own ears, as Brianna turned, moving away from the Roundhead to gain just enough distance to elude Ogden if he should lunge for her, while still remaining close enough to hurl the dirt into his face. "Juliet—she knows I despise these walls, and there are others who will suspect—"

"Suspect what? That a nameless beast-keeper hurled Lord Creighton Wakefield and his whore into a bear pit?" Ogden jeered, pacing after her like a preying jackal. "I think not, milady. I'll even hurl the pike into the pit when the bear is finished with you both, let the weapon lay there, on the bloodied floor. 'Twill be a masterful touch, think you not, devil's whore?"

Brianna bit back a silent oath, frustration tearing through her as she tried to gain distance between her and the Roundhead. But 'twas as if Ogden scented the kill, was stalking her, closing in.

"You'll not be alive to enjoy Bouret's newfound power," she goaded. "Think you Messire Mauricheau will let you live, knowing, as you do, his plot to murder one of King Charles's most honored cavaliers?"

"He'll let me live long enough to finish what we have planned—long enough to deal Galliard Wakefield and the murdering Esmeraude their deaths, and then," his lips curled, eager, demented, "once they're roasting in hell, I needs must make the new-made duke a merry widower."

Brianna felt a fist twist in her vitals, the thought of little Jolie stalked by this monster further shoring Bree's resolve to snatch from the fanatical Roundhead his intended victims. "And after you're neck-deep in blood at Bouret's bidding?" She forced herself to laugh. "You'll not get outside the castle before Bouret has you brought down."

Her glance flashed from beneath the curtain of her hair to where Creigh lay. A wisp of hope drifted free within her. The rosewood-colored waves of his hair yet tangled in disarray about his face, but his head had shifted upon its harsh bed of chains, and there was about his features a tautness, alertness, that had been absent when she had first set eyes upon him. Yet Ogden's words drove shafts of panic through her resolve.

"Think you I care about death, milady?" he said. "Even if Bouret should choose to kill me, the revenge I vowed to curse the Wakefields with will have been wrought, and naught else signifies."

"You're mad."

A slow grin spread over Ogden's face. "Mayhap I am. Mad with hate, thirst for Wakefield blood. Aye, and I 'tend to satisfy my appetites now. The bear lies waiting for its kill, milady. Who shall it devour first?" Ogden paced to the stone ledge. "The choice is yours, doxy."

"Nay, I—"

"Go to the pit's edge, or see your precious Lord Creighton hurled to its floor before you again draw breath."

Ogden started to turn toward Creigh. "Hold!" Bree hissed the word, the Roundhead's grin of triumph as he again faced her grating upon her nerves. "I'll—I'll do as you wish. Just don't kill him."

"Everything in its own time, sweeting," Ogden purred. "Just mark, each minute you follow my commands you purchase for your lover a bit more time to live. Who can say? If you do all I ask . . . *everything,* you may even use enough time that some fool will come a-searching for you both— mayhap even spare Lord Creighton the beast's rending teeth. Of course you . . . you will lie dead by then."

Her head snapped up at Ogden's hiss and she saw his eyes, glazed, demented burning into the folds of her gown. "'Twill be fitting . . ." Ogden said in a voice tinged with madness. "Seeing the flesh that has tempted to sin covered with gore, slashed until to look upon it will make even the strongest man retch. But mayhap I should take for myself the pleasure of drawing first blood."

Brianna felt bile rise in her throat, but steeled herself as the pike's point lashed the air. She started to dodge, but the weapon was too swift, the gown too heavy. She lunged for the linkings of chain, feeling the sharp blade bite into her skin, a stinging cut opening upon the curve of her collarbone as her fingers caught on the rough iron links, a half-sob of despair, fury tore from her throat as she felt the heavy links snap from her groping fingers.

In desperation, she knotted her fists together, spinning to crash them into the side of Ogden's head, but the Round-head was stunningly quick for such a large man. He evaded her blow, swinging the thick wood end of the pikestaff in a brutal arc. It slammed into Brianna's chest, driving the breath from her lungs, crashing her to the stones.

"Ogden!" Still blurred with the last clinging vestiges of his unconsciousness, Creigh's voice sliced the air. Brianna fought the pain that crushed her chest, seeing Creigh fight to struggle to his feet, fail, the bindings of chain linked heavy about his wrists, ankles, bound about his waist weighing him down.

Ogden crowed with glee, his narrowed eyes locking on Creigh with the slavering greed of a maddened boar. "Wakefield . . . 'tis God's own gift, you're awakening in time to see your whore pay for her sins. I tried to teach her the error of her ways—carved the mark of God's wrath upon her. But you chose to ignore the harlot's branding. Now . . .

now you'll see Lucifer himself tear her flesh until there is naught left but blood, aye, and the white gleam of bones."

Brianna saw Creigh try to force himself upright, staggering beneath the thick iron loopings of the chain. "Touch her . . . and I'll kill you," he threatened, struggling, Bree knew, to reach her, to place his body as a shield between her and the crazed Roundhead.

"'Tis not you who holds the power of life and death now, my high-and-holy lord," Ogden countered, his eyes sweeping from Brianna to Creigh, and back again, the pike in his hands waving dangerously at the ready between them. "The beast that lurks in the pit's depths cares naught of the Wakefields' legendary might. Will care naught when you scream as it tears your harlot's flesh from her bones. And when you, too, strike the pit's floor . . ."

Ogden's laughter echoed, demented, evil. "The bear's first frenzy will be filled, and it will take its time, most like, taking joy in dealing back to one the race of its tormentors the agony it has endured."

"Twisted bastard . . . vow I'll find a way . . ."

Brianna's heart wrenched for Creigh, as he battled the chains, lunging toward Ogden's broad bulk. But the heavy links dragged him down, cracking him to the floor with a sickening thud. Brianna started to dive for the pike, froze as its point grazed her arm. Ogden chuckled, evil, low.

"Oh, aye, Wakefield. I tremble in my boots, my lord coward. Watch now. Watch as your harlot hurls herself to the beast's jaws in hopes of gaining you time to save your worthless life."

Ogden flashed the pike toward Bree, the point jabbing close. "Do it, whore. Let your lover see you pay . . . pay . . ."

"Nay, Bree! For God's sake—"

Brianna forced her feet beneath her, Creigh's cries stabbing deep in her heart. There was but one chance, one. If it failed, she would gladly do as Ogden bid, cast herself, aye, and her babe to death's embrace if in so doing Creigh bore a chance to yet live.

Her fingers dug into the filth that littered the floor, sharp-edged objects cutting her palm, grit, slime digging under her nails as she clutched a handful of the blanketing dirt. Her jaw knotted, the gnashing, horrible sounds of the bear yet raging in its dark vortex threatening to drown her in terror.

In one lightning move she jammed herself upright, flinging the debris clutched in her hand into Ogden's face.

The Roundhead stumbled back with a bellow of fury, swiping at his eyes, only the fact that he could not see keeping the point of his weapon from slashing wide Bree's stomach. She heard Creigh's struggles as he battled to aid her despite the weight of his chains, heard his scream of rage as Ogden charged toward her, the pike clasped in his meaty hands. Bree dove for the pit's ledge, seeing the razor-sharp blade slash down, but just as it grazed her flesh Creigh smashed into Ogden from the rear, sending the weapon careening over the pit's low ledge. She saw Creigh's bound fists knot together, swinging in a deadly arc toward the Roundhead's ribs, but Ogden leapt aside, driving one heavy boot into Creigh's stomach. Bree gritted her teeth against the horrible sound of Creigh slamming to the stones a sword's length away.

A roar of feral rage echoed from deep in the blackness, ripping through the huge room as the bear hurled itself against the pit's inner wall. Yet the crazed scream from Ogden lashed her with the threat of a far greater danger.

Bree caught but a flash of glinting silver cloth, heard crashings of chains as Creigh tried to gain his feet, heard his screamed oaths, as Ogden hurtled himself toward her. The rough stone rim cracked into the base of her spine as Ogden drove himself against her, his hands knotting in her hair, gown, forcing her back toward the hellish abyss.

Bree groped for something, anything to use against him, feeling her back bent beneath Ogden's ruthless assault. In that split instant she knew she held no chance of besting the massive Roundhead, knew, also, that if she were going to be pitched to the pit's floor, she must drag Ogden as well, lest Creigh's life be forfeit.

"Bree! On the ledge!" Creigh's scream of desperation cut through her strainings of battle, her knuckles cracking against something hard, round. The chains!

The beast within the pit gave a bone-chilling roar, its huge claws raking against stone as her fingers closed around the heavy links, her flesh bruising on rough iron as she felt herself start to slip, slide over the stone. With all the power she had, Brianna drove her chain-wrapped fist into Ogden's skull, just as the Roundhead gave her a mighty shove.

She heard Creigh's agonized cry, felt the horrifying sensation of her side grating over the ledge, driven by Ogden's huge bulk. Bree fought desperately, the heavy chains she had struck Ogden with ensnaring her waist, trapping her, her weight, the weight of her heavy gown dragging her downward into the hideous emptiness below.

She screamed, the hip-level wall no barrier against the Roundhead's onslaught. Ogden cackled with sadistic glee as he forced her ever backward. His eyes seemed to consume her, glowing with an insanity that iced fear through her veins, fear, yet, stronger still, the resolve to spare Creigh this madman's vengeance no matter what the cost. She threw her weight against the Roundhead an instant, feeling the man thrust his own bulk forward as he fought to gain leverage.

A choked sob snagged in her throat as she jammed her feet against the wall. Knowing, in that instant, she had gained the only hope she yet bore to defeat the Roundhead, knowing the price of his defeat would be her own life, she gripped the chain with all her strength, hurtling her weight backward with a force she prayed would stun him, leaving him no time to release his hold upon her. She felt her momentum shoot Ogden forward, heard the scraping of his scabbard against the stone of the wall as he struggled desperately for balance. But his bulk combined with her own weight proved too great for him to stop. Shrieks of terror split the air, his arms flailing wildly as he pitched over the narrow ledge.

Bree's hands clenched upon the chains, the iron gouging deep, as she glimpsed Ogden's fingers clawing the stone, the air. Hands caught at her gown, tearing it as the Roundhead plunged past her. She screamed in horror, the image of his crazed, nightmarish face searing into her mind for all eternity as he hurtled down into the blackness.

She heard Creigh cry her name, heard chains grating against the stone wall. But she caught not so much as a glimpse of the man at the wall's crest. She clawed at the iron links like a wild thing, fighting desperately to escape the horrible thud as Ogden crashed to the floor of the pit.

"Help me! Oh, God, Wakefield, help—" Ogden's shriek

echoed up from the pit, the sounds suddenly cut off by a horrifying scream of pain, the echoings seeming to tear at the walls with bloodied fingers.

Sobs tore from Brianna's throat, as she felt her own fingers give way, felt herself falling. But instead of the hard crack of stone against her flesh, a sudden, sharp pain drove into Bree's ribs, arms. She slammed against the pit's inner wall, the stones grating against her cheek, bruising her jaw as, by some miracle, the links entangling her snapped tight, breaking her fall midway into the pit. She struggled desperately to regain her hold on the chains as she dangled, suspended against the unyielding stone endless seconds, the gruesome snarling, rending sounds, shrieks of agony that rose from below as the beast mauled its prey seeming to drag her down.

'Twas as if she could feel the bear's claws, teeth in her own flesh, tearing . . .

She clenched her eyes shut, seeing, in that instant, the image of Creigh's face, that of the babe she'd never held. Then there was naught but the hideous sensation of fingers giving way, the chain links ripping from her grasp as death's savage claws stretched out to yank her into their hellish embrace.

Chapter Twenty-five

Nay!" At the shout from above her, Brianna's fists knotted convulsively over the iron, regaining their hold for but a heartbeat. Then suddenly something hard, warm, hooked beneath her arm, yanking her upward so roughly her limb was nigh wrenched from her body.

In but an instant, she felt strong, large hands clutching her, dragging her from the snarling jaws below, felt the hardness of the menagerie floor beneath her slippers. Links of chain ground into her stomach, breasts as Creigh battled his bindings in an effort to crush her in his arms. But he could only clasp the sides of her waist in hands that bruised, yet blessed, burying his face against her tumbled hair as she cried with nigh-sick relief.

"Tigress, are you . . . are you hurt? Did he . . . did he hurt you?" Brianna heard him demand through the muffling silk of her hair.

"Bree, I thought . . . Oh God, when you fell over the side—" A harsh sound caught in his throat, and Brianna was stunned to feel his tears hot against her cheek, a wracking sob tearing his chest. She clung to him, warring to drive from her ears the beast sounds that yet rose from the pit, the sudden, more terrible absence of any sound human. Her stomach churned, a hideous montage of what might have been splashing behind her eyelids in terrifying detail.

Crushing her body against Creigh's she fought to feel naught, know naught but the life pulsing through his iron-hard muscles, wonder blossoming inside her that this most arrogant and noble of men now wept upon her breasts.

The firm-sculpted curve of his mouth took in the tip of her chin, nose, eyelids, his hungry, desperate kisses banishing the cloying feel of death's fingers upon her skin, his tears cleansing her of Ogden's touch and the horror of the Roundhead's fate. "I could've . . . strangled you with my own hands . . . when I saw you trying to drag the bastard over the wall," he said fiercely against her skin. "Christ, Tigress—"

"Thought . . . he was going to kill you . . . Had to . . . to stop . . ."

"Hush, love, it's over . . . over . . . he can never hurt you again." Creigh's voice was full of anguish, his body trembling against her. "Oh, God, Bree, I never felt so cursed helpless in my life!" His mouth came down upon hers, his tongue driving between lips open, eager, his hands clutching fistfuls of her gown just above her hips as he battled to get closer to her, meld their bodies into one. For what seemed an eternity, Bree's fingers tore at the chains that bound him, their heavy lengths fastened not by shackles, but rather by huge iron hooks worked through the wide links.

Creigh yanked himself out of the binding coils when she finally freed him, his arms reaching out, catching her to him fiercely, hungrily, his storm-shaded eyes alive with a passion that made Bree's blood pound in her breasts and that soft, secret place at the apex of her thighs.

She arched against him, desperate for the feel of him kissing her, loving her, driving away the gruesome image of Ogden's tormented face. But suddenly Creigh thrust her away from him, his hands bruising her arms, his mouth taut with grim fury.

"Damn you, Tigress," he grated. "If you ever . . . *ever* scare me like that again, I vow I'll kill you with my own hands."

Hands . . . the picture of Bouret's pale, white hands rose in Brianna's mind, his blade-thin nose, cruel lips cutting through the haze of happiness, beauty Creigh's love had spun around her, leaving love, aye, but also a sick lingering of horror and remembered fear.

"Tigress, what is it?"

"Messire Mauricheau . . ." Brianna said, the warmth Creigh had stirred in her chilling like winter wind. "'Twas he who betrayed your father and Lindley, Bouret who set Ogden to murder."

"Mauricheau? A traitor? The man is a fool, aye, and passing cruel, but he bears not the courage to prey upon any stronger than he. He but stalks the weak . . . helpless . . . bears not the wit or courage to betray a king."

"'Twas another, closer still to King Charles. Ogden said—" She spilled the entire sordid tale of plottings and murders, ambition that cared naught if it bore the blood of innocents or dragged down a noble, righteous king.

When she had done, she looked into Creigh's face. His features set in a grim mask. "There are couriers coming from Scotland tomorrow, to continue negotiating plans to launch an assault from their borders. If there be some traitor in our midst besides Mauricheau, we'd best inform the king at once. And then, by my brother's grave, I'll deal with Bouret, in my own way, with my own blade."

Brianna swallowed a lump of dread, shuddering as she pictured the knight's hands, hands that thought naught of grasping any means to meet his desires.

She shivered, sensing eyes upon her, not of the beasts yet entrapped in their cages. She turned around, eyes sweeping the huge, shadowed room. But though she caught nothing, no one with her gaze, she could not banish the feeling that someone, someone was watching as Creigh led her out into the night.

The cluster of Charles's most trusted advisors had been sequestered for hours about the ornate table that graced the room in the new wing of the castle from which Charles managed the massive hunt that had been launched to bring Messire Mauricheau to justice. And the glitter of men too oft betrayed was hard in eyes that promised no mercy.

Ever since Brianna had spilled Ogden's revelations to Charles and Blackthorne, they had paced, awaiting the news that Bouret had been taken. But as nighttime blended into dawn it seemed that the very gods cursed their efforts.

The gathering storm that drove great clouds across the sky blotted out the sun's rising, seeming to mock the distant rush of soldiers' footsteps leaving Chateau aux Marées's halls, scorn the glare of torchlight splashing the castle yard with light. And even the might of Charles's guards as a party of them made ready to sweep the island seemed dwarfed by the threatening rage of the heavens.

A quarter of an hour past, a grim-faced Galliard Wakefield had quit the chamber, claiming that he had business to attend to that might aid the search. And as the duke had left, Brianna had caught the king's eye, her back rigid against the embroidered chair, but her head drooping against her chest.

Charles had stepped over to her, curving a finger beneath her chin. He had smiled, his dark gaze so full of genuine admiration, Creigh had felt a sharp twinge of jealousy. "You have done the crown a great service this night, milady," Charles had said. "And you deserve far greater consideration than having this ill-mannered Wakefield oaf abandoning you in this cursed chair the night through." The twinkling royal eyes had flashed to Creigh's disheveled form.

Bree had nigh bolted from her chair, making, Creigh had known, an attempt to appear alert, but the king had not been fooled in spite of her protests and had banished the both of them from the council chamber with a rare royal frown.

Creigh curved his arm about her, seeking to support her as she walked down the hall, but the weariness that gripped his own aching flesh was scarce discernible in her militant step, only her eyes, dull, reddened with fatigue, betraying her exhaustion. Aye, Creigh thought grudgingly, in truth Charles had been right in commanding him to escort her to her rooms, but still he could not quell the frustration that simmered within him at being robbed of his chance to ride with the men pursuing the hated Bouret.

"A rat ofttimes returns to its hole," Charles had insisted when Creigh had pressed him to allow him to ride. "If Messire Mauricheau is yet in this castle, it may well be your lady he turns his wrath upon, as she has betrayed his evil. I need you here, Lord Creighton." Charles had used his title, bearing every inch of his towering form like a monarch. "And here you will remain."

Creigh gritted his teeth as he rounded the corridor that led to the suite of chambers that Charles's captain of the guard had directed all of Wakefield blood to lodge in. The grizzled officer had deemed that the older segment of the castle was less safe from the desperate knight, and, like Charles, Creigh sensed, expected Bouret to lash out rashly, like a savage, cornered beast.

If only the cur would dare, Creigh thought bitterly, eyes scanning the huge archways, beautifully wrought statues his mother so delighted in. Bah! He compressed his lips in disgust. Small chance the cursed Mauricheau yet lurked within these walls. Every guard Charles possessed had scoured the castle since midnight, creating, as Brianna had observed, so much noise Bouret would have had to be deaf and crippled not to bear time to escape them. And now, with the stable boy's claim . . .

Grimacing, Creigh arched his stiff neck, seeing light spilling from the chambers that had been his mother's since he had first arrived at the castle, and, across from it, the room Captain Holbey had assigned to Creigh and Bree. The stableboy's face had been pinched, frightened eyes like that of a field mouse when the hawk sweeps near. The boy, Tyler, had claimed that a man had ridden from the castle gates but moments before the alarm had been sounded.

Who, but Mauricheau, fleeing the wrath of his king, would ride out alone in the middle of the night, tearing, the lad had said, like a madman across the dangerous night-veiled fields?

"Creigh, hold," the sound of Brianna's voice interrupted his reverie, and he looked down into her face. Its usually golden-rose tint was paled with exhaustion, the wildly tangled strands of her hair dulled with dirt from the menagerie's floor. She pointed to a deserted corridor, snaking down through the shadows toward the far end of the castle. "Juliet showed me once a way to get to the stables from here. If we crept down, secured some horses, we could quit the castle in but a minute's time, hunt Bouret down between us."

Creigh felt a reluctant chuckle of disbelief rise in his throat. He grimaced. "Charles of England may seem like naught but a merry gallant to you of the fairer sex. But I vow he comes by his royal blood rightly. If he got wind of us attempting to ride with the others, he'd ordered two of his men to guard us in our room. And after . . ."

Creigh raked his free hand through his hair, pulling a face, for all the world like that of a lad cheated out of a celebration. "Nay. I've attempted to evade the royal will before, and His Majesty's reaction was not something I'd care to repeat. Christ, the last time, he nigh—"

The tale Creigh had been about to regale Brianna with stilled upon his lips, the sounds of voices, low, yet savage, raking the silence outside the open door. Creigh felt Brianna stiffen beside him, alert as he grasped the hilt of his sword. 'Twas his mother, he judged, and aye, there was someone with her.

He stepped nearer the door, slowly starting to ease his blade from its scabbard as the savagery in the voices stirred his warrior instincts. His body tensed as he recalled King Charles's predictions, and he half expected to hear Mauricheau's voice, threatening, bearing death. But the person within was not the loathsome knight. Shock surged through Creigh as his gaze pierced through the doorway, spying the somber wine-colored doublet, gray-streaked hair of the Duke of Blackthorne, his usually calm, commanding voice harsh with rage.

Creigh's fist knotted, jamming the sword back into place, and he started toward the opened portal, with a swift, silent stride. But the words spilling into the corridor stayed his feet, seeming to root him to the marble floor with secrets he did not wish to hear.

"Nay, no more, *wife.*" Blackthorne's accusation cut the silence. "You've managed to end Lindley's life, made Juliet's a hell, but I vow, I'll not stand by, silent, while you wrest Creigh's dreams from him as well!"

The laugh that rippled from the room sent an odd, crawling feeling along Creigh's spine, the sound of it the like of which he'd ne'er heard, yet one he knew as his mother's. "Tear Creighton's dreams?" she sneered. "I'm gifting him with the world—wealth, power, a princess royal. I broached the subject with Charles this eve, and he seemed truly to consider the match between Creigh and Henriette-Anne. You should be aiding me to build him to greatness instead of whining and sniveling about dreams with less substance than water, and the death of your *beloved Lindley.*"

Even through the doorway Creigh could see Blackthorne's face drain of all color. "You'll say naught of my son."

"*Your* son?" Esmeraude snorted. "The witling you cherished was none of your siring. You were but a convenient

335

weakling—choked with notions of honor, duty, to cast his birth upon. Nay, he was a bastard bred, and I cursed him from the day he was planted in my womb."

Creigh felt a fist clench in his chest, scarce bearing time to absorb his mother's words before Blackthorne's quiet reply cut through him.

"I knew from the first the lad was not of my loins. And from the day I first saw him, I blessed whoever the man was who gifted me with him."

"Then you can cast your pitiful gratitude to a comely armorer's lad who could coax ecstasy from a maid's body as readily as he coaxed a rapier from tempered iron."

Creigh winced at the venom in his mother's voice.

"If you bore any strength, ambition," she hissed, "you'd be rejoicing that the idiot bastard has died, leaving the way open for—"

The sound of Blackthorne's hand cracking into Esmeraude's face stunned Creigh, seeming to drive straight through him. He felt Brianna's hand clutch his arm, yanked free as he instinctively lunged toward the room, but 'twas as if some evil sorceress had cast a spell upon him, binding his legs, slowing them with invisible webs of confusion—anger at Blackthorne, and stark, devastating betrayal at the cold words of the mother he had worshipped ripping at his very soul.

Blackthorne's face contorted with rage as he paced toward Esmeraude, and ne'er had Creigh seen such strength in the duke's craggy countenance, nor such fury. "No more!" he flung out. "Your days of plottings are over. From the day Michel offered for Juliet's hand and I found her already wed to your cursed Mauricheau, I knew you had some scheme in mind. Yet even I never suspected to what lengths you would go to secure your ends. Lindley's *dead,* for God's sake, and the agony he endured before he—"

Esmeraude Wakefield's face paled but a little. "'Twas necessary that he die!"

"So that Creigh could be destroyed as well? You've bought him a dukedom at the cost of his brother's life, and you'd see him wed to a five-year-old child, when he bears love for a beautiful, brave lady."

"Lady? Creigh had better to mate with a serving wench than that Irish slut, and you well know it! At least they'd bear English blood, aye, and French, instead of being tainted with barbarian strains."

"Oh, aye? Tell me, *wife,* did you plan to rid him of Brianna as well?"

Esmeraude spun away from Blackthorne, but not before Creigh saw her lips press into a smirk. "She'll be made to see reason."

"How, Esmeraude? At the bottom of a cup of poisoned wine? Or had you planned to have Messire Mauricheau hurl her from the cliffs into the sea? Sweet savior, I'll murder you myself, break your scheming little throat—"

The mouth that had always seemed so vulnerable, sweet, as it had whispered declarations of love to her son, curled back in a snarl, lips thin with a cunning Creigh could scarce believe. "Oh, nay, Galliard, you'd not kill me, not kill any woman, no matter to what lengths she drove you. Not you, with your witling notions of *honor.*" The duchess spat the word, spinning to the huge gilt-framed mirror, smoothing one ice-white hand over her moon-pale hair.

Blackthorne's fists knotted, his jaw hard as granite. "Nay, 'tis true, I've not your thirst for blood. But there be other ways of keeping you from destroying innocents in the name of your own gain. On the morrow you will be escorted under guard to Chateau Le Ferre, where you'll bloody well rot until the devil comes to claim you."

Esmeraude arched a neck sinuous as one of Messire Mauricheau's adders, her eyes glittering jet as she ran her fingertips in a sickeningly sensual path down its curve to the small breasts that thrust against her night rail. "Until the devil claims me? I think I'll not have to wait quite that long," she sneered. "The moment Creighton hears of your *cruelty* to me, he'll ride to my rescue if he must bring half an army. You failed sixteen years ago to wrest Creigh from my power, and now . . ."

Her laugh raked against the painted leather walls, tearing away the veils of deception through which Creigh had always seen her, leaving her hideous, grasping to his eyes. No more the beauteous savior. "Now 'tis too late. He hates you for a weakling and a coward. Thinks you abandoned him, while I clutched him to my breasts, loved him. *He's mine,* Galliard, *mine.* My weapon to strike down my enemies, my tool to grasp the power behind the throne. And

I'll do anything—*anything*—to make certain that naught—even that Irish slut—can come between us."

"Maman." The word, once signaling his font of love unquestioned, now tore from his chest in a sound ragged with anguish, honed with rage as Creigh clutched at the brass door latch, shoving the portal to slam hard into the chamber's inner wall.

Both Blackthorne and Lady Esmeraude wheeled toward him, Blackthorne's face ill, stricken beneath its network of craggy lines, Esmeraude's that of a she-wolf suddenly caught in the jaws of its prey—yet the thing that drove spiked fists through Creigh's chest was the love his mother's face yet bore him, a love corrupt as the heart of a rotted apple, sound, beautiful when the skin veiling it was whole, but putrid when 'twas split and held to the sun.

"C-Creighton," Esmeraude cried, clutching her fists to her breasts, taking a running step toward him. "Thank God you are here—he means to imprison me, desert me—"

"'Twas you all the time," Creigh said in a voice dead of all emotion, his eyes level upon his mother's face. "You who bound Juliet to Bouret, a man you knew was a monster. 'Twas you who caused Lindley's death. Sweet God, 'til the end he was battling my cursed blindness, fighting to make me understand 'twas none of Father's doing. But nay, I'd have none of it. I was so . . . so certain that you . . ." his voice cracked, and he felt Brianna's hand, whisper-soft upon his whipcord-taut shoulder. "So certain that you loved me."

"Creigh . . . Creighton, don't listen to Blackthorne's lies; you know how he's always hated me—hated you and the special love we bear each other!" Esmeraude ran toward him, clutching handfuls of his doublet, running her bejeweled fingers over his chest in a way that turned his stomach. "Always I have loved you, only you! From the time you were a babe, you were my life—my hope. I despise Messire Mauricheau, aye, and all his cronies, and I vow to you I'll do all in my power to see them brought to justice."

Feeling soiled, strangely tainted, Creigh closed his fingers about his mother's wrists, pushing them away from his chest with a churning sense of revulsion.

"Nay, Creigh, listen to me, I love you . . . I'll tell you . . . quick, take up your sword, he lurks behind the—"

Creigh spun toward the huge arras at the sound of a hissed curse, hand locking about the hilt of his sword, but 'twas too late. His hand froze as his gaze caught the glint of two pistols at the ready in Messire Mauricheau's hands, the knight stepping from behind the shielding of tapestry, to level the weapons' deadly barrels at Lady Esmeraude's breast.

" 'Twould be most wise, *brother,* if you let your blade fall back into its scabbard," the knight said, his opaque, color-less eyes holding Creigh's. " 'Twould be a pity if I were forced to blow the Lady Esmeraude's soul into eternity, when she bears such a wealth of sins to do penance for."

Creigh's eyes narrowed upon the sharp-boned face of Bouret, his hand nigh crushing the hilt of his sword. "There are four of us, Bouret, and you bear but two pistol balls."

" 'Twill be all I need to convince my coconspirator to accompany me in my bid for freedom, aye, and to repay her in kind for the betrayal she just served me."

"I'll die before I aid you any longer!" Esmeraude shrilled. "Creighton, he forced me—"

"Forced you?" A low, evil chuckle rumbled in Messire Mauricheau's chest. "A right pretty lie, milàdy, when 'twas you who sought me out, offering me wealth untold, the hand of your mewling daughter, aye, and even a chance to gain a place in the succession for Blackthorne, if I'd but rid you of your husband and witling son. Even tonight, when Beadle came running from the menagerie telling us our plans had gone awry, you were the one who bade me stay, secrete myself away here until we might again spin our plottings. But you see, 'tis too late for us now, too late. And the one pleasure left me in this disaster you have wrought is the fact that your precious Creighton will at least know the truth about you before he dies."

Creigh's gaze shifted to that of his mother, the wild look in her black eyes confirming Bouret's accusations as naught else could have.

"Oh, aye, my Lord Creighton, 'twas brilliant, her plot to have Blackthorne and Lindley beheaded, and the delaying of the letters proclaiming my impending marriage to Juliet just long enough to keep you in a frenzy of guilt and fury at your *cruel, heartless* father, 'twas the stroke of a master."

Creigh gritted his teeth against the demented pleasure in Messire Mauricheau's face, the greed for pain, any pain, mental or physical, glittering sharp in the knight's colorless eyes. Battling to harden his features, Creigh fought to remain impassive with each thrust of the knight's verbal blade, vowing that at least in his quest to spur Creigh to horror the knight would fail to triumph.

Messire Mauricheau's lips thinned over small, white teeth, his eyes that of a beast closing in for the kill. "But most awesome of all," his voice was a low, silken purr, "was your lady mother's ploy for ridding the castle of that barbarian urchin you meant to make a duchess—"

"Nay, Creighton," Esmeraude shrilled, taking a running step toward Mauricheau. "Don't listen—"

Mauricheau snapped back the flintlock upon one pistol, cocking the weapon.

"Nay, don't—don't tell him . . ." Esmeraude stopped, a sob shaking her delicate body.

"Oh, come, now, madame, 'twill prove most entertaining to Lord Creighton here, your witty observation about the method you planned to use. What was it you said? Even if the slut manages to survive the bear's assault, Creigh'll not be able to stomach looking upon her."

Messire Mauricheau chuckled, and Creigh's gut clenched, sick with hate, the hate he had betrayed his father with, the hate, now writhing in his belly for the woman who had borne him.

Soul cold, empty as a winter sea, he flashed his gaze to Esmeraude Wakefield's delicate features, their perfect symmetry shattered by fear. "You planned to murder the woman I love in the most hideous . . ." He felt bile choke his throat, shades of the terror that had surged through him hours past in the menagerie twisting deep within him.

"Creigh . . . Creigh, I vow, I'll not aid him anymore, I'll—"

"Nay, milady, 'tis too late to play the coward. Charles's guards will no doubt be returning to the castle when they find I've eluded them yet again, and 'tis passing important that I ride to St. Aubin's Bay with all haste. Since I've now lost the hope of gaining Blackthorne through royalist means, mayhap Parliament would reward me with the Wakefield estates in return for the news I bear of the Scots' black treachery."

Creigh's eyes narrowed upon Messire Mauricheau, the

scoundrel safe across the wide expanse of room, thin lips twisted in a nasty smile. Creigh's gaze flashed to Blackthorne's, and he could see in his father roiling fury and helplessness.

"You'll be captured before you reach the sea," Blackthorne said. "Suffer a traitor's death."

"Mayhap. But before my neck meets the axe, I'll bear the pleasure of watching my betrayer suffer—aye, milady," the opaque eyes shifted from Esmeraude Wakefield's face, the loaded pistol sweeping in a slow arc toward Creigh. "My dreams are at an end. So perish yours as well."

Creigh started to lunge for Mauricheau as the pistol's aim left the duchess's chest, but he was cut off by a flash of sapphire velvet, as Brianna hurled herself in front of him. In one hideous, frozen instant, a splash of white-lawn night rail blotted out Messire Mauricheau's lean form, a wine-shaded doublet bolting after as Blackthorne catapulted toward both Esmeraude and the knight, but 'twas too late.

A scream of denial clogged Creigh's throat as his mother crashed into Messire Mauricheau, the deafening roar of a shot splitting the air, as the other pistol flew from Bouret's hand, skidding across the floor. Creigh caught a glimpse of Blackthorne sweeping it up, heard a pathetic sound from the tangle of bodies upon the floor.

Creigh shoved Brianna away from him, running where the Lady Esmeraude lay, a blossom of crimson spreading upon the fine lawn ribbons of her night rail, her lifeblood seeping from between her jeweled fingers.

"C-Creighton . . ." she managed, "C-Creighton, I . . ."

His gaze flashed to Blackthorne an instant. His father's hand clenched around the pistol pointed at Bouret's chest, Galliard Wakefield's eyes betraying the fact that he, too, knew Esmeraude's wound meant death. Yet Creigh ripped off his own doublet, pressing it to the wound in a futile effort to staunch the flowing blood. "Maman, don't try to speak. 'Twill . . . all will be well."

"Dying . . ."

"Nay. 'Tis . . . 'tis but a little wound . . ."

"Want . . . want you to know—before . . . die. Love . . . loved you, always. Did . . . all for you . . ."

The duchess's eyes held his in a desperate, death-glazed moment. Creigh felt Brianna, kneeling beside him, her fingers, gentle upon him as he reached down, smoothing back the moon-pale curls that clung to his mother's death-kissed cheeks.

She had offered up her life to save his, he thought numbly. Yet upon the delicate features, like the whisperings of a shade, he could yet see Michel's laughing countenance as Le Ferre swept Juliet about to the strains of a dance; he could see Lindley's somber face, trusting, aye, and so earnest as he turned the pages of his hymnal in a candle-lit chapel.

He wanted to feel fury, hate, wanted to feel grief, but as he reached down, closing his mother's eyes for Eternity, he felt naught but an emptiness, and a strange sense of freedom.

Chapter Twenty-six

The sea hurled itself upon the cliffs like a warrior, blind, desperate to hold aught that remained constant in a world gone mad. Brianna curled her feet beneath her skirts, watching the waves dashing themselves upon the jagged stone, feeling within herself every crash of silver water upon unyielding rock, feeling the relentless tides yank back the fingers of foam that sought to clutch at the island's rim.

Yet the desolate sound of the thwarted waves, the calls of the gulls that circled the skies in solitary paths, held not the pain that clutched at Brianna's own heart. For in all of the days since Lady Esmeraude had been buried, Creigh had not returned to Chateau aux Marées.

Bree lifted her face to the warmth of the sun, feeling the wind thread cool ribbons of salt air through her curls. A month it had been since the duchess had been interred in the Bournet family crypt, the mourners gathered around her remains, stoic, silent.

She could yet see Juliet, pale, her eyes wide, frightened, as she leaned upon the arm of her father, her gaze ever seeking Rogan, who seemed never far from her side, whilst Creigh had stood, not beside the rest of his family, but rather distant, alone, beneath the gnarled branches of a storm-struck tree.

Brianna had ached for him, ached for Blackthorne as well, when the duke had walked with a tired, wary stride to face his heir as the mourners dispersed. The two men had stood but an arm's length apart, yet separated by a gulf of pain so wide neither knew how to bridge it. Bree had wanted to draw them both into her arms, join in them the love she knew both men shared, but a hundred words, cruel, cutting, hung yet between them, drawn in sharp contrast against dark secrets stifled, hidden, explanations mayhap reasonable to a man, and yet ne'er forgiven by a child.

Even in death 'twas Esmeraude Wakefield's triumph, this breech between father and son, Brianna thought numbly, her gaze sweeping from the duke's gray eyes to Creigh's tortured ones, the legacy of the Duchess of Blackthorne.

Brianna had stepped in, trying, with Juliet, to ease the discomfort between the two, but after a few stiff, clipped words, Blackthorne had turned, guiding Juliet back into the castle, Brianna had returned to Creigh's side, tried to take his hand, comfort him, yet with a face wracked with torment, hollow-eyed with guilt, he had gently put her away from him, saying, "'Twas my doing—Michel's death, Lindley's. If I had but listened, paid heed to what was going on around me . . ." Creigh had ground his fingertips into eyes rimmed with exhaustion.

"Charles . . . the king has need of a retainer to accompany the Scots lairds to the De Carterets'—aid in settling differences between his majesty and the Covenanters before they will commit to seeing Charles crowned. And then . . . there is the business of Messire Mauricheau's trial to attend to. I offered to go, Bree. Needed to."

Drawing his velvet cavalier's hat from his head, he had crushed its brim between his fingers, turned away. But the anguish that contorted his face tore at her very soul as he said, "Dear God, Bree, how could I not have seen what my mother was?"

She had watched him swing up on a ghost-white stallion, his shoulders squared beneath a scarlet mantle, his eyes unutterably old as he spurred his mount away from the castle. She had wanted to go after him, force him to take the comfort her love could offer, to hold him while he raged, aye, and wept. But she had let him go without a word, understanding as few others could that this proud, noble man needs must wrestle his own demons.

Yet even now the memory of his face as he had ridden over the hillside made her ache inside. For instead of the bold, dashing Lord Creighton Wakefield, with his lazy, mocking smile, the Creigh who had disappeared over the horizon that day had seemed like a brooding, bitter shadow of himself. *A pagan god, cast from its temple, aye,* Brianna thought with a twist in her heart, *or like a child, wandering, lost in the darkness.*

She smoothed the violet taffeta of her gown, laying one hand gently upon her abdomen. In the weeks since Creigh had gone, she had felt signs that, of a certainty, heralded the coming of his child. A babe she now loved with the same fierceness with which she adored its father.

Four weeks past, when she had been basking beneath the light of Charles Stuart's teasing eyes, as he had told her of Creigh's love for her, Bree had been positive that Creigh would rejoice in the news that she was to bear him a child.

But now . . .

She peered out across the sun-glossed sea, forcing back the sadness that knotted in her throat. She had seen in Creigh's face such emptiness, guilt. What if he never returned?

Nay. A sorrowful smile tipped Brianna's lips. Her cavalier was far too honorable just to vanish. He bore too much belief in Charles's cause to drown in his own savage pain. And yet if he came back . . . *when* he came back . . . would he ever be able to regain the unbreachable sense of pride, lazy arrogance, deep, hidden compassion that had comprised the Creighton Wakefield who had won her heart?

She pressed her fingertips to her eyes, feeling tears upon her skin.

The sound of footsteps approaching behind her made her quickly dash away the wetness clinging to her lashes. But the crashing of the sea had so hidden the person's approach that as the world drew into focus through her tear-blurred eyes, her gaze was captured by dusty leather boots but an arm's length away, their high bucket tops lined with what had once been the most elegant of lace boot-hose, yet now appeared torn and dirty as an apprentice's garb.

Brianna's eyes leapt up along travel-stained breeches, strong hands clasping a broad-brimmed hat, its once-rakish gold plume trailing ignominiously in the dust. Then her eyes rose to the face above the jeweled fastening of a scarlet mantle—a face so pale, haggard, that tears again stung her lids. But 'twas Creigh's eyes that tore at her very soul, strong, still, aye, and noble, yet their silvery lights wrenching humbled, as they turned out across the sea.

Quelling the sob than rose in her throat, she got to her feet, the rich, lovely folds of the gown flowing down about her.

"'Tis done," he said, his voice dead, dull.

"Done?" Bree felt her throat constrict, the quiet tone frightening her more than ranting or raging could have.

"Aye. Sir Mauricheau was executed a week past, and the Scots, they are carrying word back to their leaders concerning the king's cause. Charles and the Covenanters may well reach terms after Christmastide, be on English soil by summer next."

"'Tis . . . 'tis what you've been fighting for," Bree said, watching him warily.

"Aye." He stood silent long minutes. "His Majesty has offered me a command in his army, should he launch it," he said at last. "'Twill be good once again to don armor, cross swords with enemies honest enough to meet me blade to blade."

Bree stood, trying to battle the rising sense of panic his detachment stirred in her, as he straightened his shoulders, sighed.

"But then you know that, do you not, Tigress? Understand the honest clash of steel against steel, warring for what you believe in. You know naught of deception, of lies so tangled they drag all caught within them into hell."

"I know naught but that I love you." Brianna reached out, wanting to touch him, but he paced to the edge of the cliff, staring down at the rocks far below.

"Why, Bree?" he asked, staring into the crashing waves. "When I'm naught but an arrogant braggart? From the time I was a lad, I've been so proud of who I was: Wakefield of Blackthorne." His lips twisted in pain, disgust.

"You've done the name naught but honor."

"Honor? Oh, aye, I've fought well 'neath its banner, but then, 'tis passing easy when girded in a full cuirass, while pitted against poor soldiers shielded by naught but a breast and back plate. I even deigned to cast largess to the masses,

346

prided myself upon being enlightened, tolerant. I would ever share a cup with a bailiff, race horses with a groom, yet always I was aware of who they were, who I was—bred of a line of nobles, stretching back six hundred years.

"And when I met you, came to . . ." his voice faltered, "to love you, even then my pride cursed me. I thought to gift you with my fortune and my name, as though in so doing, I would be serving you the greatest of honors. But now . . ." He turned toward her. "What can I offer you? The hand that led my most cherished friend to the headsman's axe? The heart that still burns with the knowledge that, through me, Lindley died as well. Aye, and the knowledge that the one person I trusted above all others, was in truth the greatest liar of them all, plotting death in my name."

"Your mother's sins have naught to do with the man you are."

A sick sound rose in his chest, and he turned away from Bree, as if in pain too great to share.

"Creigh, 'tis true," Brianna said, catching his iron-hard jaw in both her hands, holding him still, to peer into her eyes. "When you first taught me what love could be, Creighton Wakefield, you told me that no matter what Ogden had done to my body, he could ne'er touch my soul. That despite the scar he had carved upon me, and the maidenhead torn by his cruelty, what I offered you was precious."

"It was, Bree, the most . . . most precious gift I'd e'er been given. But 'tis not the same—"

"Nay? You told me that Ogden could ne'er take that which he couldn't touch. That my soul, 'twas mine alone, untainted until I, myself, gave of it freely. Tell me, Lord Creighton, was that some gallant lie to coax me to bed with you?"

"Damn it, Bree, of course not! Ogden *raped* you. That has naught to do with my mother's plottings, my own blind stupidity. She planned murders—yours among them—in my name. Killed as if by her own hand—"

"Aye, *she* did. In a way she raped your spirit as certainly as Ogden raped my body. She tried to tear from you things you refused to give, tried to use you for her own ends. But she failed, Creigh, failed as Ogden failed."

"Lindley lies dead, and Michel. If not for pure fortune, you would lie in a grave as well."

"But you'd not have put me there! I know that your mother hurt you, aye, and Lindley, Michel, and Juliet as well, but think, Creigh. Her evil couldn't steal Lindley's innocence, faith, by casting him to the Tower. Couldn't kill Michel's love by marrying Juliet to Mauricheau, and in you, Creigh—"

Brianna's voice caught, fierce in her throat. "Your mother could ne'er touch your honor. The honor that drove you to aid an old man, boy, and hoyden girl to escape Drogheda, when 'twould have been simpler, far, for you to slip away yourself. The honor that made you willing to sacrifice yourself for me in the Tower, aye, and the honor, compassion that spurred you to go to a king, asking for him to accept me as your love, spare me the pain of being an outcast in the world into which you had drawn me."

Creigh's eyes snapped up to hers, a dull flush staining his cheekbones, his mouth compressing into a white line. "Charles told you that?"

"Aye. And he told me as well that ne'er once, in all the years he had called you friend, had you e'er asked aught of him before. What a wondrous man you are, Creighton Wakefield, that you care naught of your own gain, but that you could take that fierce pride you bear into your hands, and offer it to a king, for me." Brianna turned her eyes up to Creigh's, unable to keep the tears from spilling free.

"Wanted . . . wanted to gift you with so much," Creigh said in a choked voice, "to return some small measure of what your honesty, innocence, courage have given to me. All my life I've lived amongst barely veiled hatred, loyalty easily given in return for riches or land. But you . . . you gave me naught but your heart. Asked naught of me but that I love you." His gray eyes clouded, bright with unshed tears. "Let me, Tigress. Let me gift you with what little the Wakefield name now means, what small worth my estates entail. In exchange for the greater gift you bear me. That of love untarnished."

Brianna reached up to that mouth, so strong, firm, laying her fingertips upon the beautifully carved curve now trembling with emotion too deep to be contained.

"Creigh . . ." His name was harsh, broken upon her lips

348

as he took her hand, sinking to one knee before her. "Creigh, nay, don't . . ."

He lifted his face, lined yet with grief, a new, soul-deep sorrow that she sensed would ne'er be entirely banished. "Marry me, Tigress," he said. "I want naught but to spend my life showering you with joy, love, filling you with sons, daughters as brave, noble as their mother."

"M-marry?" Brianna fell to her knees, capturing his face between her hands, holding the humbled silvery gaze that broke her heart. "Creigh . . . my bold, my brave cavalier . . . if you were naught but a crofter with a barren plot of ground to offer as home, I would embrace it gladly . . . love you, even as I do this day."

Brianna felt joy, mingled with a sharp tang of pain, burst within her, the two flowing into a love so deep it could still the very sea. Salty wet against her fingers came Creigh's tears, as he caught her against him, crushing her as though to draw from her strength, healing.

"I love you, Tigress," he cried brokenly against her breasts. "Oh, God, how I love you . . ."

The light from a hundred candles drove every shadow from Chateau aux Marées's chapel, festoons of gold silk gauze caught up with bright ribbon setting the dismal room aglow above a dozen of Charles Stuart's most beloved courtiers. Yet, Creigh thought, with a twist in his loins, if the angels themselves chose to grace the intricate stone arches, stiff-backed pews, none would wax as beautiful as his Tigress as she knelt at his side, wild, sweet Brianna Devlin becoming Lord Creighton Wakefield's lady wife.

A wealth of amber velvet, rummaged from Juliet's closet, turned Bree all soft, warm gold, the silk gauze and festoonings of pearls his sister had added to the ensemble glowing, luminous against the rich cloth. Cuffs of deep lace flowed like the petals of a pristine lily up from her wrists, set against satin inner sleeves, their tiny embroidered gold flowerets nestled in the wide, flowing cup of galon-trimmed outer sleeves.

But most beautiful of all, Creigh thought with a clenching in his heart, was Bree's face, bright with love, set as it was against the low, upstanding ruff of white lace. Her tawny-gold features were framed in a halo headdress of gold and pearls, that glittered not half so richly as her hair, the curls, unbound at his request, in defiance of fashion, caught back from her rose-blushed cheeks in a circlet of white lawn and lace.

Only one thing marred the perfection of the moment, one thing yet chafed against him like a wound grating against a layering of armor. His father. When they had settled upon a date—as speedily as King Charles, and the others could arrive, Bree had insisted that Creigh pen Galliard Wakefield an invitation to the ceremony as well. And the note, terse, less personal than a bailiff's markings regarding a fence row, had chafed at Creigh from the moment the message left his hand.

Your Grace,
I am taking Brianna to be my wife, in the chapel at Chateau aux Marées Vengeresses. We ask your blessing on our union.

He had scrawled the date of the ceremony nigh as an afterthought, then sent the message off, along with one, warmer far, for the king.

Three days later, the necklet had arrived, glinting gold against a bed of midnight velvet emblazoned with the Wakefield crest. And tucked within the wrappings had been a note for Brianna. She had held it out to him, asking him to read it since she could not. And he had taken it, reluctantly, every word upon the page so full of such fatherly love and acceptance, Creigh had felt a sharp stab of jealousy twist in his gut. He had jammed the missive back into Bree's hand, gritting some transparent excuse to quit the room, but even after he had raced through the castle gates astride his stallion, he could feel her watching him with those sweet, sad golden eyes.

Creigh's gaze flicked down, captured by the ornament clasped now about Bree's throat. 'Twas not a gaudy jewel, nor the ubiquitous strings of pearls or crystals the like of which was worn by the ladies at court, rather 'twas a cunningly wrought chain of topaz set in gold, each sparkling jewel held in a setting formed in the shape of a sleek golden tigress.

The king's chaplain's intonations seemed to fade, distant as Creigh's eyes fastened upon the priceless gift, given Brianna by his father, the thought of the duke, whom Creigh had not spoken to since the day Lady Esmeraude had been buried, spawning in Creigh confusion, and a longing that was nigh pain. Yet Creigh banished the stirrings of feelings yet too raw to hold to the light, willing his thoughts away from the somber man who stood, alone, at the rear of the chapel. Creigh caught the questioning tilt to Brianna's head as she regarded him, and he forced a smile again to his lips.

Suddenly Creigh heard the echoing silence, his eyes leaping up to the chaplain's stern gaze as he thrust the prayer book he held toward Creigh in a gesture that implied he had done so more than once before, and gone unnoticed. Creigh grabbed for the ring with more haste than care, his rich lace cuff catching upon the book's leather cover. The circlet of gold upon the inked page skittered across the book, nigh tumbling to the floor, but a hand flashed out, catching the ring midair with a speed that coaxed a smile of chagrin from Creigh's lips.

He took the golden circlet from Bree's palm, embarrassment, and the clinging sense of loss he yet felt about his father, fading as Creigh raised his eyes to his bride's face. All emotions melted into wonder as he took up her hand and drowned in the sweet golden lights of Brianna's eyes.

"*With this ring I thee wed,*" the chaplain intoned, gruff voice heavy with patience.

"With this ring I thee wed," Creigh repeated, his voice rough with emotion as he saw her eyes glitter with tears.

"With my body I thee worship," Creigh's voice dropped to a choked whisper. "And with all my worldly goods I thee endow."

He squeezed her hand, so warm, small in his own, yet so infinitely strong as he slipped the wedding ring upon her finger. The prayer, blessings blended together in a whirl, his heart holding on to naught but the beauty in Brianna's face, the love that shone in her eyes. Scarce a heartbeat seemed to have passed before they turned to the small group of England's most noble courtiers, Charles Stuart, resplendent in mulberry satin, sweeping from his seat of honor, to announce in his most royal tones, "My Lord and Lady

Creighton Wakefield, now the Marquess and Marchioness of Arransea."

The sound of the title jarred Creigh—Lindley's title, the estate it was spawned from one of rugged, wild holdings along the Scots border.

Creigh jerked his gaze up to first the beaming Charles, then to the dark-robed man to the rear of the chapel, but his eyes scarce touched upon the solemn gaze of his father before the bride and bridegroom were swallowed by a circle of well-wishers.

Juliet, her nose reddened with sniffling into her gold-edged handkerchief, nigh knocked Creigh over as she hurled herself into Brianna's arms, crushing the velvets as she unashamedly wept against the tawny curls.

"'Twas—'twas so beautiful . . . so . . . love him, Bree, always." He saw Juliet slip something into Brianna's hand, a sprig of tiny, fading leaves of Michel's winter-kissed roses, then spied Rogan Niall, stiff, yet his usually glowering eyes oddly mellow as he bent to brush Brianna's cheek with a kiss surprisingly cool for that of a rejected lover.

But Creigh's view of the Irishman was blotted out, as Juliet ran to him, throwing her arms about his neck as she had when a child. "'Twill give me the greatest of pleasure, watching Brianna harry you as you deserve!" she laughed. "Be happy, Creigh." Her soft fingers laid upon his lips, and Creigh felt his eyes sting with tears as she gave him a tremulous smile. "'Tis most precious, this loving . . ."

He saw her cheeks flush scarlet, but before he could speak, she darted from his arms, the merry, jesting King Charles stepping up to take her place. Yet Creigh scarce heard the royal congratulations as his gaze caught a flash of amber velvet quietly exiting the chapel, following, Creigh sensed, the dark-robed figure who had slipped away moments before.

The jealousy that had assailed him the day Bree had received the necklet twisted anew within him, mingling with a deep sadness as he pictured Blackthorne's face as it had been at the rear of the chapel, its strong lines carved with resignation, sorrow. Then, as if borne to his mind by the whisperings of time, he saw again the face that had haunted him since that long-ago day he had tossed in the throes of fever. His father, bending over him, his craggy countenance full of love, comfort. A figment of his own tortured dreaming, Creigh had thought at the time . . . and yet . . .

His eyes met the dark ones of his king, and friend, and he felt Charles's beringed fingers tighten in an affectionate grasp about his arms. "Ne'er have I exercised such witty comments to less avail," Charles said wryly, glancing back at the now empty doorway. "Go, friend," he said softly. "Mayhap you'll gain more than a wife on this day of new beginnings."

Creigh turned, striding up the aisle, a sudden alarm stirring within him, the same wrenching fear that he had felt when he had watched Galliard Wakefield ride away so many years ago. What if the duke was in truth leaving? Riding away? The note he had written to Brianna had spoken of some mission to the French court . . . some charge to raise funding for Charles. What if his father had chosen to depart immediately, feeling as though his presence caused but pain to the son who, at best, had ever seemed to loathe him?

The corridor leading away from the chapel was bright with candlelight, the magnificent window set at the passage's end a work in stained glass depicting Christ, pleading with his own father at the garden of Gethsemane. Creigh's chest constricted in relief as he saw, there beneath its jeweled light, two figures, that of a vision garbed all in gold, and a man, his black riding cloak flowing over shoulders bowed with years of suffering.

They saw Creigh not, as he watched his new bride curtsy before his father, watched the Duke of Blackthorne lift her to her feet with gentle hands. Creigh heard not what words passed between them, only saw the duke cup her face in his hands, kissing her gently on each rose-blushed cheek.

A knot strained in Creigh's throat as he saw Brianna— loving, open Brianna—catch the duke's sorrow-laden shoulders in an embrace.

Frightened, aye, more so than e'er before in his life, Creigh forced his feet forward. He saw Brianna's face angle toward him, her lips parting, eyes wide, bright with hope, then fastened his gaze upon his father's suddenly frozen visage.

Silver eyes met Creigh's, and he saw the duke gently take Brianna's hands, easing her away from him as he faced his son. The fist twisting in Creigh's belly tightened as he

353

neared, and he fought the same soul-wrenching sensation he had felt running after the duke as he spurred away from Wrensong.

"Father." The word was choked, tentative, and Creigh hated the sound of his weakness. "I see you mean to leave us."

Blackthorne nodded slowly, his face tense, watchful. "His Majesty has dispatched me to King Louis, in hopes of stirring the French to his cause. I sail three days hence."

"Three days. Then 'tis not . . . not pressing that you go immediately."

"Nay."

"I . . . Bree had hoped—I mean, there will be dancing after, in the hall after, and she . . ."

"Creigh, lad . . ." 'Twas as if every cruel word Creigh had ever dealt him was carved upon the duke's face, the mouth that had oft seemed so hard, unfeeling, appearing suddenly vulnerable, weary. Old. "I've no wish to steal joy from your wedding. 'Twill most like be best if I leave before . . ."

Creigh clenched his fists, steeling himself as he ruthlessly shoved the walls of his defenses down about the fragile feelings he yet bore his father. "Nay. In truth, 'tis . . ." he glanced down, dragged his eyes back to his father's countenance. "'Tis I who wish you to stay."

"Creigh, sweet God, lad," Blackthorne's voice was gritty with sorrow, joy.

"I want to try to . . . to make a new beginning . . ."

Creigh fought to reach out his hand to the man before him, suddenly still as if carved of stone. But his fingers had scarce begun to bridge the space between them when Blackthorne's strong arms swept out, and Creigh felt himself crushed against his father's chest.

"'Tis more . . . more than I'd e'er hoped." Blackthorne's deep voice was rough with the rakings of blade-sharp emotions. "Creigh, lad, forgive me. For all the . . . the pain I've caused you through my cursed weakness—leaving you at Wrensong, not wresting you again from Esmeraude's grasp despite the queen's command."

"Father . . ."

"Nay, lad, let me say it. I've cursed myself a thousand times for not just taking you and Lindley and Jolie when you were babes, ripping you from 'neath Esmeraude's evil influence. 'Twould have been better, far, to wander across the courts of Europe, than to allow her to tangle you in her plottings, to make you think that I didn't—"

"I thought—thought you cared only for Lindley," Creigh choked, and it was the voice of the child years past, the boy who had screamed after the father whom he had adored. "That there was something within me that made you . . . made you hate . . . when I wanted so much for you to love me."

A quiver of pain wracked Creigh's body. He tried to pull away, but Blackthorne clasped his arms, holding Creigh, facing him. "Nay, lad, don't. You were the finest son a man could've wished for. Made me . . . made me so proud."

Blackthorne's voice broke. Tears welled over his lids, tracing the crevasses sorrow had carved in his regal face. "My leaving you at Wrensong had naught to do with you. 'Twas your mother . . . your mother's incessant plotting. You were off with Charles one day, when she ordered one of her lady maids take some syllabub to the nursery with strict orders that the wench see that Lindley—and *only* Lindley— ate it. The woman tasted it, thank God, then dawdled on her way. Creigh, she nigh died. Esmeraude swore 'twas but food spoiled in the pantry, appeared most distraught. But even then I wondered . . ."

Creigh's mouth twisted with remembered pain, guilt.

"The king had just dispatched me on vital business. I could take but one of you. I chose Lindley, not because I loved you less, but because I feared for his life. And you, I put in the safest place I was able."

"Why . . . why could I not see what she was doing?" Creigh said, the sudden clarity of the pain-shrouded events glaring into his consciousness like a too-bright sun.

"Creigh, how could you have? I was a man grown, and she bewitched me one hot August night. You were but a child, caught between an evil woman and a weak man."

"I thought . . . thought you loved me not . . ."

"I know." The duke's silvery eyes were dark with anguish. "But always I carried you within my heart, lad. Always."

Sixteen years of anguish, hate, seemed to swell within Creigh, bursting in a shuddering sob that shook his whole

355

body. Blackthorne embraced him, and Creigh could feel Blackthorne's tears hot upon his face, feel the love, fierce from within his father's crushing grasp.

"Father . . ." Creigh choked out. "Forgive me . . . for all the . . . the things I've said to you—done . . ."

"Whist, lad, whist," Blackthorne said. "There is naught to forgive."

Creigh's eyes caught a glimpse of bright gold, Brianna's face glistening with tears.

"Father," he said, feeling the warmth in her eyes, in Blackthorne's embrace, healing soul-deep wounds. "Father, I love you."

A thousand tiny embroidered sailing ships tossed upon the whimsical sea of stars that spilled gold across the sapphire velvet coverlet. Brianna reached down a hand, her fingers strangely a-quiver, as she smoothed the counterpane, turned down an hour since by Juliet's maid.

Jolie herself had but exited the bridal chamber moments since in a whirl of hugs and good wishes, her eyes a-glow at the wonder she and Mademoiselle Longet had wrought in the night rail that now clung about Brianna's otherwise naked form. Silk gauze so fragile it seemed but mist from the sea drifted about tawny-gold skin, clusters of silk ribbons, soft, webby lace gathering the delicate fabric about breasts full with the promise of Creigh's child.

A fitting gown for the Marchioness of Arransea, Juliet had teased, yet the title and all it implied had dampened Brianna's soaring mood like the first frost upon autumn meadows.

She turned, her gaze catching upon a chest at the far side of the room, its surface cunningly carved with sea serpents that seemed more of a mind to carry ships safely to harbor than to crush their hulls in fierce teeth. Yet, if they had been of a mind to drive out intruders, Brianna was well certain 'twould be her the beasts would chase. For, though the few of Charles's favorites who had attended the wedding and the festivities thereafter had made her feel most welcome in their midst, doubts seemed yet to steal about her, legacy of the disastrous night of King Charles's ball.

Bree raised her eyes to the looking glass perched above the chest, seeing in the silvered reflection the same face that had been tossed back at her from the surfaces of a hundred wildland streams. Features too sharply carved clashed with the opulent quarters around her—the stubborn chin, firm mouth well used to giving orders, and the eyes that hinted at a temper of a certainty not those that should grace the countenance of a marchioness.

What would Creigh want of her, expect of her now, as his wife? He had claimed he loved her for all she was, wanted naught else; but, still, when 'neath the unforgiving eyes of his peers, would he long for a graceful belle upon his arm, one adept at dealing out witty rejoinders as they swept about ballroom floors? Would he one day regret wedding simple Bree Devlin, who bore naught to fit her for his world, saving her love for him?

The sound of the door opening made Bree turn, nervously pressing her fists to her breasts. She could feel her heart beneath her hands, leaping, bounding at the sight of Creigh framed within the entryway. The rosewood waves of his hair glistened, rough satin, around his patrician features, the roguish sensual smile formed into one of nigh boyish eagerness. He stepped into the room, balancing a long, velvet-wrapped bundle in one hand as he quietly closed the door.

"I vow I just saw my sister stealing off for a tryst with a certain flame-haired Irishman," Creigh said in a low, thick voice. "I would have followed her, mayhap called the rogue out, had I not waxed so eager for a tryst of my own."

Bree felt a shiver of anticipation go through her as silvery eyes, hot with desire, roved with agonizing slowness down her breasts, touching the rosy crests visible through the thin fabric, lingering at the indentation of her waist, before his gaze skimmed lower, hesitating long, heavy seconds upon the soft shadowing of gold pooled at the apex of her thighs.

"Sweet God, Tigress," he breathed, lifting his gaze to hers. "You are beautiful."

Brianna took a stumbling step toward him, wanting naught but to feel his arms about her, yet feeling unaccountably shy garbed in such rich beauty. "'Tis . . . 'twas Juliet's."

"You'll have a hundred the like of it, Bree, if you want them. Anything, everything you could wish for."

The doubts and uncertainties that had been nibbling at

Brianna's happiness drifted over her as she looked into his face—that of a Druid king, legend Arthur, the Cuchillain of Irish ballad. She turned away, feeling suddenly the urchin, parading about in a queen's stolen raiment.

"Creigh . . . I . . . I care naught for what coin can buy. I want naught but your love."

"I know, Bree." His hand was soft on her shoulder, as he turned her toward him. "And that is why I know myself to be the most fortunate man in Christendom this night." His knuckles traced the curve of her cheek. "God, Tigress, I cannot believe you are mine—truly mine. My *wife.*" His fingers opened, his palm splaying over her cheek, one thumb skimming the trembling swell of her lower lip. Then he bent down, his breath, warm, sweet as he tasted of her, the whisper-soft melding of their mouths seeming to blend their very souls.

"C-Creigh . . ." Brianna cried against his lips, catching his face in her hands, fighting to deepen the kiss into passion, press against the lean hardness that beckoned her, but something bumped against her hip. Creigh groaned, his hand circling her wrist, gently drawing her fingers down to flatten against his chest.

"Hold, Bree, but a moment. I want . . . God, I want you, but first . . ." he lifted the forgotten bundle he had brought with him into the room, laying it upon the oaken chest. "A fitting gift," he said softly, "for the Marchioness of Arransea."

The wondrous spell his body had been weaving about hers snapped at his gentle words, and Brianna looked down onto the velvet-wrapped bundle as though 'twere filled with hauntings, shades she wanted not to confront. But as her gaze darted up to Creigh's face, the silvery eyes were so eager beneath their lush fringing of lashes, the firm lips tipped into a smile of such love, she swallowed her fears. Taking the edge of the cloth wrapping between her fingers, she carefully unrolled the long, thin bundle, folding back the velvet that cradled it.

Dread softened into disbelief, disbelief into hope, as she freed Creigh's gift, and as the last shielding of velvet fell away, tears welled from her eyes, her heart filled with such love it seemed to fill the room, spilling out to the sea beyond. Her lips parted in awe, her fingers reaching out to touch the bright gold hilt, jeweled scabbard of the most beautifully crafted rapier she had e'er seen.

A dragon, each tiny scale of enamel perfection, gripped the scabbard in fearsome claws, its teeth locking with those of a rampant tiger, while caught between them, bold letters proclaimed some message she could not read.

She raised shining eyes to her husband's handsome face. "Creigh," she breathed. "'Tis magnificent. What—what does it say?"

"'Tis Latin," Creigh said softly, running his finger across the engraved script. *"I battle my own demons."*

Brianna felt a knot form in her throat as she remembered that distant day in Mary MacGregor's cottage, and the proud nobleman that had aided her in defeating all the terrors that had beset her then.

"I had thought to get you a bauble, mayhap a pair of earrings, or a brooch. But, after some consideration, I decided 'twould be best to see you armed again, in a manner befitting the finest wielder of a blade I have yet crossed swords with."

She flushed, glowing with joy, bubbling with laughter as she wrinkled her brow, making great show of seeming to consider some matter of great import.

"Tigress . . . what is it?" Creigh asked, puzzled. "Does it not suit?"

"Oh, aye, it suits me well enough," she said, caressing the soft swell of her stomach. "But I much doubt our sons will find it such a boon."

"Sons?"

"Aye. 'Twill be quite a blow to their pride no doubt, when I use it to school their sisters to wax as swift with a blade as they are."

"Sons? A sister? Tigress, is it . . . do you mean . . ." His gaze leapt down to her abdomen with such a mixture of shock and rejoicing Brianna's laughter broke free, and she threw herself into Creigh's arms. "Aye, my lord, I'll lay a babe in your arms after the Maying. But mark you, any daughter bred of my body will be faster by half with her sword than any Wakefield male. 'Twill be her only defense against the stubborn, arrogant, wonderful wretches that will no doubt turn her life to heaven."

"A babe . . ." Creigh smoothed one sword-calloused palm

down over her womb, the gentle haven in which his child flourished. "I vow to you that no matter what the future brings—a crown for Charles, or life in France, I vow I'll gift you and our babes with naught but joy."

Brianna clutched her arms about him, wanting to banish all the last shadings of pain from his heart, knowing her love held the strength to do so.

"I love you, milady," he whispered, his voice ragged with emotion.

"I love you, Creighton Wakefield," she cried through tears of joy too great to hold. "Even if you are a thieving Sassenach lord."

She basked in the sweetness of his laughter, its rumbling sound filling her heart, soul as her cavalier swept her into his arms, spilling them both into wonder midst the starry-gold bed.

Epilogue

London, May 29, 1660

The Marchioness of Arransea bit back a curse, glaring at the Wakefield lions emblazoned upon the fallen banner as though they themselves had dragged the huge pennon of velvet from the window overlooking London's Strand. It had taken five servants an hour to secure the emblem to iron hasps upon the window overlooking the site of Charles's triumphal procession into London. But the tawny-curled imp of two years who sat draped in the midst of her father's crest left little doubt in Brianna Wakefield's mind as to who had managed to haul down the huge square of cloth.

Blissfully stuffing one unfortunate leonine paw into her rosebud mouth, Lady Julianna Wakefield was—as her adoring father took every opportunity to point out—a most resourceful child.

Resourceful, Bree thought grimly. *She* was more of a mind to call the child stubborn, impossible, infuriating . . .

She ground her teeth, attempting for the third time to wrest the fabric from her daughter's astonishingly strong grasp, pointedly ignoring the expression of tolerance schooled into nine-year-old Taggart's features as he shook his head, ever mindful of the cavalier plumes bedecking his prized new hat. "You'd best just let her chew on it, Mama," Taggart advised sagely. "If you take it away from her, His Majesty will be able to hear her shrieking above the sound of the bells." Bree cast the miniature of Creigh a glare before turning back to her recalcitrant daughter. "Let go of the lions, Jolie love," Brianna cajoled through gritted teeth, but the babe, with a beatific smile, and her mouth stuffed with velvet, yet managed to clearly speak her most oft-used word with incredible clarity. "Nay."

The rumble of stifled masculine laughter behind her made Brianna throw a fulminating glare back at the broad-shouldered form of her husband. "Instead of laughing, you might deign to aid me—"

"What? The woman who defeated half an army crying surrender?" Creigh said, flashed her a look full of such innocence, she wanted to box his ears. "As soon as I divest Gareth and Alexander of this tart, I vow I'll rush to your aid." He bent over two identical dark curly heads bobbing about the window ledge. "It seems they have found it sore amusing, dropping cherries onto a most remarkable hat there below. I think 'tis the Duchess of Quigly's and—"

"Damnation!" Brianna burst out, as one tiny, perfect white tooth cut into her finger.

She glimpsed Creigh wheeling around, the crushed pastry held triumphantly in one cherry-stained hand. "What, by God's blood—"

"She bit me, the little wretch! I vow I'll—"

Creigh flung back his head, the whole room filling with the rich sound of his laughter, mingling with Taggart's and the twins' giggles.

"Aye, laugh, the lot of you," Bree said, sucking on her wounded finger. "But I vow I'll repay you in kind for this day, my lord marquess."

"'Tis history, Mama," Taggart said, mimicking his father's most solemn tones to perfection. "The day King Charles regains his rightful crown."

"If the king—ever does—enter the city," Bree gritted, between tugs upon the banner, "his first act of—state—will most like be to—banish the Wakefields to the farthest reaches of the kingdom."

Devlin temper flashing in Brianna's eyes, she grasped the embroidered lion's mane, readying herself to give a mighty tug that would either rip the thick velvet or pry loose Julianna's teeth. "Now—*let go.*" She levered herself backward, but instead of meeting with the fierce resistance she'd been battling each of the other times, she pulled the lion free with a vengeance. Bree caught but a flash of Julianna's cherubic lips rounding in an eager smile as her mother

362

tumbled backward, plopping onto the floor in a flurry of petticoats and satin.

"Papa!" the babe cried, stretching her chubby arms toward the towering frame of her father. "Papa! Jolie up!"

Brianna sighed in despair as Creigh swept his daughter high, the delicate ribbons the nurse had labored two hours to weave into Julianna's wild curls straggling across the babe's freckled nose.

"Creigh, 'tis hopeless. By the time Charles requested to see us, this hoyden here will have us all looking like fishmongers while Rogan and Juliet's sons will most likely have the look of little princes."

"'Twould matter not to His Majesty if Father came garbed in a brown-stuff kerchief," Taggart proclaimed, thrusting out his chest with pride. "If 'twere not for Father, the king might never have escaped Worcester, might never have lived long enough to see devil Cromwell in his grave."

"Oh, aye, your father's a hero right grand," Bree grumbled to herself. "And if the lot of you don't cease driving me to madness, he might well join the Lord Protector." But despite her biting reply, Bree's gaze locked with her husband's, beset by more solemn memories, the tangible proof of Creigh's loyalty and courage arcing in a faded scar beneath his doublet. The smile he flashed her above Julianna's ragamuffin curls held such love and tenderness, she felt it tear within her breast.

He shifted the babe in his arms, leaning over his oldest son. "Don't mind your mama, Taggart," Creigh said solemnly, laying his hand upon the lad's doublet. "'Tis just that she still waxes furious she missed that last battle. Chafes her no end that whilst young Daniel and I were off covering ourselves in glory, she was confined to the castle, scarce up from childbed."

Bree's sputtered reply about where the marquess could deposit his "glory" was lost in a squeal from Taggart, and she lunged to her feet, catching but a glimpse of Julianna's dimpled hand as it flashed out, crushing the plumes of her brother's hat in her chubby fingers.

A most unmanly wail breached Taggart's lips as he bolted to his feet, Creigh making a wild grab for the plumes as Julianna flung her little arm first back, then forward. With an accuracy that would have made Robin of the Hood proud, the broad-brimmed velvet hat flew from Julianna's hand, skimming Gareth's head as the cherished garment sailed out the window.

Bree spat a string of curses, dashing over to the ledge, but before she could even reach it, she heard Julianna's awed little cry. "Pretty, Papa. King."

The cheers from the crowd rose in a glorious clamor, even Taggart's face brightening with wonder as he leaned out the window, gazing down at the splendor below. Bright splashes of color bedecked masses of Charles's retainers; the king, his dark curls bare, his face, solemn, yet bearing regal courage, sat astride a magnificent horse, its trappings glittering in the sun.

Brianna felt Creigh's fingers, strong, warm, curve about hers, pulling her into the lee of his arm. "'Tis a new day for England," he said, his gaze following his beloved sovereign and friend.

"Aye," Brianna whispered. "And for Ireland."

She heard Gareth howl, one finger, bound with a white cloth bandage, pointing out above the crowd where something whisked through the sky. 'Twas a hat, broad-brimmed, decked with plumes, carried by the breeze above Charles's royal head. The king reached out, catching it, his head thrown back in laughter. His face angled toward the window upon the Strand, denuded of its bright lion banner.

Then Charles Stuart threw the circlet of velvet high, the wind sweeping Taggart Wakefield's cavalier hat into the cloud-studded sky, and the future.